RENEGADE

RENEGADE

⊰∞∞∞⊱

NANCY NORTHCOTT

Book 1 in the Protectors Series

FOREVER
YOURS

New York   Boston

Copyright © 2012 by Nancy Northcott
Excerpt from *Guardian* copyright © 2012 by Nancy Northcott
Cover design by Christine Foltzer, cover art by Craig White. Cover copyright © 2012 by Hachette Book Group, Inc.

Forever Yours
Grand Central Publishing
Hachette Book Group
237 Park Avenue, New York, NY 10017
www.hachettebookgroup.com
www.twitter.com/foreverromance

Originally published as an e-book by Forever Yours

First print on demand edition: December 2012

Forever Yours is an imprint of Grand Central Publishing.
The Forever Yours name and logo are trademarks of Hachette Book Group, Inc.

The publisher is not responsible for websites (or their content) that are not owned by the publisher.

The Hachette Speakers Bureau provides a wide range of authors for speaking events. To find out more, go to www.hachettespeakersbureau.com or call (866) 376-6591.

ISBN 978-1-4555-9887-8

For my guys~
Mark, who encouraged me to pursue my dream and
believed in it even during the times my faith faltered,
and
Gavin, who has always wanted me to succeed and
whose perspective was more helpful than he knows.

Acknowledgments

Along the road to publication, I've been lucky to meet readers and other writers who'll help with anything from advice and support to reading a new passage, or sometimes even the whole book, to see how it works. This is only a partial listing of the many people to whom I'm grateful.

My blogmates, the Romance Bandits, always seem to know whether it's time for a pat on the back or a kick in the pants. The Avocat Noir plot group (Donna MacMeans, Joan Kayse, Cassondra Murray, and Jeanne Adams) helped make life difficult for Griff and Val.

I belong to the Carolina Romance Writers, Heart of Carolina Romance Writers, and Georgia Romance Writers chapters of Romance Writers of America, as well as several specialty chapters, and have enjoyed the support of many members of those groups.

I've had consistent and ongoing encouragement from Nancy Knight, Sandra Chastain, Patricia Rice, Leigh Greenwood, A. C. Crispin and the DC2K Writers (Suzanne Church, Eugie Foster, Lisa Guilfoil, Scott Hancock, Amy

Herring, Teresa Howard, Alan Koslow, Aaron Longoria, Jenna Lundeen, Lynda Pickett, Gwen Veazey, and Debra Yutko), the members of Interlac, Jessica Andersen, Judith Stanton, Berta Platas, Michelle Roper, Dianna Love, Sid Barrett, Anna Sugden, Eilis and Mike Flynn, Judy Rosenbaum, Carol Strickland, Gerri Russell, Kathleen O'Reilly, Dee Davis, Julie Kenner, Elizabeth Gargano, Becke Turner, Roxann Pearson, Ann Wicker, Van Garrison, and the Davidson Wild Women beach crew.

If my first critique group, The Mystery Mavens (Paula Connolly, Dawn Cotter, Terry Hoover, Susan Luck, Cathy Pickens, Mary Tribble, and Ann Wicker), hadn't been so helpful, I might never have reached this point. They are, as Cathy once said, "a mean bunch of women," but in a constructive way. My last critique group, The Brinker Group (Paul Barrett, Dennis Carrigan, Sandy Hill, Ed McKeown, and Kim Wright), offered valuable insights in the early stages of this book.

Several people answered many questions in areas outside my expertise. Any errors in the book are due to my failure to ask the right questions, not to any mistakes of theirs. Dr. Dale Grote saved the mages' Latin imperatives from the errors my dim memory of high school Latin would have caused. Cassondra Murray and Steve Doyle helped arm and transport the mages. Without Lori McMahon, I wouldn't have known what colors Griff would use in the painting mentioned in the book. Suzanne Welch, R.N., Joan Kayse, R.N., Dr. Alan Koslow, Dr. Bonnie Revelle, and Dr. Laurie Dunn were patient with my questions about medicine and medical school.

I'm also grateful to my tireless agent, Beth Miller, who had faith the mages would find a home, and my editor, Latoya Smith, who gave them one.

Last but never least, I owe a tremendous debt to my husband, Mark, and our son, Gavin. They've never complained about juggling schedules so I could write or go to a conference. I couldn't have done this without their love and support and faith in me, and I'm glad I can now say, "Here it is. We got what we were working toward." Thanks, guys, with all my heart.

RENEGADE

Chapter 1

Not. Dead. Yet. Valeria Banning panted behind the sour-tasting gag. She still had half a chance to survive.

At least she'd helped that Mundane woman and her child escape the ghouls trying to kidnap them. And she'd killed two of the ghouls before the rest overpowered her. But now she was wounded, aching, and trussed like a Thanksgiving turkey in the trunk of their car.

Which came as no surprise. Seven to one odds were great for the seven. Unfortunately, she'd been the one in the equation, but no mage would turn away when humans were in danger. That went double for her as shire reeve, or sheriff, of the Southeastern U.S. mages' Council.

At least the nausea and chills—side effects of venom—were fading as her immune system purged her blood. The talon wounds where the ghoul had injected the venom in her back still burned like flaming acid, and that wasn't going to improve anytime soon.

Val shifted restlessly, trying to draw a deep breath. The

stuffy air didn't help. Thanks to the heat of a Georgia night in August, the sedan's small, dark trunk felt like an oven.

Best not to think of ovens. Or the fact she was mageborn toast if she couldn't remove the amulet her ghoul captors had hung around her neck, blocking her power. They'd tucked the pendant into her tank top, making it harder to shake off. Nice trick.

They likely meant to siphon her life energy, fueling their power and killing her. Or they might intend to rape her, force her to breed, as they often did with kidnapped mages and Mundanes. Ghouls couldn't breed with each other and so took captives to keep their population levels high.

Her stomach did a slow, queasy twist. She swallowed against bile and paralyzing fear. She could see the bulletin now: *Valeria Banning, age 27, KIA because she let a bunch of ghouls get the drop on her.*

Hell if she was going out that way.

First step, somehow remove the pendant, tough job with her hands cuffed behind her. Second step, get these restraints off.

Before the car stopped.

She could worry later about where ghouls had gotten the amulet. Ghouls were strong at night and weak in the daylight, bound to dark magic but limited in its use. They weren't capable of the complex magic needed to create such objects.

She tried to roll, bring her knees under her, but couldn't find her balance as the car jounced over what sounded like a gravel road. *Crap.* Breathing hard, she rested a few seconds, then tried again. And again.

If she didn't manage this, she was totally fucked.

She clenched her jaw against the pain as tightly as the gag would allow, pushed off awkwardly with her chained hands, and finally—finally!—gained her knees. Sweat ran down her face and body in rivers. She needed a minute to gather herself. If only she knew how many minutes she had.

The rough ride probably meant the driver was heading into the country. On the upside, that gave her more time to free herself. Also, heading away from town meant there would be a lot of plants and wildlife, sources of natural energy she could draw on to replenish the power the amulet had stifled.

On the ominously bad downside, ghouls only sought privacy when they wanted to play with their prey.

Her gut churned again, and a shiver of fear rippled through her. Val drew the hot, stale air in as deeply as she could. *Focus, Val. Focus or die.*

Sweat stung her eyes. She blotted it against the carpet and caught the coppery scent of blood under the more usual one of motor oil. At least there wasn't a body jammed in here with her, thank God.

The car slowed, and the bouncing decreased. Breathing through the pain, Val bowed her back and lowered her head. The pendant dropped clear of her tank, onto the smelly carpet. So far, so good.

The heavy chain slipped down to the curve at the back of her skull. Almost off. Just a little bit more.

If she could ditch the amulet and have a few minutes to recharge, she would be able to pop her shackles and transmute them into a very big, very handy knife. Good thing they weren't made of bespelled iron, just cheap ankle and wrist cuffs.

Pressing her cheek into the dirty carpeting over the spare tire, she scooted backward. The chain slipped down to the carpeting but tangled in her hair. *Shit.* She had no way to tug at it.

The car spun into another turn with the rasp of gravel spewing from the wheels. Val braced herself and tossed her head as hard as she could against the turn's momentum. At last, with a painful yank on her hair, the chain slid free.

Behind the gag, she gasped in relief. Renewed power coursed through her body, though not as much as usual. The amulet lay too near. Still, she had a little strength back.

She cracked open the cuff on one wrist, but that took more power than she'd expected.

Hell, the car was slowing. She popped the other cuffs, then lay panting, drained, in the stuffy darkness.

The car stopped. Terror squeezed her throat, and she swallowed against it. She needed a minute she didn't have to recover enough to fight. She pushed the amulet into the wheel well to hide it. That gained some distance but not nearly enough to let her recharge.

Car doors squeaked open, and footsteps crunched on gravel. Panic kicked her heartbeat up. Trying to steady it, she took as deep a breath as the gag allowed. *Do or die time.*

She flopped onto her side, hands and feet behind her, but left the gag on for the element of surprise. If she was lucky, her tawny hair flopping across her chest would hide the absence of the amulet.

When her captors opened the lid, she'd have only seconds more to prepare. She drew in a slow breath to center herself.

She'd try to knock them all back magically, then go for her sword. With the amulet off, she sensed the weapon nearby, probably inside the car. It would amplify her magic and improve her odds. Without the sword, she'd have to rely on Latin words of power to make any contact lethal. She hadn't recovered enough to shield herself or to punch a barehanded blow through ghoul shields with enough force to kill.

The trunk latch clicked. The lid rose. Redolent with the scents of earth and plants, the thick, humid summer air hit her. There was life here, and lots of it. She drew the natural energy in like a dry sponge in water and gathered herself. Moving too soon would waste her shot.

Five faces leered down at her in the waning moon's glow. They appeared human, but her mageborn senses caught the telltale scent of ammonia from the high levels of venom in their blood and saw, even in the faint light, the muddy whites of the ghouls' eyes. The four males looked to be in their thirties, with the lone woman, a busty brunette, on the far side of forty.

"Get her out," the thin, blond male on the right ordered. "I'm hungry."

Since none of the others snarled at him, Val pegged him as the leader. His grip on the trunk's edge showed his inch-long talons already deployed behind his fingernails, ready to suck out her life energy or rend her flesh.

Suddenly cold again, Val forced herself to shrink back inside the trunk. She needed all of them as close to her as possible. The female and the dark-haired, scrawny male at the rear had retreated a few paces.

"Pull the bitch out," the leader snapped.

Leaning in, one male grasped her knees while the other reached for her shoulders. She thrashed against their hands, whimpering for show, but kept her struggles to a minimum.

If she fought too much, they'd realize she'd freed herself.

As they pulled her out, she kept her knees bent to hide her unchained ankles. The leader slammed the trunk shut. The man holding her legs dropped them to grab her left arm while his buddy held her right.

They shoved her backward against the trunk. Her heart pounded like a jackhammer. They hadn't noticed her ankles—probably too gripped by power lust, and maybe too confident, to be careful. Their excitement ramped up the ammonia scent, stinging her nose.

She fought panic, tried to slow her shallow, fast breathing. The leader stepped in front of her, his dark, satisfied gaze raking over Val's body. Power flared into a muddy aura around him. His taloned hands reached for her face, and the other ghouls pressed in.

Now.

Val blew out all her stored power like a human claymore mine. The gag disintegrated. Four of the ghouls tumbled backward and fell, dazed.

The one holding her right arm rocked back but tightened his grip. His claws spiked white heat into her shoulder. She bit back a scream. Her eyes teared as magic thickened into a muddy brown shield around him. His venom shot nauseating cold down her arm and side, raising the taste of ammonia in her mouth as the venom hit her blood.

Shuddering, she turned toward him, drawing power from the swamp before the venom made that impossible. She slammed her fist through his shield. With her palm against his chest, she thought, *Morere*, for *Die*, and pictured a bursting heart.

His body jerked. Face contorting, he made a gurgling

sound. He clawed at her hand, raking it with new venom. The same sickening cold rolled up that arm, too.

She gritted her teeth against nausea. Twisted her fingers in his shirt to keep her grip.

Morere, she repeated.

Her power sputtered. Faded. His friends were stirring. *Crap.*

Suddenly, his claws retracted. His grip failed, and he fell, dead. She was free.

But his friends were on their feet.

Val stumbled over the dead ghoul and half staggered, half lunged toward the car's rear door. Yanking it open, she grinned. Her broadsword lay on the seat, its leather-wrapped hilt against the opposite door.

Footsteps scuffed behind her. She mule-kicked backward with magic powering the move. Someone whoofed.

As she dived for the sword's hilt, the female ghoul jerked open the opposite door and lunged across the seat. Her claws stabbed into Val's neck.

Oh shit, oh shit. Desperate, Val grabbed the female's wrist with both hands, but ripping the claws out could be fatal if they slashed across a vein or artery.

Other hands closed on Val's shoulders to drag her out of the car. As their claws dug in, blackness rolled over her eyes and through her soul. The female's grip tightened.

"No venom," the leader's voice ordered behind Val. He sounded royally pissed. "Carl already shot her with too much, and I'd planned to breed her. At least we can still feed."

Gasping for air, Val tried to find her feet to steady her power for a final effort. She only had seconds to do it, or she was dead.

Terror chilled her blood as the four survivors slammed her back against the warm metal of the car's hood. Tearing at her clothes, they found bare skin and sank in their claws. No venom this time, but a drain. They sucked her power like leeches, and the blackness deepened.

Six years of exile, seven friends dead, and fuck-all to show for it. Scowling, Griffin Dare pulled the two-liter Coke out of the refrigerator. A traitor still sat on the mages' Southeastern U.S. Shire Council, the governing and training body for the region's mages. That unknown bastard was working with ghouls to send unsuspecting mages to their deaths.

Griff and his team, the baker's dozen he could trust to keep his secrets, just weren't enough to turn the tide. When he'd gone rogue at twenty-eight, he hadn't dreamed his fight for justice would take this long.

He took a big swallow of Coke. Too bad high-fructose corn syrup couldn't clear the ammonialike venom from his blood. He'd acquired it, as mages often did, through ghoul-inflicted battle wounds. Unfortunately, he'd been alone, unable to reach a healer, and there'd been too much venom in him for his immune system to cleanse.

At least the soda masked the faint ammonia flavor in his mouth. Grimacing at the sweet aftertaste, he set the bottle back inside the fridge. The brief blast of cold air gave him a few seconds of relief from the night's muggy heat.

Padding barefoot across the plank flooring, he wiped sweat off his face with one arm. Only the bedroom had air-conditioning, and he rarely used it. It cut the humidity but garbled his sense of the life energy from birds and other creatures in the nearby Okefenokee Swamp. His second-floor quarters in the abandoned, run-down chair factory didn't look like much, but living near the swamp let his power continually recharge, helped control the venom level in his blood.

A sluggish breeze stirred the blue and green glass witch balls hanging at the windows, part of his defense system. A strand of his dark hair fell in his face, and he shoved it back, frowning at the police reports and newspaper clippings spread out on the battered walnut table. The recent increases in violent crime, especially gory murders, pointed to ghoul plans for something big, something involving dark powers.

Blood magic.

The dark of the moon, in just under two weeks, would be prime time for such a rite, but for what? And where would it happen?

The ghouls usually focused on kidnapping Mundanes or mages to breed, but they wouldn't need blood magic for that. Was this a final push to wipe out the mages, whose numbers had dwindled while the ghouls' grew? Even with the numerical advantage, could the ghouls manage that?

If they did, there'd be no one to stand between the ghouls and complete domination of humanity.

His second-in-command, Will Davis, was an ace researcher, with two doctoral degrees to prove it. Griff reached for his phone. Good thing using his magical tracking skills as a "psychic consultant" for the Feds had netted him an untraceable cell number.

Mage power blasted through his perimeter ward, its echo like a slap in his brain. On reflex, his personal shields flared around him, a faint shimmer in the air as he summoned his quarterstaff. The seven-foot, wrist-thick, ash shaft struck his palm, silver end caps and inlaid copper runes glowing with power on contact. He wheeled to face the threat.

The wave of power broke against his shield, then rolled past him on either side. With it came fury, fear, and a desperate cry for help.

As abruptly as it had come, it vanished. Griff remained in position with his shields up. Somewhere nearby, a mage was in trouble. Or pretended to be. How better to lure him out of hiding than to make him think a mage was in lethal danger? Shielding didn't survive translocation, so if he answered that call, he'd be vulnerable to ambush when he arrived.

Infusing emotion in a magic wave, though, required great skill, and the intensity, the terror, in the call had felt real.

A vision flashed over his sight—darkness, a pine forest. Missy, the cashier at the bakery in the town of Wayfarer, and Todd, the bakery delivery boy, kneeling before a bloodied altar.

The scene shifted. He looked down a rutted, overgrown lane as a woman in a car behind him said, "We're not having that fight now. Get in."

Then he sat in the ritual grotto at the Collegium, the mages' Georgia base, in the obsidian seat of truth, chained to it, hurting in every pore, doomed but desperate to protect a woman. From what? And who was she?

The vision winked out. Foresight was as much a curse as a gift, hard to interpret, and even harder to control. He had no time to puzzle over it now, though.

Griff shook his head, refocusing on the fading remnants of that power burst. A mage needed help. Honor, the last reminder of his old life, demanded he help, no matter the risk. He pulled power from the swamp and translocated.

Seconds later, Griff arrived in a rush of cold near the swamp, in a clearing he recognized. A clunky, blue Toyota sedan stood at the clearing's far edge, about thirty yards away.

Four ghouls pinned a feebly struggling woman against the car's hood. Her clothes hung in tatters. A tangle of golden brown hair hid her face, but her agony and the ghouls' triumph vibrated in the heavy air.

That call hadn't been a trap but a desperate Hail Mary play. Fury at the ghouls boiled in his gut.

At this distance, the woman's magic should've resonated with his, but he could barely sense her. She must be dangerously drained. He had to finish this fast, get her help.

Silently, he crossed toward them, angling left.

Enraptured by their feeding, her captors didn't notice his advance. Summoning his shield now would create a glow and alert them, and screening himself from view magically would use energy he couldn't spare in a fight with these odds. Better to rely on stealth. They weren't shielded, so he knew he could take one easily before they realized he was there.

A body lay near the back bumper, the green skin and reek of ammonia marking it as ghoul and dead. She'd gotten one. Good for her.

A widespread power blast might take them out, but if the bastards had absorbed too much of her energy, he might not have enough to stop them and stay on his feet. He spun his staff, drawing power from the life forces all around, then swung it like a bat into the skull of a thin, dark-haired male.

Crack. The impact vibrated up Griff's arms as satisfaction rolled through him. One down.

The ghoul stiffened, then crumpled. He fell, dying, his claws raking the captive mage's chest. The agony in her half gasp, half scream ripped into Griff's soul. He gritted his teeth against the echo of her pain in the magic they shared.

As Griff's shields flared around him, the other three turned to face him. Their shields sprang to life as a muddy, enveloping haze. His strike glanced off the temple of a thin, blond man. The ghoul staggered but didn't fall. *Shit.*

The trio spread out, trying to flank him. Griff backed up. Their prisoner whimpered and collapsed against the bumper. Blood seeped from wounds in her neck, arms, torso, and inner thighs. His lips tightened. He would enjoy making these ghoul scum pay.

The female ghoul flicked out a thick baton, and the heavyset blond whipped out nunchuks. The third ghoul, a burly, brown-haired male, popped a switchblade. Drunk with the power they'd absorbed from the mage, they wavered on their feet.

Nunchuks first. Griff watched them spin, timing them, then whipped the staff up against the connecting chain.

A twist of his wrist wrapped the chain around his staff, breaking the ghoul's grip, and he flung the nunchuks into the night. In the same movement, he swung the staff's low end up in an arc. The ghoul's cheekbone and jaw shattered, partial payback for the wounded mage's agony. With an outraged cry, the male staggered backward.

The woman lunged at Griff's back. He pivoted to slam a side kick into her gut. Her newly fed power hadn't stabilized, and his magic easily drove his foot through her flimsy shields. She fell backward with a gurgling sound, clutching her midsection.

Before he could follow up, the stocky knife wielder charged. Griff feinted toward the male's face. The ghoul tried to stab under the blow. Griff slashed down against the knife arm. Bone cracked at the impact. The ghoul cried out. His knife fell to the dirt.

Griff jabbed his staff's end into the male's chest, easily breaching the unstable shields. *Morere*, Griff thought. He shoved the command along the staff, so the silver end cap flared brilliant white, and into the flesh. *Sta cor*, he added to stop the heart.

The ghoul gasped before falling near the crumpled mage. With a snap like a twig breaking, his life force snuffed out.

Two parasites down, two to go.

The female ghoul jerked to her feet. Baton in a guard position, she charged. Griff started a low, fast push with one hand, then shifted the fake-out move into a whack against her ribs. He heard one crack as she lurched sideways.

Behind him, magic flared, the injured male assimilating the power he'd stolen. Griff pivoted. An arm-size tree branch smashed through his shield. He dodged, but it scraped his shoulder.

The ghouls had absorbed the wounded mage's power. Each was now temporarily stronger than he was. *Shit*. The woman shuddering against the car must've been at the upper end of the power scale.

She would be again. He'd see to it.

Her labored, whimpering breaths signaled fading strength and power. He had to finish this.

Retreating, using the swamp to cover his back, he pulled energy from the plants and animals. He focused magic through *thurisaz*, the *P*-shaped rune on his staff, amplifying his blast.

It struck the male ghoul in the chest, knocking him off his

feet, and hurled him into a live oak by the black water. He fell, twitched, and lay still. Dead.

Three down. One left to pay back.

Depleted by the blast, Griff's power sputtered. Hastily, he drew from the swamp again as a shriek of fury and pain came from behind him.

He wheeled. The female twitched in the dirt, then lay still. Behind her, the wounded mage sagged against the car hood with a switchblade in one hand. Her other hand was clamped to her eyes, and she made choked sounds through gritted teeth. Between her fingers seeped thick, muddy fluid. Venom.

If the ghoul had raked her eyes, every second counted.

Hurrying to her, he caught the coppery scent of blood under the stinging ammonia stench. He glanced at the dead female, and his lips twitched up into a grim half smile. The mage had either more strength or more guts than he'd thought. She'd stabbed the female in the kidney.

"They're dead," he told her. "You're safe now."

A jerky nod answered him. "Eyes."

"Did she scratch them? I see venom on your face." He touched her shoulder gently, feeding her power in the contact.

She gave an abrupt headshake and clenched her jaw around a sob. "Need help," she gritted out. "Healers—"

"I have some training." No way was he calling the Collegium authorities. He propped his staff against the car. "Let me look."

Gently, keeping his fingers light on her shoulder, he used his other hand to tug hers from her eyes. That full, lush mouth and determined chin looked familiar, but he could worry about that later. He brushed tangled strands of hair aside to touch the swelling around one eye gently, and she winced.

"Easy." He probed lightly with his power.

Judging by the way she squinted, she was trying to focus, to see him. He couldn't let her. At least the swelling and reactive tears would blur his features. "No scratches, but close your eyes so the air doesn't aggravate the burn."

"Need healers," she choked. "Experts." Biting her lip, she blinked at him as though trying to clear her eyes. They suddenly widened. "You look—you're— No!"

She wrenched back against his hold, swinging feebly at him with the knife. Tried to gather power for another burst.

Shit. He forced both arms behind her to catch her wrists in one of his hands. "You're safe, I swear," he said.

She'd suffered horribly, which made what he meant to do despicable, but she left him no choice. Clapping his hand over her eyes, he muttered, "*Dormi,*" and fed power into the word.

Asleep, she sagged against him, and he gathered her close. Taller than he'd thought, with a lithe build, she felt solid. Her bare arms under the blood looked toned. Her strength hadn't helped her much today, though.

He would have to call Stefan, whose healing skills far surpassed his own. Then they would figure out how to return her to Collegium circles and, if necessary, confuse her about his identity. Despite her panic, she might not have actually recognized him. She could've been hallucinating from venom poisoning.

He slid a hand under her knees and lifted. Her head lolled back against his shoulder. Her hair fell out of her face. He saw her clearly for the first time and almost dropped her.

Despite the swelling around her eyes, he knew those strong, elegant features. He'd studied them—and her—often enough.

In his arms lay Valeria Banning, his successor as Reeve of the Southeastern U.S. Shire. He'd saved a woman duty-bound to kill him.

Chapter 2

Fire seared Val's eyes. With a gasp, she jerked upright, trying to open them. Pain flashed through her body. She choked down a cry and fell back.

At least she landed on pillows and a soft mattress. Definitely not ghoul hospitality.

"Easy," a man's deep voice said at her side. A callused hand closed gently over her clenched fist. Mage power resonated in the touch. Like sunlight in her blood, strengthening power flowed from him. "You're safe now."

Truth also vibrated in his touch. Along with...worry? Regret?

Before she could probe, his hand withdrew. She couldn't sense anything now. He'd locked down his power and his emotions. She forced herself to relax.

Her eyes wouldn't open. She raised a hand to her face and gasped at biting pain in her shoulder. Her fingers touched linen. Bandages. The air smelled of lemon verbena and lavender, healing scents. Homey ones, with a hint of bay leaf—for protection?—on the pillowcase. Not hospital smells. A droning noise and a stream of cold air hinted at a window air conditioner.

"Venom in your eyes," the man said. "Sorry I can't heal them fully, but at least there's no organic damage."

His deep voice gave her a tingly sensation, like velvet drifting over her skin, and warmed her inexplicably. She pushed herself up to sit. The movement hurt pretty much everywhere, but she felt at a disadvantage lying down.

He banked pillows behind her. Awareness of him, pleasant and also somehow familiar, prickled over her skin.

"I'm Kyle Connor," he added. "You're at my home near the swamp."

"Valeria Banning." She offered her right hand. He took it in a warm, firm grip but released it too soon for her to probe. Yet the vibes of his magic felt familiar. "Have we met before?"

"We had a couple of reeve training classes together before I chose a different career. Do you remember the fight?"

Ghouls. A tall, brave mage, who looked, who fought, like...but Griffin Dare had no reason to help her and every reason to let her die. With the damage to her eyes, she hadn't seen the man clearly. Maybe Connor only resembled Dare, with the same height, lean, broad-shouldered build, and jet-black hair. "I assume you rescued me. Thank you, so very much."

Yet cold fingers of unease pinched her throat. Though her vision had been blurred from the injury, she'd seen that the man fought with a quarterstaff, an antiquated weapon almost no one used. In the Southeast, where people spoke with his accent, only Griffin Dare wielded one. She had best tread carefully.

"I'm glad your summons reached me," he said. "How did they catch you?"

"I saw a bunch of ghouls trying to kidnap a Mundane woman and her little boy in Wayfarer. I figured they meant to breed her." Remembering brought back the anger, made her voice hard. "The kid was only seven, too young to use as a breeder."

"But not too young to be a snack if the ghouls were running short on animals," he said in harsh tones.

"Exactly." She could still see the terror on the child's round face. Ghouls could digest only fresh kill. They usually kept animals for that but weren't above munching on mage or Mundane flesh if the opportunity arose. "I got them clear, killed two ghouls, but I was outnumbered."

"You took out two, and there were five in the clearing." He let out a low whistle. "Seven to one, tough odds in any case. Dicier with Mundanes to protect. Good job."

"Thanks. The woman and her child know mages exist now, but that was better than letting the ghouls take them."

As they'd taken Val's parents when she was fifteen. Her mom had headed the math department at the Collegium academy, and her dad had been the Collegium's comptroller. They'd been killed by ghouls while on a camping trip they'd taken as a romantic getaway. Val had sworn she'd fight the ghouls until her dying breath.

"Uh, where, exactly, are we?"

"At my home, as I said. I'll help you get back to the Collegium as soon as you're well enough to travel."

If he knew she lived there, he probably knew she was shire reeve. Gingerly, she moved one leg. Pain flashed in her thigh, and cool linen slid over her bare skin. Something soft but not thin, like chambray, covered her upper body. Val swallowed against a jolt of fear. "What happened to my clothes?"

"They were ruined. You're wearing one of my shirts, fresh from the laundry. Don't worry, I didn't take advantage." Her rescuer brushed his hand over hers long enough to let her sense his honesty, yet again, not long enough to let her probe. Was he hiding something, like his identity as the mage world's most notorious renegade, or was he just naturally careful?

"It's Tuesday, about three p.m.," he continued. "You've been out since a little after ten last night."

"Better out than dead. I'm very grateful, but I should report back to the Collegium."

"What you need most is rest." His voice came from farther above her now, and she had a vague, magical sense of a man's standing shape. "When the light fades enough that it won't hurt your eyes, we'll put fresh salve on them."

"There's no need for you to go to that trouble. Just give me a phone, and I'll be out of your way."

"Your wounds," he said with great patience, "were tended by an expert and will heal fully in a couple of days. Then I'll take you into town and leave you where you can call anyone you like, but I won't have the Collegium nosing into my life, Shire Reeve Banning."

"If you know who I am, you know the deputy reeves will be looking for me." Not for a few days, though, not until she was due back from vacation. For now, she was on her own. Blind, hurt, and alone. *Hellfire.*

"You won't be here that long," he said.

Because he planned to drain her of her power when she recovered? Or sell her? Cold with fear, she forced her chin up. "Look—"

"I saved your life, Sheriff." His voice hardened. "Have a little gratitude."

"Of course I'm grateful." Dread churned in her stomach, but Val could do steely tones, too. "But no honest mage would keep me here."

Of course, Griffin Dare wasn't honest, and this guy had way too much in common with Dare for her to trust him. Collegium annals labeled Dare a ghoul ally, though his killing ghouls today supported her doubts about that. In the past, he'd killed mages without hesitation. Yet he'd saved her. Why?

"I promise, you're safe." Still an edge in his voice.

"Safe and prisoner aren't partners in my universe. If you're hoping for a reward, I can arrange it."

If he killed her, would anyone really miss having her around? Gene and Zara Blake, her former guardians, and Sybil, her friend and deputy would, but no one else. She'd lived for the job, pushed loneliness aside to deal with later, and now she might be out of chances.

"I don't need a reward." Faint footsteps, as though from bare feet on wood, retreated.

"There's a bottle of water on the nightstand," he said. "You bled a lot, so drink as much as you can. Bathroom's in the back corner of the room. There's also a tub of balm on the table for the talon wounds. You can use it as often as needed. I'd offer to help, but I assume you'd refuse."

She gave him a curt nod.

The silence stretched. "I'll bring dinner soon," he finally said. "Try to rest." A faint squeak like door hinges sounded, then the click of a latch.

Val counted to ten before pushing back the covers. Although his kindness felt genuine, it didn't fit with holding her here. With who he very likely was. Trusting that kindness could be a fatal mistake.

A shiver of fear rippled through her, and she swallowed hard. She was damned if he decided to hold her prisoner. She wouldn't risk her eyes by removing the bandages, so she had to use her power to sense objects in the room. Not the ideal situation but she'd cope.

Every ward had a weakness. She would find the flaw in his.

Slamming the bedroom door would let her know she'd gotten to him, so Griff closed it softly. A wave of his hand sealed the ward and locked her in.

"How did it go?" Stefan Harper, the Collegium's chief physician and Griff's closest friend, nursed a beer at the beat-up oak bar.

"She's stubborn, as you said."

The image of her lingered in Griff's head. The rolled sleeves of his shirt revealed her slender, strong wrists, and the open neck showed the long line of her throat, a line he could capture so easily on canvas, though he would omit the bandage on one side.

The overall effect rivaled an ad in a kinky men's magazine, and he knew, after helping Stefan treat her, what lay underneath the shirt. His body hardened, but he banished the image. Hell would need heaters before she gave him the time of day.

Not that he wanted her to take that kind of interest. He was done with relationships until he cleared his name. They were too dangerous, and not only for him. He had other plans for her, if she would listen to him.

The ceiling fan stirred the heavy air but didn't cool it. He shoved his sweaty bangs out of his face.

Dark-haired and lean, Stefan pointed with his bottle. "You should knock her out, deposit her on some ER doorstep, and run like hell."

"Which helps me how?" Griff stalked across the plank flooring to the bar. He wrapped his hand around the cold, sweating beer Stefan had set out for him.

"It gets her out of here," Stefan said. "They'll come looking, you know."

"They won't find her unless I allow it. You know both this place and I are warded against scrying." Griff tapped his chest where the lapis lazuli Eye of Horus pendant, symbol of the Egyptian god of justice, lay under his shirt. The warded pendant hid him and everything close by. "Her being here changes nothing."

"Except for bringing your chief pursuer inside your home and maybe upping the bounty on your life." Stefan studied him, his brown eyes hard. "You're planning something. Damn it, if she finds out who you are, she'll kill you."

Best not to admit she seemed to have her suspicions already. "Keep your voice down," Griff said. "It'll go through the bedroom ward. You've risked enough by coming here last night and again today."

Stefan shrugged. "She's my patient. Besides, no one suspects me. The risk was yours in contacting me. Hell, I don't see how you've lived this long taking the chances you do."

"She was hurt too badly for my healing abilities. Needed the best, and that's you." Griff took a long swallow of the bitter brew. "You take chances, too, Stefan. In that, we're pot and kettle."

Stefan grunted and shook his head. After a moment, he asked, "How's your blood venom level today?"

"It's down, staying in the low teens." Any prolonged exertion, such as yesterday's battle, ramped it up. Rest and recharging pushed it down. If the venom hit fifty-six milligrams per deciliter, it would warp his physiology, and magic, permanently. He would become a ghoul.

In theory.

In fact, he would never allow the venom in his blood to turn him, even if he had to slit his own throat to prevent it.

Griff held the cool bottle against his brow. Bringing Valeria Banning here was lunacy, as Stefan said, but a slim hope beat none.

"Once we had her blood cleansed and her wounds bandaged," Stefan said, "we could've taken her to the ER at County General. I still don't see why you balked at that."

I wanted her here.

Unbidden and extremely unwelcome, the truth popped into Griff's head. She'd been the mage most likely to come after him, so he'd followed her career. Knowing the woman who hunted him could save his life someday. She'd justified her rep for guts, using her dwindling power to cover his back by stabbing that last ghoul. Besides…

"She could be a valuable ally," he said.

"You think she'll listen to you?"

"She's smart. As a cadet, she wasn't always first off the mark, but she got to the right answer faster than most."

Her parents' deaths at ghoul hands had shattered her world. She'd gone from cheerful and relaxed to driven and resolute, determined to keep others from suffering as she had.

Griff added, "She cared fiercely about justice. Apparently, she still does."

"Yeah, and one of our prime suspects is her ex-guardian."

Griff met Stefan's dour look with one of his own. "We're losing, Stefan. Despite everything we do, our numbers dwindle with each generation while the ghouls' grow. They take more Mundanes every year. More of us, too."

Stefan grimaced. "It's worse than you know. Records from that breeding nest Banning destroyed a couple of weeks ago show the ghouls have managed to bump the rate of ghoul births to captured Mundanes above sixty percent."

"Hellfire." Griff's fingers tightened on his beer in frustration. "Meanwhile, the mage gene is recessive. There're mageborn who don't even know they have powers, and the ghouls are seducing our kids with dark magic."

"All unfortunately true." Stefan shook his head. "My staff counsels the kids against it, but it's hard to resist the orgasmic kick, and tougher to believe it'll corrupt your blood until you turn ghoul. And it doesn't help that young ghouls aren't as easy to spot as mature ones."

"Yeah. Desperate times, desperate measures."

"Hell." Stefan took a long drink of his beer. "You know she's probably in there testing your wards right now. Tell me you covered that AC unit."

"Of course I did." Griff shrugged. "In her current condition, she couldn't pop an unprotected windowpane."

"That one would put her fist through the window. She'll recover quickly, you know."

"I have things under control."

"We've controlled damned little since that godawful day

you fought your way out of the Collegium." Stefan's lips tightened briefly. "If I hadn't come to you about the Council—"

"More people would've died, you among them." Griff shook his head. "We did what we had to. Now we have to keep hunting, be ready when the traitor on the Council makes a mistake."

"Preferably before you get yourself killed."

"I know what I'm doing." He hoped. "Thanks for taking Will that amulet the ghouls used on Banning. He called earlier to say he hasn't figured it out, so he's asking his parents to test it in their archaeology lab. You could take him that packet on the bar and ask him to dig into the lore on dark forces, see if he can figure out the ghouls' plan."

Stefan's grim look said the subject wasn't closed, but he set his beer down and slid off the stool. "At least the blood samples I took from her may help with the antivenom."

"How's that going?" A vaccine that could render mages immune to venom would undercut the ghouls' numerical superiority. Maybe it would even cleanse Griff's blood, however unlikely that was.

"I have a crude formula I'm not ready to test." Probing Griff's face, Stefan's eyes narrowed. "Watch yourself with her. That pretty face hides a will as determined as yours."

Griff shrugged. *Pretty* didn't begin to describe her. Now that he'd met her again, seen her courage and jousted verbally with her, *intriguing* also felt like an understatement.

"Be careful going back," he said. "As you leave, take that pot on the stove to the downstairs crew. Dumpster diving hasn't paid off lately."

"They could get an actual meal at the shelter in town."

"They want to be independent, I guess. They won't take much from me if they can avoid it." The eighteen or so homeless people living on the ground floor had created a community of sorts. He had to give them credit for trying to help each other.

Looking resigned, Stefan hoisted the pot. Griff walked him to the door and locked it behind him. The protective ward sparkled faint green for a heartbeat as Griff sealed it again.

A whisper of power, the barest hint, brushed his mind, and he smiled. She was testing the wards, as they suspected. Subtly but methodically testing. Valeria Banning had intelligence, skill, and integrity along with a lot of raw power. Even wearing only bandages and his shirt, she remained coolly self-possessed.

As for what the shirt concealed...

No. Not going there, even though the memory heated his blood. He had more important goals, and they depended on his convincing her of the truth about the traitor in the Collegium.

If he couldn't, his best hope of security lay in wiping his info from her memory, a risky process that could leave her worse than dead if his control slipped at all.

She didn't deserve that, and doing it would go against everything he believed. But if he couldn't stomach that, telling her the truth would put his life and the lives of his friends directly in the Collegium's sights.

Only an idiot, or maybe a Pollyanna, would trust her safety to the word of someone who was very likely a murderer. Sitting behind the door with one hand on the wall, attuned to the ward, Val waited for his return. She could break the window, escape through it, but she hadn't been able to sense the ground. She might be too far up to jump, and in her weakened state, unable to translocate, she couldn't outrun pursuit.

So her best chance to escape, maybe even capture the man, lay in ambushing him. Even though she still needed a few days to reach full fighting power. Magical healing could only speed recovery by so much, but she couldn't risk waiting.

The more she thought about him, the more she believed he was Griffin Dare, no matter what name he gave her. The smart play was to proceed on that assumption until she knew otherwise.

His evasion about why he kept her here could only mean he had a purpose she wouldn't like. Besides, if he was Dare, she had a duty to bring him in for execution. Even though he'd been condemned in his absence, without a trial. That went against her grain, but so did letting a man who'd killed mages roam free.

At least she had surprise on her side. One failure was enough for this week.

A failure he'd saved her from.

Okay, so maybe she wouldn't hurt him if she could avoid it.

Which was a crazy thought about a man holding her prisoner, a man already sentenced to death. Even if he had rescued her.

Dare had killed too many mages to deserve mercy, no matter what else he had or hadn't done. Five had died at his hand, including the chief councilor, as he'd fled the Collegium, and he'd killed at least two more, maybe three, since.

She rolled her tight shoulders. As a cadet, she'd met him a

couple of times, and he'd treated her, as he did all the cadets, with interest and tact, even when pointing out errors. She'd admired him, maybe even had a crush on him.

She hadn't been the only one. With his clean-cut good looks, eyes the blue of a sunlit ocean, and tall, muscular body, he'd been a walking chick magnet. And the way he moved...Even then, his skill with a quarterstaff and his tactical abilities were legend.

Then they'd become notorious. Reviled.

Val shook her head. What a waste. But maybe this man wasn't Dare. Maybe Griffin Dare was long dead, his shredded honor mere dust on a distant wind.

Yeah, and maybe she'd win the Nobel Peace Prize this year.

Once she had him secured, she could find his phone and call for backup.

A faint ripple in the warding warned of its creator approaching. She stood and hoisted the chair, grimacing at the pain in her injured arms and shoulders.

"You've been busy, if not smart," he said through the door.

Did he know she was there, or was he guessing? Or scrying? The chair's weight dragged at her sore arms.

"I know you're standing by the door, beside the hinges." Amusement warmed his voice. "Where I would."

He was laughing at her? She would kill him.

"Holding that chair has to hurt your wounded arms." He paused. "I can stand here until your strength fails. Or I walk in, you whack me, and I drop dinner to clock you with a knockout punch."

He'd be the one knocked out.

He sighed. "I can outwait you, and I'm not blind or hurt. Give it up and eat."

Her arms shook. The blasted chair felt as though it were made of granite. She couldn't hold it much longer.

Now the crazy bastard was whistling! Furious, she smashed the chair against the door. It made a satisfying crash but no cracking sound, no hint of breaking.

She was weaker than she'd known. *Hell, blast, and damnation!* Her one chance, gone. Tears of frustration welled in her eyes, stinging like new venom, and she gasped.

"What's wrong? Valeria, what is it?"

Stumbling away from the door, she choked on a sob. Hell with that. She would not let him hear her cry.

The salty liquid seared her injured eyes, and a whimper escaped. Her foot caught on the rug and she pitched forward. When her hands struck the braided fabric, it skidded. Val crashed onto her face.

Black agony rolled over her, obliterating the world. She couldn't breathe. Couldn't move.

Hands closed gently on her shoulders. Power rolled into her, dialing back the agony. Strengthening her.

"Breathe," he urged, gently turning her onto her back. "C'mon, honey, breathe." His arm slid under her legs, warm, bare skin to her bare skin, and he cradled her against his solid, cotton-covered chest.

"I'm not—your—honey," she choked. Yet she couldn't help turning toward him, resting against his strength, until the pain ebbed.

"Glad to see your grit survived the fall." He rose, lifting her easily.

She clutched his shoulders for balance and caught scents of bay leaf and sweat. His shoulders felt wide and solid—reliable, she might've said if he were any other man.

"Let's put you to bed. You've had enough exercise for one day. Then you can eat, and we'll put fresh salve on your eyes."

He wasn't even angry. What kind of weird game was he playing, being so kind?

Worse, she felt safe in his arms, as though he were the kind of man Griffin Dare once had been, the man who'd led the mage squad who'd avenged her parents.

But that was dangerous thinking. She mustn't let him confuse her. If he hadn't kept her here, she wouldn't have fallen in the first place.

If she felt safe with him, it was only because he'd rescued her, then taken care of her. Like patient-doctor dependence, a weird head game. Like Stockholm syndrome, captive attraction to captor. She had to shake it off.

"What happened?" he asked.

"I tripped." *Duh.*

He eased her onto the bed. "Before that. When you gasped and stumbled."

"I had a flash of eye pain." She wasn't about to admit she'd teared up in frustration.

He drew his arms away, straightening. For an instant, she wanted them back. *Stupid, stupid.*

He propped pillows behind her. When he drew the covers over her bare legs, the bay scent teased her nose again.

"This is your bed." Val tensed. Sleeping in his bed felt far too intimate. Too trusting.

"It's the only bed I've got. Sorry I didn't have a chance to change the linens. They've had only a couple of nights' use." After a moment, he added, "I'm taking the couch. I told you, you're safe here."

Her heart beat faster with nerves, but she had to push

him, had to know if he meant her harm. "Safe? Like a prisoner on death row?"

His frustration spiked in the magic between them, a punch that echoed in her own chest. It must be intense, or she wouldn't have felt it with her power so low and no physical contact.

"More like a witness in a safe house," he said.

"Then give me your hand so I can probe."

"No. I carry secrets other than my own." Before she could argue, he said, "Straighten out your legs. I have a bed tray to set over them."

The aromas of baked chicken and warm bread made her mouth water. Her stomach growled, but she ignored it. Chicken. Meat. *A knife to cut it.* She could work wonders with a knife.

"Napkin and spoon on the left," he said lightly. "You have chicken at nine o'clock, broccoli at noon, and a buttered roll at three. Lemonade at one o'clock beside the plate."

"It smells good." A little courtesy couldn't hurt, so she added, "Thank you." The way he'd described the food on her plate—that was a clue.

"I hope you like it. I cut everything up already, and I'm sorry, but you'll have to make do with a spoon. I'm not giving anything sharp to someone who fights with a blade."

Damn. She groped for the spoon. Could she transmute it into a blade? Rubbing her finger along the spoon as she heard him walk away, she summoned power. A bit came. Not nearly enough for a transmutation.

She sipped lemonade, and the answer hit her, the reason his description of the food mattered. Carefully she set the glass down.

The sound of his footsteps approached. A thump, then a creak, as though he'd put the chair down and sat in it. "All right?"

"Fine." Better to know what he intended than to let him toy with her any longer. "Your sister served me lemonade when I interviewed her, not long after I became reeve three years ago."

For a beat, a telltale moment, he hesitated. "I don't have a sister." His voice sounded a hair too controlled.

"You described the food locations for me easily. As though you'd dealt with someone blind before, like Caroline Dare."

"Just common sense."

"Common sense says if it walks like a duck, quacks like a duck…Few mages train with quarterstaves anymore, but you wield one as though you'd been born using it. You've expert knowledge of mage lore but don't trust the Collegium. And you know how to describe a plate of food to a blind person. Those three factors add up to only one man.

"Cut the bullshit, Dare, and tell me what you want."

Chapter 3

The silence stretched between them until fear churned in Val's gut. Had she made a mistake, pushed him too far?

"Assuming I'm this person," he said in a flat, hard voice, "what does that make me to you? I already have an idea, but give me the whole picture."

She raised her chin a notch, bracing herself for an outburst. "You're a rogue mage, a murderer several times over, and possibly a ghoul ally."

A creak alerted her as he shifted toward her, leaning so close she could feel his breath on her cheek. Her mouth went dry, but she held her position. She couldn't let him intimidate her.

"If I'm such a bastard, why the hell aren't you dead?"

"I asked you first." Thank God, her voice held steady. She swallowed to ease her tight throat.

"If you believed everything in your precious annals, you wouldn't risk challenging me. Yes, I'm Griffin Rhys Dare."

Val's heart thudded in her throat. He'd just confirmed her guess. Yet she was, for whatever reason, still alive.

"What do you want with me?"

"I want you to listen. To consider evidence you haven't seen before."

"So you're going to tell me you're innocent? I'd expected better of you."

He let out a weary sigh. "I'm not in league with the ghouls, and I never killed anyone I didn't have to."

The first part, she'd believe. But the second… "You'll never convince me the mages who tried to apprehend you were ghoul allies."

"Of course not." He sounded sad.

If only she could believe he really was.

"They were trying to capture me. I was defending my-self—and those who rely on me for protection."

"Such as?" Impatient, Val shook her head. "Regardless, you should've come in, made your case, not slaughtered—"

"We're not going there. Not tonight." His cold, hard voice warned her not to press. "I brought you here to talk to you. To show you things you can't see well enough now to read."

"So you do have a jailhouse alibi." That seemed beneath him, and his thinking her fool enough to buy it stung.

"I have the truth. If you're willing to see it."

"Right. What do you really want?"

A slight sound, not quite a sigh, came from him, as if he were hurt. Like he cared what she thought. Oh, he knew just how to play her.

"I want safety for our people," he said, "and for the Mun-danes, whether you believe me or not. Listening won't cost you anything but a couple of days for your eyes to heal. What if I'm telling the truth, Valeria? What if there's something rotten in the Collegium's heart? Can you shrug off that possibility so easily?"

What was or wasn't happening in the Collegium was her business, not his, but listening might help her better understand his angle. "I'll hear you out, but you'll have to explain right now."

Fifteen minutes later, Griff set out the files on the kitchen bar. As soon as the salve had time to melt into Valeria's eyes, he'd show her what he had. She seemed even less likely to believe him than he'd feared. Damn, but he was tired of running. Tired of fighting while innocents died anyway. Tired of winning little victories that changed nothing.

Convincing her could help unmask the traitor, give him his life back. It might even win Collegium help against whatever dark rite the ghouls planned. He'd told his team to take and interrogate a ghoul prisoner. But the Collegium mages, with their numbers, could work a lot faster.

"Dare?" She stood hesitantly in the bedroom doorway.

His shirt hung down to her midthigh, covering the bandages there but hiding little of her long, trim legs. His blood stirred, and his denim cutoffs did nothing to hide his reaction. At least she couldn't see it.

"Bar straight ahead," he said. "About ten or twelve feet, but let me help you." He'd best remember the formidable power she was recovering by the minute, and not let the sex-kitten look distract him. He could find sex in any bar. What he needed from her was belief and support.

He needed them deeply, he realized.

With one hand outstretched, she took a careful step.

"Wait." He hurried to her right side. "Give me your hand."

She bit her lip but held out her right hand. When he tucked it into the crook of his elbow, his heartbeat kicked up a notch. He hadn't had a woman's hand in his arm in years.

The trust in the gesture, however reluctant, jabbed his soul with guilt. She didn't deserve a memory blank, but if she wouldn't believe him, he'd have no choice. He carried too many people's secrets to let her go with the knowledge she was about to gain.

He led Valeria to the bar and seated her in front of the folders. "Wait while I fix the lights."

Twilight had turned to night. With indirect light, her eyes might tolerate the air and the brightness enough for her to read. He snapped on the light in the stove hood. It cast a faint glow over the papers. It would have to do.

The slight tilt of her head implied she followed his bare-footed progress around the room. When he stood beside her, she reached up to the bandages. "Now?" she asked.

"Don't open your eyes right away." He helped her remove the linen strips and cloth pads and set them on the bar within easy reach. "The stove light is on, to your left across the bar. Don't look directly at it."

"Understood." She turned right, toward him, and slowly opened her eyes. Something he couldn't read flickered in them and vanished. Bloodshot but now discernibly hazel, they regarded him intently.

His mouth went desert dry. Having her this close, looking at him so directly...if he leaned in, he could taste that ripe mouth, trace the long line of her neck, test the weight of her breasts. His body hardened, and he wrenched his gaze away.

The judgment behind those hazel eyes mattered far more

than her looks. Her choice here could help their people, maybe even give him a future.

"Do you know why I left the Collegium?"

"You claimed Chief Councilor Milt Alden was in league with ghouls." She squinted, as though protecting her eyes from the air, but her gaze took on probing intensity. "But there was no proof."

"There was circumstantial evidence. As well as my word, for all the good that did." Was that doubt in her eyes? "Damn it, I'd earned some credibility."

"I'll grant you that, but—"

Power blasted through his perimeter wards with the sick wrench inside his head that signaled ghoul magic. *Fuck.*

"Shield," he snapped, but he flung his own barrier around her in case she hadn't recovered enough. Dropping the ward around his staff, he summoned it. It struck his palm with a reassuring smack, its end caps and runes glowing.

Valeria slid from the stool. "Dare—"

One impact on his wards, one breach. Two. Three. Four. Five—

A roar shook the building. As he and Valeria fell, he snatched her close with his free arm, twisting to take the brunt of the fall. Then he rolled her under him for extra protection. Dust and fragments of brick showered down on his personal shields. At least she had the good sense not to struggle.

The building stopped shaking, but screams came from below. Terrified cries. *Shit.* He had to go.

Valeria had grabbed his shoulders. Releasing them, she said, "Thanks. What was that?"

"Ghouls." He pushed himself to his feet and gave her a

hand up. "I've made a lot of trouble for them. This isn't the first time they've hunted me." Bringing her here, though, might've left a magic trail for them to follow.

She tensed, rubbing her eyes carefully. "How many?"

"Too many."

He'd lost count but knew more had come in. A wave of his hand released the extra wards around the loft, the ones that kept her in. She could escape, and others could enter, but he couldn't sustain those wards and fight, too.

The terrified shrieks from below continued. Something crashed.

"I have to help the people downstairs, but you should be safe up here." If he could keep the ghouls away from the stairs.

She squinted against the light. "There are Mundanes here?" At his nod, she added, "I can help you. Give me my sword."

"No way." She might run. Or, once the ghouls were beaten, turn on him. He didn't want to have to fight her.

"I promised you a hearing." She grabbed his hand, opening to his magic. "If you want me to trust you, then you have to trust me."

Honesty flowed in the touch, and his breath caught at the hope it offered. He dropped the concealment on her weapon. Light shimmered in the corner, revealing the sword.

"For self-defense," he said. "I'm trusting you, and I need you safe. So wait here." He wheeled toward the door.

"Be careful," she called after him.

Surprised, he nodded and banged the door behind him. A jump took him to the stairwell landing. Below lay the corridor between the old manufacturing and storage areas.

As he leaped for the ground floor, a brown-gold blast of pure power sliced through the air. He tucked as he landed, and rolled under the sizzling beam. On his feet again, he swung his staff like an ax through the shields of the blond, voluptuous ghoul who'd launched the bolt, smashing his weapon into her gut. The woman staggered backward. Her shields dissolved.

Behind him, masonry bits and dust blew from the brick wall where the blast struck. Debris rained down on his shield and disintegrated with faint *pffft* noises. He rammed one silver-shod end of the staff into the ghoul's forehead. "*Morere,*" he snapped to make sure.

Dead, she fell. Leaping over her, he drew energy from the swamp outside. Screams came from the old manufacturing area. The coppery stench of blood.

Shit. He had to get his people out. He careened around the corner, into the former workroom, then tripped over someone's leg. Old Maureen lay by the door, neck at a sick angle, sightless eyes staring upward, and his heart twisted.

A big male ghoul with a blond Mohawk charged toward him. Griff ducked, slammed the staff into the ghoul's chest and fed in power. "*Morere.*"

Two down, about a dozen to go. Way too many. He channeled magic through the staff, blasted one ghoul. A widespread burst would hit a lot of them but not all, and would lower his power dangerously. He couldn't recharge fast enough to make that a good bet.

Against the far wall, the two young runaways, Hector and Rosa, lay still, bleeding from throat wounds. Dying. The other men and women struggled to get themselves and their children to a gaping hole in the wall. They dodged ghouls, stumbled over broken furniture and dishes. He had to reach them, cover their retreat—

Behind him a ghoul approached. He pivoted to meet the threat, too late. Talons punched through his shield and raked across his back.

The floor vibrated. Screams and crashes rang in the air. Val reeled against the bar, her sword dragging on her arm like a battleship's anchor. No way could she fight with it.

She laid the weapon down. She hadn't even felt its presence earlier, a sign Dare was better than she'd realized. But nobody was good enough to take on a large group of ghouls alone, especially with Mundanes to protect.

He'd looked surprised, even wary, when she asked for his trust. That reaction had stung, but he'd probably be dead by now if he were less careful.

Fear for him knotted her gut. Traitor or not, he'd braved dangerous odds to save her. He was braving worse ones for those Mundanes now. She had to help him, give the Mundanes the best chance she could.

She drew energy from the swamp. New power coursed through her body, but more like a summer-dry creek than the torrent it should've been. It would just have to do.

The air burned her eyes, made them tear. She rubbed them carefully. Her vision was a little blurry, but she could see well enough to fight.

Magic roared through the building, a widespread burst. Dare wouldn't risk that unless he was desperately outnumbered.

The fading magic of his blast skated across her skin, and she opened to it, drinking it in to quicken her own power and strengthen her. She couldn't fully recharge until her wounds healed, but every bit helped. Val grabbed a butcher knife from the kitchen and sped down the stairs.

They ended in a corridor. A big, male ghoul staggered against a door frame to her right. The muddy whites of his eyes were filled with rage. He was huge, and she was so weak.

Fear gave her a jolt of adrenaline. Val charged. The ghoul swiped his talons at her face. She ducked and stabbed under his arm, punching power into the blade. "*Morere.*"

With a gurgled cry, he slumped, dying.

She yanked the blade free. Val jumped over a female ghoul's stinking corpse, then a Mundane woman's body, and ran into a wide room with high, narrow windows.

The air reeked of ammonia from dead ghouls. About a dozen bodies lay scattered amid jumbled furniture, broken crockery, and cardboard boxes. Eight were ghouls, their skin already turned faint green in death.

On the far side of the room, three big males stalked Dare. Bleeding gouges on his chest and arms had his blue T-shirt in shreds. Sweat poured down his face. He stumbled backward, haggard and too pale, shielding a little brown-haired girl. Sobbing, she scrambled behind him.

His strain to keep up his shield thrummed in his magic and felt like a drain in Val's chest. Her heart plummeted. Translocating someone else you weren't touching took far more power than shifting yourself. She was too weak to shift the child clear. So was Dare, or he would've already done it.

In seconds, the ghouls would corner him, but she could even the odds. Buy time for the girl to run.

Dare's eyes met hers, and he gave her a slight shake of his head. Val ignored it.

Intent on him, the ghouls hadn't noticed her. She crept up behind the nearest one, feeding power to the blade, and stabbed at his kidney. His shield deflected most of the blow. He spun around to face her.

Dare whipped his staff toward the male on the far end. The ghoul's shielding blunted the hit, another sign of Dare's fading power.

The ghoul facing Val had a shock of inky hair and a face that looked as though it'd been mashed together. With lightning speed, he whipped his bludgeon at her head. Only a leap backward carried her out of its crushing path.

The ghoul shot venom out of his talons. *Shit.* Ducking, Val pushed into a backward shoulder roll and evaded his swiping follow-up.

Heart pounding, she kicked out his right kneecap, but her power sputtered. Once more, maybe twice, she could punch through that kind of shielding. Then it would be game over.

He crumpled, bringing him level with her. She dived for him and flipped the knife into her left hand as her right forearm blocked his strike. She stabbed with all the power she could draw. "*Morere*," she gasped, and the blade rammed home.

He shuddered and spat blood before going limp.

Panting, Val dragged herself to her feet and wiped her stinging eyes. Where was Dare?

There, jerking away from a scrawny, brown-haired male. The ghoul's power blast struck Dare's bloody chest and flung him backward. The staff flew from his hand as he hit the ground hard, with an agonized groan.

The ghoul darted past him, toward the screaming, scrambling child. The little girl tripped, but quickly pulled herself up and dodged a swipe of talons before darting between two cardboard boxes. The ghoul flung them aside, scattering clothes across the floor.

Stumbling toward them with her lungs aching and her heart in her throat, Val couldn't reach either of them in time. She had nothing left, only the barest of shielding.

Dare was closer but so still. Had they killed— No, she realized with a gasp of relief as he groaned and pushed himself onto an elbow.

The ghoul cornered the child and loomed over her, extending talons.

"Dare!" Val screeched, pointing.

His head whipped around. His lips tightened. Then he was gone. Vanished.

A heartbeat later, he reappeared kneeling between the child and the ghoul, his body hunching over the tot, sheltering her as the talons swiped downward.

No! Val's heart tore as the ghoul clawed new gouges in Griffin's bleeding back. She gathered herself and leaped forward, driving her blade between the ghoul's shoulders.

"*Morere,*" she gasped. He arched with the blow, reeled, and fell. Dead.

She twisted out of the way. No more ghouls, thank God. She couldn't have done that again.

Fighting to breathe, aching all over, she blinked her stinging eyes clear and looked for Dare. He knelt a few feet beyond the body, shuddering in pain and bleeding from multiple wounds. He cradled the wailing child in his arms, a child with big, mournful eyes and shabby clothes.

He'd been willing to die for that little girl. If Val hadn't reached them in time, he would have.

No traitor would take such a risk.

The Collegium annals contained only one side of the story. Dare had been a hero once, had acted like one now. Maybe there was more to his claims than she'd wanted to believe.

"Griffin?" She touched his shoulder gently, and his pain flashed through the sympathetic bonds of shared magic. Shaking with it, she managed, "They're gone."

He gave her a single jerky nod.

The sobbing child clung to him, tiny fingers digging into his arms. "Gray," she wailed into his shoulder.

"Gray?" Val raised an eyebrow at him.

"Later."

The child's weight on his injured chest had to be torture, but he closed his arms around her. He even kissed her tangled hair. "It's all right, Molly," his voice rasped.

The child sobbed into his shoulder, and he patted her back absently. Above her head, his eyes scanned the disordered, stinking room.

"We're clear," Val said.

He studied her with a wary expression. "Good thing you didn't leave."

"I gave you my word."

His eyes warmed, and one corner of his mouth crooked up. She couldn't resist smiling back at him.

"Guess I have to trust you now," he said. "I'm not used to it. Trusting, I mean."

"I guess not." And she shouldn't trust him without reservation, but he was courageous, she had to give him that.

He'd changed from the man she remembered. His face was still handsome in a clean-cut way, with its strong jaw, high cheekbones, and straight nose, but he now looked more austere. More controlled. Shadowed by pain, his ocean-blue eyes scanned the room, alert for any danger. When he looked at her, though, the blue softened in a way that made her heart skip a beat.

He stared at her quizzically. "What? Did I grow an extra ear or something?"

"No, I—"

"Molly?" A woman's hesitant voice came from behind Val. "Oh, Molly-love!"

A thin, bedraggled woman in her midtwenties climbed through a hole in the masonry. The woman ran toward Griffin, and he handed the child to her.

"Mama," Molly sobbed. "There was bad men."

"I know sweetie, I know." The woman pressed her lips to Molly's hair and choked, "Thank you" to Dare.

He waved away her gratitude. In the fluorescent lights, his skin looked ashen. "We have to go," he said painfully. "All of us." He scrubbed a hand over his face. "Others will come."

Oh, crap. Val's relief evaporated. Of course the enemy would return. They'd found a feeding ground, one with mages they could draw power from or breed.

The stench in the air from human death and deteriorating ghoul corpses burned her nose.

As Molly and her mom gathered their belongings, Val crouched beside Dare. His glance skimmed her bare legs, and the heat in it made her breath hitch.

He grinned despite the shivers he was probably trying to hide. "I like the new take on combat gear."

"Your pants would've made the wrong fashion statement. Besides, I was in a hurry." She brushed his tangled hair off his face. His skin felt clammy. Cold. A bruised knot marred his temple, and she didn't have the power to fix it. "You need a healer."

"You okay?" Although he blew out a ragged breath, his grave eyes stayed locked on her face. He touched her shoulder, and her heart beat faster.

"Nothing new." Compared to everything else, the scrapes from diving at that ghoul were too minor to count. "I'm fine, just, well, surprised by you." She took his hand, and the pain searing him flashed into her. Val bit back a gasp. How did he breathe through the white heat in his chest?

When he tried to pull free, she laced her fingers through his. "Mages' creed, remember? We fought together. We handle this together, too."

Shock rippled over his face, vibrated through the touch. Behind it lay sweet, warm pleasure. "You're already hurt. You don't need this." But he stood with her and let her draw his head against her shoulder, sighing when she rested her cheek against his hair. He set his hands at her waist.

"I can deal," she said. "Take what I'm sending you." If only she had more to give, to push back the acid that pulsed inside him.

Because of his wounds, she kept her body clear of his, cupping her hands around his elbows as they both drew power from the swamp outside. A group would've formed a circle, arms around each other, to share energy and ease pain. For the two of them, this would have to do.

Tender concern, almost affection, seeped through the pain. There was also…yearning. His? Or hers? It had to be his. She hardly knew him. Couldn't afford to feel such things for him.

He might not be a traitor, but that didn't mean his claim of a traitor in mage ranks had been right. His current heroism didn't make him faultless in the deaths of those who'd tried to stop him, but she would give him the hearing she'd promised.

Her sense of his pain ebbed, not because it eased but because he damped it. "Griffin—"

Sounds came from behind her. Footsteps. Someone gasped. She would've turned, but Griffin's hold tightened.

"It's okay. They live here." He lifted his head, his eyes warm despite the pain tightening his features. "You risked your life for them."

"I was only doing my job." She made the words light, trying to ease away from the intimacy created by sharing energy and pain.

"Yeah. Still. Thank you." The warmth in his eyes deepened. Softened. His glance dropped to her lips.

Kissing him would be too easy. And so very stupid. The shire reeve had to walk a line. Val stepped back. "We'll see to things here, then talk."

"Okay." Dare's gaze held steady as he caught and quickly kissed her hand.

Heat rolled up her arm, and into the depths of her body. Her fingers tightened on his, but he released her. An unwelcome twinge of loss nipped her heart.

"We have to get these people out of here," he said. "The community shelter in Wayfarer will take them in, at least for a while. I'll make the call." He turned away, swaying.

Val fought the urge to steady him. He needed skilled

medical care, the kind available only through the Collegium. If she took him back with her, though, some on the Council, perhaps even her mentor, Gene Blake, would insist on his immediate execution. If she didn't and the Council learned she'd let him go, she would share his death sentence.

Chapter 4

The pickup truck hit a pothole, and Griff bit back a groan. So much for staying under the radar. There were too many people involved in his business now, including one who continually surprised him. Even with Valeria sitting by his side, gripping his hand as he braced himself against the pain, he still couldn't believe she was helping him.

Bringing in the mage world's most-wanted fugitive would make her a law enforcement superstar. His wounds would've given her the perfect excuse. Instead, she'd bandaged him up and, over the past two hours, helped him evacuate his surviving tenants to the Wayfarer homeless shelter.

They'd gone ahead in the shelter's vans. He lay on his mattress in Miss Hettie Telfair's truck bed. A local retiree, Hettie used the truck to haul whatever needed hauling for her gardens, the shelter, or anyone who needed help.

Lying on his side so nothing touched his wounds, he was as comfortable as he could be for the moment. He had not only Valeria but Hettie's big, panting golden retriever, Magnus, for company. But the truck would never be a smooth ride. Or a fast one.

Not like his car, a black Dodge Charger. Todd Claypool, the bakery delivery boy, was driving it into town for him. "Todd...better not...try for any speed records," he muttered.

Breathing hurt. So did talking, but he could manage with shallow breaths and short phrases. He needed the distraction.

"Guys and their cars." Valeria laughed, and the warm, rich sound shot straight to his groin. Griff swallowed a curse.

"I'm sure your baby will be fine," she said.

"It better be." He took a slow breath in and let it out. "Not much farther."

"I wish I had more power to share."

"You've been generous already." She'd locked down her emotions now, distancing herself, but she'd treated him earlier like someone she respected. She couldn't know how much that meant to an outcast.

"Why Wayfarer? What made you settle here?"

"I wandered into it. The people are laid-back. Accepting." Hettie and the shelter director, Unitarian minister Marc Wagner, had become his friends. He'd known they would come tonight, but the other volunteers had been a heartwarming surprise. "I could help here."

"Like working with the kids at the homeless shelter."

"Right."

"Reverend Wagner said you're great with them."

Before he could reply, the truck hit another bump. Pain spiked through him, and he bit back a grunt.

She gripped his shoulder. "Steady."

Her other hand, holding his, tightened in support. She obviously didn't regard him as evil incarnate anymore, so that was progress, but would she actually listen to what he had to say?

The taste of ammonia lay bitter on his tongue, an ominous sign of high venom levels in his blood from the new wounds and the power drain of battle. The venom was also making him queasy and cold. He needed to see Stefan as soon as he could, without alerting Valeria. He wasn't trusting her with anyone else's name. Not yet.

Magnus poked his cold, wet nose at Griff's chin.

Valeria pushed him firmly away. "Down, boy," she said, and Magnus laid his massive head on his paws.

Moving carefully, Griff scratched the dog's chest with his free hand. Magnus thumped his tail and rolled over to give him better access.

Valeria gave Griff an appraising look. "Reverend Wagner says you're a good guy, that you do magic tricks for the kids. Pretty risky choice."

"It's perfect cover. Hiding in plain sight." Marc knew Griff's secrets, so he'd given Valeria a plausible story. Hettie hadn't known but now, unfortunately, would expect explanations. So would the authorities, if not for the friends Griff had called, while Valeria was busy downstairs, secretly clearing away the ghoul bodies and burying the Mundanes.

"Speaking of hiding," she said, "Reverend Wagner called Stefan Harper, who also promised confidentiality. Dr. Harper's on his way. He's the best. You'll be all right, Griffin."

"That's…a risk for you."

"Not much of one." She glanced out at the night. "We'll talk about all that when you're patched up. Meanwhile, can you give me the lowdown on Miss Hettie?"

"Retired lawyer." The truck bounced over a bump, and he gritted his teeth. "Social activist," he ground out around the burning pain in his chest and back.

He could picture Hettie striding past the shops on Burke Street, Wayfarer's main road, in Earth shoes with her gray braid hanging down the back of her unstructured tunic, the dog trotting beside her. "Granddad would've said she's a pistol."

"Packs one, too. Nice SIG Sauer nine millimeter. That's an odd thing for an activist to carry."

He would've shrugged, but it would hurt. "She lives out in the country alone. I've done work for her." A mural for her dining room, a big job that had netted him not only three months' living expenses but a friend. "Rented a room for a while."

"She's very fond of you." Casually, Valeria added, "So's your sister. I went to see her, as I said."

He'd learned not to think about Caro, not to miss her. They'd been so close once, even though he had all that power while she had only the ability to sense color by touch. Yet she'd never resented him, never complained.

"How was she?" he asked.

"Did you know she was married, to Rick Moore?" When Griff nodded, Valeria continued, "They seemed very happy, but she was not exactly welcoming to me. More like defiant. She insisted we were all wrong about you."

The words shot into his heart and twisted. Damn, he missed Caro. Too bad he couldn't risk even a phone call.

"Your parents were a tougher book to read, very stoic. That's probably where your grit comes from."

"They're the best." Even if they despised him now.

"They're bewildered. Hurt, I think, and maybe a little angry that you didn't come to them for help. Your father, especially."

That implied they'd had faith in him, at least for a while. Unless she was playing him, digging into his soul to find the weak spots so she could talk him into giving himself up.

"Nothing to be done," he said. It was safer for them if he stayed away. No matter what that led them to believe.

"Lawyers like your dad don't seem to subscribe to that."

Griff said nothing. Thinking about his family involved too many might-have-beens and if-onlys.

As though Valeria knew it, her fingers tightened on his. "That little girl, Molly, called you Gray."

Magnus batted at his arm, and Griff realized he'd stopped scratching. He sank his fingers into the dog's soft, thick coat and indulged the beast.

"Walker. Gray Walker. Alias." He could give her that one. Simon Ishmael, he wouldn't risk. She'd packed his art supplies, but that didn't mean she would realize he earned money by painting. And it wouldn't tip her to his off-and-on gig with the Feds.

"It helps if I know what to call you in front of people."

"My mage friends called me Griff." He used the past tense deliberately. Better not to alert her he still had mage friends.

A shadow came into her eyes, but she didn't look away. "I like you, Dare. I respect some of the things you've done, but let's hold off on crossing the line into friend territory."

"Valeria, I swear to you—"

"Don't. I'll look at what you have, I promise, but don't ask me to accept anything without proof."

"You'll have it."

Streetlights lined the road now. The two-story shops of Burke Street, some brick and some wooden structures, came into view. The shops were closed, but lights shone in the upper windows, in the apartments where the shop owners and tenants lived.

The truck swung into the bumpy alley alongside the Wayfarer Community Shelter. Griff swore between his teeth, and Valeria gripped his shoulder in silent encouragement.

The truck stopped at the shelter's back door. Squeaks heralded the cab doors opening, and then Miss Hettie and Marc lowered the tailgate. When Hettie snapped her fingers, Magnus jumped out.

She climbed in to kneel beside Griff, peering over gold, wire-framed trifocals. "You still with us?"

He mustered a grin for her. "Yes'm."

"Magnus and I could take care of you just fine, but these other folks seemed to think you'd be less trouble here." Hettie snorted. "Trouble! Time comes I can't handle a banged-up man, I'll have to move into town myself."

Marc climbed in beside her, his lean face surrounded by the usual crop of unruly brown hair. "We set up an air mattress in my office. Can you climb out, or should we—"

"I'll manage."

Moving ramped up the pain. Griff set his jaw. All he needed was a few seconds to get out of the truck.

His wounds screamed, but he made it to the ground, then up the steps, into Marc's cramped office, down onto the air mattress with Valeria at his side.

Her eyes were bloodshot. "You should at least wear my sunglasses," he said.

"I'll put some salve in before I go to bed." She patted his shoulder and leaned back against the desk.

From this angle, he had a close view of the way his chambray shirt draped her high, round breasts. *Shit*. Wounds generally trumped horniness. Why didn't they tonight? Swearing silently, he closed his eyes.

When he opened them again, Valeria was gone. Miss Hettie sat beside him with Magnus, as usual, by her side. The pair of them and the mattress filled the narrow floor.

He must've zoned out.

"Water?" she asked.

When he nodded, she handed him the cup and straw. "That's a nice girl you got there, levelheaded. Polite. Even if she did try to give me some moonshine about a bear."

Staring over her glasses, she informed him, "I've lived 'round about the Okefenokee all my life. Seen bears and their handiwork. You don't want to tell me what tore you up, fine, but don't try to sell me that bear story."

"Okay." Normally, Hettie would press. She must be cutting him a break because he was hurt. "And she's not my girl." That little twinge of pain must've come from his wounds. Or from sexual frustration. "Where'd she go?"

Hell if the pain wasn't worse. The ammonia taste, too. It practically seared his mouth. His blood venom must be way up. Where was Stefan?

Hettie set the cup aside. "The doctor's on his way in, so she left to give you privacy. Marc set her up in the playroom. Kids're in bed, she'll have quiet. Looks fair done in herself."

Valeria didn't want Stefan to see her. She didn't need to hide, but Griff couldn't tell her that. Not without Stefan's consent. He had to protect Stefan, too.

Shit, what a web of protective silences. It was hard, sometimes, to remember where they intersected.

"You know," Hettie said quietly, "I've always known there was something different about you, Gray. That's your business, but if you ever want to tell me, remember, I know how to keep my mouth shut."

"I know." He squeezed her hand. "Thanks." But there was no sense bringing his trouble to her doorstep to worry her or, God forbid, endanger her in some way.

Someone tapped on the door, and Stefan walked in. "Ma'am, Mr. Walker, I'm Dr. Stefan Harper." Hettie introduced herself and Magnus. Stefan shooed them out politely, then knelt by Griff's side.

"Banning came through for you. I admit I'm surprised."

"You don't…know the half." She'd risked her life for his tenants, was risking it for her word to him. Hell of a woman.

Stefan set out a small boom box. He punched a button, and soft, slow violin music filled the room. As he took cleansing wipes and bandages from his bag, he wove his power through the music, wrapping the melody around Griff's mind, distancing him from the pain.

Stefan lit a lavender candle, and the sweet, healing scent filled the air. Griff drew it in, let the magic in it bolster him. Stefan's low, soothing voice detailed his progress as he worked. Griff drifted with the music and the sound of his friend's words.

Maybe Valeria would sit for him, let him paint her someday. Sap green flecked with gold and burnt umber would work for her eyes. Naples yellow, highlights of burnt umber and sienna for that beautiful fall of hair. Cadmium red mixed with white for the rose in her cheeks and lips.

Yeah. Like that would ever happen.

"Easy," Stefan murmured. "I have to remove these bandages, and they're stuck to you." Lukewarm water and a soft hint of power slid over Griff's skin, tamping down the pain. Until Stefan lifted the makeshift bandages. Fire blazed over Griff's back.

His fists clenched on the edge of the mattress. "Holy fuck," he muttered through gritted teeth.

"Sorry, bro." Stefan held a hand above the abused skin, easing the agony with more magic. "This is bad, but I guess you know that."

"No shit." As Stefan probed, Griff set his jaw and breathed through the hurt.

"I'm worried about your systemic venom levels," Stefan said. "I'll take a blood level in a bit. Before I do any healing, I want to draw the venom with an herbal plaster. This'll take a while."

Griff answered with a grunt. The sooner they started, the sooner he could have the conversation that might give him back his life.

An hour later, Griff's chest and back still burned, but not as much as his need to see Valeria. At least he didn't have the venom-based taste of ammonia on his tongue.

"All done." Kneeling by the mattress, Stefan switched the music to something quiet with acoustic guitars, something familiar.

"Did you write that?" Griff asked.

"Yep, so if you don't like it, pretend you do. Either way, it should help the healing. Let the lavender candle burn until it gutters out."

"Right. Thanks."

Marc tapped on the door and entered. "Will and Lorelei are here. You up to seeing them?"

"Sure." He hadn't expected them, though. Was something else wrong? Griff forced himself up to sit cross-legged. Rather than focus on the throbbing in his back, he concentrated on breathing.

Marc reached for the knob. "I'll send your guests in, then check on Ms. Banning."

When he opened the door, the newcomers walked in. Lorelei Martin, a petite brunette, led the way. An unusually large, blue tote hung from her shoulder. Griff noted the faint outline of her crossbow on the fabric.

Behind her came Griff's second-in-command, tall, blond historian and archaeologist Will Davis. Will was also the Collegium's assistant loremaster and like a brother to Griff. Marc closed the door as he left.

"Not many Mundanes we can trust." Stefan glanced at the closed door, then at Griff. "It was a lucky day for all of us when Marc found you wounded by the road and brought you here."

"Not many Mundanes who would believe us, anyway." Griff nodded a greeting to the new arrivals. "You know, it's weird how easily Marc accepts all this, but I'm not complaining."

Hettie might listen, too. She already suspected.

Lorelei glanced at the burning candle, one she'd probably supplied Stefan with. "I brought another if you need it. Just made a batch for the shop."

"That one should do it," Stefan said, "but thanks."

She set her tote on the desk, with a clunk that confirmed

it held her crossbow, and perched by it. She peered at Griff. "You look better than I'd feared, pal."

He mustered a grin. "Better than I expected, too."

Will dropped onto the floor beside the air mattress. "I haven't had time to do much digging on the things Stefan brought me. I have ideas, but I'd rather wait until I've done some research."

"Dire ideas, judging by that frown." Griff glanced from Will to Lorelei. Lorelei lived in Savannah, and Will lived at the Collegium, in the coastal marshes north of Brunswick. Yet they'd arrived together. "So if you two have nothing to report, why are you both here? To be sure I'm breathing?"

"More or less." Lorelei smiled at him. "Since Dan was out of town, I talked Will into being my arm candy for the River Street Vendors dinner. It was winding down when Stefan called Will."

Will sighed. "I had to wear a necktie, but the food was decent. Just remember, when I need a date for some godawful boring thing, you owe me."

"Oh, like you wouldn't just whistle up the woman of the moment," Lorelei said, rolling her eyes.

"I don't take them to boring dinners. It would spoil my image. So you owe me, and so does your honey. Being a Mundane doesn't mean Dan can't—"

Grim-faced, Marc slipped inside and shut the door behind him. He carried Griff's laptop under one arm.

The anger in his eyes had Griff's gut knotting. "What is it? Collegium?"

"No, thank God. But Banning's gone."

"What?" Griff stiffened. Shit, had she changed her mind about hearing him out?

Marc continued, "With downloads of your files." He snapped the computer open and handed it to Griff.

A document filled the screen. *Since you're unwell, I've copied your evidence. You'd best hope it supports your story. If not, you have a head start, with my gratitude, and we're even.*

You owe the reverend for a blank CD.

"No signature," he noted. Nothing to tie her to the note. Smart of her. At least she'd bothered to leave a message, but she was gone, with enough information, if she chose to use it, to hunt him and his friends down and kill them all.

Chapter 5

Val's blue Mustang ate ground when she wanted it to, but tonight she kept it a few miles under the speed limit. With her eyes still less than a hundred percent, caution was the order of the day.

Lucky thing the shelter was just a few blocks from the Goddess's Hearth Café, where she'd parked her car before the clash with ghouls that had led to her capture and Griffin's rescue. So much had happened since yesterday's dinner, it seemed a lifetime ago. A bit of magic to retrieve the magnetic box holding the spare key under the frame, and she'd hit the road.

The fifty or so miles from Wayfarer to the Collegium took about an hour to drive at this speed. She glanced at the dashboard clock. She'd been driving about forty-five minutes. Soon she'd be home, could see whether Dare's info had any value.

Until then, she should stop thinking about him. Stop thinking about the way he moved, stop remembering the heat in those blues eyes while he stared at her legs, the gentle grip of his big, strong hands. *Just stop, damn it.*

But she'd noticed, even though she hadn't realized it at the time, how good that long, lean body of his felt in her arms, the way he'd fitted so snugly against her, when he covered her for those few seconds after the attack.

Heat bubbled low in her belly. She swore silently and tried not to fidget. Her wounds still ached, and her eyes stung.

Running out on him felt cowardly, but what if his claims didn't hold up? Would she have to fight him? Her mind shied from that. Better to look at the evidence for herself before hearing what he had to say. Of course, the *Caudex Magi*, the code of laws that governed mages, counted his courage and compassion as evidence, too.

She would never forget what he'd risked for that homeless child. No matter what he'd once done, or why he'd done it, such a man would never betray his own kind. That didn't make his actions six years ago right, though.

And here she was thinking about him again. Scowling, Val shoved him out of her mind.

The headlights struck the side of a familiar stone gateway ahead. Val turned into the Collegium compound driveway, under the archway that read GEORGIA INSTITUTE FOR PARANORMAL RESEARCH, the cover that hid the mages from their Mundane neighbors. The mage guarding the wrought-iron gates, a slim, dark figure in the night, waved the car through.

Ahead lay the four-story, ivy-covered walls of the Collegium's main building. It held the administrative offices, classrooms, and dormitories, as well as quarters for department heads and Council members.

Val's heart lifted. She was finally home, back to the place she'd grown up. Safe.

She parked behind the big stone building and hurried inside, up the stairs and across the marble-floored atrium lobby. Her rank merited a large suite on the ground floor. She could dig into Dare's files in comfort and privacy.

"Val?" someone called behind her.

She winced. Pasting a smile on her face, she turned to greet her chief deputy, Sybil Harrison. "Hey, Syb. Wow, you look great. Special date?"

"Not as much as I'd hoped, no." Sybil's blond hair, free of her habitual ponytail, lay soft and fluffy on her shoulders and across the spaghetti straps of a green silk sheath. Her brown eyes narrowed as she scanned Val, taking in the boots, man's cutoffs and chambray shirt, the plastic bag of medical supplies, and the sword Val carried instead of wearing.

"I'd say I hope your date was hot," Sybil said, "since you're wearing his clothes. But if he's the cause of your bandages, I figure he's dead. What happened?"

A friend did not involve a friend in illegal secrets. Val shrugged, managing not to flinch. "Had a little trouble with ghouls. The clothes belong to the guy who helped me out of it."

Sybil grinned. "So I repeat, was he hot?"

Extremely, but that was better not considered. "I didn't notice. We had other things on our minds."

"You look beat, but I want to hear all about this."

"Tomorrow. I promise."

"Well, okay." Sybil hesitated. "There's been some fallout while you were gone. The Council had some complaints about the problems on that last raid."

Val bit down on a surge of anger, then let out a deep breath before she could trust her voice. "Since when is wiping out a ghoul nest a problem?"

"It's the informant's disappearance that's the problem. Plus the fact the raid put some people on the disabled list." Frowning, Sybil added, "We can go over all that later. Do you need help with anything?"

"No. Thanks. I'm going to crash." Any other reply, and she'd have to ask Sybil in to chat. Val couldn't sleep until she checked out Dare's information.

Val and Sybil said good night, and Val hurried down the corridor to her own quarters. Fatigue thrummed in her bones, beat in her blood. Yet the memory of Dare's ravaged chest haunted her.

She couldn't let sympathy sway her opinion of him, but her heart softened at the memory of Griffin lying in the truck's bed, jaw set against the pain. She'd liked the way he'd kept his warm, strong fingers entwined with hers.

With the goal of playing on her sympathy, maybe.

Well, that was a no-go. Once she saw what information he had, she would decide whether to listen further or drag his ass out of that shelter for a reckoning.

She palmed the lock-plate scanner, and the door to her one-bedroom suite clicked open. As she entered, the bed beckoned, its smooth sheets and soft, forest-green quilt a haven. The idea of a shower also felt tempting, but that would mean balm and clean bandages and a lot of fuss. She had work to do.

She turned on the computer, which sat on its rosewood desk by the window, and let it boot while she started coffee.

Rubbing her stinging, weary eyes, she fed the CD into the

drive. She clicked on a file at random, enlarging the view to reduce the strain, and started to read.

At first glance, it looked like just another report, a description of a raid on a ghoul breeding nest, the one that'd been mysteriously destroyed outside Jacksonville, Florida, last year. But this wasn't the official report. And he had data on nests she didn't know about.

How did Dare know about these ghoul nests that weren't on her maps? Why wasn't the intel and recon division of the shire reeve's office spotting them? She would check them out, of course, but his data looked solid.

If he had detailed info, why the hell didn't she?

Her eyes burned. She should rest them, but she had to know what else was in his files. Scrolling down, she noticed Dare—or someone else—had inserted comments in red, notes detailing suspicions about a possible traitor, indicating where the various councilors had been, as well as how much they'd probably known. There were cross-matches of different data files on the ghoul nests, on mage raids that failed.

He suspected a current councilor was the traitor. But how could that be? Councilors went through testing that made the CIA's look like a college mixer. Yet his notes were too logical to dismiss.

It could be a lie, a setup created to distract her. The sheer volume of the files argued against that, though. How had he gotten so much info on the councilors, anyway?

He had to have help inside the Collegium. Under her nose. *Damn it.* If he'd spotted these inconsistencies, why hadn't she?

Feeling sick, Val pushed away from the table. Coffee wouldn't help her aching body, but it would keep her brain going, at least for a while. Her vacation officially ended in two days. By then, she needed to cover everything on that disk.

Early the next morning, the phone jolted her awake. She grabbed it. "Banning."

"Tia Corbett, ma'am, officer of the day. We have a situation."

"Go ahead." If Corbett thought this was worth interrupting the last of Val's official leave, the *situation* was grim.

"Daniel Goodwin, son of the Northeast Shire high councilor, was kidnapped from a bar parking lot in Milledgeville by ghouls. He seems to have been intoxicated. His girlfriend, who's also a mage, Lucy Jones, escaped but pursued in his vehicle. Ghouls drove a Ford F-150, green, didn't get the tag. She lost them just west of Milledgeville, off Georgia 212, near Lake Sinclair, when her car skidded off the road. No serious injuries to her."

"Okay. Stand by a sec." Val glanced at the map on the wall above her desk. There was no ghoul nest marked in that area, but Dare's files had noted one. She used the search function to bring it up.

Yep, there it was, near the Oconee National Forest and Milledgeville, a breeding center masked as a camp for recovering alcoholics. Addicted dark magic users, more like, but they'd probably taken the boy as a breeder. Well, not for long.

Trusting untried intel was risky but better than searching blind for a young mage about to be violated or killed. To be on the safe side, she'd take superior numbers.

"Corbett, scramble eight squads, full combat gear." Forty mages should easily trump twenty-eight ghouls, especially with daylight on their side. Ghouls were weaker during the day. "Call up helos with a medical support team. I'll be right down. I want us airborne in forty-five minutes."

Val hung up and yanked her gear from the closet. This rescue couldn't be put off, but she could've used some time to think. She had to talk to Dare, find out more about the information contained in his files.

Thinking about seeing him should not give her the warm fuzzies, blast it. She couldn't fall for him. His certainty reminded her too much of her ex-fiancé, Drew Sampson, who'd constantly tried to steer her away from the dangerous parts of a deputy reeve's job. He'd taken risks as a quick-reaction force fighter but wanted her to go into forensics, not enforcement. The conflict had eventually destroyed their relationship.

Once she'd straightened out the problems with her department's intel and had time to think about a relationship, it wouldn't be with a guy who had an agenda. A guy who didn't know how to compromise.

Been there, done that. Getting involved with a renegade would be totally insane.

Even a brave one with hands that were both strong and gentle. And eyes that could heat her up with just one look. And the chivalry to catch her as they both fell, to take the brunt of the impact and then shelter her with his body.

Crap, crap, crap. Lack of sleep was making her moony. She had to stop thinking this way.

Before leaving, she would hide the disk, just to be on the safe side. There would be time when she got back to worry about Griffin Dare.

* * *

Where the hell was Valeria? What was she doing? Seated at Marc's desk, Griff shoved his cleaned breakfast plate away. He'd searched magically for a vision of her off and on throughout the night, with no luck. That probably meant she was within the Collegium's screening wards, but doing what?

Surely she'd had time to see he had information worth discussing. He could give her more he hadn't written down.

He shouldn't feel so eager to see her again. Dumbass. She was a potential ally. She could never be anything else to him.

He ran a hand over his face. Waiting purely sucked.

His phone vibrated on the desk. He picked it up, checked the caller ID. Javier Ruiz, the wiry, dark-haired mage whose tax accountant business in Athens gave him the flexibility to chase ghouls.

Griff flipped the phone open. "Yeah, Javy?"

"Chuck and I caught a prisoner." Javier's tenor drawl held deep satisfaction. "Stopped him snacking on a paper delivery boy near the college campus."

"Good on two counts." Chuck Porter, former NFL wide receiver, security agency owner, and interim athletic director at Walmer Lawrence College, considered ghoul hunting almost as fun as football. His tall, burly frame and dark skin contrasted with Javier's wiry build and olive complexion, but the two made an effective team. "Y'all learn anything?"

"Nothing useful."

Hell.

Javier continued, "Chuck has football staff meetings coming up, what with the season starting, but I'll keep looking."

"Take someone with you. Hunt in pairs, Javy, always."

"Except for you," Javier said in a dry voice.

"Benefit of being in charge." Anyone caught with Griff by the Collegium would receive a death sentence. He wouldn't let anyone risk that for something as minor as trying to take a random ghoul captive. "Try Tasha Murdock. She's between decorating jobs right now. Anything else?"

"Not so far. I'll call Tasha. We'll get something, boss, just might take us a while."

They had little more than a week before the waning moon went dark and conditions became optimum for blood magic. "Okay. Watch your backs."

They signed off. Brooding over ghoul mysteries, Griff took his breakfast tray to the kitchen and set it down without bothering the busy volunteers. He headed back to the office, although the wise play would be to leave, and soon. Until he spoke to Valeria he'd stay there, where she could find him easily. He knew it was risky but he was tired of running.

He had to figure out another way to reach her. Careful of his wounds, he leaned over the silver bowl on the desk. Infusing power into the pure springwater it held would make it show what he asked for, unless what he sought was hidden by magical screening. He wouldn't be able to hear anything, but he might get some idea about Banning's intentions this way.

A wave of his hand, a whiff of power, and the surface of the water gleamed. Turned foggy... *Yes!* He'd found her.

He set his hands on either side of the basin, leaning over it, and increased the power. The water's surface turned misty white, thickening and solidifying until he could feel the connection in his bones, and then the surface slowly cleared.

The bowl's center showed figures in dappled green mage camo crouched in a woodland glade of pine trees, oaks, and maples, the colors mirrored by the garments. There she was, at the front of the group.

So she hadn't come after him. Griff smiled. Maybe trusting her wasn't such a long shot after all.

He looked closer and squinted. Surely she wouldn't have gone charging after one of the nests on his list. Not without detailed recon of her own. Unless this was field training—but wait. He could see her team in the scrying.

They weren't screened. If he could see them, so could anyone else with magical gifts.

Shifting the angle of view, gut tight with foreboding, he spotted a red, windowless shed with a blue roof. He knew that building, part of the ghoul nest near Milledgeville, home to a couple dozen ghouls. The compound included two well-guarded breeding sheds and stock pens to supply the ghouls with fresh meat.

There's no way she'd go into something like that exposed. She must think she was screened, and that meant she'd walked into a trap.

So Dare was right about the nest. Clearly some butts in intel and recon needed rousting. One this size should've generated enough police reports to draw attention to it.

Val opened her magical senses, checking the area. Birds and small animals brushed over her awareness. No prickles that would signal ghoul presence. Screen ward in place. But that odd tingle…

She glanced left, at Senior Deputy Harry Parker. Fortyish and experienced, he made an excellent squad leader. "Check the screen, Harry," she murmured.

His eyes lost focus. Awareness of him brushed her senses

as he extended his own. "Something weird, but the screen's okay."

Once they broke cover and started moving, the screen wouldn't hold. By then, they would've seized the advantage.

"Thanks. Get ready." As soon as she blew the fence, he would shear off the back of the breeding shed. The noise would signal the team on the far side to free and stampede the animals as a distraction. The rest of her group would hold the flanks while she and Harry evacuated the captives.

If Dare was right about the nests on his list, he might be right about other things, including the gut-wrenching claim about a traitor.

Closing her eyes, she reached deep inside to muster the power she needed. It built within her, warm, fizzy and gold. Colors supposedly weren't tactile, but the buildup of power always felt golden to her.

With mages mustering their magic all around her, the radios weren't reliable. She stuck up a closed fist so everyone could see it. She spread her fingers, then folded them down to signal five…four…three…two…

Suddenly the world exploded around her with a deafening roar. Then dirt, bark and oh, God, bodies slammed into her, hurling Val into the mages at her right. Her head hit the ground, dazing her despite the magic-infused Kevlar helmet.

She tumbled blindly. At last, she came to rest on her stomach with a heavy weight on top of her.

Trap, her brain struggled to process. *Move or die.* The ground had been mined. Ghouls had never done that before.

The weight on top of her was soft, and the acrid stench of blood stung her nose. She turned, reached out with a raw, scraped hand and found Harry with half his face blown off.

Her stomach revolted, but fierce yells yanked her back from illness.

Yells? In the compound.

Val shoved Harry's body off her. Scrambling to her knees, she magically shielded herself and flung what power she could at the fence.

Around her, mages jerked upright, shielding as they recovered. Others struggled to rise, groaning. Or lay too still, too silent. The sight stabbed grief and guilt into her throat, but she had a job to do.

Meanwhile, medevac should be rushing in. If only they could translocate, but that destroyed magical shielding, and materializing without it in a battle zone was suicide.

The compound yard held squat barricades that hadn't been visible before. A couple of dozen ghouls knelt behind them with leveled automatic weapons. *Shit!*

"Fall back," she shouted, then loosed another, more scattered burst of power to pass through the chain link of the fence and explode the bullets the ghouls fired. She didn't have the range to reach the weapons themselves.

Some rounds blew in midair, flares of silver and red that sent shrapnel pinging off the fence or clattering off the buildings. Others zinged unhindered toward her deputies as the *brrrrrrr* of weapons fire continued.

Concentrated automatic weapons fire could penetrate magical shields, and kill a mage. But it couldn't destroy a ghoul unless it came from a mage-crafted firearm, and those were about as common as snow in Miami since ghouls targeted mageborn gunsmiths.

She yanked her sword from the scabbard, drawing power and focusing it through the blade as her team's crossbow quarrels shot past her. "Longbows," she shouted. "Loose at will."

Arrows flew up and into the compound, rained down on the defenders, but not nearly as many as there should've been. That scattering couldn't come from more than three bowmen. Three, out of eight. *Hell.*

She sent more power streaming from her blade into the compound. The four-mage medevac team and the reserve force, six mages, charged into the clearing. Val knelt with the reserves, forming a human wall to pour destructive energy at the rounds flying their way while their comrades translocated out.

Guilt beat at her brain as she tallied the numbers, living and dead. No one would be left behind for the ghouls to drain, breed, or eat.

Almost done, the last ones were leaving. She backed up, wincing at a flash of pain from her left ankle. The reserves, still miraculously intact, moved with her. At least the ghouls weren't charging.

A little farther, just a little, and her group could translocate directly to the choppers. Still no pursuit. Strange, but she'd take what they could get and be grate—

The ground under her detonated, the shock wave flinging her toward an oak tree. Twisting, she managed not to hit with her head, but her chest slammed into the trunk. Even her vest couldn't keep fire from exploding inside her, and then darkness swallowed the world.

Frozen in horror by the scrying bowl, Griff watched Valeria slam into the oak's broad trunk. The impact knifed into his heart, crushed the breath from his lungs.

She dropped to the ground like a wet rag and lay motionless. "Move," he snapped. "Move, damn it."

She had to be alive.

Ghouls poured out of their compound, charging the survivors, and he swore. His fists balled. She was almost two hundred miles away. He couldn't translocate that far. No one could. He could only stand there and watch while—

A silvery wave of mage power swept the clearing and flung back the ghoul attack. A clump of filthy, bloodied survivors ran to their comrades' aid. Two of them picked up Valeria. Another pair grabbed the tall man who'd fallen beside her. A pair of medics in stained camos grabbed another.

The others, with help, flashed away while a mere three haggard, dirty mages, one with an arm in a makeshift sling and another leaning on a tree-branch crutch, covered their retreat. A crossbowman staggered up to join them, a woman. Swaying on her feet, she fired behind their power blasts.

Griff followed the group carrying Valeria until, in midstep, they winked out of sight. Screened. Effectively this time. The rear guard followed.

A moment later the ghouls raced into view, but the survivors were already headed home.

He forced himself to breathe. The helos wouldn't reach the Collegium for an hour. An hour to return home, longer before Stefan would have time to tell him whether she—and so many others—lived or died.

Live, he willed her. *Whether you help me or not, you have to live.*

She would never have attacked with an unscreened force. She'd walked into a trap. And where had all those ghouls come from? Had the nest grown? Or was it reinforced?

The screened, potent ghoul defenses, the swift response of the defenders, the ready counterattack, meant her targets had known she was coming. She and her force had been betrayed, as he and his once had been.

His fists balled again. He knew the pain she'd feel, the grief and guilt of unnecessary loss, knew them as only someone who'd led others to their deaths could. If she lived, she would need someone who understood that, and he would be there for her.

If she lived.

Chapter 6

Griff paced the shelter common room's worn, beige linoleum. He'd volunteered to give art lessons to keep his mind clear, but it wasn't working. Good thing for him the two girls and three boys seated at the long, wooden table seemed absorbed in their pictures.

In the room's far corner, several adults occupied chairs around a television. *Entertainment Tonight* blared from the set.

Griff walked back to the battered table and leaned over the seven-year-old girl's shoulder. "Nice flowers, Josie. I like the red."

She beamed at him from under curly blond bangs. "It's my favorite. Thanks, Gray."

He wandered around the table and absently returned little Molly's smile. Will had called, told him Valeria had attacked the nest to rescue a kidnapped college student. That explained why she'd gone there, but where the hell had all those ghouls come from? Was his info outdated, or had someone reinforced the nest? He would ask Javier to check on that.

God, she'd hit that tree so damned hard, and so many of her troops had died. Those deaths would screw with her head more than anything she personally suffered.

Griff glanced at the clock. Eight thirty. He should've left hours ago, in case she blamed his info and sent mages after him, but he hadn't been able to make himself go until he knew she would be okay.

Marc walked in from the hall doorway. "The softball crew's back, so you have five minutes, kids. Then it's lights out upstairs."

A chorus of groans answered him.

In the doorway, Todd Claypool, the blond, lanky delivery boy, waited. His kid sister, sandy-haired, thirteen-year-old Robin, stood at his shoulder. They'd taken a couple of the shelter's middle schoolers out for a round of softball with the town kids.

Robin grinned at Griff, her brown eyes dancing. "Are we in time for magic tricks?"

The kids set up a clamor for their favorite tricks. Smiling, Marc cocked an eyebrow at Griff. "We can push bedtime back a few minutes for magic."

Marc might pretend he was doing it for the kids, but he seemed to enjoy seeing the tricks. Maybe that was because he knew they were real magic.

The coin trick was a favorite, and it wouldn't take long. The usual, Mundane version worked by sleight of hand, but Griff used translocation. The coin vanished because he wrapped power around it, shifting it out of reality and through the space between life and death to reappear wherever he directed it.

"Well," he started, and his pocket vibrated. He tensed. "Sorry, but I can't tonight. I have to go, kids. I'll make it up to you." He shot an urgent look at Marc, who shepherded the disappointed children out of the room.

The kids went without too much muttering. They knew he'd make good on his promise.

Griff glanced at the caller ID. Stefan's number. Praying for good news, he whipped the phone to his ear and stepped onto the deserted front stoop. The muggy air felt heavy, but he hardly noticed. "How is she?"

"So you heard about this morning's little problem." Stefan sounded bone tired, and no wonder. His medical team couldn't magically heal large numbers of severe injuries at one time. They would've had to stabilize the worst, operate, and then do a partial healing, with more rounds of magic work to follow.

"We lost twenty-three," he said.

Twenty-three dead? Griff's breath froze in his lungs.

"But the patient you're worried about," Stefan added, carefully avoiding names, as usual, "will recover."

Griff's breath rushed out of him. He dropped down to sit on the concrete steps. "From…?"

A pause, as though Stefan debated with himself. "Multiple rib fractures. Impact damage to internal organs, though the vest diffused the force. Face and body contusions. Torn ligament, left ankle. Bad abrasions on the hands. She's asleep, and I'm keeping her that way until morning."

Griff stared across the street at the weekly Wayfarer *Oracle*'s plate-glass front window. All that, and she'd lived.

But twenty-three dead? Holy hell.

If only he could see her. Touch her and see for himself that she'd recover.

"The thing is," Stefan was saying, "the Council didn't

know about that ghoul nest. Before she left, she refused to say how she'd heard of it, so they're gunning for her." His voice hardened. "They may replace her as reeve."

"The hell they will. I'll…Shit." Griff could do nothing, as they both knew.

"Exactly." Stefan paused. "Once I'm out of the way, they'll hammer her."

While Griff sat here, feeling helpless. He had to do something.

"She may have to give you up to save herself," Stefan said. "Go to ground and stay there."

As if he could do that with her in trouble because of him. She might blame him, understandably. "Admitting she talked to me and didn't kill me outright would only make her problems worse. She'll hold."

What would that cost her, though? The Council wouldn't accept silence from her, not with so many dead.

"Maybe she'll stand firm." Stefan yawned. "Either way, don't get it into your head you can help her, Sir Galahad. If they have any idea you're involved, that you give a damn, she'll go from victim to bait in a heartbeat."

Stefan was right.

"I know. Thanks, Stefan. Get some rest."

"Eventually."

They said good night. Griff leaned back against the warm brick wall. His brain churned like the Chattahoochee in flood season. Valeria was in the Council's crosshairs because of him. If she continued to protect him, would they put her under ritual questioning? Would she resist?

If she did, and they forced her, that would leave her worse than dead.

His jaw tightened against a curse. He couldn't help remembering how bravely she'd confronted him at his loft. How she'd rushed into a battle armed with only a kitchen knife and saved his life. Little Molly's, too. How she'd embraced him after the fight, as though no cloud lingered over his name.

He'd gotten her into this mess. Somehow, he had to help her out of it. Even if that meant taking her place in the crosshairs.

It hurt to breathe.

Trying to keep her breaths shallow, Val opened her eyes. Pale blue ceiling. Pale blue curtains walling off a narrow space. Beeps and clicks. Monitors. Soothing violins playing softly. Antiseptic smells. The Collegium clinic.

But how?

The explosion. A tree coming at her, and before that—

A sob welled in her throat, scalding her chest. She gulped it back but couldn't stop the tears trickling from the corners of her eyes. Her deputy reeves, so many blown to bits. She'd led them into a fucking trap.

Dare had marked that side of the compound as vulnerable, hadn't given any warning of those defenses. Magically screened defenses, magic that must've caused the tingle she and Harry— Oh, God! Harry. His poor face blown off.

The sob this time escaped. Shaking, she bit her lip against the pain. Must be broken ribs. Maybe other damage.

She wiped away tears with her IV-free hand. A hint of something lemony, familiar, brushed her nose, but she'd figure that out later. Whatever damage she'd suffered could be no less than she deserved. This was her fault.

Was Dare's intel outdated? Or had he held something back? He was slow to trust, or he'd have died long ago. Regardless, the choice had been hers. So was the burden of the result.

Even if Dare had deliberately baited her.

But why would he? Her breath caught at the memory of his grave blue eyes looking down at her. *I need you safe*, he'd said. He'd seemed sincere about wanting her help, had felt that way to her magical senses.

He had no reason to set a trap that would kill her. She'd warned him she would check out his information. He had to know she would do that herself, just as he would've in her place.

"No," Dr. Stefan Harper said outside the curtains. "Absolutely not. She'll require at least one more round of healing, probably two, and she needs rest before we proceed."

"This is urgent, Doctor. Surely she can interrupt her little nap to answer a question or two."

Crap. That harsh, scathing bass belonged to Councilor Otto Larkin. He not only looked like an English bulldog but had the tenacity of one.

"The explosive force," Harper said with strained patience vibrating in his words, "disrupted their bodies' energy centers. With those centers out of alignment, magic doesn't flow properly. Healing takes longer. Realigning is a slow, delicate business, and you're delaying us."

"This comes first," Larkin bit out. "We've lost more than twenty mages because of her incompetence, and by God—"

"Shut up," Harper snapped.

He said something else she didn't catch. More than twenty dead. Over half her task force, nearly a fifth of the total cadre.

Incompetence didn't begin to describe her folly.

"If that must wait, it can," Gene's voice said. "I'd like to see her, see for myself how she's doing."

A beat of silence, and then Harper said, "If she's awake. Try anything else, though, and you're out of here so fast your eyes'll cross."

He slipped through the curtains. When his gaze met hers, he asked softly, "Do you feel up to seeing Councilor Blake?"

Val nodded. "I don't want him to worry."

Harper looked at her a long moment, his doubtful expression urging her to change her mind, but she didn't waver. At last, frowning, he walked to the curtain and opened it an inch. "Chief Councilor Blake. You have two minutes, no more."

He stepped back to let Gene enter and closed the curtain behind the short, stocky man. Harper followed him in to stand at her shoulder like a rottweiler on guard.

Below Gene's shock of graying brown hair, his blue eyes regarded her with concern. He took her IV-free hand in a gentle grip. "Valeria, my dear. I'm so glad you survived."

"I'm sorry," she choked. "So sorry."

He opened his mouth as though to say something, glanced at Harper's stern face, and cleared his throat instead. "We'll discuss that later. Is there anything you need, my dear?"

A do-over, but no one could give her that. "No. Thanks for coming, Gene."

"I had to see that you were all right. Zara sends her love, too. Get well, Valeria. That's your job for now." He patted her hand and walked out.

She'd let him down, and the knowledge burned in her throat. He'd supported her for the reeve job. Now he probably regretted that.

Quietly, Stefan Harper said, "He's right. Your only job now is recovery. We're going to move you to a room in a few minutes, then do another round of healing on those ribs. Then you need to sleep. Figuring out what went wrong can wait."

For him, maybe. Not for her. She had to get out of there to find answers.

A gentle hand stroked Val's hair back from her brow. The touch carried such concern, such tenderness, that she turned her face into it. A hand was holding hers, too, in a warm, comforting grip.

With a sigh, she opened her eyes and looked straight into Griffin Dare's worried blue ones.

He'd come. He would help, she thought foggily, lifting a hand toward his cheek. Then she came fully awake and froze. Would he help, or was she wrong about him? Had he set her up after all? Come to finish the job? Was he even real, or a dream born of her need for answers?

His face hardened. He lifted both hands and stepped back. "If you want to push the call button, I won't stop you."

She glanced at the buzzer beside the pillow, confirming he hadn't moved it. If she pressed it, he had no chance of fighting his way free again. He couldn't translocate out, either. Collegium buildings were warded against all forms of translocation except short, line-of-sight shifts within the buildings.

Maybe she should be afraid, but seeing him so concerned,

remembering that feeling of comfort from his touch, kept her hand away from the button. Besides, he could've killed her while she slept if he'd wanted to. "What are you doing here?"

"I had to see you. Had to know you were going to be okay." He shoved his hands into his pockets, his voice flat. "I never intended anything like this. You have to believe me."

"How did you know something had happened?"

"I was curious about what you meant to do. I scried for you. Saw the whole thing."

"That's impossible. We were screened."

Anger flashed in his eyes. "I figured you thought you were, but you weren't, and that means you walked into a trap. When you hit that tree..." His lips tightened, and he shook his head.

"I checked. Harry checked— Oh, God, Harry." The grief welled up in her chest, into her throat, filled her tearing eyes. She glared at Dare's blurry image and fought the mind fuzz of pain medication.

"A trap? Whose?"

"That's the question of the hour." He leaned over, close enough for her to see his stony expression through the tears. He took her hand and let her sense his honesty. "Not mine, I swear to you. I didn't know there were that many ghouls there."

Maybe she was as gullible as a fish rising to a lure, but she believed him. Should she have sensed the danger? Saved her team? A sob broke from her throat. Shuddering, she grabbed fistfuls of the covers, fingers digging in, and squeezed her eyes shut.

"It wasn't your fault." He wiped her tears away with his

thumbs, cradling her face in his hands. "You didn't do this. Remember that."

Gripping his sturdy wrists seemed like the only natural response. How had he known she felt responsible?

She tried to stop the tears, but the flow was too strong. Yet he didn't try to pull away. He lowered his forehead to hers and gathered her as close as the bed rail allowed.

Again, his hold brought comfort. He smelled of bay leaves and some kind of spicy soap. She slid her arms around his neck.

He made a wordless sound. Something clanked, and the bed rail went down. Then his weight sank onto the bed by her hip. Carefully, he drew her up to hold her closer. She nestled against him, clinging. He brushed a kiss over her hair and then rested his cheek against it. For the first time since the world exploded, she felt safe.

Long minutes later, the tide of grief finally ebbed, leaving her weary and desolate. "Thank you," she said into his warm, solid shoulder.

"It's little enough to do for you." He kissed her temple and stood. Raising the bed rail, he said, "Get well, Valeria, and we'll nail the bastards together."

Saying this next felt scuzzy. Ungrateful. And yet, she had to be honest with him. "Dare…I haven't made up my mind yet. About your claims. I have questions for you, but I can't think right now."

"Understood." If he was disappointed, it didn't show in his face or his calm voice. "When you're ready, leave the Collegium, and I'll find you. I'll be keeping an eye out."

Val nodded. "How did you get in here, anyway?"

"Slipped through the boundary wards, which I have to say

wasn't easy, screened myself, and sneaked into the building as a visitor left. Since I was inside the wards, I could scry to find your room. A bathroom sink isn't the best bowl, but it'll do." A wry smile quirked his lips. "Then I caused a tiny, harmless equipment malfunction to get in here."

"Just to be sure I was okay?"

"I had to know."

His sincerity vibrated in the magic between them. Warm, soft pleasure brushed her heart, but she lowered her eyes. She couldn't afford to trust him completely, not yet.

He waited until she looked back at him. "The Council will want explanations, along with the chance to do some posturing. Be very careful what you say, Valeria. Don't mention a trap. Don't accuse anyone of anything, and if blaming me will make things easier for you, do it. Just please don't set them on the people in Wayfarer."

"I wouldn't. But if I name you, they'll hunt you down."

"I'm used to that." He cupped her cheek, his eyes solemn. "The last thing I wanted was to make trouble for you."

She squeezed his hand. "I believe you." Even if that made her the fool of the year, everything in her said he'd told her the truth. "You should go. Be careful."

"Always." A half smile crooked his lips, and his eyes warmed. Her heart kicked. He tipped her chin up and kissed her.

His mouth was firm, warm, and gentle. Heat bubbled low in her belly, and she lifted a hand to his face. A long moment later, he raised his head. His fingers brushed her cheek.

"Watch your back." He turned toward the door and vanished in midstride, screened.

"You, too," she murmured. The door opened just enough

for him to slip through and then closed silently.

Val lay back on her pillow. Her fingers tingled with the memory of beard stubble under them, and his bay scent lingered in the air. Kissing him back probably hadn't been smart, but she didn't regret it.

Now, though, he'd given her a lot to think about. Who could have laid a trap for her, and why?

Four days later, Val walked into the boxy, paneled Council chamber in the tan shirt, brown trousers, and brown boots that were her regular uniform. A day in ICU and three more in a bed had left her impatient and antsy, too aware of all the work she had to do.

The first order of business should be condolence notes. Then she would roust intel and recon and burn their butts about not doing their jobs. Next, if most of the survivors were out of the infirmary, she would call an after-action meeting, a roundtable on why so many things seemed to go wrong.

Before seeing to those important tasks, however, she had to meet with the Council and somehow explain herself.

Gene gave her a slight nod that eased some of the tension in her neck. He, at least, still believed in her.

On the front wall, behind the Council, portraits of past councilors gazed dourly at the room. Maybe that was why this chamber always felt oppressive.

The Council members sat in a horseshoe, the five elected high councilors in the middle and the ten department heads who made up the regular Council at the sides. Gene occupied the chief's center chair.

Dare had warned her to be careful. He suspected one of

these people was a traitor. If someone had set a trap for her team, was it one of them?

At least no replacement yet sat in her regular seat on the right end, next to Teresa DiMaggio, the weaponsmistress. Her salt-and-pepper curls were jumbled, as though she'd been sparring earlier. Stefan Harper's chair also stood empty, probably because he couldn't leave his patients yet.

Gerry Armitage, the loremaster, sat in his usual spot on the left. With his flowing white hair, kind face, and wire-framed glasses, he looked like he'd come from central casting to play a distinguished scholar. He had the keen mind for such a role, too. He gave Val a cool nod of greeting.

She sat at a small table facing the Council's long, curved one and took a deep breath to steady herself. They would give her a hard time, especially since she wouldn't say how she'd known about the nest, but shire reeves had presided over worse disasters than this and kept their jobs.

"You understand," thin, unctuous Albert Dutton said, "that this hearing is convened to determine your fitness to retain the office you hold and, more specifically, whether you were derelict in your duty four days ago?"

"I do." If they charged her with dereliction, removed her from office, she couldn't argue that she didn't deserve it. She could only hope to sway enough of them to her side. She owed her dead reeves vengeance, and she could get it more easily as shire reeve.

"Well, then." Dutton smiled. "Walk us through the events following your return from vacation, please."

She obliged, keeping her voice calm.

Blond, thirtyish Pansy Wilson said coldly, "You claim a

mage helped you rescue a couple of Mundanes and tipped you off to the Milledgeville nest."

"That's correct. I'd intended to check it out, but Daniel Goodwin's kidnapping—"

"We've scried your vacation." Otto Larkin's bulldog face twisted into a smirk. "There's no indication of anyone contacting you, or even approaching you, until you returned here last week."

Val kept her eyes level on his. "As I was about to say, Councilor, the kidnapping made quick action necessary. As for your not seeing the mage who helped me, you know ghouls screen their kidnappings to avoid detection."

"Yet this rescuer didn't give you his name," Gene said slowly. He hadn't spoken before. His gaze probed into hers, and Val didn't dare look away as he added, "Even though he gave you his clothes and bandaged your wounds."

"Some mages, as you know, prefer to live quietly. Some even forego credit for good deeds." At least her voice sounded composed, despite the anxiety tightening the back of her neck. "He'd helped me against the ghouls. I was willing to accept his anonymity in exchange for information."

Frowning, Otto said, "But it wasn't reliable, was it?"

"In many respects, yes, it was. I can't blame my informant if his information was outdated."

"Outdated in fatal ways." Elayne Smith's alto grated, and loathing burned in her eyes.

Well, she couldn't loathe Val any more than Val despised herself. Those mages' deaths weren't on Smith's conscience.

The short, graying arborist, Lew Ardmore, leaned forward. "We also scried the raid. Why were you not screened?"

"We were." Val tried to look surprised, as though she

hadn't already heard about the screen from Dare. "Or we thought we were. I checked, had Harry check, too. Harry Parker."

Who was dead. Around a fresh stab of grief, she ground out, "There was this odd tingle, we both noticed it, but the screen felt fine."

Judging by the councilors' grim expressions, that wasn't good enough. Had she missed something? Should she have placed more significance on that tingle? Sensed the nest's hidden defenses? She would probably wonder for the rest of her life.

Gene leaned out from his seat in the middle to look along the table. "Deputy Arbaugh, the scout, confirms that he, too, believed the strike force to be screened. Odd magics sometimes occur near ghoul nests. He, like Sheriff Banning and Deputy Parker, didn't consider the odd tingle he sensed important."

"We have only her word on Parker's opinion," Larkin said. "If you think she's told us the truth about this so-called tip, you're getting senile. We can jail her for lying to us, and I say we should."

Chapter 7

Val's stomach churned with sick dread. If they arrested her, questioned her magically, she wouldn't be able to hold back anything, including her contact with Dare. They'd kill her for hiding that, not just fire her.

But she couldn't give him up. She wouldn't. Not when she didn't believe he'd caused this tragedy.

Gene shot Larkin a hard look, and he subsided. "Does anyone else have a question?" Gene asked.

After a few moments of silence, he turned to Val. "Shire Reeve Banning, please step out. We'll call you back in a few moments."

With a nod, Val went out to the hall to sit on the hard bench by the door. That had gone very badly. They might well fire her, and then what would she do?

Sybil came around the corner and sat next to her. "I hope you told them something that helped."

"I told them what happened, but they didn't seem to like what they heard."

The centrally located Council chamber had its own lobby,

an atrium with a skylight and plants that always felt inviting. It was also a frequent cut-through for those coming into the building from outside. A stocky deputy reeve in khaki fatigues walked into the building and down the corridor. He didn't even glance her way. *Shit.* Not that she blamed him.

"At least you're talking to me, Syb. That's something."

After a moment, Sybil said, "If you didn't act like you're hiding things, it might not be as bad. But you seem to, and with all those people dead…" She shrugged.

"Yeah." Val sighed. "I can't give them what I don't have, you know." If they fired her, what would she do? Go be a Mundane cop again, as she had been before becoming shire reeve?

The door warden poked his head out. Holding the door open, he said, "Shire Reeve Banning, they're ready for you."

Val blew out another breath that didn't slow her pounding heart and rose.

Sybil said, "Good luck."

"Thanks." Val walked into the chamber to learn her fate.

The councilors, even Gene, looked grave. The soft thud of the door behind her and the warden's presence at her back seemed suddenly ominous.

The table she had used was gone. She had to stand in front of the Council members. This must be how the Roman victims had felt awaiting the lions, alone and very exposed. She glanced at Gene, who looked sad, and her throat tightened. Her chest felt as though a lead ball filled it.

"Sheriff Banning," he said, "this Council is unanimous in finding that you have not been candid with us."

He paused, letting his words sink in. "You leave us no choice but to hold you responsible for the fatal errors in judgment regarding Tuesday's raid. Such deceits and mis-judgments are not acceptable in a mage entrusted with high office. However, because of the proper precautions taken in executing the raid, you are not charged with dereliction of duty."

The heaviness in her chest eased.

"However," he continued, "we can no longer trust your loyalty or your judgment. Pending further investigation, you are suspended from your position as reeve of the Southeastern Shire."

Seething with frustration and anger, Val headed for her suite.

She'd almost reached her door when Gene called out to her.

"Valeria?" He hurried down the corridor. "A word, if you please."

The last thing she needed was a scolding, or company, but she forced a polite tone. "I'm heading out for a few days, Gene. I have a lot to do first."

"This won't take long." He followed her inside. "I hated to vote against you. I hope you understand that I couldn't support you in the circumstances."

"You have to do what you think is right." As she had. She glanced around the familiar suite. If she couldn't clear her name, she'd lose the right to this place that had become home.

He took the nearest armchair. "Please sit down, my dear, and listen."

She wouldn't get rid of him until he'd had his say. Reluctantly, she perched on the couch.

"You should know, Valeria, that the department heads

have agreed not to hire you for any other position during your suspension, if you're thinking along those lines. Your presence here has become awkward. Besides, you might do better to take some time away, as you said you intended to."

The condemnation in his face jabbed at her, made holding her silence that much harder. He'd always been so proud of her.

Were they kicking her out in hopes she would lead them to Dare?

She rubbed the ache between her eyes. "Gene, I think you should go. As I said, I have a lot to do before I leave." Like writing those condolence notes.

He sighed heavily. She hated disappointing him, but telling him the truth would put him at risk, too.

"I have something for you," he said, "from Zara and me." He drew a wrapped box out of his pocket and handed it to her. "No matter what my office requires of me, you're very dear to us. You know that. Zara sends her best. She's sorry she can't come back from Egypt to see you."

"There's no need for her to." A lump rose in Val's throat. "You know I hate letting you down." She opened the box. A quarter-size moonstone pendant in a delicate, silver setting lay inside. "It's beautiful."

"There's a protection charm on it," he said. "I hope you'll wear it in good health."

"Yes. Thank you, Gene." The kindness in the gesture wrenched her heart. She had to swallow hard before adding, "Thank Zara, too. Please."

"Of course. I couldn't vote to support you. I can, however, shield you. If you will only cooperate with us, give up this misguided effort to protect this man, attitudes will soften.

You used to confide in me," he said. "Trust me, Valeria. Let me help."

For a moment, she was tempted. He and Zara had helped her through the darkest days of her life.

Then she remembered Dare's visit and the trust he'd placed in her. *If you want to push the call button, I won't stop you*, he'd said. He'd risked his life to see for himself that she was okay. To warn her.

"Valeria." Gene gave her an encouraging smile. "Tell me who he is, where to find him."

"I've told you." She stood and paced to the window. "I don't know who or where he is."

Gene sighed. "Until you can be more forthcoming, don't expect much of a welcome around here."

"I see." All or nothing, then. "I think I'll go out to Gran's old cottage at Lake Pearson. Do some thinking."

Dare had said he would keep an eye out, would come to her if she left the Collegium. If he didn't show, she'd hunt him down and drag answers out of him. Shire reeve or not, she was still a mage. If there was a traitor in the Collegium, she'd find him—or her.

"Well." Sadly, Gene shook his head. "I'll see you when you return, then. Time and perspective will do you some good." He walked out of the room.

Val forced air into her tight chest. He'd been like an uncle since her parents' deaths, had encouraged and advocated for her. Now he didn't trust her.

Feeling sick with worry, she packed a bag, stuffing the CD with Dare's info on it into a side pocket. She'd given Dare the benefit of the doubt, and that choice was biting her on the ass. His information had better be worth all this trouble.

* * *

Griff knocked on the door of Valeria's lake cottage. No McMansion for her. Nothing pretentious about the compact, one-story building with weathered wooden siding and a dark green roof.

Only silence answered his knock, yet her blue Mustang sat in the driveway. She must be around somewhere. He'd scried her yesterday and had seen her here. This was a perfect chance for them to talk.

Waiting for her to recover, he'd kept busy interrogating ghouls Tasha and Javier caught. But the prisoners had known nothing. Whatever the bastards were planning for the dark of the moon, they'd kept the knowledge tightly restricted. At least there were five less ghouls in the world.

Now Valeria was out of the infirmary, out of the Collegium. Accessible. Would she trust him now as she'd seemed to the other night? Or had she decided to blame him instead? If so, this could be a trap, but he had to risk it. He'd done what he could in the smart department, setting alert wards on the road in both directions.

He knocked again. Still no answer. Maybe she'd gone out on the water.

He walked back down the slope, past his black Dodge Charger and her Mustang. With the lack of rain lately, the water level had dropped, exposing a strip of rocky red clay along the shoreline, wide enough to make a path. He shaded his eyes against the sunset and peered down the shore.

A woman in brief, blue running shorts and a light blue tank jogged toward him, sunglasses on, tawny ponytail swinging behind a navy blue Georgia Tech Yellow Jackets ball cap. A pale pendant around her neck flashed in the sunlight as her long legs ate ground.

Her head lifted. Relief and inexplicable joy roared through him, hardening him, an instant before his mind caught up with his eyes.

Valeria. He took a quick step, then another, before his wits kicked in and stopped him. She didn't trust him fully, had said she had questions. Besides that, she might regret that kiss the other night. He couldn't regret it, but he had to admit it'd been irresponsible. Drawing her into any kind of personal involvement would be unwise for both of them. He was not only a fugitive but had potentially dangerous ghoul venom polluting his blood.

He shoved his hands into his pockets. Hellfire, he was glad to see her healthy.

Breathing hard, she halted for a long moment before walking slowly toward him. The sunglasses hid her eyes, and she wasn't close enough for him to get any sense of her feelings through the magic.

"How are you?" he asked.

"I've been better."

Into the awkward silence, he said, "Pretty necklace. Moonstone?"

"Yes, thanks. Come in, and let's get out of the sun."

As they walked, Val glanced at Dare's tall frame, now clad in jeans and a weathered, blue chambray shirt with the sleeves rolled up above his corded forearms. The cotton sat snugly across his wide shoulders and chest.

Heat that had nothing to do with exercise bubbled low in her belly. Her blood seemed to sing in her veins, and she couldn't take her eyes off him. She took a slow breath and let it out.

He looked tired, as though he'd pushed himself too long on too little sleep. He'd been wounded recently, too.

He was alive, though, while too many of her deputies were dead.

His visit to the infirmary, his warning—okay, yes, and his kiss—hadn't strayed far from her mind in the days between. But she couldn't afford to trust him blindly.

She squared her shoulders. "You have to let me probe your mind."

His face tightened. "I told you—"

"Yeah, now I'm telling you, over the bodies of my dead deputies. I believe you about last week's disaster, but I told you I had questions. I'm wrestling with whether you're a good guy who was right all along, or someone who made a series of tragic mistakes." If only she could read his frown, know what he was feeling or thinking. He'd pulled himself in magically, hiding his emotions.

At last, he gave her a curt nod. "I'll let you probe, but you'll stick to my motives, my feelings and intentions. You go farther than that, and I'll slap you back so hard you won't see straight for a week."

"Fine." Did he really think she'd just fish around in his head, that she had so little integrity?

She led him to the covered patio under the porch overhang—bright floral cushions on the wrought-iron loveseat and chair, a matching glass-topped table, screening trellises on the sides for privacy. A restful spot, usually, with a view of the water.

When she perched on the love seat, he folded his tall

frame onto the cushion beside her. His wide shoulders crowded her on the narrow bench. Silently, looking at the lake and not at her, he offered his right hand.

She clasped it between her two and closed her eyes, then opened her senses to feel the sturdy structure of bones and muscles, the power crackling in his nerve endings. When she touched it, she caught a quick, electric tingle that made her breath hitch. Dimly, she felt his fingers wrap around hers.

He didn't try to block her. The path to his mind opened, and she rode that current of power back to it. Summoning the memory of that moment in his loft, before the attack, she homed in on it. Felt the memory take shape.

Then she was fully in the moment, seeing her battered face through his eyes and feeling the pain of loneliness he tried to deny, the frustration of his inability to find a traitor he believed betrayed the mages. His admiration for her.

Her heart thudded hard against her ribs. Could he feel her rush of pleasure? Her eyes flew open to meet his dark, uncertain ones.

"Don't stop there," he murmured, and the words echoed in the power linking her mind and his.

Another memory engulfed her, one he offered. Through his eyes, she saw the Council chamber. Tall, scholarly, graying Alden, the chief councilor, sputtered in outrage over Dare's accusation of treason. Other councilors shouted at Dare, refusing to listen.

A hard, dark flash of precog certainty ripped through Dare, the knowledge Alden would escape, that there would be no justice for the dead deputy reeves. Alden blasted green power straight at Dare, who ducked, rolled, and came to his feet blasting silver energy from his staff. Struck in the chest, Alden fell, dead.

Deputy reeves broke free of their shock to charge Dare, their leader. He mowed his way through them, killing four, and the pain he'd felt, the helplessness, frustration, rage, and grief, all thrummed in her veins as they had in his.

It was too much. Her mind jerked free of his.

Both his hands now held hers, and the shadow of that old pain haunted his eyes. It also echoed in her heart.

Their people had branded him a criminal, put a price on his head, forced him to live on the run, yet he still cleaved to his oath, his vow to protect them. Even when that meant killing the ones who came after him, men and women who had been his aides but also his friends.

With his pain echoing in her, Val touched his cheek. "Griffin, I'm so sorry. I don't know what else to say. You deserve…so much better."

Surprise flared in his eyes, and he drew an audible breath. "I never thought I'd live to hear any mage say that to me."

A quick flash of insight hit her, of the constant wariness and lack of hope that had dogged him for six years. "Griffin, I…"

Nothing she could think to say seemed good enough. She gently pressed her lips to his.

The touch sent a flash of desire through her. Shaken, she pulled back to stare at him. The kiss in the infirmary hadn't felt so intense.

He looked as stunned as she felt. Surprise vibrated in the air between them, and then his eyes heated.

Playing with fire, she thought as his head came down, but she couldn't resist tipping her face up to meet him. He kissed her, a brush of warm, soft lips. Her breasts tightened.

Their lips parted, fused, tongues fencing with frantic need as the kiss deepened. She twisted onto her knees to face him fully. When he did the same, his hold tightening, her breasts flattened against his muscular frame, and the hard bulge at his groin pressed into her core.

He felt so good against her. So right. Needing more, she tightened her grip on his shoulders. Ran her hands down the sculpted planes of his back, his arms.

He trailed hot, fast, tongue-flicking kisses down her neck. As she quivered with pleasure, he took her mouth in another deep, possessive kiss. His hands cupped her butt, pulling her against his erection.

Val gasped, felt herself go damp, before another searing, insistent kiss flooded her senses. His hands roamed, molding the curves of her hips and ass, her breasts, stroking pleasure into craving. This was going too fast, rocketing out of control, but she couldn't bear to stop him. Instead, she kissed his neck, nibbled his jaw, his ear.

He pressed hard, fast kisses over her face. When he sucked the pulse point under her ear, she moaned as greedy, needy pleasure made her clutch at him. He palmed her breast through the tank top. Her nipple tightened, and desire again flashed through her. She gave a choked cry, arching against him.

As he kneaded her flesh, she cupped his erection through his jeans. He groaned into her neck. Thrust against her hand.

When she breathed into his ear, he shuddered. His hold tightened. She nipped his jaw, her lips rasping over the stubble there.

He dragged his open mouth down her neck. Clutching

him for balance, she slid a hand under his shirt to stroke his warm, muscular chest with its soft dusting of hair, and the flat pendant lying over his heart. The washboard divisions of his abs tensed at her touch.

He made a choked sound, pressing against her, and she clung to him, wanting him. Needing him.

At the edge of her neckline, he licked the valley between her breasts. Val shivered. She held his head to her, her fingers deep in the thick, inky silk of his hair. He gripped the tank's hem, pulling it up.

If she didn't stop him now, the tide of pleasure and need would overwhelm her.

"No," she choked, and she caught his hand. Breathing as hard as he was, she jerked backward. Guilt and longing tore into her. "No. Griffin, we can't do this."

Chapter 8

Valeria's pained expression hit Griff in the heart. How the hell had he lost control so fast? The kiss in the infirmary had been sweet, but this one had set him on fire.

One kiss, one taste, and all he'd been able to think about was *more*. He was rock hard, aching to have her. Instead, he released Valeria abruptly and stood, stepping away to face the water while he took control of himself. His heart raced, and he gulped in air.

"Right," he ground out at last. "The shire reeve can't fuck a fugitive." That last word had never tasted so bitter, but he swallowed it. Fact was fact. He knew from past experience what a relationship with him could cost her. He ran a hand over his face. "I apologize, Valeria."

"Don't." She took a ragged, audible breath. "Please, don't. I started this."

"Maybe, but I kept it going." He'd also taken it farther.

His hands still held the feel of her. He jammed them into his pockets. If she knew about the venom in his blood, she wouldn't want him to touch her. Maybe she had a right to know, but telling her now, when she was on the brink of trusting him, could blow any chance of getting her help.

"Besides, I'm not reeve right now." Staring out at the lake, she spoke in a grim, hard voice. She'd fisted both hands on her knees. "I'm suspended, likely done."

"What? When did this happen?" He sat beside her, folding his fingers over her tight fist, and tried to settle his breathing, reorient his brain.

They're gunning for her, Stefan had said. Why hadn't he mentioned this little detail?

She flicked a glance at him and then away. "I can't be of much use to you now, I'm afraid."

"Never mind that. What happened?"

She shrugged but didn't look at him. Didn't take his hand but didn't move hers, either. "I screwed up. Mages died."

"They can't blame you for that ambush. The Council always wants a scapegoat, but anyone with any tactical sense should realize you walked into a trap."

"Thanks for calling it that." She stared out at the water, and the light caught lines of weariness in her beautiful face. "Most everyone else is calling it my fatal fuckup."

"What happened at the debriefing?"

"There wasn't one. Most of the survivors were in the infirmary." Her lips parted, as though she meant to say something else, but she only shook her head.

With two fingers, he gently turned her chin so she faced him. "What aren't you telling me?"

Her face stayed calm, but pain lurked in her eyes. "It doesn't matter."

"If it didn't, you wouldn't hold back." Their gazes locked. A faint hint of defiance in her expression put a different cast on things. His breath caught. "Are you…protecting me?"

"I'm doing my job. What used to be my job anyway."

"That's not an answer." Had she lost her job because of him? His gut took a sick twist.

She hesitated. At last, she said, "They think I haven't been candid about where I got my information."

"Because you haven't." Confirmation flashed in her eyes. Hellfire. "I never meant to make trouble for you. I can't tell you how sorry I am."

"Thanks." Another little shrug. "Looks like I won't be able to help you clear your name."

"Damn it, that doesn't matter now. You matter." He waited until she looked at him again. "What you've lost because of me matters."

Her lips trembled. She pressed them together and, at last, turned her hand over to grip his. The contact warmed his heart as she said, "Thanks for that."

He gently brushed a strand of hair out of her face. "I remember finding you in the gym one day when you were a cadet, about seventeen or so, I think. I asked you why you were pushing yourself so hard, if you wanted to be an Olympic athlete. You smiled, but I could tell you were serious when you said you didn't care about gold medals, that you wanted my job one day."

Her smile didn't reach her eyes, but they softened. "I remember. You told me to keep pushing, and I'd get there."

"And you did. You became shire reeve at age twenty-three, two years earlier than anyone else ever has." He gave her hand a quick squeeze. "Sometimes, you just have to keep pushing until you get where you want to go." Even when you didn't see a clear path forward.

She cocked her head, studying him. "Is that how you've kept going so long?"

"I'll see that your name's cleared, Valeria." Instead of answering her question, he kissed her knuckles.

Her fingers tightened on his, and desire slammed through him. *Crap.* He'd never responded so quickly, so intensely, to any woman.

Clearly oblivious to her effect on him, Valeria held their joined hands on her smooth, firm thigh. Leaning back against the cushions, she said, "As for what just happened—I can't have sex with you, Griffin. Even though, obviously, I want to."

Her cheeks flushed, but she kept her gaze level on his. "I know now what kind of man you are, but it's too much, too fast."

"Fair enough. Smart, too." At her inquiring look, he added, "I'm not the best guy to get involved with."

At least her hand still gripped his. She'd given him her precious trust, a big risk for her. "I came to help," he said. "If you're up for it, let's go over the battle. Maybe together we can figure out how they fooled you."

"Together," she repeated. A shaky smile curved her mouth, and her eyes warmed. "You know, you're the first person to offer something constructive."

"I live to kick ass and take names." He grinned at her. Her answering smile lit her face, and he fought the urge to kiss her again. Instead, he said, "Going out for dinner's too risky, but I could pick up something."

"Nothing's close. I have chicken and veggies we can toss together while we talk. I just need a few minutes to shower and change."

He followed her inside, his mind already slotting into strategic mode. Who stood to gain if she left?

Talking to Griffin was dangerous, Val concluded as they washed the dishes after dinner. He'd focused, listened, and mulled things over while they ate. She could grow to like talking with him far too much.

"That was a great meal," he said. "Your idea of tossing something together is more like what I'd call serious cooking. I'm guessing you either like to cook or hate eating takeout."

"Both, thanks. My mom loved to cook. So did my dad. Zara and Gene, not so much." Thinking of her guardians, remembering Gene's disapproval, made her throat tighten. Maybe he would relent if she could show the ambush wasn't her fault. "So I cooked a lot. It made me feel closer to my folks."

"It paid off for you."

Smiling her thanks, she accepted a wet plate from him and rubbed a dish towel over it. Gran had installed a dishwasher, but using it for such a small load seemed like a waste.

The economy of movement in Dare's fighting style translated to this task, too. His large, tanned hands scrubbed a pot and ran water over it as efficiently as his hold on his quarterstaff had shifted during the battle. As smoothly as his touch had glided over her body a little while ago.

She yanked her gaze back to the now dry plate in her hand. Putting it in the cabinet, she felt his gaze on her. She cut her eyes at him in time to see one corner of his mouth crook upward.

"What?" she asked. Maybe he wouldn't notice, in the fading light from the kitchen window, the color rising in her face.

"Nothing." He shook water off the pot in his hand and reached for the towel she'd set aside. "I like looking at you. Working with you."

"We work well together." No way he could miss her blush now, not when her cheeks felt so warm. She held out her hand. "I'll do that. I'm drying."

"It's the last." He gave the pot a final wipe and passed it over.

Their fingers brushed on the handle. Desire sparked in his eyes, turning them a rich azure, and her breathing stopped.

Griffin abruptly turned away from her. "Let's work with your whiteboard. Map things out."

"All right." She stooped to put away the pot. He was respecting her boundaries. She should appreciate that, not wish he wouldn't. Not think of dropping them herself.

Yes, he attracted her, as he would any breathing woman. But *baggage* didn't begin to describe what he came with, and getting involved with him would destroy her last shreds of credibility with the Council.

Wineglass in hand, he studied the whiteboard on its easel by the bookcase. His position gave her an excellent view of the chambray draping his broad shoulders and the denim hugging his taut, lean butt.

Geez, Val. Grow the hell up. She grabbed her own glass of sauvignon blanc and joined him. "See anything?"

"Nothing new." He rubbed his free hand over his chin. "Any chance there'll be a follow-up strike?"

As he always had required. "I didn't order one, though I don't know what my replacement will do. To be honest, we don't have the trained manpower for that." Again, guilt stabbed into her heart.

"We lost the people I'd have chosen—the best—" Their faces flashed across her mind's eye. She couldn't breathe. Couldn't finish.

"Sometimes," he said quietly, "being in charge sucks."

"Yeah." No one had ever shared that particular pain of loss with her, but he had losses of his own. His matter-of-fact sympathy eased the jagged edges in her soul.

Gene had claimed to care but hadn't offered comfort, yet this renegade's mere presence bolstered her.

"We'll solve this. I swear we will." Griffin gave Val's shoulder a quick squeeze.

Desire ignited in her core, but Val only nodded. She had to think, not dissolve into hormonal goo, so she kept her eyes on the board. "We have to figure this out. I owe my fallen comrades that."

Yet he'd been working alone for six years without ending the problem. Could the two of them succeed where he'd failed?

"Griffin, did you ever think that maybe working in the system would've been a better choice?"

His body tensed. "Not if I wanted Alden to pay for what he'd done." He glanced down at her with hard eyes. "Do I regret the mages who died? Damned straight. But I can't change what happened."

Whoa. Big NO TRESPASSING sign there. Maybe that was best since, as he said, he couldn't undo anything. Still, working within the system might ultimately be his best hope of vindication. She would have to raise that carefully.

"Okay." She shrugged. "Just asking."

The tension in his body eased. He glanced at the diagram of the attack and then at her. "Was there something special about this nest, a reason you didn't take it out two years ago?"

"I didn't know about it." She frowned at the board.

"I leaked you that information," he said, the words crisp with impatience, "via Tina Wallace."

Stunned, she stared at him. "The pot dealer near Scottsboro?" Just a couple of miles from Milledgeville and the nest. "Tina's a reliable snitch. Or was." Until she disappeared. "She...Griffin, are you sure?"

He raised an eyebrow. Of course he was sure.

"When did you send the tip?" she asked. Dread of his answer twisted in her heart.

"Mid-April, year before last." His eyes narrowed, concerned. "Valeria, what is it?"

She took a shaky breath. "Tina disappeared about that time. I figured she just moved on, maybe because the Mundane sheriff was getting suspicious."

"But maybe not," he said softly. "You think not."

"If she'd come in with a tip like that, and someone didn't want me to know..."

"Too much of a coincidence," he said.

"Yes. I didn't look for her. God, I wish I had. You had several nests listed that were new to me, and now you tell me this. Another witness recently disappeared. Seems there're even bigger problems in intel and recon than I suspected."

Fighting for control, she turned away from him. A kick in the face would've shocked her less than this kind of betrayal. Her chest felt tight, and her stomach roiled.

He stepped closer to grip her shoulder, but he didn't use

magic, only warm, solid, steadying contact. She covered his hand with hers. For just a moment, she let herself lean against him.

"Treachery is never easy to believe," he said. "Or to understand." He drew her close with an arm around her waist and rested his cheek against her hair. "Take a minute."

There spoke the voice of experience. He'd lived with treachery for years now, had lost those he cared for to it. Maybe her stomach would settle if she didn't think. Relaxing against him, she closed her eyes and took deep, slow breaths. In, out. In, out. No thinking.

The churning in her stomach lessened, and her breathing steadied. Now she noticed the warmth of his muscular frame, remembered the feel of it under her hands, the feel of his hands on her.

She also sensed the desire he held in check. Heat sparked low in her belly. Letting him hold her felt so good.

As though he caught her reaction in the magic, and he likely did, his fingers caressed her waist. He rubbed his face lightly against her hair.

If she kissed him now, when she was hurting so much, she probably wouldn't be able to stop. And that would be a mistake.

She jerked away from him. "I need water." The words emerged low and smoky. She didn't dare look at him. Instead, she stalked into the kitchen.

He didn't follow. In the corner of her eye, she saw a muscle work in his tight jaw. He took a big gulp of wine. She turned her back and headed for the fridge. Putting ice in a glass, running the water, taking a swallow steadied her.

When she returned to the living room, he gestured at the

board with his wineglass. "Why are mages protecting ghoul nests? And why would the ghouls suddenly think to plant mines on their perimeter?"

"I'd love to know. Of course, they could've gotten the idea from any number of movies and TV shows."

"Those kinds of shows have been around for years. So, again, why now?"

"Could there be something special about that nest? Something they don't want anyone to find?" She rubbed a finger along the cool rim of her glass. "The ghouls who captured me had an amulet that blocked my power. If I hadn't gotten it off before the car stopped, I wouldn't have lived to call for help."

He raised an eyebrow. "How did you remove it if you were bound?"

Val grimaced, pushing away the shadow of remembered fear. "Rolled to my knees, bent over, and let gravity do its work."

He captured her arm, ran his hand lightly down it, just for a moment, and her blood seemed to sizzle. Thank God, he'd looked back at the diagram.

She ached to touch him, to draw his strong body close again, but how pointless was that? Most likely, common troubles and isolation drew them together, a bond that wouldn't last.

But the comfort of having someone believe her, believe *in* her, could seduce her so easily. Was it the same for him?

"And where," he muttered softly, "did they come up with such an amulet?" His brows knitted together. "I've suspected they've been working up to something big for quite a while. Something involving dark magic."

"Well, that's never good."

They stared at the board in brooding silence.

"Anything special about that kid," he asked slowly, "the one you went to rescue? Besides his grand poobah mom?"

"Not so far as I know. Why?"

He frowned. "Have you ever felt a tingle like that before?"

The look on his face as he set his glass on the bookcase made her want to run. Instead, she clenched her fingers on the stem of her goblet. "No, I haven't. Have you?"

"Yes, when I led my team into a trap." He gripped Val's shoulders, as though to brace her, and the hardening of his face sent dread rippling through her. "What you felt," he said, "that tingle, came from the mixing of mage magic with ghoul."

"Well, of course." Val frowned. "Ours and theirs hit—"

"No, honey." Regret darkened his eyes, but his expression was grim. "I mean mage magic joined with ghoul against you."

She stared up at him. He couldn't have said what she thought he had.

"I had the figures on that nest right," he continued, his eyes level on hers. "The number might've fluctuated a little, but not that much. Mages and ghouls reinforced it. Together they trumped your team's power, pierced your screen, and hid the ghoul defenses. No matter how little you want to believe it, mages helped the ghouls kill your team."

Chapter 9

The only good thing about emergency surgery was that it kept a man's mind off idiocy like politics. This afternoon's Council meeting had been one prolonged irritant, like a boil on the butt.

Scowling, Stefan flopped onto the couch and pulled out his recorder to dictate the surgical notes. At least he wasn't writing another death certificate. Deputy Reeve Selena Vale had suffered multiple gunshot wounds at Milledgeville but had responded to on-scene treatment. She'd been stable until the sudden drop in blood pressure today.

That bleeding artery was fixed for good this time, but he felt tired down to his bones, ready to turn in even if it was only ten fifty. But surgery always left him too wired to sleep. At least living at the Collegium meant he didn't have to get in a car and drive after a long procedure.

He clicked the recorder off and stared at the blinking message light on his desk phone across the room. Whatever it signaled could wait. Anything urgent would've come over his pager. Or been relayed to him after surgery.

Email could wait, too. He'd far rather look at the screen saver slide show of his sister, Annie, and her husband and kids than read a bunch of carping about the Council choosing Joe Healey as acting shire reeve, or whatever else lurked in his inbox.

Someone knocked at the door. This late, it could only be a friend or, God forbid, a councilor. Pulling himself off the couch, he extended his magical senses and recognized Will.

When Stefan opened the door, Will stood in the hall with a folder in one hand.

"Dr. Harper, I know it's late, but I thought you'd want the preliminary research on the use of ancient herbal magic for internal injuries right away."

"Yes, come in. Thanks."

With cover for their meeting thus established, Stefan locked the door behind Will. No one in Griff's circle socialized without a business excuse, especially since they both had links to Griff. Stefan had worked with him when he was reeve, and Will had stayed with the Dare family as a kid when his parents were on archaeological digs.

"Have a seat," Stefan said. "Beer? Or something else?"

"Anything but coffee, thanks. I've had enough of that for one day." Will handed over the folder.

Stefan tossed it on the coffee table en route to the fridge. He grabbed a beer for Will and one for himself.

After passing Will his bottle, Stefan spread the papers from the folder on the coffee table. Handling them while he and Will talked would give the appearance the conversation was about the papers. Since scrying didn't carry audio, no one would know what he and Will really discussed.

"So," Will said, "Joe Healey? I couldn't believe the

Council chose him as acting reeve at the meeting this afternoon. He doesn't have Banning's ability to think creatively. Or anything near her drive. Never distinguished himself in any way."

"Except his knack for kissing the right political asses." Stefan dropped into the easy chair at a right angle to the sofa.

Will took a long pull on his beer. "Yeah. Gerry's pissed. He wanted Sybil Harrison or, if she's considered too close to Banning, Deke Jones."

"So did I." Stefan and Gerry Armitage, Will's boss, often saw eye to eye. "But Otto Larkin pushed hard for Healey." Stefan pulled papers out of the folder and leafed through them as though reading. "I thought Teresa would come across the table at him for a minute, there."

"I would've liked to see that." Will grinned. Teresa DiMaggio, the stocky, middle-aged weaponsmistress, had definite opinions and little patience for bullshit.

"I was hoping." The print on the pages blurred. Stefan rubbed his weary eyes. "Anything on that stuff Griff sent you?"

"Not much. I got a line on a guy in Finland who may be able to help. He owns a lot of old books, he says. Even some papyrus scrolls." Will sighed. "Ever think about where we'd be if the ancient library at Alexandria hadn't burned?"

"No. I'm not a geek." Stefan grinned over his beer. "Knock yourself out, though."

Will not only loved mage lore but could name every development in the history of Superman since *Action Comics* No. 1 in 1930-whatever. He could also rattle off a list of which Jedi carried which color lightsabers in the *Star Wars* movies.

Will smirked at him. "Want to hit the gym, see how it feels when a geek kicks your ass into next week?"

"Nah. Can't stand to hear you scream like a little girl." If only. Stefan could hold his own in magical combat, but Will was better. And had a second-degree black belt in jeet kune do.

"Dream on, Doc."

Before Stefan could respond, someone knocked at the door. Stefan glanced at Will in shared concern and went to answer the knock.

Gerry Armitage stood in the hallway. Judging by the grim look on his face, the news wasn't good.

"We could've used your level head in Council just now," Gerry said. "You won't believe the crap that's coming down."

Hell. Now what? "Come in, Gerry. Have a seat. What Council meeting?"

"It was called suddenly." Settling on the couch, Gerry glanced at the blinking message light on the phone. "Guess you didn't hear about it."

"I was in surgery." Foreboding gnawed at Stefan's throat.

"I would've gone with you, Gerry," Will said.

Gerry shrugged. "You were deep in medical research. That's more important. Besides, you don't have a vote."

"What happened?" Stefan demanded.

Gerry blew out a hard breath. "I could use a beer if you can spare it."

"Sure. Will, do you mind?"

"In Blake's defense," Gerry said as Will headed for the kitchen, "he's very worried about our former shire reeve, about her evasiveness."

"We all are."

With a nod of thanks, Gerry accepted his beer from Will, who sat beside him. "The long and short of it is, Blake authorized Healey to spy on Banning. Gave her some sort of necklace that penetrates shielding, lets them scry."

"That's outrageous," Will said as Stefan snapped, "What?"

"Several of us objected, but they did the scrying again so we could all see. Damn it, I thought Banning had a brain between her ears." Gerry took a long, slow drink.

"What has she done?" Stefan managed not to look at Will. He couldn't give the game away. Had she given Griff up? Set the Council on Marc and the shelter?

"She was with some guy. Tall, dark haired," Gerry said as Stefan's blood chilled. "His face was blurred, but for just a second—while they were, ah, heavily engaged—it blinked clear. I'd swear the son of a bitch looked just like Griffin Dare."

"That's not much to go on," Will said.

"It was enough for Blake and Healey. They've sent two squads to her place at the lake to arrest them both."

Oh, fuck us all sideways. Stefan couldn't help looking at Will. They had to get Gerry out of there so they could warn Griff before it was too late.

"This is like something out of a nightmare." Val stared at the councilors' names and the list of ghoul nests Griffin had written on the whiteboard. They'd been talking about this for over an hour, and it still didn't seem any more real to her. "Mages working against their own kind to help ghouls!"

"I know how you feel." Staring out the window, he shook his head. "Just as you know we can't duck this. We have to stop it. What you said about disappearing witnesses means the corruption spreads farther than we knew."

He turned, anger evident in the taut lines of his body. "One of our kind has sent our people to their deaths, not once but several times. And almost killed *you*. I want the bastard."

He tipped up her chin, and the gentleness of his touch contrasted with the steely resolve in his eyes. His fury for Val warmed her, made her pulse quicken. Awareness of his touch rippled through her body. So tempting.

His hand drifted along her jaw, his thumb caressing her cheek. She caught his wrist and gently pulled it down to his side. Yet her fingers lingered on his arm long enough for his eyes to darken. Her heart stuttered.

Stupid, she reminded herself, and jerked her gaze back to the board, to the name Americus. "If there's a large ghoul nest outside Americus, there would be lots of missing persons' reports from the area around it. Someone had to have picked up on that. And hidden it, damn them. We should check it out." She circled the name, underlining it in her mind, too.

"No one would do that," he said, "without support from above, from a councilor. At least, not successfully for very long."

The pain of that truth felt like a boulder in her chest. Swallowing against it, she wandered to the kitchen. Since the water hadn't settled her gut anyway, she'd gone back to wine for the mellowing effect. She poured more of the pale liquid into her goblet and went back to the living room.

Griffin was staring at the floor, looking frustrated and weary. He ran a hand through his hair.

He'd lived with this, fought the ghouls and defended against an enemy he couldn't find, for years while the people he protected vilified him.

"How do you keep going?" she asked. "You could create an identity somewhere, make a life for yourself."

His head lifted, and he turned a surprised look on her. "Somebody has to do it. Why not me?"

Her heart turned over at his answer. The simple, selfless courage in his words stole her breath away. She couldn't form a reply, and the look between them held. Yearning fluttered in her heart.

His gaze fell to her mouth. If he touched her—

Griffin looked away and cleared his throat. "Besides, I won't let the bastards beat me." He frowned at his empty goblet. "Is there any more wine?"

"Couple of glasses' worth." As he walked into the kitchen, she asked, "Speaking of making a life, how have you survived all this time? Or shouldn't I ask?"

He poured his refill and strolled back into the room. "You saw the paints at my place by the swamp. I sell my work when I can. Thanks to a college roommate, I have an off-and-on gig as a 'psychic consultant' for the Feds." When her brows rose, he added, "I'm a tracker. Comes in handy sometimes."

Most mages had the average skill set, basic magic use, and could refine it with practice, though some mages excelled more in particular areas. A rare few had special skills, like tracking or increased ability to scry, translocate, or even shield.

"I had a tracker on my staff," she said. "One I thought I could trust. He works in intel and recon."

They shared a grim look, and he said, "We're going to

straighten this out, Valeria. The bastards will pay."

She, too, wanted payback, but the idea of chasing it for years with no help seemed impossible. She ached for the loss and loneliness he'd endured. "Griffin, I wish—"

"Don't. It doesn't help."

He took a long swallow of wine. "It's a hell of a mess. I should've left you out of it."

"It's my job. Or was." Val shook her head.

"It will be again," he said, and his eyes were hard. Determined. On her behalf.

No one had cared that much about what she wanted since her parents' deaths. Even Gene and Zara, supporting her for the job of shire reeve, hadn't shown this kind of determination. Griffin's expression was stony.

Looking at the board, she took a deep breath to steady herself. She hadn't met a man she'd wanted to touch, to have touch her, in a long time. Why the hell did he have to be the one?

"Someone," he added, "obviously tipped the ghouls at Lake Sinclair. But there's nothing to tie anyone on the Council to that. Let's run it down anyway. What does Blake say about the ghouls?"

Nothing like hitting the sore spot, the man whose good opinion she'd lost, first. "He hates them. He did worry about wasted resources from some of my raids, but he never actually tried to stop them. Though I heard some of the Council—don't know who—were unhappy about the one I led a couple of weeks ago."

Val stared into the golden depths of her goblet, detesting what she had to say. "Gene wanted me to put more effort into keeping kids away from dark magic, arresting dabblers.

I'd hate to think it's because he wants to protect the ghouls."

"Of course you would." Griffin's face was kind as he added, "The chief councilor has access to a lot of information, in every department, but that doesn't mean he's a traitor."

"Alden was the council chief."

"Yes, and that experience taught me not to jump without concrete proof. Blake wasn't on the Council then. Now maybe he's just juggling priorities. Elayne Smith was on the Council as quartermistress six years ago, is High Council now, and she loves secrets and intrigue. Seems to hate the ghouls but has been known to say we should consider a truce."

"She still does," Val said, "but she has the sense, or seems to, to realize that's unlikely."

She frowned at the whiteboard. "Pansy Wilson is new to the High Council. She loves gossip and backstairs dealing, but never says much about ghouls and doesn't seem to have any sympathy for them."

"What about Otto Larkin?"

"He's so generally disagreeable, it's hard to know what he thinks about anything. And Dutton blows with the prevailing wind." Val shrugged. "Nothing definite on the High Council, then. I've never heard anything about ghouls from the department heads that struck me as odd."

"Still, we might be able to narrow the field if we—" His head snapped up. "Shit. We have to go. If you have a go bag packed, grab it."

"What? Griffin, what is it?"

"Mages coming this way. Two cars. No, damn it. Three." He stepped away from her. "Valeria, move!"

If the Council needed her to come back, they would

phone, not send cars. But..."How would they know you were here?"

"My screen may not be as good as it usually is. Or something's interfering. Do you have anything that would do that?"

"No, I..." Her stomach knotted as intuition hit. Gene had given her that pendant despite his disapproval. Her hand went to her throat, but she'd left the pendant off after her shower. Was the *protective spell* on it just for protection? It had to be. He wouldn't spy on her. Would he? Maybe to keep the Collegium safe. If so, that didn't make him a traitor.

"Valeria?"

"I don't know, Griffin. Just go. Now. They have no quarrel with me." He knew far more than she did about the problems within the Collegium, so his freedom was more important than hers. Somehow, she would talk her way out of this, cover his back. Buy him time.

She tugged him toward the door. "I'll throw them off."

"Good luck with that. If they already know I'm here, they'll kill you."

"I'll manage."

"Like hell." He yanked his arm free. "I won't leave you. You come with me, or I don't go."

If she left with him, she would also be a fugitive. Was she ready to take that irrevocable step?

"Decide fast," he said. "If we're staying, you need to call for backup, report I'm here, and then bash me in the head, before they arrive."

His grim face meant he was in earnest, that he would sacrifice himself to protect her. If she stopped to think about that, the enormity of it would paralyze her.

"I keep a bag packed." Even though she now had no job requiring it. "Habit, you know? I'll grab it."

"Hurry. They're about a mile away. The dirt road is slowing them down, but they'll be here pronto."

Left alone in the sitting area, Griff erased the whiteboard with a wave of his hand and summoned his staff from beside the table. He and Valeria couldn't take on a group the size of the approaching one without using lethal force. He already had too many mage deaths on his conscience and didn't want any on hers. Their best chance of escaping was to sneak clear before the deputies arrived.

Most likely, the approaching units had orders to kill him and secure Valeria, and he'd have no chance to protect her. Unless he pretended to take her hostage, made them listen to him before they started blasting.

Valeria hurried back into the room with a small backpack over her shoulder and her broadsword at her hip. "By the way, Griffin, I won't let you sacrifice yourself to save me. Not ever. I can look after myself, and I know we can find a way to make the Council listen to us."

Yeah, right, but arguing would waste time and breath. So would stopping to think about the longing her loyalty stirred in his soul.

They hurried out of the house. Valeria locked the door with a jolt of magic so they wouldn't have to stop. That lock wouldn't keep mages out, but it would slow down other intruders.

"You drive my car," he said, "if you can handle a stick shift. I have things in the trunk I can't lose. Besides, I can build a stronger screen if I don't have to divide my attention." She could probably feel him building it already—a glamour of absence, of transparency and illusion, one layer at a time.

He could fire energy bolts to blast their way to freedom, a tactic he didn't want her using. He was already an outcast beyond redemption. No sense making her road back any harder than it had to be.

She tossed her bag in the rear seat of his low-slung four-door while he propped her sword between the gear box and his leg, with his staff stuck between the seats in easy reach.

"Leave the lights off," he said as she started the engine, "and go around your car, down to the water. Head left along the exposed lake bed to your neighbor's boat ramp. Then pull up a few feet and sit until the Collegium SUVs go by."

"Then we drive onto the road behind them, moving out while they move in. All without bringing your screen close, where they might sense it." Shifting into first, she arched a brow at him, her face barely visible in the darkness. "Smart."

"Thanks. Once we get around that bend up there, out of their sight, turn on the lights and drive like hell. Engine's a V8, so it's got muscle."

What they'd find at the entrance to the lakeside community might pose another problem. No tactician with a brain would leave that unguarded. But they'd swim that river when they reached it.

Unfortunately, they couldn't hide behind a screen and put up a deflecting shield at the same time. But if the screen worked, the shield wasn't necessary. He pushed the glamour a little farther out. Slow, steady expansion was key.

Valeria steered between pine trees and down to the red clay edging the water. As she swung left, onto the bumpy surface, his screen brushed something—a tingle—power. Mages coming along the water's edge on foot. They would feel the screen.

"Shit," he snapped. "Floor it!"

Her lips tightened. The car surged onto her neighbor's lawn with a roar, and a bolt of blue-white energy shot past the rear bumper. "I'm going to the road. The ground's too uneven for us to make time here."

"I'll keep the screen up so they can't peg us exactly."

Another blue-white streak ripped by, this time in front of them, as a pale green bolt zoomed toward the rear window. The mages must've homed in on the screen's energy. Griff dropped the screen and flung a personal shield around himself and Valeria. The tingle rippling over his skin meant she was also shielding.

The rear window exploded. Shrapnel bounced off their personal shields. They traded a grim look.

"Those shots come close enough to the fuel line and they'll blow the engine." She had a white-knuckled grip on the wheel.

"Just get to the road." He threw more power into his shield.

The nearest SUV was merely fifty feet away. The intense power he felt building inside it had to come from at least five or six mages.

Valeria swerved wildly and careened onto the road. Just ahead, the other SUV was pulling a three-point turn. One closing fast, the other angling to intercept, and the one that had come in from the other direction gaining.

Shit. Griff aimed his staff out the back window. The runes and end caps glowed. He pushed his power into the staff through the P-shaped rune, *thurisaz*, for pure might, to trigger a blast from the end cap. Using the rune amplified the power but drained him faster.

With an earthshaking, deafening boom that shattered windows in nearby houses and made his shielded ears ring, the gravel surface erupted. The lead SUV flipped.

Valeria gaped at him. "What the—"

A bolt of blue-white sizzled past the car. Way too close.

"Not now." Griff closed his eyes. Centered. "There's a kill switch for the engine, that red button by the ignition. Punch it."

"But that'll—"

"Do as I say!"

Valeria hit the button. The engine roar died abruptly, but momentum carried the car forward.

He gathered more power, drawing from the grass and trees, the fish in the lake, even the night bugs stirring around them.

"Griffin, damn it—"

"Hang on," he bit out. His neck hurt. His chest cramped. He centered his power, surrounded the car with it, and reached for the space between life and death.

His control wobbled, felt dangerously shaky. But if this didn't work, they were dead anyway.

Chapter 10

Reality whirled away with speed that pressed the breath from Val's lungs. Blind and deaf in the icy cold, she fought terror an instant before realizing they'd translocated. Then the car popped back into reality. Headlights rushed toward them as she discovered they were on the wrong side of a forest road. Yanking the wheel to the right, toward the correct lane, she hit the gas. Nothing. *Hell.*

"Key," Dare gasped as she reached for it.

Brakes squealed. She turned the key and the engine caught, but the other car was veering into the open lane. It passed them with a long, hard blare of its horn and an angry shout.

"Shit," Val muttered. If she tried to say anything more right now, she'd blow like a volcano. Of course he'd killed the engine before translocating, but she hadn't realized that was his plan. Nobody she knew had ever translocated an entire car.

She swung into the correct lane and drove forward. There had to be a place she could pull over and get a few things straight. He'd flipped that SUV like a toy. God only knew if the mages inside had shielded in time.

God, she'd trusted him. Started to care, maybe more than— *No, nuh-uh, not walking that path.*

"Should've…warned you." His soft voice rasped.

"Should have done a lot of things." She shot an angry glance at him, and her anger evaporated as her heart plunged into her stomach.

Dare slumped in his seat, eyes closed, head lolling against the headrest. The green glow of dash lights showed beads of sweat on his upper lip and temples. His chest rose and fell in fast, shallow breaths.

No, no, no. He couldn't have blown himself out. Could he? "Griffin?"

His throat moved in a hard swallow. "I'm okay. Just…need a minute." Another swallow.

When she touched his cheek with her knuckles, it felt clammy. Like a ghoul's—but that was ridiculous. Sick people had cold, clammy skin, too, and he'd drained himself dangerously pulling this stunt.

He caught her hand to kiss it, and her heart skipped a beat. Despite the anger still seething under her worry, she squeezed his fingers before she drew her hand back.

Everything he'd done, he'd done to save her. She would remember that when they talked, but he'd better not order her around like that ever again if he wanted her help.

Of course, she needed his help, too. Val sighed.

Distrusting Gene went against the grain. Maybe he hadn't always supported her ideas. Maybe she'd occasionally felt as though he were manipulating her, not an unusual move for a politician. Still, he and Zara had treated her as though she were their own. Reluctantly, feeling ungrateful and overly suspicious, she'd left the pendant behind. Just in case.

For better or worse, she was allied with Dare. They had to find a way to make things right.

"Where are we?" she asked. He would recharge faster in a place thick with life, with energy he could safely draw from.

"Should be about a mile from the lake, maybe less." He ran a hand over his face.

"But I don't recognize anything, and I've explored all around the lake cottage." Translocating a car a mile would be a record.

He frowned into the darkness. "Then I don't know where we are," he said slowly. "Sorry."

"We'll figure it out." He must've sent them quite a distance, maybe farther than any mage had ever achieved. Just how strong was he?

"Watch for a road sign," she said.

He nodded but didn't look any better. Drawing more power than you could handle could burst a blood vessel or create a systemic effect similar to an electrical short or induce knee-buckling fatigue.

"We need a place to crash," he muttered. He shook his head and blinked, as though he were having trouble seeing.

"Yeah." Val kept her tone easy despite the way his gesture pinched her heart. "Once we know where we are."

She hoped there wasn't any physical damage from the overload.

"How have you managed to stay hidden these last six years? Have you shielded yourself? Can you shield us now? Or are we busted, with helos on the way?"

"We should be okay." He fished under his shirt and drew

out the pendant she'd felt earlier. "I have warding stones to put around whatever place we stop in for the night. Meanwhile, this is specially warded. As long as we're within fifteen feet of it, we're covered."

She glanced at it. "Is that an eye?"

"Of Horus, the Egyptian god of justice. It's made of lapis lazuli." He tucked it back into his shirt. "We should also disable the GPS on your cell phone. You can't use it, or they'll be able to track you. I can do it magically if you give me the phone."

She reached behind the seat, fished in her bag on the floor, and handed him the phone. "The sooner the better."

If anyone had told her she'd be on the run with a fugitive, she would've said they were living in Loony Land.

The headlights struck a green rectangle with white lettering—a road sign, finally! BICKLEY 3, it read.

Val gaped at it. "Bickley is twelve miles from the cabin."

"And you've driven, what, about three?" His eyes reflected her astonishment.

"You sent us six miles. Six times the distance any mage ever attained with a freakin' paperweight, and you did it with a car, two people, and gear." A chill ran down her spine. "Griffin, what are you?"

"Stronger than I knew, I guess." Again, he ran a hand over his face. "I don't know how I did it. My record with a car is about a mile. I just wanted us safe."

Nothing about him hinted at evasion or deceit. Val blew out a breath. "Okay," she said. "We'll worry about it later. One thing at a time, and rest comes first. Beyond Bickley is Abner Wade State Park, a great place to recharge."

Rest would also give her time to think, something she

badly needed if she had to accept that someone she'd trusted for most of her life was a traitor.

"I paid with cash." Griff climbed back into the car. Valeria looked strained, and no wonder. She'd come to grips with a lot today. "Remember, no credit cards from here out. Those are traceable."

"Right." She grimaced as she put the car in gear. "I only have about seventy-five dollars on me. That won't go far."

"This place is pretty cheap. We're in cabin six, on the left side. As for money, I have a couple of hundred, and I can get more." Through the untraceable account he'd gotten from the Feds. "Don't worry, Valeria. I'll get you home soon."

For now, though, that translocation was catching up to him. His eyelids felt heavy. Gritty, too. Fatigue thrummed in his muscles and knotted his gut.

Worst of all, the ammonia taste in his mouth was so strong, it backed up into his nose. *Shit.* If he turned ghoul, what would happen to her? She'd burned her bridges tonight because of him. His choices had led to too many deaths, including two close friends and the woman he'd loved. Somehow, he would keep Valeria safe.

She backed out of the parking space, and he flipped open his phone. Stefan or Will might be able to clue him in on how the Collegium had tracked them. The message icon appeared on the screen. He checked his voicemail.

"Mages coming," Stefan's voice said. "Get out now, both of you. They found you by scrying through Banning's pendant. The Horus charm mostly blurred your face, but it failed for just a second, enough time to let them suspect who you were. Get rid of her pendant."

Well, shit. The Horus pendant's screen had probably failed when she'd cupped him. His intense reaction to that could've broken through. But he couldn't tell her the truth without risking Stefan's cover. He glanced at her throat. "What happened to your necklace?"

"I left it at the lake." She shot him an uneasy glance. "It was the only new thing I had, the only way I could think they might spy on us."

"Smart move." He tried to keep the relief from his voice. She'd made a tough choice, and it showed in the unhappiness shadowing her eyes. He longed to comfort her, but hugs wouldn't solve their problem. After tonight, she'd have no reputation left. He couldn't let her pay any more than she already was for giving him a chance.

She drove into a gravel parking lot surrounded by a dozen or so small huts. Judging their color at night was tough, but they looked slightly run-down—a bit of paint peeling here, an uneven roof shingle there. They'd definitely seen better days.

VACATION CABINS, the sign had said? More like garden sheds for the Bates Motel. Still, obscurity was good for fugitives.

He and Valeria climbed out of the car and unloaded their gear. He jammed the key into the lock, turned it, only to have the door stick. *Bates Motel*, he thought again, and put his shoulder to the wood. His weight, more than his strength, forced the door open.

Great, a musty smell. Better not be from the body of a mummified old lady. Frowning, he stepped inside and found the light switch.

Dim yellow light issued from a floor lamp by the window

to his left. Cracked leather armchair on one side of it, worn green-cushioned love seat on the other against the wall by the door. Spindly coffee table in front of the love seat. Kitchenette to his right. Bed across the room.

One bed.

Hell. "I didn't think to ask about the beds," he said. "I'll take the couch."

She squeezed past him to set her bag and sword down. "It's way too short for you. We'll share the bed." Her lips quirked up in a wry smile that didn't reach her eyes. "I promise not to molest you."

If only she would. Even half dead and totally exhausted, his body responded, and he swore silently.

"No argument." Her firm tone underlined the words.

So the shire reeve still lurked inside her. Good. She'd looked so discouraged earlier. But sleeping next to her was dangerous for his peace of mind. Undecided, he stared at the love seat.

"Can the chivalry," she said. "I need you functioning. You won't be, without real rest, and you're too tall to get it there. Unless you want me to take the couch?"

"No way."

"Okay, then." Her stern gaze locked on his face, no yielding in her eyes.

He drew on the last dregs of his strength to firm his voice and almost winced at the spike in ammonia taste, a reminder he was no good for her or any other woman. She deserved better than a fugitive who could turn ghoul at any time. "Okay. Thanks."

She nodded, but grief darkened her eyes. Helpless to fix it, he clenched his fists at his sides. She probably felt more alone now than she ever had, even when her parents died. A corner of his soul he'd learned to ignore knew that aching loneliness, that desolation of being an outcast. He hated it for her.

"Before we settle in," she said, "I have to tell you, I was seriously pissed when you flipped that SUV."

"What, you wanted me to wave toodles?" He fought back a roar of impatience. "I had to stop them."

"I know." She blew out a heavy sigh, her eyes tired and pained. "I said I *was* pissed. While you were checking us in, I realized you had little choice. You've spent years battling mages who should've been your allies." Her lower lip trembled, but her voice stayed firm. "I need to stop thinking of the Collegium mages as my teammates. They're not anymore."

No, and the bastards had been ready to kill her with no questions asked. But his anger wouldn't help her now. He brushed her hair back gently. "It never gets easy."

At least the last dregs of his power kept him on his feet, though not for long. And tonight had jacked up his blood venom levels. He not only tasted ammonia but felt rage bubbling in his veins.

"We need to get a couple of other things straight." Her eyes narrowed. "First, while I'm glad you've recovered a bit, you don't give me orders."

The hell he didn't. "Back atcha, babe." He could do narrow eyes, too.

"Do not *babe* me in that snide tone. Second—"

"You're not my mother, my nurse, or my boss, so stop acting like you are." Hell, a minute ago he'd been glad—

"When you're teetering on your feet, you need at least one of those. Don't be an ass, Griffin."

He raised an eyebrow, daring her. His hands balled into fists. "Want to rephrase that? Babe?"

Snapping with irritation, her eyes skimmed over him. "What's the matter with you all of a sudden?"

Ammonia burned the inside of his nose. Red haze washed across his vision. His fists tightened. His body twisted, left foot edging forward, right arm drawing up and back to punch.

Valeria balanced on the balls of her feet, hands rising. She was set to meet him, but by hell's bells, he'd teach her not to boss him around. He'd saved her stubborn life. She should be on her knees, thanking him. Stripping for him. Spreading for him. He'd make her beg once he'd wiped that pained look off—

Pained?

Pained. Despite her set expression, her eyes were mossy wells of aching disbelief. A moment more, he hovered between fury and guilt before the guilt won. The rage abruptly drained.

"Oh, shit, I'm sorry." He dropped his hand, made his body relax. "Valeria, I'm sorry."

She kept her ready stance. "In the last five minutes, you've gone from looking half dead to threatening to hit me, and now you're slumping and sorry. Which will it be five minutes from now?"

"Semiconscious, probably, and still very, very sorry. I'm tired from the fight and the car. When I'm tired, my temper is damnably unsteady." Because fatigue let the venom level in his blood rise, but he couldn't tell her that now, not after the day they'd had, the danger they'd faced.

The way he'd threatened her.

He owed her the truth, had meant to tell her at the lake. Maybe he was a jerk not to do it now, but if they could pass a peaceful night, maybe she'd be more inclined to trust him, not fear him, when he explained.

She studied him, her face still uncertain. "Okay. This time. Any new insights about how you threw us so far?"

"I don't know how I did it. I wish I did." Could it be the venom in his blood? Could there be any benefit to that? "I've never done anything even close to that before."

"Well. We can kick that around in the morning." She hesitated. "I have pajamas I'd planned to sleep in. Are you okay with that?"

As in, able to control himself? The question stung, but after his temper fit and almost punch, he deserved it. Trying for normal, he asked, "Any chance they're red lace and skimpy?"

Her lips twitched, as though she bit back a smile. "Sorry. Yellow cotton shorts and T-shirt. With daisies."

"Beats my black gym shorts." He smiled, tried to make it teasing. Maybe that slight upward curve of her mouth was a good sign. "Valeria," he said seriously, "you can trust me. I swear you can."

Her smile faded. She gave him a level, warning look. "I hope so. We should call it a day. Everything will look better in the morning."

Despite her upbeat tone, doubt shadowed her eyes as she turned away, and with good reason. The hunt for him would include her now. He'd gained her as an ally in a way he never would've chosen. *Damn it.*

He fished the warding stones for the cabin out of his bag to set at the building's corners. First thing tomorrow, he'd have to take a blood level. He should do it now, but digging the kit out, running the test, would lead to explanations he'd rather delay.

Maybe he should send Valeria away, no matter how she reacted when he told her. He'd nearly clocked her tonight. What if his control slipped again, when he was stronger? What about the pain in her eyes?

He cared about her, so he should think of her, not his need for an ally, his need for—

No. Not going there.

Morning, he thought, as he set the first ward. In the morning, he would tell her everything.

Val awoke to faint morning light filtering through the curtains. Despite what she'd said to Griffin, their situation didn't seem any better. And her eyes felt gritty. No surprise, considering that she'd slept like a horror movie heroine, starting at every creak of the run-down cabin, at the brush of tree branches over the window above the bed, at the strange dreams that haunted her sleep.

Griffin still slept. Breathing quietly, he lay on his back with his face turned toward her. On his chest rested the flat, golf ball–size Eye of Horus pendant.

She fingered it cautiously, and the high level of warding magic it contained zinged against her fingers. No wonder he'd eluded all searches. Even unwarded, that symbol was a protective charm, one sometimes invoked against hostile scrying.

In the dim light coming through the curtains, he looked less drawn and tired than he had last night. And no longer scary.

What had turned the ardent lover, the gentle, courteous man who'd treated her wounds, the brave one who'd risked his life for her and for a homeless child, into an arrogant, menacing bully? No matter what he said, fatigue alone didn't explain it. Something was going on with him, and she had a right to know what it was.

Despite her concerns, the sight of him sleeping, defenseless, made her want to shelter him. Last night had been too tense for a good night kiss, but she'd wanted one. Still did, even though they'd both backed off from near kisses at the lake. Still, she wanted to run her fingers through the dusting of dark hair on his chest and trace the sculpted planes of muscle underneath.

Last night, she hadn't noticed the scars below his left shoulder. Four parallel marks almost as long as her hand scored the tanned surface of his upper chest. Talon marks. He wouldn't have scars if there had been anyone around to heal him. Instead, he'd had to fight the venom in his system, enduring the burning agony of those wounds, alone.

Gently, she brushed tumbled jet-black hair off his brow. He sighed but didn't rouse. She let her fingers drift down, toward the shadowy stubble lining his jaw. He had such a strong face. A strong heart. A strong sense of right and wrong, which made his temper fit last night even more baffling.

Val sighed and scrubbed at her tired eyes. Maybe a shower would clear the cobwebs from her brain.

She padded into the bathroom and shut the door. The doctors had healed the serious damage from that disastrous raid but left the minor problems to resolve on their own. After her shower, she would need to reapply salve on her scraped hands. Most of the tub she'd brought from Dare's was gone. She would finish that, then dip into the supply Stefan Harper had given her when she left the infirmary.

She turned the water on to let it heat. Giving it time, she dug the two tubs out of her toilet kit. They looked the same. Weird. She'd packed so quickly to leave the Collegium that she hadn't noticed.

She unscrewed the top of one and found it nearly full, the surface smooth. This was the newer one, its lemon verbena scent refreshing. Finishing one before starting another was more efficient, so she opened the other tub.

The same scent of lemon verbena wafted across her nose. Val frowned, staring at the tub. Healers mixed their own salve. Lemon verbena was popular for its healing properties, but no one used the same proportion as anyone else.

Cautiously, focusing on the degree of scent, she sniffed the tub in her hand, then the other. The same scent touched her nostrils. The shades of pale yellow matched. The mixtures were exactly the same.

An expert tended you, Dare had said, back at his place.

Not just any expert, either. The Collegium's chief medical officer was in league with Griffin Dare. No wonder Dare knew so much about the Collegium operations, had such detailed intel.

How many other insiders had he co-opted? One was too many, a sign of poor attention to the Collegium's own backyard by her, the Council, and the two shire reeves between her and Dare. The blasted place might be one big leak of information.

Val's lips tightened. He believed his cause was just. She was beginning to think so, but there was still the little matter of his going scary-weird on her. That, too, they would settle this morning.

Griff forced his heavy eyelids open. Valeria was already up, and the shower was running.

He plucked his watch from the bedside table. Six fifty. Seven hours of sleep should've brought his blood venom level down a good bit.

Still, morning had arrived. He had no right to delay the reckoning any longer, not with Valeria's fate also at stake.

Yet he couldn't resist brushing his fingers over the dent in her pillow. Her light, honeysuckle scent caught in his nose, banishing the residue of ammonia that lingered there. He closed his eyes and could, for a heart-stuttering instant, feel her body in his arms, her lips on his.

She deserved to know what she was dealing with, including his venom problem. He rolled out of bed and scrounged in his bag for the kit.

Seated on the couch, he set the toximeter and a cotton pad on the rickety coffee table. With the lancet poised over his finger, he hesitated. If this was as bad as he feared it might be…He triggered the blade. It snapped against his finger, and a drop of blood welled from the tiny cut.

The shower stopped. A moment later, the bathroom door opened. Still in her pajamas, with dry hair, Valeria marched toward him. "What are you doing?"

"You didn't want a shower? Or is something wrong with it?"

The cotton shorts bared most of her legs while the T-shirt draped the firm curves of her breasts. Those tanned, toned arms would feel smooth against his mouth. Under his hands.

In his dreams, maybe. Once he told her the truth, his chances of touching or tasting her were gone forever.

"Griffin, are you diabetic?"

"I wish it were something that ordinary." He turned on the toximeter and let the droplet of blood fall onto its gray central screen. The blood disappeared. Green rippled outward from the point of impact, then black, and he held his breath.

"Then I repeat, what are you doing?"

Praying. "Hang on a sec."

Above the screen, the readout started to blink. A number formed, ten, but the readout was climbing. Thirteen, twenty-four, twenty-nine, thirty, thirty-eight—oh shit, never that high before—forty-one, and his heart hammered in his chest. At forty-four, the numbers stopped blinking. Forty-four, a scant handful shy of the fifty-six marking the point of no return. The fifty-five he'd privately sworn was his limit.

It must've been in the fifties last night. He and Valeria were both lucky he hadn't tried to kill her.

"Griffin." She sat next to him, laying her hand on his forearm. Her touch ripped through him. It felt so sweet. He couldn't bear to think that in moments she would withdraw it forever. "What's wrong? You seem so...rocked."

More like doomed. Steeling himself, he looked into her worried hazel eyes. "I'm not diabetic, but I do have to check my blood levels daily. For venom."

She recoiled, her eyes wide. She snatched her hand away from him, and his soul ached with the loss. "Venom," she choked, "but only ghouls—"

"Yes. Only ghouls have venom in their blood, and I'm teetering on the edge of becoming one."

Chapter 11

Val stared at Griffin's grim face. She must've misunderstood. He couldn't have said—

"Could you repeat that?" Her voice sounded tight, achy, like her chest suddenly felt.

"You heard me."

"But that's impossible. If you were about to—you were so rational last night, so gentle and strong. If you were a ghoul, you'd be…" Then she remembered, and the protest died.

"Also as I was last night." Wearily, he ran a hand through his hair. "I would give a year of my life for that not to have happened. When I'm tired, the venom in my blood goes up. The more I overexert, the faster it spikes."

"'Overexert,' as in flinging a loaded car six miles. Blowing yourself out." Damn it, he'd gotten worse saving her.

"Or when I draw power faster than I should. But yeah, looks like I did have a blowout." He reached for her hand, but stopped, balling his fist on his knee instead. She couldn't bring herself to wrap her fingers around his.

"I meant to tell you this at the lake, then they came

and—hell, it's the story of our dealings, my meaning to tell you something and an emergency interrupting. I swear, if not for that, I would've told you before I let you throw in with me."

The man she'd had dinner with last night would've told her. The one who'd almost hit her, maybe not. "What brings the level back down?"

"Rest. Frequent recharges." He rubbed the heels of his hands against his eyes. "That's why I was living near the swamp. In that kind of atmosphere, with so much life around me, the recharge became unconscious, almost constant and without hurting anything. That's the healthiest I've been in a couple of years. Venom-wise, anyway."

"Except you're tired a lot, aren't you? Tired and discouraged." She had no idea where that insight had come from, but it rang true. And made her heart ache for him. "Lonely, too. Why else would you kidnap the shire reeve to talk to?"

Griffin shifted to face her, and his drawn expression confirmed her guess. "I hoped you could quietly help unmask the traitor, but the attack on my place screwed up my plans. I'm sorry I dragged you into this unholy mess."

"If you're right about there being a traitor on the Council, the more people we can 'drag in,' the better."

She hesitated, hating this topic as he must, but she had to ask. "How close are you to turning? I didn't realize the process could be tracked."

"I didn't either, not until it happened to me. It started with battle wounds I had no one to heal."

Venom wounds were an occupational hazard of fighting ghouls, but there was always a medical team on hand to take care of the venom as well as the actual wounds.

Unless you were a renegade.

He must've suffered horribly, and she hated that. "So the venom was too much for your system to handle, and you had no one to purge it."

"Right." He let out a heavy sigh. "Barring battle damage, I thought mages got venom in their blood from repeatedly working dark magic." His frustrated gaze fell to the floor. "Hell of a way to find out you're wrong."

"Yeah." He had venom in his blood but was now, again, the man who'd kissed her so passionately and touched her so gently. The man who'd been willing to die for her. If he were more ghoul than mage, he would've abandoned Val to her fate last night. For that tender, thoughtful man, she bit back her revulsion about the venom and took his hand.

He inhaled sharply, the muscle working in his jaw for a long moment. Then he raised her hand to his mouth and, still not looking at her, kissed it.

The gesture stabbed into her soul. There was too much good in him for her to write him off.

At least this morning Griffin's hand, like his lips, felt warm, not cold and clammy. She laced her fingers through his, a silent offer of support. "You said you were teetering. What does that mean?"

He turned the little gadget in front of him so she could read the green forty-four on the gauge. "The level has never been that high," he said in a grim voice, "and after the way I treated you last night, and considering that sleep brings it down and I've slept several hours since, I was probably on the edge of tipping over, of being done."

"Define 'the edge.'" Odd, how steady her voice sounded when her breath wasn't working quite right.

If he turned ghoul, she could probably handle him. But losing him, seeing the ruin of all that strength, that courage and kindness…She couldn't allow that to happen.

"Fifty-six is the lowest blood venom level measured in any ghoul, so that's probably the point of no return. At least as far as my doctor, who's something of an expert, knows."

"Yes." Val watched him closely. "Stefan Harper is the world's foremost expert."

Griffin's fingers tensed, but his blank expression didn't change. Casually, he said, "Can't argue with that, but it's not as if I can consult him again."

Though she had expected him to stonewall, his evasion still hurt. Of course, her refusal to trust him fully until last night had to be rankling him.

She couldn't control what he saw in her eyes, but she kept her voice and gaze level. "The time for you to lie to me, Griffin, is over. If I'm going to help you, I need the truth. Always. In return, I'll be honest with you. I'll trust you completely."

The appraising look between them held until her neck felt tight. At last, he raised his eyebrows. "If you had any sense, you'd bolt out of here, turn me in, and try groveling as a path back into the Collegium. Valeria, if I tip without warning, I could kill you."

"If," she repeated, shrugging. That clutch in her chest, that lift at the sudden, amazed light in his eyes, didn't bode well for the state of her heart, but she couldn't abandon him. "Besides, since this mostly happens when you're tired, I'm pretty sure I can take you."

His expression turned grim. "You have to promise me something. If you ever look at me and you know I'm not myself anymore, that you're looking at a ghoul, you won't question me, won't test me, won't stall to consult anyone. You'll take a kill shot without hesitating."

"I can't just—"

"You have to. Or else, I swear, I'll leave you here." When she shook her head, he added, "If that moment comes, you won't be wrong, Valeria. You've seen enough ghouls. You'll know. Hesitate, and I might kill you. Or worse."

"You wouldn't." Last night, he'd stopped himself.

"I'd like to think not, but the numbers don't lie." He nodded down at the gauge. "Last night came way too close to violence to ignore. Promise me, Valeria."

"After you saved my life, risked your own to come tell me that a catastrophe was not my fault? You were willing to die to protect me if I refused to run with you last night. And don't think I didn't notice you set us up so only you fired at the Collegium mages. I can't kill you. I owe you too much."

The mere thought of taking his life made her breath hitch, her soul flinch. Val swallowed hard. "There has to be another way."

"If there were, don't you think I would've found some hint of it?" He shook his head. "Ghouls are a perversion of magic, an unnatural bane inflicted on us and on Mundanes. I've spent my adult life battling them. If you were in my shoes, would you want to live as that?"

"No, but—"

"There are no 'buts.' As the saying goes, you'd be doing me a favor."

Heart aching, she looked into his dark, agonized eyes. Behind his unhappiness lay resolve. He truly wanted this.

"All right," she said. "I promise." But if that moment arrived and she had any other choice, she would not sacrifice him.

"Okay, then." His solemn stare seemed to pierce her soul, to see beyond the brave front she'd put on. "One way or another," he said, "I'll make things right for you with the Collegium. You'll go home again."

"We will. Right now, though, you'll call Stefan Harper about the fastest way to bring your blood levels down."

"Valeria—"

"The truth, remember." She explained about the identical salves from her stint in the infirmary and her stay at his place. "Before you point out that Harper could've shared what he mixed, recall how you always told reeve cadets not to trust coincidence."

His jaw tightened. He looked away, and she could almost hear the cursing going through his brain.

Tapping his chin with one finger recaptured his attention. "I can keep secrets," she said. "You brought me into this, so why can't you trust me?"

He threw her a frustrated look. "I told you not all my secrets are my own. I can't reveal anyone else to you unless that person consents. I'll call my doctor. My friends."

"Fair enough. I'll even take a shower and give you privacy for that. Then, unless Dr. Harper says otherwise, we're going in search of food—the refuel part of blowout recovery."

"Sounds good." He stood with her and remained standing as she walked toward the bathroom.

"Valeria," he said as she reached the door, "there's something that might make you feel better about your promise, something you have a right to know anyway."

His face was set in grim, purposeful lines. "I check my

blood level faithfully, and I won't let it reach fifty-six. If it ever hits fifty-five, I'll commit suicide."

Hard to believe, Val thought, as she watched Griffin drive down the winding road an hour later, that he'd so calmly said, *I'll commit suicide*. How unfair that he had to face this venom problem along with everything else.

She knew as well as anyone, of course, that *fair* wasn't a standard the universe particularly noticed. Yet he seemed to cope amazingly well.

To his credit, he'd always been resolute. Focused. He couldn't have survived this long on the run if either of those traits had changed.

Everyone had a breaking point, though.

He glanced at her. "What're you thinking?"

"Considering various problems. What you said last night about the ghouls and dark magic is scary as hell. If I'd known, I would've put deputies on it. You've found nothing?"

"Nothing specific. If you'd put people on it, depending on where their true loyalties lay, they might've covered it up."

"Or killed any witnesses. God, I hope that isn't what happened to Tina and this latest man, Jim Barcan. His tip led to my raid two weeks ago, but now he's vanished."

"After we eat and recharge, I'll see if I can track them." He turned onto a side road and glanced at her. "In his message last night, Stefan confirmed that your moonstone pendant let the Council scry us. It's good you didn't bring it."

For a moment, she couldn't breathe. Gene trusted her even less than she'd thought. "It was a gift," she managed at last. "From Gene. I swear I didn't mean to lead them to you."

"Easier ways to do that if you'd wanted to." Shaking his

head, he added, "I'm sorry, Valeria. I know he and his wife are important to you."

More important than she was to Gene, apparently, and the knowledge burned deep in her soul. "If his trust is so easily lost, I never truly had it."

They drove another mile or so in silence. At last, she turned in the seat to look at him. "I hate to say this, I really, really do, but I think someone on the High Council, not just one of the department heads, must be involved. They subverted my department. That points to someone doing it who outranks me as department head. Only the High Council members hold that power."

"Could be someone else, but my gut says you're right." Griffin nodded to a green highway sign. "Carson, Georgia, population three hundred. It's a little after eight. Probably not much open besides breakfast places."

Around the curve lay a typical little Southern town. One-story shops with large front windows lined the high-way—mostly brick, a few wood, many with aluminum awnings in front.

At the far end of the street, the road forked. A small patch of parched, brown grass in the fork held a statue of a Confederate soldier with the Stars and Bars on the pedestal. Above him hung the only traffic light in sight. As Griffin had predicted, the shops weren't open, but a few cars sat by the curb a couple of blocks down.

"This place looks familiar," he said, staring down the street. "I think I came through here a couple of years ago." He pulled up to the curb behind the other cars.

LOU'S, read the sign hanging under the flat aluminum awning two doors down. A painting of a BLT on white bread sitting by a glass of iced tea brightened the blue-on-white sign. That had to be the diner the motel clerk had recommended.

Here and there, straggly tufts of grass grew in the sidewalk cracks. Some of the shop windows bore smudges and streaks, as though no one had washed them lately.

"It looks like the kind of place people go mostly through, not to," she said.

"Yeah, it does."

Val let her fingertips brush the screened hunting knife she'd strapped to her belt. His dagger lay at the small of his back, also screened. They probably wouldn't need weapons for breakfast among Mundanes, but you never knew when you might encounter a supernatural menace.

She climbed out of the car and waited for him. Looking at his tall, strong frame and his confident stance, she never would've guessed he carried potentially fatal venom in his veins.

He smiled at her, giving her pulse a giddy hop, as she fell into step beside him. Their shoulders bumped, and her face warmed.

He inhaled sharply. The glance he flicked her was hot, and Val's mouth went dry. Good thing they were about to be among people.

When Griffin pushed the two-panel, glass door open, a bell jangled above it. The smells of bacon, toast, and coffee tickled her nose, and her stomach growled.

He held the door for her but edged inside in front of her. Val resisted the urge to poke him. She didn't need him to protect her. When she stepped around him, she noticed what he must've already caught, a vague, disquieting sense of something not quite right.

His raised eyebrows offered her the choice, retreat or stay and investigate. She hesitated, but they needed food, had no other options nearby. Once they'd finished recharging, they could pin down the problem here. She walked farther inside, and the bell jangled again as he closed the door behind her.

Four empty booths ran along the plate-glass window to their left. The place was only about twenty feet square, with a pass-through for the kitchen behind the counter on their right. Opposite the booths stood a blue laminate counter with a cash register at the end near the door. Half a dozen stools covered in cracked, red vinyl offered counter seating. Three men sat on the middle stools, one in worn blue coveralls with faded grease stains, two in jeans and denim work shirts.

"Mornin', folks." A thin woman with fading reddish hair sauntered up to them. She seemed normal enough, complete with a welcoming smile. "Y'all want the counter today?"

"A booth, please." Just enough power laced Griffin's words to defy argument.

Smart of him. With the weirdness in the air, sitting with their backs to the room was too risky.

For a heartbeat, the woman's eyes narrowed. Darkened. Cold like the winter wind prickled along Val's neck, and she eased a hand toward her knife.

The woman's face resumed its bored look. With a shrug, she grabbed two menus from a stack by the register and led the way to the booth farthest from the door.

Griffin slid onto the seat facing the entry. He would be the one to see and counter any approaching threat. Protecting her again. They really had to talk about that.

The waitress laid down the menus. "Two coffees?"

Griffin waited for Val's nod before he said, "Sure. Thanks."

The waitress strolled away. One of the men at the counter, a lanky ash-blond, gave them a hard, speculative look.

Maybe he didn't like outsiders. Maybe he was just in a bad mood. Or maybe he was trouble. She gave him her sunniest smile. He stared through her, but she held the look until he turned away.

"Problem?" Griffin murmured. He laid his hand over hers on the table.

Power of the dyad, she remembered, lacing her fingers with his, letting their power touch and entwine. The contact reinforced their power. It would also let them hear each other's thoughts, if his weren't closed to her now.

"Yes, but I'm not sure what," she whispered.

The waitress brought their coffee, and the two leaned back breaking their connection. "Haven't seen you through here before. You folks going into the state park for a hike?" Her face smiled, but her watchful eyes didn't.

Griffin gave the waitress a relaxed smile. "My girl and I thought we'd find a romantic spot to camp. Any suggestions?"

"You want to be careful," the hard-eyed man in coveralls at the counter said, "in the park." His gaze also held a snake's warmth and raised that brief, nasty chill. "Get a map so's you don't lose your way." His gaze ran over Val, not lecherous but assessing.

She tried for perky and clueless with her smile this time, and that seemed to satisfy him. He turned back to his meal.

Val fought back a shudder. The vibes in this place felt like tiny spiders crawling over her skin.

Griffin sipped his coffee and frowned.

"The breakfast special's good," the waitress said.

He reached for a menu. "We need a minute."

The waitress shrugged and walked back behind the counter.

Staring at the window, at the faint reflections of the men at the counter, Griffin breathed, "There's blood in the coffee."

Val nodded, but wanted to check for herself since she knew the venom in his system might affect his taste buds. She tipped her cup until coffee touched her lips. An acrid, coppery taste lay under the standard diner brew. *Crap.* Lowering the cup, she asked him, "Now what?"

"I'll probe."

She reached for him, squeezed his hand to indicate agreement.

His power and hers mingled, reinforcing each other and again deepening her awareness of him, of the appealing way strength and tenderness blended in him. Of the attraction between them and the way his feelings mirrored hers. Val took a breath, staring at the table to steady herself.

Griffin kept his eyes on the menu, but his senses brushed hers as he reached out. He touched cold that echoed faintly in her mind with a hint of brimstone. Dark power. Unmistakable but impossible to gauge without giving themselves away.

He tensed, and their eyes locked across the table.

These people could be Satanists or demon hosts, possibly even unwilling demon servants, known as thralls. Satanists and demon thralls weren't that big a problem, but five demon hosts could take the two of them, depleted as they were, without breaking a sweat.

They both knew it, but she leaned closer to whisper a reminder. "They're serving that brew to Mundanes. We have to stop them."

"We will. But only we know about this place, so we can't afford to try and fail."

The grim, irritated look on his face echoed the mood in the magic between them. "Don't worry," he murmured, rubbing his thumb over her hand. "We'll come back when we're recharged enough for a fight." He reached for his wallet, mouthing, *On three.*

Val's heartbeat kicked up, but she squeezed his hand hard and fast, shifting her balance forward. He held a five in his hand as he silently counted. On three, they both pushed out of the booth. He angled his body between her and the stools.

As they came abreast of the burly, dark-haired man nearest the door, all three men slid from the stools, flanking them.

A triad trumped a worn-down dyad. *Shit.*

"You didn't pay." The dark-haired man grabbed at Griffin.

Griffin sidestepped. As he yanked her behind him, closer to the door, Val drew her knife. She dropped the screen on it and stepped out from behind Griffin with her weapon in sight.

"Money's on the table." Griffin also drew, revealing his dagger.

"Hey, now!" The waitress dashed out of the kitchen.

On her heels came a burly, blond man whose apron and red-faced, sweaty appearance marked him as the cook. He gripped a cleaver in his fist. "Where y'all goin'?"

"We have to be somewhere." Val let her voice go flat, watching them all.

"We don't want trouble." Resonant with power, Griffin's voice carried a hard, lethal edge. "But if you do, we'll oblige."

Chapter 12

Griff kept his senses open, alert for reinforcements threatening him and Valeria as they backed out of the door. When she hit the street, she turned to cover their rear.

No one tried to stop them, but the five inside watched with cold, predatory eyes. Nausea from the dark influence raised a bitter taste in Griff's mouth. He and Valeria had run from one problem smack into another.

They climbed into the car, and he cut a U-turn away from the curb. Valeria twisted in her seat, watching behind them, until the turn of the road hid the town.

"I'm surprised they let us go," she said. "They likely meant to trap us with whatever was in those mugs. We should've gotten the coffee to go, for a sample."

"Asking for that would've given them too much time to think, maybe try a different ploy." He eased back on the gas. "Maybe they didn't try harder to stop us because they figure someone else will happen along. I doubt they wanted us in particular. Unless the motel clerk who referred us there is in with them, but that feels like a stretch."

"Wouldn't take much bespelled blood to knock out a normal person. A Mundane probably wouldn't even sense it, just think it was bad coffee. But why? Could it be related to your idea about ghouls and dark magic?"

"I don't think we should assume it isn't. Those people obviously aren't ghouls, but if not, then what are they?" He turned onto the main road. "Whatever this is, it has to be stopped. Too bad we don't have backup closer."

"The Collegium could send helos," she said. "If word reached the right people." Before he could speak, she held up a hand to stop him. "If ghouls are allied with mages, someone at the Collegium could be in on this, too. I know."

"I'm sorry. I wish we could trust them."

"If ghouls are using Mundanes to work dark magic, they're planning something big. I haven't heard of anything like that since my history of magic class. We need someone who can dig into the old records."

He pulled into a gas station parking lot, backed into a space that gave them a view of the entire lot and the road, and fished his phone out of his pocket. "Luckily, I have someone who can research that."

"You have an expert in ancient magics on call?"

He cocked an eyebrow at her. "If you consider the assistant loremaster at the Collegium an expert."

"Will Davis? How many people do you have inside, anyway?"

Judging by her scowl, she was wondering how blind she'd been. "No one in your department, but I can't give you a number. Only a few have agreed to let me name them."

"Because they don't trust me." She blew out a hard, audible breath. "Fine."

"They'll come around." He drew his phone from his pocket. "Give it time."

"I understand their reasoning, but if ghouls are pulling Mundanes into dark magic, time is the one thing we don't have."

"Can't argue with that."

Griff watched her from the corner of his eye as he punched in numbers. No speed dial for him. Too easy for anyone else to use if the phone fell into the wrong hands. He deleted the call history, manually and magically, after each call.

Valeria sat still, her gaze scanning the lot and the road. She probably had no idea how the morning sunlight turned her eyes green-gold and put gilded highlights in that fall of dark blond hair. How its play on her body accented the high, firm curve of her breasts under the green V-necked top.

He remembered the feel of those curves too well. Too bad exploring them again would be incredibly stupid.

The phone rang, yanking him away from dangerous thoughts.

"Yeah." Sounding sleepy, Will answered. Griff could almost see him shoving his hair out of his eyes.

"Morning, Sunshine. Can you look up something for me?"

"After coffee. What is it?"

He told Will about the encounter. "See if you can find any record of ghouls using Mundanes to work blood magic. Or of ghouls using Mundanes for blood magic. Also, check out the missing persons' reports near the Abner Wade State Park, for people who disappeared on hiking trips and anything weird to do with Carson, Georgia."

"Blood magic." Will now sounded not only alert but grim.

"Putting this together with my other research, we should meet, Griff. As many of us as can get there. Maybe at Tasha's river cabin."

"It's that bad?"

"It's that complicated, and easier to explain once. Though some of us will have issues with Ms. Banning coming along."

"They'll just have to trust me on that. Set the meeting for two this afternoon. Meanwhile, Valeria and I will shut that place down as soon as we can. I'll also have the team see if they're serving that nasty brew anywhere else around here. We need to figure out how widespread the problem is."

Griff snapped his phone shut. "If you need help and I'm not around, go to Stefan or Will. Marc Wagner knows everyone on my team. He can contact them if you ever need him to." He explained about the meeting.

"But some of them don't trust me, Griffin, or you would've told me who they are."

"They trust me, I trust you, and so will they as soon as they realize you're in this with us now. Judging by the tone of Will's voice, it's time to cut to the chase on this problem."

She looked doubtful, but he wasn't finished. He reached into his pocket. "Hold your hand out. I have something for you."

When she turned her palm up, he laid the lapis lazuli pendant and its cord on her palm. "You don't have to take it."

Wary now, her eyes lifted to his. "An Eye of Horus. Like yours."

"I keep a couple of extras on hand. It activates when you're wearing it. All of my team members have them. It'll hide you from most scrying."

She said nothing, just stared at it. Had he offended her?

"It doesn't commit you to anything. Doesn't mean you've turned against anyone." He took her hand, rubbing gently. "It's to keep you protected, safe."

Finally, she looked at him, her eyes soft. "Thank you…for sharing your secret." She slipped the cord over her head and tucked the pendant into her shirt.

Their gazes locked. The warmth in her eyes heated his blood, and the car suddenly seemed close. Intimate. Desire hummed in the air between them. If he kissed her, he knew, she would welcome him.

That was a very bad idea, especially for her. Nothing about involvement with him could help her.

He wrenched his eyes to the side and started the engine. "The clerk mentioned a McDonald's on the main highway. It's farther away than that diner, but the coffee's probably better."

His voice sounded hoarse, tight. He cleared his throat. "And the drive-through cashier won't care if we order six breakfasts."

"You and Will seem very close." Valeria's voice sounded light, but she stared through the windshield, not at him. Bright pink bloomed over her cheekbones.

His fingers itched to trace it. He tightened his grip on the gear knob instead. "Will spent a lot of time with my family when we were kids. His parents were always traveling to some archaeological site or another." He'd been the second mage, after Stefan, to say he had Griff's back when he went rogue.

But that was enough personal info. "I know a great place we can recharge in the forest. There's a creek with a big, flat rock by it to sit on."

He planned to paint that spot someday, when he could

count on not having to pack in a hurry and run. "You can just sit if you don't want to wade." He swung the car onto the road.

"I get a boost from the earth," she said, "and from trees especially."

"This spot should work for you, then." Some mages had an affinity for one of the four elements, earth, air, fire, or water, and so recharged better with a boost from that element. Spirit mages were rarer but could get the boost from all elements. Others, like him, had no particular affinity.

Valeria shoved her hair back, and he longed to touch the soft strands. He had to look away as she asked, "Are you a water mage?"

"I like the feel of the water, that's all. Helps me think." Let him imagine it was cleansing his soul.

"Considering the morning, we should do a lot of thinking." She shifted in her seat to look at him. "I heard what you said about checking out those towns. Unless your team is much larger than I think, that'll take them a while."

"Not much choice, though." He cocked an eyebrow at her. Was she backtracking about trusting the Collegium?

"No," she agreed sadly, "no choice."

He turned his attention back to the road. The handful of his team available would have a lot of ground to cover. He could only hope Valeria's conflicted loyalties wouldn't add another problem to the list.

Icy water burbled around Griff's calves. His bare feet sank into the stream's muddy bed with each step. Breakfast had provided a much needed energy boost.

Now, with midmorning sunlight through the tree limbs

casting alternate patches of silver and shadow over the lazy current and washing the purest form of natural energy over his back, his power levels rose steadily. Too bad his mood didn't.

Valeria sat on the flat rock by the stream and splashed her toes in the icy current. She was taking him on faith, trusting him, as she'd promised. Somehow, he had to make her situation right. But how could he do that now that she was known to have fled with him?

"Griffin? Do you want to talk? Or should I watch the sky through the trees and leave you alone?"

Hands on his hips, he faced her. "I hate that you can't go home because of me."

Valeria shook her head. "A traitor in the Collegium is what's keeping me from my home, not you. Besides, I won't leave you. I'm in this until we finish it."

His heart lifted at the words and at the sincerity vibrating in the magic between them. One thing he'd learned was never to take loyalty for granted. Unfortunately, her loyalty put her too much at risk.

"I appreciate your support more than you can know, Valeria. But one woman I cared about died because of me. I'm not going for two." The rage and bitterness and grief of that day flooded through him again.

She pushed off the rock and waded toward him with determination that didn't slow for the mud and stones under her bare feet. "I read the file. Her name was Allie Henderson. Brunette, age twenty-six, instructor in botanical magic at the Collegium and your lover of more than two years. One of three mages you're said to have killed since you've been on the run."

"That doesn't bother you, thinking I killed her, and then Sykes Mitchell, who'd been my friend?"

"Sykes killed Allie," she said, her voice calm and her gaze steady, "and you killed Sykes."

"What?" Stunned, he stared down at her. The sunlight on the water seemed brighter, the rush of the stream over the rocks, musical. He'd never expected anyone outside his tight circle of comrades to believe that. "How did you know?"

"From the blast patterns. Allie had a narrow energy burn slashing her torso from left shoulder to right hip, and Sykes was a left-handed swordsman. He died from a focused blast at point-blank range, round burn, as from a staff." Her face softened, as though she sensed the pain thinking of that day always gave him.

"That's not the official story." Yet the sincerity in her eyes blanketed him. It soothed the gnawing bitterness inside him.

"That account never rang true to me. First, you don't need to take someone else's weapon when you have your own. Second, they died too close together, Allie first and Sykes a few seconds later. For you to have been disarmed, used his weapon, then recovered yours so quickly…impossible."

"Yet the story persists," he said bitterly. "People think I killed her because they want to."

"It's the easy path, especially for those who don't know you. I've been in your head, seen your integrity, and that brings me to the third, and most important, reason to believe you're innocent. You loved her."

But now he loved…*Damn it, no.* He didn't. Couldn't. He was overreacting to the circumstances. Valeria was brave and intelligent and kind, and she deserved better than anything he could hope to offer.

"She wouldn't give up on me," he said, "even after I ran. Even though people ostracized her for it. She didn't realize Sykes followed her that day. He and I fought, and she stepped between us, trying to stop the fight. If Allie hadn't loved me, she wouldn't have come to me. Into the line of fire."

Where Valeria now stood. *Hell.*

"I'm sorry for that, Griffin, for her sake and yours. I'm sorry about all of it. But you must know that's not your fault, though I realize that doesn't stop you from hurting over it. You're a man who protects, first and always."

"I try." Was she implying that was a flaw?

Valeria sighed and crossed her arms. "We aren't lovers, but you habitually put yourself between me and danger. You need to cut that out, by the way. I can handle myself."

"Not if there's a nasty surprise waiting. If I'd sent you home after that fight in the swamp, you'd be where you belong."

"And I'd still be wondering why little things keep going wrong with investigations. Things I didn't think much about before seem sinister now." She frowned at him. "This is not something I tell everyone, but I need you to understand if we're going to work together."

When he nodded, she said, "After my parents died, I was afraid all the time."

Griff shook his head, starting to speak, but she overrode him.

"Anger at the ghouls only took me so far. I was terrified in combat training. Every time someone took a swing at me, I wanted to run. I had to learn not to retreat, to counterattack instead. It was something I had to do."

"You did it brilliantly." What she'd said increased his respect for her. Although the set look on her face discouraged comment, he said, "Valeria—"

"I'm not finished. Just listen, please. When you step in front of me, it's like you're disrespecting me."

"That's crazy. Of course I respect you. But you're here because I got you into this. I'm responsible for your safety."

Her lips compressed into a tight line. Staring down at the burbling water, she shook her head.

He raised an eyebrow at her, waiting. He was talking sense, and she should pay attention.

At last, she said, "Maybe that's the rule in your world. In mine, the person who makes the choice is responsible for the result. I chose not to turn you in after that fight at your place. I can't go home until I know where the problem in the Collegium lies. When I do, I can prove I'm not a traitor. I can prove you're not. Then you can go home, too. Finally."

His fists clenched in frustration. "Let's not forget the long odds on that last one."

She took a deep breath and blew it out audibly. "Did you kill Corin Jacobs?" Her voice carried an edge of impatience.

"No," he snapped, knowing she wouldn't believe him.

"Didn't think so." Valeria nodded.

Stunned, he stared at her. "Everybody thinks so."

"I don't. Not lately, anyway. You have too much honor to blast a friend in the back."

While he was still trying to absorb the fact that she believed him, she continued, "Ritual questioning isn't always bad, you know. It can be a path to vindication. You're not guilty, so why not take the plunge, clear yourself? You could've done that years ago."

"That's what Corin thought. He tried to arrange it. Then

he called me, told me the Council wanted to agree but only to draw me in, that I shouldn't bite. And some bastard killed him while we were on the phone. Killed him with an energy blast from a staff, Valeria, and everybody blamed me."

He couldn't look at the pain in her eyes, couldn't see it and know it was for him. He turned toward the bank.

She caught his arm. "I'm sorry. I can't imagine how horrible all of this must've been."

Her touch stirred his blood. He looked down into her appalled face. Her eyes were dark with pain that echoed in the magic. She was a breath away from moving into him, to comfort him.

A flicker of encouragement from him, and she would. He could feel her longing in the magic, her desire to hold him, to ease his pain. If she did, he wasn't sure he could stop there. He sure as hell didn't want to, and she probably wouldn't ask him to.

Because she felt sorry for him. Not acceptable.

"Thanks, but I don't need your pity."

As she recoiled at his curt tone, he jerked his head toward the bank. "Let's go. We're recharged. We can scry those people in the diner and see what we learn."

"Fine." She slogged toward the large rock.

The stiff line of her body screamed that he'd hurt her feelings. She didn't deserve that. But he wouldn't apologize. Keeping some distance was best for both of them.

A short time later, Val knelt opposite Griffin on the flat rock with his silver scrying bowl between them. He looked grim and had said little since they'd stepped out of the stream. Maybe it was better that way. A man who couldn't accept sincere expressions of sympathy—not pity, never pity—had way more issues than she wanted to deal with.

Besides, over the long term, his protectiveness would make her nuts.

They set screen wards and scried back in time to see what happened in the diner after they left. The waitress, cook, and customers stood in a clump, pointing at each other and gesturing.

Val frowned at the image. "When demons enslave people, make them thralls, they don't usually have the kind of independent thought it takes to argue."

"Not usually. Of course, Satanists and demon hosts don't have any trouble arguing."

More back and forth, and then the three customers departed. They got into a pickup truck in front of the diner and drove away, out of town and onto the highway. The other two closed the diner.

"Maybe they're not local," Val said. "At least with the diner closed, we don't have to worry about Mundanes for a bit."

"Maybe." Shrugging, he added, "Various dark rituals could create that sinister feeling around them. It isn't necessarily ghoul-related, let alone demonic."

"But still nasty."

"Agreed. We'll know more when my team finishes their canvass of the area coffee shops and after we interrogate one of those suckers. Best to do that before midnight, given their ties to dark magic."

"I'm for it," she said. "And a sample of coffee."

"Absolutely." His eyes met hers in shared resolve.

For him, too, action must be better than just sitting

around. At least he was talking again. Hard to work with someone who wouldn't speak.

"I'd thought we might look for Tina," he said, "but we don't have time now. We'll get a sample of that coffee and head for the rendezvous."

As they cleaned the bowl and packed it along with the warding stones, Val couldn't help watching his shoulders flex under his shirt.

He didn't say a word or look at her. A muscle worked in his jaw. Awareness rippled through the magic between them.

They started back down the trail. Walking was better exercise than translocating.

Maybe an innocuous conversation would ease the strain between them. "How does tracking work, anyway?" she asked.

"I reach for whoever or whatever I'm hunting. I never exactly learned it, kinda stumbled into it as a teenager, looking for our dog after he'd wandered off."

"That's a rare talent," she said. "I wonder what that says about your elemental affinity."

"No idea." He grinned at her again, kicking her heartbeat up.

There was nothing surly about him now. In fact, he'd gone back to being way too appealing.

"That's the second time you've asked about affinity," he continued. "Is that your version of 'What's your sign?'"

Maybe he was trying to lighten the mood, make up for being a jerk. Guys weren't much for apologies. For the sake of teamwork, Val smiled, playing along. "No, I'm just nosy."

"I don't think I have a particular affinity." His grin faded.

"Let's hope the diner staff left enough of the tainted coffee when they closed to give us a sample."

Val nodded. Better to focus on the mission instead of her mercurial companion. If a brilliant man like Will Davis said there was something to worry about, this afternoon's meeting could bring dire news.

Chapter 13

Val's stomach fluttered as she and Griffin materialized in front of Tasha Murdock's log cabin outside Waynesville. After a quick swing by the diner to grab a coffee sample, they'd driven to Waynesville, parked in the lot for a nearby recreation area and translocated to get there. Everyone else would also park elsewhere, choosing different places, before translocating.

A mostly pine forest blocked Val's view of the road, but sunlight glinted off the Big Satilla River beyond the house. This would be a restful spot if a person came for a casual visit.

She summoned a confident expression as they stepped onto the low porch. Griffin was vouching for her here. For his sake, she wanted these people to accept her.

He raised his hand to knock, but the door swung open. A tall woman stood in the opening. She wore her auburn hair boy-short except for bangs that framed her eyebrows.

"Come in," she said.

Griffin hugged her. "Tasha Murdock, Valeria Banning."

"Nice to meet you." Their hostess extended a hand, but

her cool, blue eyes flicked over Val's face, assessing.

Screw with him, Tasha's look said, *and you're toast.*

"Good to meet you, too." Val answered that warning look with a level one.

After a moment, the other woman nodded slightly. "We'll sit at the table. Grab a soda or whatever off the bar."

"Thanks." That was probably as close to a seal of approval as Val could expect. That was fine. She and Griffin weren't an item. As long as his friends could work with her, they didn't need to like her.

She stepped into a cozy seating area furnished with an overstuffed couch and armchairs in earth tones. The bright chintz curtains and unpainted, golden-brown log walls with white chinking created a homey atmosphere at odds with their owner's frosty greeting.

Griffin didn't seem to have noticed the byplay. His hand at the small of Val's back urged her toward Stefan Harper and Will Davis, who stood by a large, plank dining table at the far end of the big room. Beyond it, sodas, chips, and dip sat on a counter dividing the kitchen from the dining area.

Stefan and Will smiled a welcome that eased the chill of Tasha's reception.

A petite brunette came out of a door near the kitchen and offered Val a friendly handshake. "Valeria. I'm Lorelei Martin. Nice to have you with us."

"I've been in your shop. It's great." Val smiled. At least this woman seemed to think her arrival was a good thing.

"We try." Lorelei patted Val's shoulder and squeezed past her to grab a Sprite from the bar.

"Welcome to the club," Stefan said with a wry grin and a brief hug that surprised her.

"The danger zone, he means." Will also grinned as he grabbed her in another quick hug. He kept an arm around her waist. "Food's over here. Tasha makes great salsa."

At least these three accepted her. A rush of pleasure warmed her cheeks and eased the tension inside her.

"Okay, break it up." Smiling, Griffin grabbed the neck of Will's shirt. "No copping a feel off other team members."

The look he directed at her was possessive. Heat bubbled low in her belly, and wasn't that stupid of her since he hadn't acted like he wanted her earlier, by the stream? What was he doing?

Will shrugged off Griffin's hold and smirked at him. "Well, I sure as hell don't want to feel *you* up."

Speak for yourself, Val thought. Her mouth went dry at the thought of exploring Griffin's lean body again.

"You know you want me," Griffin replied. "Wuss."

"Pitiful comeback. Just pitiful." Shaking his head, Will grabbed a Coke. "No Pepsi, as usual. Geez, Tasha, when are you gonna wise up?" He sighed heavily.

"We drink Pepsi when it's your turn to buy," Tasha said. "If you don't want Coke or Sprite, there's water."

"Which is better for you anyway," Stefan added. He grabbed a glass from a cabinet and filled it at the sink behind the counter. "You won't catch me rotting my teeth with all that sugar."

Will toasted him with the Coke can. "Live dangerously, why don't you?"

Griffin tugged Val toward the table. "We'll start in a minute." He took the chair at the head.

She nodded and dropped into the seat next to his. He was so relaxed with these people, and they with him. She'd never had that kind of camaraderie. Thoughts of their encounter at the stream flooded her mind again.

She should be glad he'd turned her away. His protective-ness a reminded her of Drew.

Then there was the small matter of the venom in his blood. Nothing about him said *good relationship candidate.* Yet she'd never felt so drawn to a man this quickly.

Just how much did she care about him, anyway?

Too much.

Especially for a man she'd believed was a traitor until a few days ago. Way too much for a man who, no matter how much she wished it, might never be able to return home. And definitely too much for a man she might someday have to kill.

Crud. Caring for him was just idiotic.

Griffin patted her knee under the table. "Okay?"

She had been until he touched her, until that bolt of pure need flashed up her leg. She couldn't do anything about the color probably rising in her face, and instead mustered a smile. "Just thinking," she said quietly, so the others wouldn't hear. "You're lucky to have such great friends."

"I know. It sucks that Will has to be extra careful since he's known to be close with my family." He paused. "They can be your friends now, too, you know."

If only that were true, but the kind of bond he had with them didn't develop in one afternoon. How many times had they risked their lives together? Stefan and Will must take risks regularly, helping Griffin while living at the Collegium.

Someone else knocked on the door. Tasha opened it and grinned. "Hey, Javy."

A slight, dark-haired man exchanged hugs with her.

"Sorry I'm late. Chuck can't make it. Football practice is in full swing, but I'll fill him in."

"Hey, Javy." Griffin stood. His hand on Val's shoulder steadied her as the newcomer's dark, inscrutable eyes surveyed her. "Javier Ruiz, Valeria Banning."

Javier offered his hand. "Good to have you aboard." The words were proper, but the tone reserved judgment.

Val shook hands with him. "Thanks."

Lorelei dropped easily into the seat beside her. Will took the foot of the table, and the others filled in the sides.

Griffin nodded to Will. "It's your show. Go ahead."

Will shoved his longish blond hair back absently. "First, I looked at the police reports and news clippings you sent me, Griff. The increased crime rate could be from normal nutso behavior during the hot, humid days of summer. That stuff's always especially bad around the full moon. There might be some blood magic—compulsion spells, revenge, that kind of ghoul or demonic dabbling—thrown in."

Griffin frowned at him. "You wouldn't have asked for a meeting if you thought that was the answer."

"No." Will grimaced. "The alternative is much worse. I've done a lot of research on this, and the blood in the coffee and the dark influence you felt in the diner worry me. These crimes might be normal, as I said, but they generate fear, panic, and anger. Those emotions feed Chaos magic."

"Which is what?" Stefan asked him.

"It's an ancient form of dark magic that lets the wielder violate the laws of nature. It's also associated with demons from the Void between worlds. It's how they've opened their portals into this dimension, with Chaos magic wielded by willing servants they're somehow recruiting on this side."

"Any signs of this magic in use?" Frowning, Javier drummed his fingers on the table.

Will shook his head. "Not that I've found. Except a lot of weird stuff is happening around the swamp, and swamps are full of splices, places where the Veil between worlds is weak."

"We know what a splice is," Griffin said. In professor mode, Will tended to explain everything.

Will shrugged. "Just reminding you. Maybe, seeing as how this stuff is most intense in the towns around the swamp, the ghouls are trying to set up a demon gate."

"How do they do that?" Val asked.

"A splice is a normal portal between dimensions. Lower level demons—we'll call them earthly for convenience since they're from this dimension—can use those to reach our realm.

"Making a Void demon gate requires two things," Will said, "a splice and a portal, usually a black crystal orb charged with stolen souls, which allows access through the splice to areas that are normally out of reach. They'll have to prime it by adding souls for a week or so before they mean to open it. If they fuel it with blood, put enough power behind it—"

"And have help from the other side," Lorelei added.

Will gave her a nod of acknowledgment. "They can let earthly demons from darker planes of existence into ours. Think of a splice as a collapsed tunnel. Expanding it to allow travel within our dimension isn't that hard. But with enough power, they can extend the splice, open the interdimensional Veil and let demons in from the alternate dimension the ancients named the Void. Questions?" He glanced around.

No one spoke, so he continued. "Of course, Chaos magic

lives up to its name, not only in violating the natural order but in being extremely difficult to control. It's possible they'll screw it up and eliminate the problem."

"But you don't think so," Tasha muttered. "Hell."

"Apt choice of words," Will said in a dry voice. "The last Void demon gate opened on Cyprus in June 1347, following one in the Gobi Desert in 1320. These incursions unleashed Void demons and brought the Black Death, first to China and then to Europe."

Frowning, Tasha said, "My history's vague. Does this connect to something else?"

"Cycles of plague persisted intermittently until the early modern period. The Void demons also triggered various European conflicts and fed the religious wars."

"And then the Burning Times?" Stefan asked.

"Yes." Will gave him a grim nod. "Like the mageborn needed more trouble. Just to confuse matters, earthly demons can come through those portals in droves."

"Can earthly demons take hosts?" Val asked.

"Oh, yeah." Will grimaced. "I've been emailing with a guy in Finland who owns very old texts. He says the main way to tell an earthly demon host from a Void demon host is the eyes. The whites are red in hosts of earthly demons, a weird lavender in those of Void demons."

Frowning, Valeria said, "The people at the diner looked normal. They just…felt wrong. So what does that mean?"

Will shrugged, his eyes worried. "Maybe they're allied with demons. Or ghouls, however unlikely that seems. I'm just guessing, here."

A tense silence settled over the group.

* * *

Griff scanned the solemn faces around the table. Void demons, figures out of distant history, hadn't been on his radar. He'd figured he and Valeria faced earthly demon hosts today. Instead, he and his friends might be facing the worst problem in centuries. Sort of like the difference between dealing with a hand grenade and a nuclear weapon.

Everyone at the table, no matter how shaky their knowledge of history, knew Void demons had decimated Europe's mages while the ghouls had multiplied. The mages had never again reached their former numbers.

The effort to eliminate the demons had exposed magic users, leading to the witchcraft persecutions and burnings that had driven the mageborn into hiding and given the Burning Times their name. *Please*, Griff thought, *let it be something else. Anything else.*

His eyes met Will's grim ones down the length of the table. "Any unsuccessful attempts at opening gates?" Griff asked.

"Those tend not to go on record," Will noted, "owing to the participants dying in the backlash. The old records could probably help if we had them."

Those had been lost or destroyed during the Burning Times.

Lorelei leaned forward. "I've had visions of something dark and cold, with purple and red streaks. Could be a Void demon, Will says, but it could also be something else. It brings terror, which would fit with what he says about Chaos magic. I saw you with it, Griff, though I couldn't tell where you were. Have you had any visions?"

"Not of anything like that." Griff blew out a breath. "I hope you're wrong, Will."

"Earthly demons," Javier said, "we can handle, right? We *do* handle them."

"At last we finger a bright spot." Will raised his Coke can in a congratulatory salute. "Odds favor demons along with their hosts or allies only when they have superior numbers or face depleted mages. Earthly demons hate working together, are only halfway stronger than an averagely gifted mage and, like ghouls, tend to rely on brute force over strategy."

"Their mistake," Tasha said with a fierce smile. "With a little luck, a combat-trained mage can take three or four ghouls. Their impatience and lack of interest in training undercuts their strength. Please tell me Void demons have the same issues."

"Aaand the bright spot fades." Will sighed. "Void demons are sly, unified, and much stronger than any mage triad. Some of their human allies, though not all, have wielded enough dark power to overwhelm their mageborn foes."

"Is there any way to know what the ghouls intend?" Valeria asked. "You've given us options, Will, but nothing definite. From what you've said, opening a gate can bring either type of demon."

"A gate through the Veil requires a lot more power, but the methods are the same. If you smell brimstone, that's a sign of Void demon influence if not actual presence. Charnel house reek, decaying flesh, signals earthly demons. Also, Void demons, like earthly ones, guard what they consider theirs. Only Void demon wards, according to my source, are a lot nastier. He didn't say how." He flashed her a wry grin. "I think we've had enough bad news today, anyway."

The grin faded as he said, "But putting all of this together is giving me neck prickles. My new buddy in Finland says it gives him prickles, too. We need to be vigilant, all of us. Griff, did you get that coffee?"

"A diluted sample. They'd washed the urn but left some residue. I hope it'll be enough. We'll scry it tomorrow at dawn."

"By then, we should have an idea how widespread the stuff is," Javier said.

"Don't test the coffee before dawn," Lorelei added, "any of you. I'm guessing you don't intend to, but don't be tempted." She looked around the table. "With all Will has told us, any time other than dawn, when dark magic is weakest, is too risky."

"Agreed," Griff said. "Anyone want to add anything?"

Most of the group shook their heads. After a moment, Will said, "Walk out with me, Val."

That didn't sound good. Griff stood. "I can—"

"If I'd wanted you," Will said, raising an eyebrow, "I'd have asked for you. Ms. Banning?"

She followed him without a backward glance. Griff watched them go. Will didn't keep secrets from him, so this must be something Will thought she should know first. If he wanted privacy, it had to be something bad.

Val let Will lead her through the pine trees behind the house, toward the river. What could he have to say that he wouldn't say in front of Griffin? Did he intend to warn her off his friend? If so, he didn't have to bother, not after this morning. She might want Griffin, but she didn't mean to act on that desire.

At the water's edge, Will turned to her. "You're good for him."

Of all things he might've said, this was one she hadn't expected. "No warning, no 'screw with him and you're done for' routine?"

He grinned, though the humor didn't reach his eyes. "That's more Tasha's deal. But even she can see his mood's more up than it has been in quite a while."

Warmth flicked over Val's heart. So she'd helped him. Good. "He's a fine man. He deserves better than he's had."

"Yeah." Will looked out over the water. "It weighs on him, especially the mages he killed."

"Why are you telling me this?"

"Tromping on his privacy, you mean?" When she nodded, he said, "There's a light in his eyes when he looks at you that I haven't seen in a long time. If anyone can teach him to hope again, you can."

Val sighed. "That's a heavy load, Will, and I don't think he wants comfort or encouragement from me. He's very…closed in, sometimes."

Will was giving her his blessing, and that meant a lot. He was also giving her way too much credit. She'd tried to help Griffin this morning, when her heart felt shredded over his losses, only to have him snap at her and pull away. She wasn't putting herself out there to get smacked again.

"I know how he can be." Will picked up a rock and skipped it over the water. "Three jumps. Not bad." He turned another stone over between his fingers. "There's something else. Stefan's telling Griff, but I wanted you to have some privacy when you heard it."

"That's the main reason you asked me to come out here."

The realization gave her stomach a sinking feeling.

When he looked at her again, his eyes were grim. "There's no way to ease this blow, so I'll just say it. The High Council has issued a warrant for your arrest on charges of aiding and abetting a fugitive, resisting arrest, and treason."

Val stared at him. God, she should've expected this. Should've seen it coming. If only she'd stopped to think. But she hadn't, and the news hit her like a bolt of lightning.

"I'm sorry," he said.

She nodded at him, forcing words through her tight throat. "Thanks for letting me know."

Griffin materialized at her side. He reached for her with his face hard, eyes blazing. "Valeria, honey, I—"

"Don't." She drew a breath that felt as though knives raked her lungs. "Just don't."

She couldn't accept comfort from a man who rejected her concern for him. With her chest heavy and her eyes stinging, she walked down the bank to get as far away from him as she could.

Chapter 14

Two hours after leaving Tasha's, Stefan sat in the Council chamber listening to a lunatic proposal. Joe Healey had pushed more than half the Council into supporting his insanely dangerous counterstrike against the ghouls.

Stefan's eyes met Will's disgusted ones briefly. Maybe they hadn't credited Healey with enough drive. Or maybe he really wanted to keep his temporary job.

Stefan stared hard at him. "Joe, what makes you think you have enough deputies to storm any nest after what happened to Banning at Milledgeville?"

"Northeast Collegium has offered us some fill-ins until our injured recover, and the Midwest has said—"

"Not what I meant," Stefan snapped. "Ghoul defenses cut Banning's group to ribbons, and you want to attack this place near Americus just because it was described on her whiteboard as a breeding center? For all you know, you'll be as vulnerable as she was."

A few heads nodded. A couple of councilors rolled their eyes.

"You're not a tactician, Dr. Harper," Healey began.

"No, I'm the man who patches up the tactician's wounded."

Lisa Turner, the plump, graying-blond headmistress of the academy, leaned out to look at Stefan. "We have to do something. Those ghoul bastards are laughing at us. Payback provides not only retribution but intimidation."

"Only," Gerry Armitage said, "if the payback succeeds. I agree with Stefan. This is too risky."

"Far too risky," Gene Blake said. "Joe, we've no business borrowing personnel only to put them at risk."

Healey's grin looked sharkish. "With the Milledgeville nest abandoned now, the Goodwin kid may be in the Americus one. Northeast wants payback, too. They're on board."

Well, of course they were, with their high councilor's son a prisoner.

"For all you know," Blake said, "this is a trap. Dare might have left that on the board for your people to find."

"He'd erased the board," Healey returned. "We scried back in time half an hour to see what'd been on it. Earlier, he and Banning had up diagrams of the Milledgeville raid."

"That isn't enough to warrant launching an attack," Teresa DiMaggio, the stocky weaponsmistress, said. "Anybody ever stop to think maybe Dare told Banning something worth listening to?"

"More likely, he conned her." Healey glared at Teresa. "Somebody'd put a circle around Americus. Might be where Dare and Banning are headed, to take refuge with his ghoul buddies."

"That's a ridiculous leap." Teresa spoke a beat ahead of Stefan's heated, "Or maybe they're just checking it out."

Teresa sounded pissed. At Healey? Or was she defending Griff? Some mages, a minority but better than none, still didn't think Griff deserved to be ranked with demons on the listing of evil menaces.

"Really, Joe," Pansy Wilson said. "No one ever proved Dare was allied with ghouls." She flung up a hand to stop the arguments coming from several councilors. "However, if this is a breeding nest, it's as good a candidate as any for the place the ghouls are holding young Dan Goodwin. We owe it to the Northeast Collegium to recover him and punish his captors. I see no reason not to proceed."

Several heads nodded. Damned overeager idiots.

"We should table this," Blake said. He glanced down the table and got a few nods of agreement. "I'll call the Northeast high councilor and convince her this raid's too dangerous for her son."

"I call for a vote," Healey snapped.

Blake narrowed his eyes, but Healey didn't seem to notice. *Fucking ambitious bastard.* Stefan glared at him.

Blake shrugged, his face hard. "We'll vote, then."

There was no way to tell from the debate or the votes who might have a secret agenda. Stefan listened grimly to the tally. He didn't know enough to judge whether someone's reluctance came from a desire to protect that nest or some other reason, like basic common sense.

In the end, the Council approved the raid. Stefan couldn't believe it. Would this force also walk into a trap, or was there a chance for a straight fight here? Either way, there would be mage casualties tomorrow.

Will caught his eye as the room emptied. "I have those

sources you wanted, Dr. Harper, the ones on ancient mass-healing techniques from Asia."

"Good." Stefan glanced at the infirmary director, Dr. Callie Malone. "We're going to need them."

"Yeah." Callie scowled at the departing councilors. "I'll go start prepping the infirmary, Stefan," she muttered.

"Thanks. I'll be down in a few." Stefan cocked an eyebrow at Will. "If Will has time to give me his insights on the best articles to start with, maybe we can have an edge tomorrow."

"I can do that," Will said. With cover for a talk thus established, Stefan and Will followed Callie out.

In the hall, Sybil Harrison stood, arms crossed at her waist, staring at nothing. Misery vibrated in the magic around her.

Stefan touched her shoulder lightly. "Deputy Harrison, are you all right?"

She raised anguished eyes to his face. "The deputies chasing Val last night saw Griffin Dare with her. Dr. Harper, she's so levelheaded. She's nobody's fool. How could she do something like this?"

"I'll catch up to you," he told Will, drawing Harrison back into the empty meeting room.

"Is it possible—could he have bewitched her?" the chief deputy asked. Hope flickered in her eyes.

"I doubt it." He squeezed her shoulder as the hope died. To keep her from sensing anything from his touch, he tucked his hands into his pockets. "Maybe it's as Teresa said. Maybe Dare told Ms. Banning something worth listening to."

She gave her head a vehement shake. "That's ridiculous. Dare's… You know what he is."

"Yes." Better than she did. She was Banning's friend, but that didn't mean she was open-minded about Griff. Even more important, though, she was Stefan's patient, and she needed something to hold on to. He chose his words with care. "At least, I know what we say he is."

"'What we say'? Everyone who was there that day saw him kill Alden and the deputy reeves who tried to stop him. Are you saying we're wrong about him?" She almost seemed to hope for a yes. She must care a lot about Banning.

He shrugged. "I think we sometimes rush to judgment. It's a normal human reaction, and we're no different from Mundanes in that regard, especially when our world has been jolted and we're frightened. That was the situation six years ago."

That was no more than others said, if rarely. His response should be safe.

Harrison stared at him thoughtfully. At last, she said, "I just hope she's okay."

"So do I." If she was, Griff was, but Stefan had to warn them. Whatever Griff and Banning were doing, for whatever reason they'd circled the name Americus, they'd better stay away from that nest.

Griff watched Valeria covertly as they walked along the second-floor gallery at the Big Satilla Motel. The slanting afternoon sunlight cast harsh shadows over her face, highlighting its tight, pinched look. Not that he blamed her.

She'd called the Collegium home her entire life, and now the High Council, and most likely, much of the Council, had turned against her. Because of him. That burned. So did her suffering on his account. He'd wanted to comfort her, and she'd walked away. But she had no one else now.

They both needed rest, the final part of recharging, before

they searched the homes of the people from the diner. Those houses might well contain dark magic traps. Facing them at less than full strength would be suicidal, but the tension in her body meant sleep wouldn't come easily for her.

He opened the door and stepped back to let her in. She gave him a quick glance in thanks as she walked by. They set their gear by the low, fake-wood dresser. The room wasn't great, but it was better than last night's cabin. At least this place smelled and looked clean. He'd stayed in worse. Yet he suddenly hated it.

She deserved luxury. The Ritz Carlton on Atlanta's Peachtree Street. The Westin Peachtree Plaza with its revolving bar, skyline view and plush beds. The Waldorf Astoria in New York. She should be with someone who could give her those things, who wouldn't have to hide her in motels one step up from rat traps.

She stood in the center of the room as though she didn't know what to do next. Finally, she sank onto one of the beds, her gaze distant and unfocused.

He couldn't stand by and do nothing. He knew that kind of disillusionment, of having those you'd trusted and served despise you.

"I'm sorry," she said, visibly gathering herself. "For being so shaky."

"Give yourself a break." He knelt in front of her and took her hands, felt her misery through the connection. "The hits have been nonstop these last two days, and you're still standing."

"More or less." Her lips tightened, and she shook her head.

Standing, he said, "Come here," and tugged on her hands. She let him pull her upright but looked wary. "I'm okay."

"You're not." Her eyes were huge in her pale face. Staring into them, willing her to trust him, he slid his hands up to her shoulders and tugged. "Come here, Valeria."

With a strangled gasp, she fell into his arms. He closed them tightly around her, and she pressed her face into his neck. His heart thudded in his chest. Resting his cheek against her thick, soft hair seemed natural. Inevitable. She shuddered, fighting tears.

Fucking bastard traitors. Just how many of them were there, anyway? He tightened his hold, wishing he could take away her pain as well as the danger.

"I can manage," she choked, pushing against him.

"Sssh." He pressed a kiss to her temple. "You've had two days from hell. There's nothing wrong with needing to lean on someone once in a while."

She looked directly into his eyes, her own bright and watery, but focused. Defiant. "There's nothing wrong with letting someone share your grief for your lost friends, either."

Her expression held no pity, only concern that made him ashamed of his earlier reaction, but he wasn't going to spew his feelings all over her. Wallowing in them just gave them more power.

"Okay," he managed at last. He couldn't think what else to say. At least Valeria seemed satisfied, lowering her head to his shoulder again.

She wasn't only letting him hold her now but was holding him in return, with her arms locked around his waist. He slid a hand into the silky strands of her honey-brown hair, stroking. Easing her, he hoped.

As they stood together, tender warmth stole into his heart. He'd had no one to offer him the simple comfort of an embrace in years. He held her closer, breathing in her honey-suckle scent.

Gradually, he noticed her firm breasts pressed against his chest, her belly against his. Memory taunted him with the feel of her curves under his palms, the taste of her skin on his lips. His blood stirred. He should step back before his body betrayed him, but his hands refused to slide away from her.

Valeria lifted her head, a questioning look in her soft, warm eyes. Maybe he was crazy, maybe he'd regret this, maybe he was taking advantage, but he couldn't stop himself.

He lowered his head and kissed her.

Her lips parted on a sigh that made him hard instantly. Her hands slid up his back, stroking in a caress that was tender, like her lips against his. They were unbearably sweet and had him aching for more.

Deepening the kiss, he plunged his tongue into her warm, soft mouth, stroking and claiming. Her tongue met his, welcoming him, igniting his blood. He barely heard the faint, wordless sound she made as she tightened her hold on his waist. Her body sagged into his, yielding, and he burned for her.

Kissing Valeria's neck, reveling in her gasps of pleasure and the feel of her fingers roaming his body, he caressed her smooth hips, ripe breasts. Every touch ratcheted up his craving for her. She slid a hand into the back of his jeans, inside his briefs, squeezing his ass while her other hand slid up his back.

Kissing and touching, exploring each other, they tumbled onto the bed. He yanked her shirt off and finally got to run his mouth down those gorgeous arms.

"So sexy," he murmured, watching her.

Valeria flashed him a grin before she tugged his head up to kiss him.

Through the lacy cup of her bra, he stroked her nipple, and it pebbled under his hand. She gave a wordless cry, arching her back in a silent plea for more, and her hips ground against him.

His cock throbbed with the need to be inside her. His heart ached for that too, for the chance to express with his body the longing he felt when he touched her.

As they shoved off their remaining clothes, her hands glided over his chest and belly. She trailed slow kisses along his waist, traced his abs with her tongue and made him shudder with need. Her skin felt soft and warm. He kneaded the plump, smooth mound of her breast and gloried in the way her breath hitched.

Her fingers closed around his cock and lust blinded him. Thrusting against her hand, he rolled her onto her back. He tasted the light salting of sweat on that long neck of hers, and she whimpered.

She flicked her tongue over his ear, the touch shooting straight to his throbbing cock. He couldn't touch her enough. Taste her enough. When he lifted his head, her smile knocked away the last shadows of the day's worries.

They rolled together over the bed, learning each other's bodies, laughing at each other as their legs tangled. When he thumbed her nipple, Valeria gasped and clutched his shoulders. He slid his arm under her, arching her body so her breasts lifted.

Val stroked Griffin's cheek as his fierce, demanding gaze locked on her face. "God, you're so beautiful," he muttered.

As the words seared her heart, he closed his mouth over her breast.

Her senses reeling, she clutched his head to her. Then he slid his fingers between her moist folds. Stroked. Delved.

Her hips jerked in response, and another whimper escaped her. Caught in the arc of pleasure from his mouth and hand, she could only cling to him and accept what he chose to give.

He raised his head, leaving her nipple tight and wanting. "You're so hot and wet for me."

"Only for you," she gasped, hips lifting again in a silent plea. She hadn't meant to say that, didn't know where it had come from, but she'd worry about it later. She was tired of fighting the attraction between them, especially now, when she'd felt so alone and needed his affections.

His eyes fired, possessiveness glinting in their depths. He lowered his head to her other breast, licking, nibbling, tasting. Finally, he sucked as she writhed under him.

She slid her hands into his hair, then caressed his chest and shoulders as his thrusting finger made her core throb with need. She'd never craved anyone, ached for anyone, more than she did this man. She needed him now.

He slid another finger into her, and she shuddered.

"You like that?" he asked, his breath teasing the sensitive bud of her nipple.

"Yes," she moaned, pressing against his hand.

He lightly kissed taut, aching breast, still stroking her core, and then the other. She struggled against the tide of pleasure. Reaching down, she found him again, thrilled at the need that flared in his eyes.

He leaned over her, and she caressed a path up his corded

arms to the soft hair at his nape. His mouth caught hers in a blazing kiss as his weight settled in the cradle of her thighs. Val nipped his shoulder, slid her hands over the firm muscles of his back and ass.

Kissing her neck, he let out a ragged groan. She pushed his shoulder, and they rolled together.

Straddling him, she closed her fingers around his hard, smooth erection. She stroked him as she worked her way down his body, touching and tasting and reveling in the way his muscles tensed under her lips and hands.

"You're gorgeous," she said.

He winced, as though she'd embarrassed him, and she felt her heart soften. "I'm just a guy." He rolled her beneath him. "You're the beautiful one."

With heat flashing through her, she dimly heard him say, "Someday, I want to paint you."

Griffin rose above her to trail kisses and caresses down her body, leaving little streaks of heat where he touched and yearning where he didn't.

Aching to have him, she tugged on his hair. "Come here."

He flashed a grin that was a blend of mischief and desire, a fleeting glimpse of the younger, more easygoing man she remembered. "Not finished here."

Before she could reply, he leaned down and kissed her sex. Pleasure ripped through her like an energy bolt, arching her back and tightening her nipples. Val let out a choked cry.

His palms slid up her inner thighs, caressing her and spreading her wide. "Gorgeous," he said. He brushed a soft, slow kiss into the crease of her thigh. "You smell like paradise. I'll bet you taste even better."

Her belly clenched with wanting.

He slipped his hands under her thighs, up to her breasts to tweak the nipples, and she moaned, holding his hands to her.

"I love when you do that." He brushed his lips over the folds of her sex. "The way you respond so completely."

"I want you inside me."

"Soon, honey." Watching her face, he licked her cleft.

Blinding pleasure shivered through her. She held on to his shoulders. His soft, warm tongue stroked between her folds, across her clit, inside her. Again and again. Every touch of his mouth, every flick of his tongue on her most sensitive flesh shot alternate bliss and craving through her.

Magic sparked around them. Need tightened her belly until she gasped his name, the sound a caress and a plea. He pushed her over in a rush of heat that stole her breath away.

The sweet tremors eased. Her breathing slowed, and she opened her eyes to find Griffin cradling her close. The moment imprinted itself on her heart, the cool sheets under her, the warmth of his body against hers, the tenderness in his deep blue gaze.

She brushed her fingers over his jaw, and his eyes locked with hers. He caught her hand to kiss it.

"I have condoms," he murmured against her knuckles.

Val smiled. "I'm on the pill, so no worries."

Watching Val's face, he positioned himself over her. He eased into her, the fullness of his cock giving her pleasure yet making her want even more. His tender look gave way to fierce possessiveness that made her heart pound and her body clench around him.

He moved slowly until he was fully sheathed inside of her. He withdrew himself to thrust again, faster this time, so her back arched and a moan of pleasure and need broke from her throat. He thrust again, faster.

The craving had bite now. Val thrashed beneath him. "More! Griffin…"

He groaned, thrust harder. Deeper. Her hips pumped to the rhythm he set. She could feel how much he wanted her, and that made her want him even more. His smooth skin covered hard muscle, but his lips felt soft against her neck.

When he raised his head, his taut face above her and his flesh within her consumed her world. The magic sparked again, bright behind her eyelids, feeding the tension, the hot need coiling her.

So tight. So close to the edge.

He shuddered, then thrust again, whipping white hot pleasure through her, shooting her into sweet oblivion as he cried her name.

Slowly, the hot rush faded. She surfaced to find they were still joined. Griffin's ragged breathing brushed her cheek, but he'd pushed himself up on his elbows, taking his weight off her.

Val had to swallow hard and draw a deep breath before she could speak. "Come back," she said, caressing his cheek.

He smiled, kissed her shoulder, and rested his head in the curve of her neck. His heart hammered against her while her pulse echoed in her ears. His body was warm, faintly damp with sweat from their joining. She wrapped her arms around him and pressed her cheek to his.

Griffin raised his head. She smiled, and a slow, tender smile widened his mouth. He rolled to the side, pulling her with him. Val nestled against him and let her fingers drift softly over his strong jaw.

He switched off the bedside lamp, leaving the room in the dimness of sunlight filtering through cheap drapes. "We should sleep for a while. We have a busy night ahead."

Searching the homes of the people from the diner. She let him settle her against his side. He pushed her hair back with a touch so gentle, so tender, it made her heart yearn.

She couldn't afford to yearn for Griffin. To want him. To feel any more than she already did. So why did lying here with him feel so right?

He drew back to look into her face. "Let's take this one day at a time. See how it goes."

It was almost as if he'd read her mind.

"Works for me." She slid an arm across his chest, savoring its soft dusting of hair, and he tightened his hold on her.

One day at a time, indeed. With the mages hunting them and the ghouls summoning dark forces, every day would be a bonus.

Chapter 15

The summer night was muggy, but little shivers of dread rippled under Val's skin as she and Griffin waited, screened, under an elm tree in Carson. Modest bungalows and small post-war ranches lined the street. Lights burned in a few of the houses, but most were dark, including the diner owner's house three doors down.

Once the neighbors were in bed, she and Griffin would break into their target and search. With just over an hour until midnight, they'd be at a slight but manageable disadvantage if they encountered dark forces. Better to deal with that, though, and have the Mundane neighbors in bed, than risk their involvement if she and Griffin had to engage the people from the diner.

The streets were empty. Most residents had gone to bed for the night.

"Lights went out next door to the target." Griffin nodded down the street. "When the neighbor across the street turns in, we'll move."

"Right." She didn't think she could stand finding evidence

that tied the tainted coffee to mages. On the other hand, solving a big problem involving dark magic or—worst case scenario—Void demons might open the way for him to return home. To at least have the chance to explain his side of the story to the Council.

But dark magic could kill hundreds of Mundanes, as well as honest mages, before his crew got a handle on it.

"Interesting," she said softly, so the words wouldn't carry through her screen to any unexpected passerby, "that there were two different coffee urns, one with that bloody residue in it and one plain."

"Yeah." Frowning, he stroked her shoulder absently. "Maybe only people who're passing through get the nasty stuff."

"But that means they're being selective."

"Did you notice, there are no pets of any kind wandering around, not even cats?"

Val kept her voice low. "Lots of rats, though. Ugh."

"That's why I looked for cats." He gave her arm a reassuring squeeze and grinned. "Don't worry, hon. I'll protect you from the big, bad rats."

She wrinkled her nose at him. "Wiseass."

"Always." He kissed her quickly. "Light just went out across the street. Let's go."

They strolled down the sidewalk with their magical senses alert but detected nothing abnormal. No wards had protected the diner, so maybe there would be none here. Their absence was encouraging. As Will had said, demons of any sort guarded what was theirs.

At the target house, a Craftsman bungalow, Griffin halted. "I'll take point," he murmured.

"On the grounds of being a guy?" Val raised an eyebrow and put a chill into the soft reply.

He answered in a tight, irritated whisper, "On the grounds of my ranking you, Banning, by both time in rank and in the field. I take point."

Going into a fight arguing disrupted teamwork. Val shut up, for now. Considering the friends Griffin had lost, maybe his protectiveness made sense, but his lack of trust in her skill could prove fatal someday.

She stood by one of the porch pillars to keep watch while he checked for door wards. The screen she and Griffin shared concealed them both from Mundane eyes, so she drew her sword, raising it in the guard position.

"Nothing," he said softly. A faint click sounded, like a latch sliding back. He eased the door open.

No strange smells drifted out of the house, no eerie sense of presence. "I get nothing," he said. "It's empty."

Val backed toward him so she could keep her eyes on the street. "Trap empty or just empty?"

"That would be the question." Staff at the ready, copper runes glowing softly, he slipped inside.

"Do you think they left because of us?" Val slid in after him. The house looked tidy, the wood floors shiny with wax. The living room's modest furnishings could've belonged to any blue-collar family in America, but the place felt empty, as he'd said.

"No brimstone stench from Void demons," he noted. "Or charnel reek from earthly ones. But if not demons, what?"

Val shrugged. "Let's check the house and the other two homes anyway, cover our bases."

"Agreed. My gut, though, says the threat probably moved on."

But to where? she thought. They separated to search.

In one of the bedrooms Val found a scrap of paper about the size of her palm on the floor between the bed and nightstand. "Griffin," she called, "come look at this."

He hurried in from the other room as she reached for it. "Wait, let me get it!"

"I'm shielded." As he must've noticed. She picked up the paper and felt, through her shield, icy cold roll over her hand. "Don't touch it unshielded. Look at these weird runes."

He looked over her shoulder. "I don't recognize them. I'll take a photo and send it to Will."

As he pulled his phone from his pocket, it rang. "Stefan," he said, eyebrows rising. He flipped open the phone and leaned down so she could hear. "Hey."

"I don't have much time. Healey scried what had been on Val's whiteboard. He's convinced the Council to authorize a raid on the Americus ghoul nest at daybreak tomorrow."

Val scowled at the phone. "He doesn't have the personnel for that."

"He's borrowing them. Northeast wants payback, if not actual recovery of the Goodwin kid. I have to go prepare for casualties and hope to hell I don't have any."

Griffin looked as appalled as she felt, but he said only, "Good luck, bro. I'll call you tomorrow."

"Wait. There's one more thing. Will picked up from the deputy reeve grapevine that Healey did some scrying, figured out you rescued Val near Wayfarer because that's where she disappeared under screening. He thinks you've got 'a hidey-

hole' there, and he has reserve deputies looking for it and
you. Stay out of Wayfarer."

"Right. Thanks."

As Griffin signed off, Val muttered, "Hell of a time for Joe
to start thinking logically."

"Hell of an idiotic idea for that raid, too." He took the
photo, transmitted it, and pocketed his phone.

She touched his arm. "Griffin. I have to go to Americus."
That would delay analyzing the blood-tainted coffee, but the
diner was shut down so it wasn't an immediate danger. It
could wait. "I have to warn them if they're walking into a
trap. Maybe I can help them, but you're a high-value target. I
know you won't want to, but you should wait for me somewhere."

"Oh, like that'll happen." He frowned down at her.
"Honey, I've been a high-value target for years. I know how
to watch my ass. If those mages are heading into an ambush,
they need all possible hands."

"Not yours. It's too dangerous." She should've known he'd
react like this. Should've just sneaked away on her own. "I
wish I hadn't said anything."

"Yeah, well, that ship's sailed. Besides, I would've said it if
you hadn't. Even though you're a pretty valuable target, yourself." He paused. "In fact, we may end up distracting them
instead of helping."

"I know, but we *have* to try."

"True...Okay, we go, on one condition." His face hardened. "If things get tight for us, and I say we leave, no argument. We can't afford to have either side catch us."

"Agreed."

* * *

Floodlights shone through the pine trees, illuminating a cleared area around the ghoul nest's double chain-link fences. Nothing moved in that space. Overhead, the stars were fading, the sky easing from night black to deep gray.

Griff crouched in the scrubby undergrowth with Valeria. Seeing her this tense twisted his heart. He'd had years to adjust to the idea of a traitor on the Council, to being an outcast. She was dealing with a lot in very little time.

She glanced at the sky. "Almost daylight, a good time to set up an attack. Let's work our way around to the other side."

They'd already checked one part of the nest for land mines and other traps but found none.

"I'll take point," he said. As she opened her mouth to argue, he added, "If any mages are already here, better they see me than you. My rep's already crap."

"Which I'm trying to change, if you'd pay attention. Besides, my rep's crap now, too, you know."

"I know. We'll talk later." The vision she offered, of exoneration and even acceptance, tempted him. Her faith in him, her hope for change, reminded him so much of Allie, who'd died because of those traits. He wouldn't let that happen to Valeria.

But if he could go home…

Yeah. As if. Pipe dreams only led to trouble.

The dirt road to the nest came into sight, and something niggled at his magical senses. He stuck out an arm to stop Valeria and said softly, "Check our screen."

Her face tensed, but she nodded. Opening his own senses, he felt the whispery brush of hers.

Beyond that lay a nasty, weird tingle. Mage magic and ghoul mixed. *Hell.*

Her face set in grim lines, and her pain vibrated in the magic between them. "Like before," she muttered. "Bastards."

"I still don't sense explosives, though, so that's good."

From the far side of the camp came the *kra-kow* of a massed energy blast. The attack had begun, so the time for warnings had passed.

Another energy blast came from the left side of the camp, then another from the right. Then another in front of them. The mages were hitting all sides of the camp. Did they have enough people to do that safely?

"They brought a large number of mages," Griff noted. "But do they know they're up against their own kind, too?"

Valeria chewed her lip. "If we join this fight, the mages will turn on us sooner or later. Can we help them enough to be worth the distraction, not to mention the risk to us, before they spot us?"

"Maybe if we go in with mages from somewhere else. They might not recognize us." He didn't have to tell her the newcomers would be mixed in with the Southeastern deputies. He studied her worried face. "You want to try it."

"I can't stand the idea of another massacre."

Neither could he. "We'll go, then, but the moment they come after us, we're out of here."

"Absolutely."

They exchanged a grim look. "Be careful," she said, before kissing him quickly.

"You, too. Let's go." If only he could hold her just a second longer, but any time wasted might cost them their lives.

Shielded, they ran toward the sounds of battle.

The deafening *brrrr* of automatic weapons fire meant multiple armed defenders. Mage energy in a rainbow of colors clashed with brown-gold ghoul power in the air. A stocky female mage, shield shimmering around her, gutted a ghoul the old-fashioned way, using only her sword. Ensorcelled arrows arced toward the ghoul compound, exploding against ghoul shields.

There were no defending mages in sight, but he could feel their power, even their conflicted emotions inside the compound, damn them. They might not like helping the ghouls fire on other mages, but they were doing it. Why?

Valeria stepped up beside him. "Do you feel that mage energy inside?" she shouted. Energy crackled along her sword. When he nodded, she whipped that power at the nearest gun emplacement inside the fence. It exploded, and a feral grin lit her face.

Exultant, he took out another gun emplacement the same way. As he turned to her, ghouls raced out of the nest, blasting muddy gold energy. From behind Griff, mages came running towards them. He stepped in front of Valeria to attack the nearest ghoul.

"Crap," she muttered and swung left to meet another ghoul attack.

"It's Dare," someone shouted. "Nail him."

Story of his life, and he was damned tired of it.

Blue energy zipped from his left. Diving clear, he tucked and rolled. A woman and three men in mage camos, shielded magically, charged at him.

"Valeria, let's go!"

She didn't answer, and he wouldn't leave without her.

He rolled to one knee and focused power through the staff's slanted *X* rune, *naudhiz*, to keep the force at the minimum necessary to stop them. The burst knocked them down. And out, he hoped.

A dozen or so mages still stood, firing on the enemy.

Where the hell was Valeria? Gripped by fear for her, he peered through the energy haze.

Val's energy blast knocked three charging ghouls flat on their backs. A chill flickered over her neck and she spun around to see a ghoul almost on her. She ducked his blast and stabbed through his shields, gutting him.

Where was Griffin? How had they gotten separated?

"Over there," someone shouted. "Dare. Get the fucker!"

The words rang above the din of battle. For a single instant Val's heart stopped. Her blood chilled. She'd known the risk going in, had blocked it as she always did before a battle, but she couldn't block it out now.

He could die out here.

She couldn't, wouldn't, lose him.

Oh, God, where was he?

Translocating in a battle zone was dangerous. Shielding dissolved during the position shift. But she had to reach him quickly. She picked a spot in the direction the mages who'd yelled his name were heading, then translocated. Emerging several yards ahead of them, she spotted Griffin six feet away on her left. Thank God.

Shielding again, she fired as she ran to him, a focused beam of blue that illuminated the ghoul it struck. "We have to get out of here," she shouted. A sweep of her blade laid down a wide scythe of repelling power and blew two shielded mages backward. "We're distracting the mages more than we're helping them. I don't want to engage directly."

"I don't either. Flash to the car, and I'll—"

A flare of brown-gold energy burst through the woods, behind the mage forces. Ghouls in black skinsuits charged, muddy yellow energy pouring off them, stabbing into the mages. Cutting them down.

Ghouls could not translocate. If they were behind the attackers, they'd been lying in wait all along. The traitor mages' power must've kept her and Griffin from sensing them.

She and Griffin exchanged one enraged look as they fired together at the ghouls. Behind a large oak lay a figure in mage camos, face concealed by the tree. Val darted around it.

"Darren," she gasped. She dropped to her knees by the young man who lay sprawled out on the ground, bleeding from his belly.

Griffin sprang to cover her as she checked the wound. It was too severe for her to heal with a simple spell, but infusing healing energy would mend some of the damage. It might keep him from bleeding out. The young mage's eyes opened slowly, dark wells of pain in his brown face.

"Be still," she said. "Let me—"

"Bitch." He shoved her hands aside. His face contorted with the effort of forcing out words. "Set up...you...traitor."

Her chest tightened as though he'd punched her.

Griffin fired at the advancing enemy, and her skin tingled as he drew more power from the woods. "She's no traitor, kid."

The mage spat. "Bast—bastard."

"Let's go," Griffin said. "Valeria." The mages were scattering. A couple of dozen ghouls were advancing, now within thirty yards.

She stepped up beside him to whip an arc of lethal green energy at the ghouls. Two stumbled backward as it rebounded against their shields. One fell.

To Griffin, she said, "We can help Darren if we get a little space."

"Risky, but saving even one matters." He locked an arm around her waist. "Grab him."

Val bent to grip the wounded mage's arm with her free hand. Griffin's power surged, and he flashed away with them.

As they emerged in a clearing, he surveyed their surroundings. "We're on the side where the mages left their helos, about fifty yards from the action. Should be far enough." He took up a guard position facing the battle.

Darren moaned, but he didn't seem to have the strength to fight her off any longer.

"I'm no more a traitor than you are, Darren." She crossed her hands over the bloody wound.

"*Sanere.*" A brilliant silver light flowed over the young man's torso. Though she couldn't heal him completely, she had provided a stopgap until the medics reached him.

She leaned down, panting, as she grabbed her sword. "I am no traitor, but you need to find out who is."

"The mages are retreating," Griffin said. "We should, too." He locked an arm around her, building up power. "Going," he snapped, and flashed them out.

They materialized halfway down the mountain. Breathing hard against rage that threatened to choke her, Val pushed away from Griffin.

"We have to get out of here," he said behind her. "Valeria? You okay?"

"Yes." *Damn, damn, damn.* "Knowing mages would help ghouls kill our own kind is one thing, but seeing it…"

He drew her into his arms, and she dropped her face onto his shoulder, drawing in his familiar scent. They were safe, for now.

Griffin was safe.

The fear she'd pushed back tightened her throat and chest. With it came painful clarity. She was in love with him. Couldn't allow anyone to harm him. What the hell was she going to do now?

Chapter 16

Sure you're okay?" Frowning, Griffin tipped Val's chin up to peer into her face.

"I'm fine." She stepped clear of him, lowering her eyes in case her roiling emotions showed. He wouldn't want her to love him, to have any deeper ties to him. She wasn't thrilled about it, but she wouldn't run from it, either. She would, however, pick her moment for telling him.

"That kid was only saying what he'd been told, honey."

The memory burned, but she nodded. "I know how it looks. Of course Darren thought I lured them there."

Griffin dropped a kiss onto her forehead. "After that healing, you should rest here. I'll go back, see if there are captured survivors I can shake loose. It's daylight. The ghouls will be weaker."

"Even so, the odds are too one-sided." The enemy would be on guard. Worse, any mages he freed would turn on him at the first opportunity. "Besides, we don't know there are captives. We're leaving. If we run into trouble along the way, I don't want you waiting around for me. Leave me if that's what it takes for you to get yourself to safety."

"No chance." He crossed his arms over his chest, his face stony. "I got you into this, so I'll be damned if I don't see you clear of it."

Her pulse quickened. She set a hand on his chest and felt his sudden, sharp intake of breath. "Is that the only reason?"

"It's reason enough…but no." He pulled her to him, and his mouth covered hers in a hard, deep, possessive kiss.

Val held him close, relishing the strength of his body as he held her.

The kiss broke, and he brushed his mouth lightly over her forehead. "Let's go."

The more Val thought about the battle and the discoveries of the day before, the angrier she became. She paced the room she shared with Griffin at the small, shabby Rest Rite Inn with fury simmering deep in her gut.

He'd said little since the battle, mostly letting her fume. Now he sprawled in a chair, seemingly deep in thought. "What forces do the reeves have left?" he asked.

"Not enough to do anything that matters." She glared at the AC unit under the window. Kicking it might make her feel better, but then they'd have to pay for it. Besides, it was cooling the tiny room and bath even though it wasn't cooling her temper.

Over its hum, she added, "Damn it all, they didn't counterstrike after that disaster at Milledgeville, but they sent a team—wasted a team—*damn* it! How have you stood it all these years? How did you learn to walk away, to go on?"

"As the old cliché says, you do what you have to." His voice was harsh, but his eyes were full of regret.

She blew out a hard breath. "That sucks."

"No argument here."

He caught her arm and drew her down onto his lap. "Let's forget it for a while," he said before pressing his lips against hers.

The hard, blistering kiss triggered an eruption of heat in Val's belly, and her blood seemed to sing in her veins. She gasped. His tongue slid into her mouth, plundering, demanding more.

She ran her hands over the broad, warm expanse of his back and pulled his shirt from his jeans. Her fingers fumbled for his belt buckle.

He palmed her breasts, and her brain fogged. When it cleared, she lay on the bed, with Griffin tugging off her shirt.

"If they'd hurt you out there," he said in a raspy, strained voice, eyes burning as he yanked her jeans and panties off, "I'd have blown them all to hell."

She stared at him, stunned, and he kissed her again. When he covered her body with his, the weight of his muscular frame ignited her entire being. She clutched at him, ran her hands over his back. Today was theirs. Just the two of them now, no politics, no battles, no deaths.

"Shirt," she managed, tugging it as he kissed his way down her neck. "Jeans, too."

He removed her bra before he pushed himself to his feet. "Remember where we were."

Remember? She always would. The possessive, almost fierce look on his face shot straight to her heart. Smiling, she traced the edge of one of her taut, aching nipples with a fingertip and savored the desire blazing in his eyes.

He dropped his shirt, and she let her gaze roam the sculptured lines of his chest and arms. She knew how those curves and planes felt against her skin. How they tasted.

Aching with the need to touch him, she said, "Hurry."

He pushed his pants down and stepped out of them. Below the hard plane of his belly, his cock jutted from its nest of dark hair. Her inner muscles tightened.

She sat up, reaching for him. Setting a knee by her thigh, he leaned down to take her mouth in a greedy kiss. He lowered himself on top of her, pressing her back into the bed with nothing between them now. His hard chest flattened her breasts, its soft dusting of hair teasing her nipples, and his erection pressing into her mound.

The simmer in her rose to craving. Val moaned, holding him close as she turned her face into his neck and nibbled. Shuddering, he made a wordless sound that deepened her pleasure.

"You go to my head like a drug," he murmured, cupping her sex. "Seductive. Sweet." Suddenly, he groaned. "I can't wait any longer."

The words made her own need spike. She writhed under him, her hands roaming his body. "I don't want you to."

Watching her face, he slid inside of her.

"Yes," she gasped, lifting to take him in deeper. "Griffin."

Possessive triumph filled her heart and glinted in his eyes. She twined her legs around his hips, taking him all the way. Still, she wanted more.

His mouth found the tender spot at the hinge of her jaw and sent flash fire through her, tightening her body around him.

Val whimpered at the hard heat of him filling her. Having him inside of her felt so good, so right. As nothing ever had.

I love you, she thought but knew better than to say the words aloud. He'd shown no sign of feeling the same way, and telling him how she felt would only make things awkward.

He nuzzled the curve between her neck and shoulder, then nipped it gently. Quivering in response, she slid her palms over his sculpted shoulders and down his firm sides.

Maybe she could memorize the feel of his weight on her and the bulk of his arms around her. The hard, precious fullness of his flesh in hers.

He lifted his head. The blue of his eyes darkened and softened, and her heart swelled with love for him.

"Griffin," she murmured. She tugged his head down, angling her own so their lips met, opening for him.

The kiss was long and deep and sweet, drawing her in—drawing him in—until the magic they shared vibrated with tenderness, with longing and possibility. Without breaking the kiss, he drew back. She whimpered her protest into his mouth, and he surged forward.

When he lifted his head again, his pleasure lit his eyes. Need rolled through the depths of her body. He drew back again, his craving etched in the taut lines of his face as desire clenched her lower body and rocked her hips upward.

Back and forth they went, moving together, each sensing the touch the other wanted, and pleasure became need became desperate passion. Still the look between them held, exposing her reactions to him and his to her and drawing the two of them closer.

The sounds of their ragged breathing, the mingled groans and cries of pleasure as their pace quickened, the scent of him on her, all went straight to her heart. Yet Val wouldn't look away. She couldn't.

He pounded into her, hard and fast, giving in one instant and taking, making her ache with desire, the next. Fierce with possession and demand, his eyes burned into hers, and still she wanted more.

Frantic, she met his thrusts, bucking urgently beneath him. The shared magic between them sparked and built in the air, in her soul, until she not only saw the pleasure in his face but felt its echo in her own body.

She sensed him reveling in the fullness of her breasts under his chest, the way her taut nipples rubbed him as he rode her, the grip of her thighs on his hips. Even as he withdrew, she ached for him to thrust back into her, to feel her soft, wet heat sheathe him. He was close to coming, she realized, fighting it for her sake. Wanting her to tip first.

It was too much, almost overload, but she still couldn't look away. Legs tightening around him, body arching, Val gasped.

With a groan, he thrust deep, grinding their bodies together. His head snapped back, his eyes blanked, and then the tidal wave of shared pleasure crashed through her. Behind her eyelids, red became black became golden starbursts and then faded into sweet nothingness as her climax ebbed. Still she felt him with her, floating and savoring together.

When the world faded back in, their bodies were still joined. Griffin's face rested in the curve of her neck. His warm, uneven breath whispered over her shoulder, and his heart pounded hard against her chest.

A faint sheen of moisture coated their bodies, companion to the musky, delicious sex aroma in the air. Together, their heartbeats slowed. Their breathing eased, and his flesh slid from hers. Val's lips curved in a contented, easy smile.

Despite everything that had happened, in this place, in this moment, only the man in her arms and what she'd shared with him mattered.

Drowsily, she slid her hand up into his hair to stroke it. She loved the feel of the inky black, thick, soft strands under her fingertips. Val sighed. If only they could hold on to the rightness of this moment. But maybe feeling this way was a leap, beyond what he wanted.

His lips moved against her neck in a lazy kiss. "It's not a leap," he said softly. "It's just complicated."

Her heart skipped a beat. "I didn't say that aloud."

He raised his head. They stared at each other.

"Weird," he said at last, shifting off of her. He settled at her side, close, but not touching.

"Very weird." She eyed him carefully. Right now, she didn't mind a little distance. "Has this ever happened to you before?"

"No. I can't explain it. I wanted to be as close to you as I could, feel everything, while I made love to you, but I didn't try to do anything magical."

"Neither did I. But you've just summed up what I was feeling, too. Except I felt the magic building between us in a way it never has before." Wrinkling her nose, she added, "Not that I have a lot of experience. Either way, this awareness is new to me, too."

He brushed her hair gently out of her face. "I haven't been with many women since Allie died. I'd forgotten how sweet this could be."

He'd loved Allie. Maybe someday he would love Val, too. "So what are we going to do about this?"

He raised an eyebrow. "We go with it. Test it. See how far

away we can sense each other, catch specific thoughts. How we can block it for privacy in our own heads. It could be useful."

Val smiled. "You sound just like you used to when you told us how to test weapons capabilities."

"Old habits." His face softened, but he frowned. "If someone had offered me a link like this, I would've turned it down. I'm surprised it doesn't bother me, that I actually like the idea. If it bothers you, we'll focus on blocking it."

"Uh-uh. No way. Like you said, it can be useful." Hesitantly, watching him, she added, "Besides, I like being close to you this way."

His smile lit his eyes. "Me, too." He nibbled her lower lip.

Desire spiked downward from the contact. Val sighed, sliding her arms around him, and he deepened the kiss.

Griff's phone rang. He lifted his head and swallowed a roar of frustration. "Shit. Somebody's timing sucks."

"But you need to take it." For them both, duty came first.

When he answered her with a rueful look, she suggested, "When you're finished, join me in the shower?"

"Count on it." He watched her walk into the bathroom as he dug his phone from his jeans' pocket and flipped it open. "Yeah."

She truly had a fabulous ass, toned with sweet curves. His hands still felt warm with the memory of it.

"Your companion," Stefan said carefully, crashing Griff back to Earth, "may be interested to know the morning's casualties did not include Sybil Harrison. Also, one of the young deputies asked me privately if he might've hallucinated. He thought you and Val helped him."

"We did. Good that he remembers. Maybe it'll change his views." Though Griff wouldn't count on it. "Somehow I doubt the rest of your news is as cheery."

"Only if ten dead, six critical, and five walking wounded, including Harrison, qualify as cheery. But everybody, living and not, made it home."

"Then it's cheerier than it might've been."

"I guess so." The silence seemed pregnant.

From the bathroom came the sound of the shower running.

At last, Griff said, "Just spit it out."

"Hell. There's no way to make this any prettier. You and Banning are now officially the Bonnie and Clyde of our world. She supposedly has been your slut—their word, not mine—for years, which explains the operations that went wrong on her watch."

Rage ignited in Griff's veins. His hand tightened until the phone creaked.

"It's amazing," Stefan continued, "the number of studly young dudes who're now admitting they tried to hit on her without success. Obviously, they failed because she was too busy putting out for you, the bad boy. Not, as previously assumed, because she lived for the job."

"Fucking bastards," Griff spat out.

After a moment, Stefan said, "They tried."

"Ha. Ha." But the grim attempt at humor relaxed a little of the tight, angry knot in Griff's gut. "Anything else?"

"Will says he's still digging, has some interesting stuff on demon portals he'll send to your email. Lorelei says no news is good news."

"Thank them for me when you can. I guess your wounded

must be stable if you can take a break to call me."

"Mostly." Stefan hesitated. "Harrison is out for Banning's ass, wants it in the most painful way possible."

"And so history repeats itself," Griff said softly, thinking of Corin, who'd wanted Griff's ass in the same way.

Griff hadn't told Valeria the whole story. Corin had tracked him down to arrest him. They'd fought, and Griff had nearly killed his friend. Desperate to avoid that, he'd agreed to surrender if he was guaranteed a chance to offer his proof, either in the obsidian seat or under ritual questioning by mages of his choice.

Corin had died trying to get him that chance.

"What happened to Corin wasn't your fault," Stefan said.

"Still have to live with it, though."

They signed off. Griff frowned at the phone. The scapegoating was bad enough, but now Valeria and Harrison paralleled him and Corin in the same pattern of friendship shattered, the same road to confrontation.

He scrubbed a hand over his face. Helping him was costing her a lot. She probably wished she'd never gotten mixed up with him or his fight.

Chapter 17

The knock on the bathroom door made Val jump. "Come in," she called over the sound of the water. "You really don't need to knock, you know."

The magic seethed with Griffin's worry, doubt, and anger. Something must've happened, something urgent. She pulled back the flimsy, gray-white plastic curtain. "What's wrong?"

He walked in, still naked and scowling as though he wanted to smash something. "That was Stefan."

"What's happened?"

He climbed into the tub and pulled her close, his hold gentle despite his fierce expression. "First, Sybil Harrison was in that battle this morning."

"What?" Val's heart lurched. "Is she all right?"

"She had minor injuries. The team this morning took casualties but left no one behind."

"That's something. What about the rest?"

"Ten dead, six critical, five with minor injuries, including Harrison, but no one's missing."

"Thanks." No use asking for names. They were people to her, ones she ached for, but he wouldn't have known many of them.

Now that he'd delivered his news, he looked uncertain. She could feel his anger but sensed it wasn't directed at her. "Why are you so pissed?"

He hesitated. "That can wait. I have something important to tell you." His grim eyes scanned her face, and he gripped her shoulders. "Harrison is blaming you. I'm sorry."

She needed a moment for the words to sink in around the stab of pain in her chest. Finally, she said, "From where she's sitting, she has a right to."

"We'll see that she learns the truth." He drew her close, and she leaned into the comfort of his warm embrace. "Corin Jacobs had been my friend since we were five. He was to me what Sybil Harrison is to you. I will help you fix this somehow."

"We'll fix it together." She glanced up at his solemn face. "Things always look worse when we're tired. Let's take a shower, get some rest." Val turned to grab the soap. "You'll have to crouch for the low shower head."

Griffin tugged her back against him, his erection hard and warm between her buttocks as he slid his palm over them.

"Nice," he said, his voice husky. "Very nice."

His touch sent tremors of pleasure through her. Val lost the soap.

"Yeah, about that," she said. Steam rose around them, a tamer warmth than the inner heat from his body at her back. She wiggled free to face him and set her hands on his shoulders. "You seem to like taking charge at these moments. Now, it's my turn and you're going to cooperate."

"Am I?" A crooked grin tugged at the corners of his mouth, and his eyes lit with mischief.

"Yes, if you want there to be more of these moments." Smiling, she let her hands roam over the sculpted contours of his body and delighted in the hitch of his breath, the quick contractions and releases of his muscles. "I promise you'll like it."

She pressed her mouth to the scars on his chest. His heart thudded against her palm.

"Yeah," he said hoarsely, hands gliding over her wet flesh. "I can go with that."

"Good." Val closed her fingers around his hard, smooth erection. Stroking him, she trailed kisses over the soft line of hair leading down from his chest, over his taut abs and lower.

His hands slipped into her hair, caressing. The slide of his fingers, the tiny jerks of his body, the hot craving flowing through the magic, all delighted her. Made her want more.

On her knees, she slid her lips down the hard length of him. She would never forget the throbbing of his flesh in her hand, the knowledge she could give him such intense pleasure. She took him in her mouth, and his pleasure rocketed through them both.

Again, their eyes locked and the heat in his gaze made her inner muscles clench.

"Valeria—sweet—" Warning edged his raspy voice. His eyes glazed.

Fondling him, she moaned in acknowledgment. Griffin shuddered again. He braced one hand on the wall, gripping the curtain rod with the other. His hips jerked. He choked out her name as his release flooded her mouth.

Val swallowed, milking him. Loving how she made him feel.

Breathing hard, he tugged her up for a long, deep kiss. "That's unbelievably sexy, the way you taste."

"Back at you."

He nipped her lower lip, and his arms closed around her. Long moments drifted by as they held each other in the steam.

"I like the way that feels," she said, "the contentment coming off you."

"Good, because you're the one who caused it." He rubbed her back with long, slow strokes, resting his cheek on her damp hair. Slowly, his body tensed.

"Now I feel your worry." She drew back to look at him. "What is it, Griffin?"

He ran his knuckles down her cheek. His mind gave off wary vibes, and his face was resolute. "I care for you and I know you care for me. You're sweet, you're beautiful, and you're loyal. If I have to stay in exile, I don't want you sharing it."

"Not your choice." If ever a man needed the healing power of love, this one did. Confessing her feelings would complicate a situation that was already a mass of tangles, but she couldn't help what she was about to say.

Taking a deep breath Val looked into his eyes. "I more than 'care for you.' I think I'm in love with you."

His face tightened. The flicker in his eyes, in the bond between them, might have been joy, but he locked his emotions down too fast for her to be sure.

Disappointment stung, but she'd expected it. She said nothing, waiting for his response.

After a moment, he drew a deep breath. His eyes were pained. "I can't say what you want to hear. What you deserve to hear."

Can't or won't? she wondered, but she kept her voice even. "I didn't ask you to. My feelings for you or yours for me, whatever they are, don't change what we have to do." She kissed him lightly.

He shook his head. "You'll be shire reeve again, and I'm still a fugitive."

"For now," she agreed, "but Griffin, brave, steadfast Griffin, at heart you're still a shire reeve, too."

His eyes widened in shock. She felt it break free of his pent-up emotions as the truth of her words struck home.

"Christ," he muttered, drawing her close again, "I can't believe you see me that way."

"I would bet everyone who knows you sees you that way."

Her strange new connection to him betrayed the pain his face did not. And probably let him see that her heart ached for the losses that had pushed him to this point.

She let her fingers drift along his jaw. "You carry a lot of guilt. A lot of grief. But I believe in the future, so let's take things one day at a time, as we agreed."

"Fair enough."

And better than nothing. She slid her arm around his neck, resting against him for a long moment, cherishing the contact.

"I should've waited," he said abruptly. When she looked up, into his tormented face, he continued, "When I told you I couldn't work within the system, I wasn't entirely honest. I did think about it, just not until it was too late. I should've watched Alden, built a case. Taken my time. I might've avoided having to kill my deputies, losing Allie, Corin, and Sykes."

"Maybe. But if you had, how many more mages would Alden have betrayed to their deaths? You might be standing at the Collegium now but wishing you'd taken the bastard down."

"I wish I knew," he muttered.

"Of course you do. And we will avenge our dead." She kissed him quickly. "We should finish this shower and get some rest."

"Nice word, 'finish.'" He tweaked her hard nipples and pleasure weakened her knees.

She clung to him to keep from falling. "That isn't what I meant."

"Yeah." He grinned at her. "Too bad your turn's up." Cupping her buttocks, he lifted.

She grabbed his shoulders, locking her legs around his waist for balance, and he drove into her. His power rose, warm and tender, to meet hers and the explosion at the end hit harder and rocked them longer. In the sweet, lazy aftermath, Val rested peacefully in his arms.

Carefully, Val lifted a slice of fully loaded pizza over her shoulder so Griffin could take a bite. Sitting between his thighs, leaning back against his warm chest while they fed each other pizza and Coke in bed was a little loony, not to mention messy if they weren't careful. After the tension of the last few days, though, they were entitled to indulge a little.

"Hey. Hold your hand still." He steadied it with a light grip on her wrist and bit into the pie. "Thanks," he mumbled.

"You're welcome." She twisted to grin up at him. "You know better than to talk with your mouth full."

One side of that firm, luscious mouth quirked up in a smile. He swallowed and licked tomato sauce off his lip. The gesture flicked heat between her legs, and his eyes glinted as he sensed her reaction. "Caught between the requirement of a thank-you and the food-in-mouth rule. I'll make it up to you later."

"Count on it." She slid a hand along the sheet over his thigh and smiled when the muscles tensed. "For now, though, I'll settle for some Coke, please."

She felt him lean sideways to grab the big cup off the nightstand. A moment later, he held it in front of her face. She reached for it, but he pulled it away.

"Uh-uh. I have to deal with your pizza-feeding technique, you can deal with my holding your Coke."

She rolled her eyes. "This was your idea, remember." But she set her hand gently on his wrist and let him tip the cup for her. When she tapped his hand, he lowered the drink.

"You know, I never ate pizza naked before."

"I know how to show a woman a good time." His palm flattened on her bare stomach and he kissed her shoulder lightly. Lips moving in a tickly, tingly caress against her neck, he murmured, "I could show you an even better time."

Val moved the pizza out of range and encircled his neck with her arm. "Well…"

His phone rang. The sound knotted her gut and wiped the smile off Griffin's face. Reluctantly, he grabbed the phone and glanced at the caller ID.

"Will," he said, holding it so she could hear, as he punched the button to take the call.

"Hey," Will said. "I have to make this fast. The weird stuff is escalating, in all the towns around the Okefenokee."

What weird stuff? Val asked Griffin through the mental link they'd formed.

Reanimated animal corpses, eerie lights at night, he replied.

Will continued, "There's definitely a dark influence at work. Increases in domestic violence and petty crime, too, though that, as I said, could just be from a hot, humid summer."

Griffin exchanged a grim look with Val. "What's Healey doing about it?"

"He sent reserve deputies to all those towns, including Wayfarer. They're checking out the reports, scrying for repeated or intense use of magical power, but also they're still looking for you. You both should stay out of that area."

"Got it," Griffin said, which was not the same as agreeing to stay away.

They signed off. He lay back on the pillows and held out an arm for her. "My appetite's gone now."

She settled against his side. "What can we do about this? Anything?"

"Nothing that isn't already being done." He stroked her arm absently, but frowned. His mind felt distracted, and no wonder. Wayfarer was his home.

"We'll figure it out," she said. "Somehow, we'll figure it out."

Shortly before dawn the next morning, Val and Griffin reached the flat rock by the stream, a spot she already considered theirs. They'd tested their bond earlier, found that it had a range of more than a mile. When they had time, they'd see how much farther it would reach. Now sunrise approached, and they had a dangerous scrying to perform.

The predawn air was cool. Val kept her chilled hands in her hoodie pockets while Griffin filled his silver bowl with pure, clean water.

Wiping the outside with the linen cloth, he nodded toward the gray eastern sky. "Sun's rising." He lifted his worried eyes to her face. "I wish this didn't have to be on you."

He set the bowl on the rock, in line with the rising sun, and warded the rock. A chilled breeze sent ripples over the surface and tousled his hair. He shoved it back absently.

Val shrugged despite her uneasiness. "We work with what we have." Blood magic required blood to uncover it, and the venom in his might taint the unmasking spell. At least he accepted that he couldn't protect her from this task.

She pulled her silver dagger out of her belt sheath, pricked her finger, and squeezed three large drops of blood into the bowl. The droplets formed pink ripples in the clear water.

She and Griffin turned to the horizon. Griffin uncapped the thermos, holding it ready. The purest power in nature was the first light of day. They would use it for this risky scrying.

The golden glow of morning cast silver ripples over the stream, spreading toward the rock. When the sun cleared the horizon, its light struck the bowl. Griffin tipped a small splash of tainted coffee into the water.

The brown liquid swirled around the blood trails. Val breathed on the water, sending power into it, and the surface took on a reddish glow. The bowl shook.

She kept her eyes on the water, but Griffin's hand caught hers. Strength flowed in the contact.

The liquid in the bowl swirled. Darkened. In the center

appeared a dark crystal orb that pulsed with purple-red fire. Around it drifted blackness deeper and colder than night. A stench of sulfur rose from the bowl. Her nose wrinkled.

Griffin's hand tightened on hers. From a great distance, he said, "Valeria. Honey."

She answered him. Or thought she did. The chill wafted into her, calling. Compelling.

Evil.

Tensing, she tried to draw back, but her body leaned closer to the pulsing glow. Someone called to her, as the orb's light flared, washing over Val's body with icy fingers that sickened her.

She screamed inside her mind and yet, craved its touch.

A strong, woodsy scent smacked her nose. Cedar and sage warred with sulfur, and the world spun.

The blackness vanished. She cried out in protest even as she shivered in relief. A crazy jumble of green, blue, and brown reeled across her vision, and she closed her eyes against it.

"Valeria, no. No." Griffin's voice held a panicked edge. "Come on, Valeria. Come back. Look at me, love."

She opened her eyes. Griffin sat cross-legged on the stone, cradling her in his lap. At his side, a bundle of herbs smoldered. The ward was gone.

Val drew a shuddering breath.

"It's okay." Holding her face against his shoulder, he muttered, "You scared the piss out of me."

"I'm cold." Queasy.

His arms tightened around her. With her face turned to the curve of his neck and shoulder, she inhaled his bay scent. "It's a summoning spell. It's really…vile."

"Yeah." He stroked her back slowly, soothing. "Take your time, honey."

"We don't have much time." Straightening so she could look him in the eye, she gripped his shoulders. "The summons is for midnight at the dark of the moon, four days away. In Wayfarer."

Chapter 18

The faces of Griff's friends in the town flashed through his mind—Marc, Miss Hettie, Sally at the Crystal Grotto, Ben at the newspaper. Damned if he'd stand by while some dark force preyed on them.

Now, though, Valeria needed to recover. She was shivering, and a cold current of fear ran through their bond, muted as though she tried to hide it.

He kissed her temple. Only something very powerful could affect a fully trained, fully powered mage this badly.

She burrowed against him. "Cold. So cold."

"We'll fix that." He stripped off his denim jacket and wrapped it around her. With no cell reception, he couldn't call Stefan and feared he might need to.

She huddled into the jacket, pulling it up around her ears. The bluish tint to her lips sent fear crawling up his spine. He rubbed her arms and legs, feeding her power. If only he had agate or carnelian to amplify her magic and strengthen her. "This is your last stab at something like this. Next time, it's my shot."

"We can fight about that when the time comes." She burrowed into his shoulder again. "Too tired to fight now."

Gradually, the shivering stopped. Valeria sighed, nestling against him. "Better now," she mumbled. "Sleepy."

For good reasons or bad? He stroked her cheek. "Look at me, sweetheart."

"Hm?" Blinking, she lifted her head to peer at him. Her eyes looked normal, more brown than green today, but clear, the whites unsullied.

He kissed her lightly. "Just checking. Let's go."

Clinging to him, she got to her feet. Still, her fatigue beat at his bones. Fighting that darkness had exhausted her. Good thing the car was just at the bottom of the trail. He scooped her up in his arms.

"I can walk." Her eyelids snapped open, then sagged immediately.

"Humor me."

"Mm-hm." She yawned and slid her arms around his neck. In moments, her deep, even breathing signaled that she slept.

His magical senses detected no one nearby. Griff held her close and translocated to the car. No way would he take her into the realm of this summons, but he had to go. Wayfarer was the closest thing he had to home, the people in it were his family. If evil was lurking, he'd do anything to keep the people he loved from it.

Icy darkness flowed around Val, caressing her body, stroking her soul with chilled fingers of dread. She fought to move. If she could just break free. Cry out. Anything.

If only she weren't so weak. Hunger gnawed at her soul. She looked down at herself, found her arms and legs gaunt.

Wasted. When had she last eaten? Too long ago to remember. Those who defied the darkness received no rewards, but she couldn't give in.

But she was so tired of fighting.

An icicle stabbed through her heart, and her mouth opened in mute torment. This was punishment for her resistance.

As before, her body arched, impaling her further, and she finally screamed, a shrill, agonized ripping of sound from her throat that went on and on and on, each twist of the icicle driving it higher as she helplessly clawed at the intangible thing piercing her chest.

Suffer, mage bitch. The voice sounded like cracking ice, but it trembled with power. *Suffer as all your kind will.*

Something grabbed her. She lashed out, but the blow had no strength. The darkness swirled around her, so cold—

Valeria. A man's voice. Strong. Warm. *I have you, honey. It's okay. You're okay.*

Struggling, she reached feebly for him but caught nothing. He would never find her. In all this darkness, how could he?

Despair bit at her soul like a serpent, and she wept, silently and without tears. She hadn't had water in so very long.

Valeria. I'm here. Look at me, love. Turn to me.

He can die with you. I'll devour you both, as my kind always has.

No, damn it. Valeria. He touched her hand at last. Her face. Her mouth. She couldn't see him, but she felt his warmth. Heard him say, "Come on, honey. Come back to me."

"Griffin," she gasped, knowing him at last.

"Yes." He sighed, a sound heavy with relief. "I'm here. Wake up, honey, please."

Light. At last, light.

She forced her eyes open. He leaned back against the headboard, cradling her in his arms. She let out a sob of relief, and the pain vanished. Real tears squeezed out of her eyes.

She wiped her face against his shoulder. This was real, he was real.

But the dream lingered in her bones.

Stroking her hair, he kissed her temple and kept his lips against it. "You with me now?"

She nodded. "It was so real. Too real." She swallowed hard, not liking where this was going, and held him tighter. "Visionary."

"Shit." For a long moment, his eyes searched hers. "I was talking to Stefan when you started whimpering, so I asked him to hold on. Let's see what he says."

When she nodded, he picked up his cell phone from the bed by her hip. He held it between them. "Stefan, she seems okay now, but that was one hell of a dream."

Stefan replied, "I heard your conversation. That's a magical problem, not medical. Will can help you with that better than I can. For tonight, burn cedar and sage and be sure the smoke goes in all corners of the room. Make valerian root tea."

"I don't carry that." Griffin arched an eyebrow at her.

Val shook her head. She didn't have it either.

"You can use commercial chamomile or peppermint tea," Stefan said. "Infuse healing energy in it before you drink it, both of you. Valeria should take a cleansing bath, using whatever healing herbs you have, and you should charge the water with golden power through the healing rune on your staff. If you have blue chalcedony, be sure it's magically charged and put it between your pillows to protect your minds in sleep."

Val squeezed Griffin's shoulder. "Did you tell him about the summons?"

"I told him everything. While you were out, Tasha called in to say they'd found tainted coffee, all of it containing summonses to Wayfarer, in five nonchain diners near the swamp, though not in Wayfarer itself."

"Are they okay? Did it affect them badly?"

"Two of them, yes, but they're okay now. Lorelei figured out a way to test it with quartz and she had no ill effects."

"That's good." Val nestled against Griffin's shoulder. "I wonder why they didn't find the tainted coffee in Wayfarer."

"Will thinks the demon servants, if that's what they were, probably didn't want to take someone from a small town where a missing person gets noticed. Anyway, the team shut those places down, took a couple of prisoners, only to have them spontaneously die."

"Well, that's rotten luck," she said. "And too coincidental."

"Agreed." His eyes hardened. "We're up against something big here."

Not to mention the problem in Wayfarer. "May I talk to Stefan?" When Griffin passed her the phone, she asked, "What's the status of the search around Wayfarer for us?"

As Griffin muttered, "Hell with that," his friend said, "One of the Collegium mages also happened across the bad coffee. Healey's sending as many veterans as he can muster to Wayfarer, with orders to scry for heavy magical activity, including the type a portal would cause. The town's crawling with deputy reeves now, so stay away from there."

Stefan paused. "And good luck with Griff on that one."

Judging by Griffin's set face, he would ignore any such advice. He held out a hand for the phone.

She thanked Stefan and passed it over.

As the two men signed off, she took Griffin's hand. Despite the tension in his body, his fingers curved around hers.

"Your home is threatened," she said, "and you want to defend it. You're tired of running, especially when people you care about need help. I get that. All of it. Really."

"Right now, I'm more concerned about you." His worried eyes searched her face, and he brushed back her hair. "How do you feel?"

"Tired. Hungry." Snuggling against his warmth, she added, "A little scared, partly because it seemed weirdly familiar. Did you hear it say it would devour our kind as its kind always had?"

He nodded. "It seemed familiar to me, too, but I can't place it."

"Old legends? Ancestral memory?" She turned her head into his neck, taking refuge in its warmth and familiar scent. Bay was not only a masculine herb but a protective one.

His arms tightened around her. "All of this fits with what Will said about Void demons. You were in a Void-like space."

They sat holding each other, trying not to think about what such a vision could portend, and she suddenly realized the room wasn't familiar. They'd checked out of the Rest Rite that morning. "Where are we?"

"The Holiday Chalet off U.S. 23. Used to be part of some castle-themed chain, by the look of it."

"Thanks for taking care of all that."

He tucked her head under his chin. "I'd like to take you someplace elegant—fancy bathroom, puffy beds, room service. Someplace paying in cash isn't acceptable and guests stay the whole night. But right now, I'll go find what Stefan ordered and bring back food. Or we can go down to the highway and eat. There're places busy enough to minimize the risk of being spotted."

"Let's go. A change of scene will help shake this off."

"I'll burn the cedar and sage around the room before we go, so we come back to something free of bad vibes."

"Good idea." His mouth pressed against hers and she opened to him, poured herself into the kiss.

He groaned, slanting his head to deepen the contact. When the kiss broke, she smiled at him. Relief flashed into his eyes.

"That's much better," she said. "How about we come back after dinner, do what the doctor ordered, and then make some good vibes of our own?"

"Sounds like a plan. But I want a date for that fancy hotel. You and me as soon as we can."

"Future thinking. I like it."

He kissed her again and tugged her off the bed. "Let's purge the room and go."

He hadn't actually said he would stay out of Wayfarer but they'd deal with that later.

Remembering the dream, she shivered. *What in God's name are we up against?*

Contentment required some adjustment, Griff decided, watching Valeria. Oblivious to the babble of voices around them and the movements of the dinnertime crowd to and from the salad bar, she closed her eyes and made approving noises over apple pie from the dessert rack.

He watched her and wondered what the future held for them. He didn't trust readily anymore, but he trusted her.

With a sigh, she opened her eyes. "This pie probably came out of a box, but it's sweet and gooey and just the thing I needed after the couple of days we've had." She cut off a bite-size piece. "Here, taste."

Because she was smiling and cupping her hand under the fork, he let her feed him the pie.

Smiling into her warm, happy eyes, he tasted cinnamon and nutmeg along with apple and surprisingly flaky crust. "Pretty decent. I thought you'd go for the chocolate, though."

"I don't like all that whipped cream where meringue should be. Want some more?"

"I'm good, thanks."

She wrinkled her nose at him. "Lucky for you, 'cause I was going to tell you to get your own pie. When it comes to desserts, my sharing capacity is limited."

"I'm wounded." Grinning at her, he used one finger to swipe a trace of pie filling from the edge of her plate and ate it.

This was normal, he suddenly realized. All over America, couples and families like the ones here went out, sat across laminate-covered tables set with cheap silverware, tasted each other's food, and teased each other. He'd almost forgotten what this was like.

With her, he could have pockets of normalcy, time just for them. God, he wanted it. But not if that meant she had to stay in exile with him. And there was still the matter of the venom in his blood.

She deserved to have her love returned, and even more, she deserved a love that wouldn't complicate her life. He couldn't give her that.

Her brow furrowed in a quizzical look. "Something wrong?"

"Nope. Just tired." To prove it, he smiled at her. "I like watching you eat."

"You envy my pie. I can tell." She waggled her fork at him.

The corners of her eyes crinkled when she smiled like that, and his heart felt about as solid as the pie filling. He wanted to stroke those lines, feel the joy radiating out of her eyes. Later, he would. In bed.

He kissed her hand, and they smiled at each other.

"Will also called while you were sleeping," he said. "He found several reports of disappearances in the swamp and nearby state forests. We think the diners are staffed with demon servants giving the tainted coffee to people already away from home, less likely to be missed right away."

"Smart."

"Yep. He says a portal orb like the ones commonly used to open the Void can accept only a few souls at a time. Otherwise it overloads, so they need to allow time for the priming, with the final priming done where it's going to be used. The summonses in the coffee at the other diners were for staggered times, all during the next four days, and all for Wayfarer. That probably means Wayfarer is where they plan to open the demon gate. So if we can figure out where they mean to do it, exactly, we may be able to stop the priming and destroy the thing before more people die."

"In Wayfarer. Griffin, I understand, but—"

He held up a hand to stop her from arguing. "Will deciphered that piece of paper you found in the diner cook's house. Those runes are like the dark counterpart of Ogham script, an ancient Celtic way of writing runes. If his translation is right, you found a chant that's used to help prime a demon portal with stolen souls. We have no choice."

Chapter 19

Griff eyed Valeria's set face. "You know you'd go if this was your town."

"I understand your need to help."

"But?" No matter what she said, he was going, but he'd hear her out first.

"You know already. There are Collegium mages all over the area. They're a danger to you, to us, and they can muster the numbers to handle a portal."

"If they're in the right place at the right time, and with no traitors in their midst. We can't count on that. I have to go, but I want you to stay out of there, wait somewhere safe."

"Be serious." She narrowed her eyes at him. "Besides, nowhere is safe for either of us right now. If you're determined to go, I'm going with you."

He shook his head. "Not acceptable."

"Precisely. You don't accept the idea that I'd take a big risk to watch your back. I feel the same way about you."

"I won't abandon them. Come on, let's take this outside."

He dropped a dollar on the table for the busboy and caught Valeria smiling at him. "What?"

"Most people wouldn't think about the busboy." She slid her hand into his.

He shrugged. Tipping was a habit, not a grand deed of chivalry, but he supposed she was right.

In silence, they walked outside.

"You don't trust the Collegium," she said as they crossed the parking lot, "but you know they won't let anything dark attack Mundanes. Don't you?"

"They don't care about that town the way I do."

"Undeniably not." She laid her hands on his chest, her eyes grave. "I don't want you to go, and you don't want *me* to, and neither of us has the power to stop the other. Though I have to point out that all your friends would be on my side."

"That's low." But knowing she was right turned his tone wry instead of angry.

"If the town weren't overrun with mages right now, I wouldn't argue. But they're looking for intense uses of magic. We can assume a portal would take a lot of magic, but what if you're in a fight and use a large amount of magic for that? Or to translocate several times? We don't know how they're defining 'intense.' So can't we make a deal—I won't go if you won't?"

"Even lower." He studied her for a long moment but saw no sign she'd yield. "What if I ask Will to keep me posted? As long as things in Wayfarer don't go south, I'll stay out. That's the best I can do."

"I'll take that." She kissed him gently. "Let's go find the supplies the doctor ordered and finish off our evening."

He opened the car door for her, closing it behind her.

She'd played him like a drum, his smart lover. Only his refusal to put her at risk had compelled him to agree to her terms. He should resent that, but knowing how much she cared blunted his temper. He climbed into the car and reached for the key. "That tea should be avail—"

Brilliant light flashed into his eyes. Sunlight. He wasn't in the car anymore but in a cemetery, wearing a suit and standing by a fresh grave. Hettie's name on the tombstone. *Fucking hell.*

The scene changed. Facing an eerily quiet mob, Marc retreated up the shelter steps, a silver cross held straight out in one hand and a Bible tucked against his heart in the other. The crowd flanked him, advancing with slow, determined steps. He stood in the doorway now, but they were close—so close—ghouls?

Shit, they had that dead-eyed look of the people in the diner. Reaching for Marc—grabbing him. Purple-red glowed around their fingers.

Purple-red fingers? Will hadn't mentioned— Silver light flared, silhouetting the attackers, and the scene changed.

In a modest living room, little Molly cowered behind her screaming, scrambling mother, Cindy, as a purple-eyed mob crashed through the door. A big man flung Cindy aside and grabbed Molly. He bared pointed teeth as the child shrieked.

"Griffin! Oh, God, Griffin!" Hands on his shoulders. Valeria, trying to help.

"No. Have to see." Struggling to hold the vision, he groped for her wrists, found them, shook her off. The steering wheel and dashboard showed through the scene.

Hettie stood in her front yard, firing her ancient shotgun as a ragged mob advanced on her. Overhead, the waning crescent moon cast an eerie light over the scene. She backed toward the porch steps ten feet away. Eight.

As the vision wavered, she passed Magnus's broken corpse. Blood and a black, tarry substance stained the retriever's golden coat, and his head lay at a nauseating angle. Hettie reached for the door, turned, and the mob lunged.

But where had they come from?

A barn flashed into his sight, one he'd painted. The one at the old Adams farm, a mile from Hettie's place.

The vision died. His heart pounded and his mouth felt dry, as though he'd run a long, desperate race.

Valeria's hand caught his in a hard grip warm with power and concern. "Hey." She peered into his eyes. "You okay?"

"Yeah, I just— Shit, the moon." He dug his phone from his pocket. "It's a waning crescent, same as the vision. Hettie's in danger. Maybe others are, too."

"What happened?"

He explained everything.

"You're about to tell me the deal's gone south, that you're going and you don't want me to go with you." Her steady gaze never wavered, and she sounded calm despite the circumstances.

"Right on all counts." He started the engine. The sooner he got on the road, the better.

She laid a hand on his. "The thing is, you need backup, and I need to help. If we're together, we can watch out for each other."

Unfortunately, he couldn't argue with that.

Peering down the rutted, overgrown lane, Val shivered. The sycamores and live oaks, with shadowy Spanish moss hanging from their branches, made the place look like a horror movie set. Knowing midnight would arrive in about twenty minutes didn't make it any better.

Griffin parked in underbrush just off the lane so no demon servants or ghouls would spot the car.

She climbed out into wintry air. In August? "Do you feel that? Cold power."

"Yeah. It's familiar."

As in her dream, though neither of them said so. They held their weapons ready, drawing magic into them, and crept down the long, bumpy drive. Her blade and the runes on his staff glowed faintly with the power influx.

Tires crunched on the dirt road. Val slipped back into the trees with Griffin as a green SUV drove down the lane and into the woods. They followed it.

It's getting worse, she noted, *the chill.*

For me, too. He caught her arm to stop her. *You had closer contact with that dark energy than I did. If you feel anything weird, anything beyond a chill, pull out.* Before she could protest, he added, *You can't watch my back if that thing's screwing with your head.*

Too true. *Okay.*

They rounded the bend behind the overgrown ruins of a house, and the chill deepened. The air felt like a late autumn evening, far too cold for August.

There's a little hollow back here, Griffin said as they passed a shadowy structure that was probably the barn he'd mentioned on the way here. *Feels like the chill's coming from there.*

The SUV that had passed them was parked just ahead.

A man and a woman, the pair from the diner, emerged.

They dragged out a nightgown-clad young woman. Made her walk between them.

Shit. Griffin's eyes narrowed. *That's Missy Jones, from the bakery.*

The girl's eyes were wide, and her mouth worked furiously, as though she fought to speak.

Val glanced at Griffin, whose face had gone taut with anger.

His fury echoed in their bond. *My team said Wayfarer was clean. How the hell did Missy drink that crap?*

Val had no answer, squeezed his arm instead.

The breeze pressed the young woman's nightgown against her body. Shivering, either from the chill or from the terror coming off her in waves, she walked mechanically between her guards. Big tears welled in her eyes and ran, unwiped, down her pale cheeks. At her sides, her fingers curled into claws, as though she desperately struggled to move them.

Her guards forced her into the trees, apparently going downhill. Following, Val and Griffin had to deepen their screens, muffling the sounds of their footsteps.

Other people moved through the trees alone or in small groups. One trio marched a light-haired teenaged boy, looking about sixteen, before them. The youth, too, lurched when he walked, fingers clawing uselessly, in an apparent struggle against the force driving him forward.

Todd Claypool. The bakery delivery boy, Griffin supplied. *Shit. I'd bet he and Missy went on a delivery run together, stopped somewhere and were grabbed. Or drugged with something more immediate than the coffee.*

With Griffin in the lead they trailed their quarry down the hill, to a shadowy clearing the sliver of moon did little to illuminate. As people reached the bottom of the hill, they formed a loose circle around a large, flat stone.

An altar, and not to anything good. To Val's mageborn eyes, the miasma of death around it hung dark and ominous and nauseatingly clear. *I count fifteen*, she told Griffin. *Plus the prisoners.* Too many for the two of them to take out in one blast, even though they were nearly at full power.

The guards pushed the woman and the boy to the altar, sliced into their prisoners' palms, and rubbed the wounds over the rough stone. That had to hurt, yet despite increased shuddering, neither prisoner made a sound.

Griffin, we can't just sit here.

No, he sent, and his anger pulsed in the thought, *but let's see what they mean to do.*

In the circle below, the guards pushed the shaking, weeping captives to their knees. A man stepped out of the circle a large sack in his hands. From it he pulled a basketball-size orb of dark crystal. Purple-red light pulsed inside it and cast a vile glow over the group in the dell.

Val swallowed against bile. *That's what I saw in the scrying.* She glanced at Griffin and caught his grim nod.

The man dropped the sack. With the orb in one hand, he circled the kneeling prisoners, then grabbed Todd's hair and yanked his head back.

"This one first." His words vibrated with malevolent power. He set the orb in the bloody smear on the altar.

Work your way down and to the left, where Missy is, Griffin directed. *You take her. I'll take Todd. When I fire, jump in, grab her, translocate to the car with her. No checking for me, no waiting, no close fighting if you can help it. Grab and go.*

Reluctantly, she nodded. Below them, the leader's head

lifted. He sniffed the air, then stared straight at them with reddish eyes set deep in a pale face. Val's heart lurched. Power washed up the hill and over their screens.

With his staff at the ready, Griffin glanced at her. The back of her neck itched as he drew power for additional concealment from the trees and the creatures of the woods and soil.

Val drew power into her blade. At least the swamp's nearness would feed their magic.

The boy's guards forced him back across the altar with his head by the orb. A woman sauntered toward him.

The leader turned to watch as the woman straddled the boy. She pressed Todd's bloody palm to the glowing orb and pulled a long, serrated knife from her skirts raising it high above the boy's chest.

Shit, no more time. Griffin lifted his staff, aiming at the knot of people by the altar. The power building in the weapon crackled across Val's skin as she tightened her grip on her sword.

Go, Griffin said, and fired.

Chapter 20

Val materialized behind the kneeling girl—Missy, Griffin had called her—as his dazzling silver bolt struck the leader. The man reeled into the woman straddling the boy, knocking her aside. They fell in a tangle.

The black orb on the altar pulsed with a sick, purple-red light. Waves of dark power rolling off it raised the hair on Val's neck and arms. The chill iced her blood.

For an instant, she saw herself on that altar, as her soul screamed in agony and something dark and formless rose from the orb.

A scrawny woman grabbed Val's arm, and adrenaline banished the chill. Striking back with power, she saw the woman's reddish eyes, a sign of earthly demon possession, just in time to bite back the instinctive *morere*. Unfortunately, killing a host only set a demon free to roam.

Val blew out power, bowling over three of the demon-eyed crowd. The boy, Todd, crumpled to the ground, panting and wild-eyed. Over him stood Griffin, whose face looked pale in the pulsing light. Had that thing mentally attacked him, too?

No time to worry about that. She blasted back a stout man and woman. As she drew power from the surrounding woods, she used the flat of her blade to knock back a thin, red-eyed man.

A female ghoul leaped at her. Val slashed a backhanded, diagonal blow to gut her, caught the scent of ammonia. Demon hosts and ghouls together were a damnable development.

Missy's guards wheeled toward Griffin, hands rising, and lost their hold on her. She screamed. Val grabbed the back of her nightgown.

A burly man rushed Griffin. Griffin pivoted to block a dagger strike as another man, slim and balding, rushed him from the other side. *Damn it.*

But she had to go while it was clear. Lips tight, Val knocked back the balding man with a snap kick, then flashed away with Missy.

They appeared behind the car, in the trees a few feet from the road. Still shrieking, Missy struck out at Val, at the air, at herself.

Val grabbed her, slapped a hand over her eyes, and fed in power. "*Dormi*," she ordered.

As the poor girl collapsed, Val caught her, easing her to the ground. Her face bore tear streaks and, at the corner of her mouth, a dribble of saliva. Still breathing hard, Val dug a tissue out of her pocket and wiped Missy's face. Maybe waking up safe would calm her.

Grab and go, Griffin had said. He should've returned by now. If he'd been overwhelmed, he could be lying on that vile altar now.

She opened her mind and reached, carefully so she didn't

distract him. There he was, alive but under attack.

Val couldn't help him. A mage's first duty was the protection of Mundanes. She'd learned that along with the alphabet and had always lived by it.

Griffin also held to that, even when the odds were against him, even when answering a call for help or taking in a bunch of homeless people could draw attention and jeopardize his hiding place. No wonder she'd fallen in love with him.

She had to do her duty, even when it ate at her heart. So many things could go wrong in that clearing, not least the numbers tide. *Watch your back*, she thought, and was filled with dread when only silence echoed in her mind

There're far too many, Griff thought, blasting back a ghoul trio as they charged him. He tried to grab the crystal orb, but Todd clung, shivering, to his leg with ghouls and dead-eyed Mundanes rushing them from all sides. He couldn't even get a clear space to translocate.

At least Valeria had followed orders and should be safe now.

He blasted another two. Eerie cold hit the back of his shield, and the stink of brimstone blew around him. From the orb? Or one of those people?

He turned, shot out a wide-spread blast, and rammed the staff into someone attacking him from behind. The crystal fell off the altar, out of reach. Maybe he could come back for it. He had to move. It was now or never.

He locked his free hand on to Todd's neck and flashed out.

They arrived beside the car. A gasp drew his attention left.

Valeria hurried toward him, her face drawn in the faint light. "I was so worried," she said.

"Me, too." He wanted to grab her, kiss her and feel her warm, uninjured body in his arms, but they still had to secure the orb. He eased Todd's grip from his leg. "How's Missy?"

No sense mentioning the weird moment of déjà vu when he'd seen Missy and Todd by the altar. That sequence of visions, just before he met Valeria, had been ominous, but he couldn't let that stop him from protecting his town.

"Sleeping," Valeria said, with emphasis that implied she'd put the girl out. "Pretty shaken up, but I don't think she's hurt. At least, not physically. She's in the car."

"Good. I'm going back, see if I can get that crystal."

"Griffin, no—"

"Take them to the shelter in Wayfarer, before those things come after us. Do it, Valeria." Without giving her a chance to argue, he flashed back into the clearing.

As soon as he arrived, he shielded. The demon hosts were scattering, but that purple-red light through the trees had to be from the orb. It silhouetted the running man who carried it. The light also gave Griff a target. Drawing power from the swamp, he fired a hard blast. The figure stumbled.

The others stopped and turned. He had to get that orb and get the hell out of there. He risked translocating to where the man he'd blasted lay. Griff checked him. He was unconscious, not an obstacle.

The orb had fallen a few feet away. Now he had to figure out how to touch the damned thing. This close, its influence ran ice down his back and bile through his throat.

Footsteps behind him. Demon hosts coming. No time.

Drawing as much energy from the swamp as he could hold, he picked up the orb. A thousand icy daggers stabbed into his flesh. Gritting his teeth, he translocated back to the end of the drive.

There sat Valeria in the car, with Missy asleep on Todd's shoulder in the back.

Griffin scanned the driveway for enemies.

"We're clear. Get in."

"Not with this thing. I'll meet you at the shelter."

"We're not having that fight now. Get in."

A sudden inrush of power crackled in the air. Mages, two, four, more, too many to count, materialized into the driveway. Each held a sword or pike rippling with magical energy and pointed at him. At Valeria.

Her horrified eyes met his, and he could no longer deny the truth stabbing into his heart.

"I love you," he said, whipping power around her, and flashed her as far away as he could.

"No!" Val appeared beside a deserted road as a fist of fire crushed her chest, stealing her breath.

The pain came from Griffin. The mages were firing on him, killing him, and everything in her screamed. She had to stop them. Had to help.

Struggling for air, desperate to stay conscious, she fell to her knees, then crumpled to the ground. Val dug her hands in the dirt to fight the pain that had her knees drawing up to her chest and tears flooding her face.

If she could help—use their bond to somehow feed him power…*I love you*, he'd said.

Her heart broke and she choked back a sob.

I love you, too, Griffin. I love you. She put what power she could behind the words. Love was a power, too.

As though a switch had flipped off, her awareness of him vanished. Gasping, with her breath coming in sobs, Val pushed herself up. The echoes of pain still throbbed in her bones. If it was that bad for her, how horrible, how much worse, had it been for him? Was he dead? Or behind wards?

Please, not dead. If he'd died, wouldn't she have felt that?

He'd shifted her clear of the mage perimeter. Why hadn't he come with her? Because he couldn't translocate himself very far with the orb? Or because he wanted to be sure she was clear?

Please, please, let her not be the reason. She couldn't stand being the reason if he died.

Todd and Missy, at least, were safe. The mages would see to that.

She wiped her face with the heel of her hand. Aside from the cell phone in her pocket and the dagger at her belt, she had nothing, but she'd better get under cover fast. She had to stay free to help Griffin. The Horus pendant would deflect scrying, but she screened herself to make doubly sure.

Executions traditionally occurred at midnight, and that time had passed. Hurrying into the trees, she glanced at her watch. Twelve forty-three, so she had a little less than twenty-four hours to work. Was that enough time? She couldn't rescue him alone, but maybe she could with his team's help.

Unless the mages had already killed him. *Oh, please, no.*

Not even being tied up in the ghouls' car trunk had made her feel so helpless, so frightened.

Better to focus on what she could do than on the very bad odds against rescue. She had none of his network's numbers. Calling Stefan or Will via the Collegium line could expose them.

But Griffin had said Marc Wagner was part of the team, and she did know the name of the shelter in Wayfarer. Directory assistance would have the number. Val pulled her cell phone out of her pocket.

Griff surfaced, pain throbbing in his bones. A grunt escaped before he gritted his teeth against the agony. He tried to breathe through it.

Of course, surfacing at all was a surprise. He'd expected kill shots. Would've preferred them. Instead, the mages had used stun shots that battered his body but left mild, if widespread, energy burns that only delayed the inevitable.

The high security cell hadn't changed since he'd last put someone into it. Black walls, bespelled iron over steel, recessed lights. Warding tingled on his skin. A shackle of ensorcelled iron anchored his left ankle to the wall and stifled his magic. If any cell was escape-proof, this one was.

His chest tightened painfully, and he drew in a slow breath. There was so much he still wanted to do.

At least Valeria was free and she knew he loved her.

I love you, too, Griffin, she'd thought to him. *I love you.*

Hearing that again was worth the agony, worth surviving to face the extremely nasty proceedings ahead. At least he could die knowing a woman like Valeria Banning could love him.

Loss raked his heart, and he drew a sharp breath against it. He'd known better than to hope, after all. But it was ironic that he should die only after finding something, someone, he wanted so very badly.

He would do what he could, take any chance, to make Valeria look like an innocent. Maybe he could convince the

Council he'd manipulated her. That would piss her off, but he'd sworn she would have her life back.

Stay safe, he thought to her, though he couldn't sense her. The wards surrounding the Collegium likely blocked contact with anyone outside them. Good thing the Council didn't know about his bond to her. What they couldn't see, they couldn't use to hurt her.

He could only hope his death wouldn't flow through that bond and harm her. Surely the mages would ward the site of his execution. They wouldn't want to risk a last, wild burst of magic hurting any of them.

At least Todd and Missy would be safe. Unless the car's engine had blown when he flung magic inside it to snatch Valeria. But the mages would've contained the damage, protected the Mundanes. He could probably trust them for that much, and, unless they were all in league with the traitor, to contain the orb. He and Valeria had accomplished something important at the end, shutting down that portal.

Maybe knowing he loved her would be some consolation. Or maybe it would make the loss worse, but he'd had to tell her. In that last moment, knowing he would never see her again, he couldn't hold back the words.

He'd wanted to nail that bastard traitor himself, exact justice for his dead deputies. For the friends who'd died because of him. But Will would see it through. His friends would help Valeria if she let them, Stefan especially.

"Bastard's awake," a gravelly voice said outside the cell. "I'll fix that."

"Leave him alone, Mitch," a woman ordered. "We're doing this by the book."

Mitch. Corin's brother?

"Too bad we didn't get Banning, too," another male voice muttered.

"That stupid slut," a deeper male voice said. "Bitch has been holding out on us. What a waste of those round tits and long, sweet legs. That ripe mouth, made for sucking—"

"Could you be any more crude, Parker?" a different woman demanded as Griff bit down a surge of fury.

"Hey," the man answered, "mage woman, any woman, spreads her legs for a murdering traitor, she's no better'n a whore."

"So she's an idiot," one of the women replied. "Doesn't make her a slut."

"No," someone else said, "but the way Healey and the Council saw them going at it at her lake house does."

Griff winced. *Shit.* He'd damaged Valeria's reputation more than he'd realized.

"Can it," Stefan's voice said, "and get back to your duties. You can speculate on your off hours."

He wasn't their direct boss, but he was a councilor. Muttering, the deputy reeves dispersed, except for the two women guarding the entrance.

The door ward dropped, and Stefan stepped through, his face bland. The ward hummed as it rose again behind him.

Because of the guards outside, Griff held back his smile of greeting. At least he'd have one last talk with Stefan.

Stefan sat by him on the bunk. "Mr. Dare, I'm here to check you as part of the admission process. Let's get those burns tended."

Griff cocked an eyebrow at him. "Kind of a waste of effort. Considering."

"Procedure," Stefan said crisply. In a low voice that

wouldn't carry, he said, "Griff, I'm sorry I ever got you into this."

"Not your fault," Griff murmured, peeling back the gray coverall. "Believe it, Stefan."

Shaking his head, Stefan touched Griff's shoulder, and healing energy flowed over the raw skin, cooling and soothing. "Sit and let me do this."

"How long was I out?"

"About five hours. It's almost dawn." In a soft voice, he added, "I'm also feeding you power. You need all you can muster. They plan to put you under ritual questioning without letting you answer the charges against you first. We had a battle in the Council about that, and about your right to a lawyer under the *Caudex Magi*."

"Nobody would take my case anyway," Griff said, but an icy fist twisted in his gut. The nasty vision of him in that chair was coming true. The mages would chain him to the obsidian seat of justice with councilors probing his mind. He would either break and betray his friends, or hold, and have his brain scrambled.

He wouldn't betray his friends.

"Guess they see no reason to bother with procedure since I'm already convicted."

Stefan snorted. "If the three chicken-shit abstainers had voted our way, you would have your chance."

"Not a surprise. They're politicians." But a tiny corner of Griff's soul could still feel the sting of disappointment, of disillusionment, that the organization he'd served failed to live up to its principles. "Thanks for trying, though."

"Had to take a shot."

"What happened to the portal, to the people it ensnared?"

"Missy and Todd are safe at home. The captive souls have been liberated to pass to the next plane." Stefan shook his head. "Tragic for them."

"What about the people summoned for the dark of the moon?"

Stefan shrugged. "Gerry Armitage thinks destroying the orb kills the summons. Either way, we'll know soon enough. There's a guard there now, but the people in that circle escaped. The mages were too busy with you to catch them. They're not a current threat. For now, Griff, your situation is priority. Lorelei's here. Will and the rest are inbound. Val says she loves you and you're to hang on. She has a plan."

Valeria. Griff's heart jumped, and his throat closed. To see her one more time, to touch her, but no use wishing for that. "Tell everyone to stand down. It's too dangerous for them to be here, especially if I crack under questioning."

Stefan raised an eyebrow. "I'm sure they'll pay as much attention to that advice as you always have."

"Bite me." Griff smiled as he said it. He'd been damned lucky to have Stefan and the others as friends. "Seriously, no stupid chances."

"No stupid people involved." Along with the healing energy, Stefan fed him power. "Out of your hands, bro. Park the control freak and trust us to be smart. Will says to tell you, if Val's plan fails, he and Tasha have a backup."

"Magic can't even dent these walls."

"Will says C-4 might." Stefan raised his voice to add, "All done here."

"Thanks." Griff tugged the coverall shut. "Stefan," he murmured, "you have to stop them. When I'm gone, they're the only hope—"

"Dr. Harper, what are you doing?" Gene Blake, chief councilor of the Collegium, glared through the door ward's blue sheen.

Griff's fists balled. He'd like to pound Blake for the pain he'd caused Valeria.

"I'm tending my patient." Stefan gave Blake a cold stare.

"We need him for questioning," Blake said. "You're making him better able to resist."

Stefan shrugged. "Under the *Caudex Magi*, only those fit in mind and body can undergo ritual questioning."

"This is Griffin Dare, for God's sake, a cold-blooded killer. Nobody gives a damn. They want him dead."

"Very likely." His voice hard, Stefan rose. "They may not give a damn about him, but they care about us. About who we are. If we throw away the rules because they're inconvenient, what protection do any of us have?"

"Bullshit."

Gerry Armitage stepped into view. "Ease up, Blake."

"Properly healing even minor wounds requires rest to complete." Stefan spoke to Gerry, not to Blake.

"Too damned bad," Blake snapped. "We're taking him now." The ward dropped. Mitch Jacobs, Corin's brother, and three other burly deputy reeves stalked through the portal.

Stefan stepped in front of Griff. "I won't certify—"

"Doc. It's okay." Griff tugged him aside. He had to protect Stefan, keep him safe to carry on the fight. "Now or later makes no difference to me."

At least he had a fresh infusion of power. That should help him hold, protect his friends. Go with his head high.

He turned a level, cold look on Blake. "We all know where

this train stops. No sense prolonging the journey. I waive any right I have to a delay on medical grounds."

"So you consent?" Blake's eyes gleamed as the guards moved in with their shackles.

"I don't consent, but I know it doesn't matter since I'm already condemned. We may as well get this part done." While the power infusion from Stefan was fresh.

The guards drew his hands behind his back, snapped the shackles on his wrists. Another traded the wall shackle for a hobble, but with a chain long enough for shuffling steps.

I love you, he thought, even knowing Valeria wouldn't hear it through all the Collegium's wards.

The guards pushed him out, and he held on to the image of her. She was a gift beyond measure, a reason all by herself for him to stand firm. And he would. He would protect her.

No matter what it cost him.

Chapter 21

Standing room only, Griff noted as the guards chained his arms behind the ritual grotto's ancient obsidian seat. How many of the two hundred or so watchers had come to have their hatred confirmed? How many might actually have open minds? He would probably never know.

The ceiling was fifty feet over his head. On three sides around him rose tiers of granite benches, all full now, with the doors behind the highest row. Below the ceiling, a mural ran around the chamber, depicting the heroic deeds of ancient mages. He'd been in this room for his ritual fledging, his acceptance as a full mage. For his appointments as a deputy reeve and then, five years later, as shire reeve.

Tonight he'd be back here to die. Unless they decided to roll right into that.

Dread rolled ice down his back. He forced himself to breathe. As a distraction, he surveyed the room. Torches in a chandelier overhead provided the only light and cast eerie shadows over the spectators' faces.

Down the wall at his back trickled a waterfall. Earth, air,

fire, and water, the four base elements, made up all the room's furnishings. No synthetics here. He planted his bare feet on the chair's base and reached into the earth to ground himself as best he could with the shackles stifling his power.

Most of the Council filed into the first row, six feet above the dirt floor. Stefan looked grim, Loremaster Gerry Armitage solemn, a few others neutral. Healey gave Griff a hard stare. The rest of the Council looked at him with undisguised hatred.

If only he knew which of them was the real traitor. Blake and Otto Larkin walked down to the earth floor and stood facing the assembly. "We're met for the ritual questioning of condemned murderer and traitor Griffin Rhys Dare. As is our law, I, as chief councilor, will be one of the questioners. High Councilor Larkin was chosen by lot to be the other."

The two men walked to obsidian squares set on either side of Griff's seat.

Griff's heart hammered in his chest. He fixed his eyes on a point at the back of the chamber. Control was everything. He had to keep it or Valeria and his friends were doomed, and there would be no one to expose the ghouls' ally.

He drew a deep, slow breath, blanking his thoughts, in the instant before Blake and Larkin each gripped one of his shoulders. Their two minds pushed at his. He let them past the first barrier. No point wasting his strength on the outer shell. Instead, he drew what earth power he could, summoned fog in his mind, and spun it into a wall around his thoughts.

The councilors didn't dillydally with questions but went straight to probing. They wanted his team. His friends. He let them find the innocents, the town, the ones they wouldn't hurt. Not Marc.

As though sensing a weak spot, Larkin pressed. *He's holding back. Someone in that town knows something.*

Griff focused on the wall of fog.

Valeria, Larkin snapped.

Griff couldn't help it, couldn't block it fast enough. A flash of her face, of his love for her, slipped out. *Shit.*

Blake and Larkin attacked that slippage.

Griff slammed his walls up. The questioners' power built until his skull felt too full, pressure making the bones throb. Their hands tightened on his shoulder.

Sweat trickled down the side of his face. They already figured he and Valeria were lovers, but he wouldn't give them anything else. Maybe they hadn't caught her love for him. Or their bond.

Something there, Larkin sent. *Something more.*

Nothing, Griff thought. Blank. All blank. He fixed his eyes on the wall, his mind on the image of Merlin over the door. Tried to steady his breathing.

He has helpers, Blake thought. *We have to root them out.*

The pressure in Griff's head spread down his neck and into his chest. His heart spasmed.

I'm no traitor. He pushed the thought at them, hurled it against their attack with all the certainty he could muster. *A councilor is.*

At least they had to feel his belief, not just hear his words. Larkin paused. A ripple of surprise, almost belief, leaked out of him.

Bullshit, Blake snapped. His fingers bit into Griff's shoulder.

Blake slammed his mind against Griff's, and Griff's failing power faltered. Desperate, he tried to draw more.

No go. Shackles blocked it.

He tasted sweat on his upper lip, ammonia on his tongue. So much for that power infusion.

Don't let him con you, Otto. We have to break this murdering bastard.

There was a flash of something in Blake's mind—ghouls, in a meeting with him—then suddenly, fear and guilt flared as Blake shielded his mind. So Blake was the fucking traitor, but Griff couldn't focus on that. If he dropped his walls, tried to reach Larkin, the questioners would rip into his mind and find everything. Hellfire and damnation—

Remember those he killed, Blake urged, and Larkin's resolve firmed.

Power like a sledgehammer crashed against Griff's mental walls. A wave of agonizing pain rolled through his head. He choked, barely held, his body arching in his tormentors' hold. His blood roared like floodwaters in his ears, trickled from his nose.

The pain increased. Blinding. Lancing through his body. Cramping his shoulders, his legs, his feet. He gritted his teeth. His fists clenched on the chains as he put everything he had, everything he was, into his mental walls.

He could feel his fate now. This was the end.

At least the pain would end, too. And he would win. They would break his mind, not his will.

His friends, his love, would be safe.

Valeria's face jumped into his mind. She would be his last sane thought. With his love for her bracing him, he waited.

Gradually, he realized he could still think. Still had his

walls up. Could hear and recognize his ragged breathing, his pounding heartbeat.

From far away came Blake's voice, "What do you mean, you let his lawyer in? He's not entitled—"

"It was that or the Glynn County Sheriff's Department." Payne's voice. "And the *Savannah Crier*. And the Wayfarer *Oracle*. They had a report we kidnapped this bastard. Damn it, Gene, listen. We let the lawyer in or half the Mundane world pries into our business. And the lawyer's threatening to go to the All-Shires Council."

"The murdering son of a bitch isn't entitled to a goddamned lawyer," Blake roared.

"Yes, he is." A man's cold, hard voice came from the room's upper reaches. "Under the *Caudex Magi*, he is, just as he was six years ago, and that's the last time you insult my wife."

Insult his wife?

It couldn't be.

Panting, Griff forced his eyes open. Sweat trickled into them. It stung, blurring his vision. Six years had carved new lines in the tall man's face, but Griff couldn't mistake the strong, clean-cut features so like his own or the gray eyes looking coolly down at him.

In the doorway behind the uppermost seats stood Stuart Dare, attorney at law in both the mage and Mundane worlds. Griff's father.

Maybe they'd scrambled his brain after all, Griff thought, and he was hallucinating. He couldn't be walking through the Collegium hallways with his father, who seemed as oblivious to the six-person squad of reeves escorting them as he did to Griff's shackles.

Gerry Armitage had asked Griff if he accepted his father's representation. Griff's need to protect his family had given way before the plea in Stuart's usually stern eyes. Griff had said yes, so here they were.

In a charcoal-gray suit, white shirt, and navy blue silk power tie, with his bland, semibored courtroom face on, Stuart might've been pacing the halls of the U.S. District Court in Atlanta instead of walking beside his condemned son.

There was more gray in the black at his temples now, and Griff got no vibe from him at all. But he'd come. He'd calmly handed Griff a linen handkerchief, just like the ones he'd always carried, to wipe the blood from his nose and made the guards leave Griff's hands free until he finished.

Griff's throat felt suspiciously tight. He cleared it. "Dad, what are you doing here?"

"I've warded a room so you can meet with your legal team in privacy. Best not to talk until then."

Legal team? How had he acquired a legal team? Hettie was a lawyer, but she didn't know his dad or know about the Collegium. Or hadn't, anyway. This must be Valeria's doing, the plan Stefan mentioned.

Thank you, love, he thought, trying not to send her the thought. Why bother, with wards between them? At least she'd stayed away. It was far safer here for his dad than for her.

They rounded a corner into a short hallway, and Hettie—looking very lawyerly in a navy-blue pantsuit and carrying a tan leather briefcase—rose from her seat by a doorway at the corridor's end. When she stood, he could see the slender, dark-haired woman sitting by her. Smiling a welcome even though she couldn't see him, his sister, Caro, also stood.

Griff's heart took a weird leap that managed to be happy

and painful at the same time. He grinned at Caro and Hettie.

His father caught his arm. "Easy, son. Almost there."

Only then did Griff realize he'd been about to break into a run that would've sent him straight to the ground because of the shackles.

"I believe you know Ms. Telfair," his dad continued. "Caroline is our legal assistant."

Valeria had given him one hell of a gift. He hadn't thought he'd see his family again, but here were Dad and Caro.

The group surrounding him reached the doorway. Hettie eyed the nearest reeve, a short, muscular young woman, with disfavor. "You're blocking me from my client, Officer. Move it."

"Take those shackles off," his father ordered. "I need his hands free so he can write."

And hug his sister, Griff thought. And Hettie. And, if his dad would permit it, his chief counsel.

"Leg ones stay on." A tall reeve behind him freed his hands.

"If they must," Stuart said.

The circle of reeves opened a path to the doorway, and Hettie eased Caro in front of her.

"Hey, sis." Griff relished the words.

With a gasp, she flung herself at him. He caught her, lifting to bring her head to his shoulder, and held her as her arms locked around his neck.

"Hey, Goofball," she said into his collar.

As he laughed, she ran her hands over his face, "seeing" him. "You need a shave." She kissed his cheek, hard, anyway.

He planted an equally emphatic kiss on her forehead. "You cut your hair. I like it."

She smelled of roses. She'd always smelled of roses. The memory threatened to fracture his control. He held her tightly before he set her down, keeping an arm around her.

Hettie kissed his other cheek. "Let's go in, boy, and get started while your daddy tends to some procedural issues."

"What procedural issues?"

Stuart raised a jet eyebrow. "The sort you used to call 'lawyer crap.' I've got this, Griffin. You go do your part."

"Yes, sir," he replied, but he couldn't help grinning. Nobody was better than his dad. Maybe, just maybe, he had a chance to live through this.

Waiting in the conference room, praying Griffin's father succeeded in stopping the Council's torture, Val tried to steady her breathing. Griffin would be furious that she had come.

Tough.

She drew a painful breath. They were mind-bonded lovers. That made them mates under mage law if they both acknowledged the bond, according to what his dad had told her earlier. If Griffin expected her to bail when he was in trouble, he really didn't understand her at all. She couldn't live with hanging back when his life was in danger.

The door swung open. He stepped inside, and love flooded her. His shock at seeing her reverberated in the bond as she forgot everything but how glad she was to see him alive and sane. She sprang into his arms.

I love you, she told him as their mouths fused and their bodies strained together. Now that they were both inside the Collegium wards, nothing blocked their bond.

I love you, too. He lifted his head abruptly, stepping back even though he kept his grip on her arms.

Their bond vibrated with shared desire, with his longing to lay her down on the table and seal the words they'd said. But he frowned at her. "You shouldn't be here."

So they were down to it already. But she couldn't hold back her grin at seeing him. Touching him. She finger-combed his damp hair from his face. "Miss Hettie, didn't I tell you he would say that?"

"I believe you did." Hettie gave him one of her decisive nods. "Val came to me first, knowing I'd want to help you, no matter what your father decided. When she told me the truth about you, it really wasn't much of a shock. More like 'Oh, of course.'"

Smiling, she added, "Val orchestrated this whole thing, including the media nuisance."

"I stayed behind when your dad went to get you," Val said, "because I knew you would kick up dust about my being here. I didn't want us dealing with that out there."

"Kick up dust"? Try a fucking mountain. His eyes narrowed. He shot her a steely look she met with a level, unyielding one.

If you thought I'd desert you, she told him, *you're nuts.*

"I like her, Griff," Caro volunteered before he could reply. "So do Dad and Rick. Mom's in L.A. for a gallery show of her sculptures, but she ditched that and is grabbing the first plane back. She sends you her love."

"This isn't a family reunion. This is serious."

"We all get how serious this is," Val said. "That doesn't make us any less happy to see you, especially since you're still alive."

"You think I'm not glad?" Despite his scowl he pulled her against him, running his hands down her arms in a caress. "I would've given anything to hold you just once more, but I didn't flash you out of that circle so you could walk into a damned cage."

"I'm not walking into one. Any guilt I have is dependent on yours, on my 'aiding and abetting' you, as your dad expressed it. If you aren't guilty, my love, I'm not either. And we both know you're not."

He shook his head but apparently realized there was no going back. She had something important to ask him, anyway. "Speaking of your getting me away, you could've gone, too. Why didn't you?" They had more immediate problems, but she needed to know.

"My power was down from shielding against the orb, and I knew I'd need a lot to shift you because we weren't touching. I didn't know how big a perimeter the mages had established. I didn't want to risk not sending you far enough."

"I knew it." It hurt her to know he placed so little value on his life.

Honey? He ran a hand lightly down her arm.

She stepped back, shaking her head. Softly, she repeated, "I knew it." *The mages wouldn't have thought to erect a perimeter wider than a mile. You sent me four. Half that would've kept us both free. You could've escaped, but you were so determined to protect me that you sacrificed yourself when you didn't have to.*

He seemed startled. Giving off a defensive vibe, he pulled back from the bond. His face hardened. *I'd do it again.*

I know. But I don't know how you expect me to live with that.

"I had to make a quick choice. Let's not fight about it."

"I realize there's no point," she said, her voice flat.

He frowned at her, worry shadowing his eyes. She had to shake off this mood, focus on more immediate concerns. He needed her support. Anything else between them could wait.

If he was acquitted, *when* he was, he might relax enough to let go a little, to stop being so unnecessarily protective.

"Valeria, we—"

"Anyway," she added in a brisk tone, "I'm safe enough, Griffin. I walked in here openly."

"After helping Marc push some media into the Collegium's face." Hettie gave him a fierce grin.

"I think Marc liked doing it," Val said. "Right about now, your dad's giving the Council a tiny taste of the hell they deserve. It'll be fine."

He drew her close again. "You walked in openly, but you aren't walking out, are you?"

"Not unless you do."

"Damn it, Valeria."

She kissed him quickly, then longer. "Everything will be fine. I know it will."

Her hands slid down his back. On a sigh, he pressed his mouth to hers, stroked her from neck to hips, then back again.

She deepened the kiss, and he seemingly forgot his concerns. Hettie cleared her throat. Val and Griffin turned to see that she'd set out a legal pad and was sitting behind it, pen in hand. Beside her, Caro sat, aiming a contented half-smile in his direction.

"You have to understand," Caro said, "none of us expected to see you again. Val and Hettie came to me early this morning, then Rick and I took them straight to Dad. Oh, and

Rick said he's in your corner, but he's staying out of the way for now. Anyhow, Dad didn't take much convincing. You know he's the best, Goofball. It really will be fine."

"I assumed he believed I was guilty."

"Because you never gave him a reason to think otherwise," Griffin's sister said. "All he needed was a reason."

Val cocked her head. "Why does she call you Goofball?"

"It's a long story," he said. As Caro opened her mouth, he added, "One we're not telling here."

Their father stepped into the room, looking satisfied. "Not quite what I was hoping for, which was Valeria released on her own recognizance, but pretty good. She's in guest quarters with us. Griff, your trial starts first thing tomorrow."

"Tomorrow." Stunned, Griffin turned to Val. "I didn't expect to have tomorrow."

"'Only a day away,'" she quoted around the lump in her throat, "but a very precious day."

"Damned straight." He squeezed her shoulder, and she slid an arm around his waist.

"You were entitled to a damned trial." His father's eyes looked like granite chips. "They had no right to condemn you in your absence. I tried to stop it then, but Alden's death allowed them to ram the conviction through."

"You tried to stop it?"

"Of course I did." The words sounded clipped, impatient. "You're my son. I knew you must have had a solid reason for what you'd done. But a lawyer can't just volunteer to represent someone. The accused has to accept representation, even when a family member tries to hire the lawyer, as your bondmate did today."

"What? You revealed the bond?" Griffin's head jerked toward Val. "The risk—"

"Don't start," she said, with steel in her voice.

The hell I won't. Valeria, you—

Stuart Dare cleared his throat. "Our defense, besides your own account, Griff, will be to sandbag the tribunal with your good character. The people in Wayfarer have been told you're applying for membership on the institute's board. Some of them are coming to testify for you."

Raising an eyebrow, Griffin asked, "What do Mundane witnesses have to do with Alden being a traitor? Or whether or not someone else is?"

"Mundanes can't prove anything about Alden. However, the *Caudex* allows a great deal more leeway for character witnesses than the Georgia Rules of Evidence. Under our rules, character speaks to judgment, to the accuracy of your perceptions. It's particularly useful when actual evidence is thin on the ground."

Hettie beamed at Griffin. "Marc has the Wayfarer angle covered. Peace and love and sunshine don't run the world, but those of us who believe in them learn to tell the hard cases from the good. You're the good, and all of Wayfarer knows it."

"By tomorrow evening," Valeria said, "everyone will."

If only, he thought to her.

Believe, Griffin. Val squeezed his waist. *Have hope. I do.* But there was something else in his mind, something he hid from her. *Griffin?*

Later, love. I'll tell you later. The thought had an ominous undercurrent.

"You'll have to go back to your cell," his father said, "but for now, sit down, son. We have six years to cover and not all that much time."

Griffin waited for Val to take her seat, then took the chair beside her.

She laid her hand over his on his knee. He had a fighting chance now, and they would make the most of it.

Chapter 22

Fear jabbed at Val's heart, kept her pacing the conference room. Morning had come, the day of Griffin's trial. That was enough to worry about, but her concern over whatever he'd refused to tell her yesterday had grown through the sleepless night.

He'd said he would tell her, but there hadn't been time. Whatever it was, he'd blocked it from her while they were together. The wards around his cell had interfered with the bond after that.

His father sat at the table, sipping coffee and scanning the notes on a yellow legal pad. Did he know what Griffin wanted to talk about?

Griffin hadn't answered when she'd asked him how he thought she could live knowing he would sacrifice himself for her even when he didn't have to. She took a deep breath and pressed her hands to her eyes. Could he really not know she'd rather die than have him sacrifice himself for her?

Stuart cleared his throat. "We have an excellent shot, Val,

better than I have with most of my Mundane clients." He looked composed, as though Griffin were any other client. Only the tension around his eyes, if she looked closely, betrayed his concern.

"Because of the chair and its truth auras," she said.

"That and the Mundanes who'll speak for Griffin today. No ghoul ally would ever have done the things he has for them."

"He thought Alden could beat the chair, deceive the auras. He saw it in a precog flash."

"He saw Alden free and himself dead in that flash. Maybe there's a way to beat the chair, but there was a bigger problem legally. Griffin had no firsthand knowledge of Alden's treason. No one did. It's a requirement for accusation. He saw the result correctly but didn't see the reason."

Griffin's mother, Lara Dare, slipped into the conference room. The tall brunette with eyes the blue of Griffin's and streaks of gray in her hair had arrived late the night before.

She smiled at Val, who nodded a greeting. Griffin's family accepted her with surprising ease. Maybe they realized she would do anything to help him.

"I left Caro and Hettie with the people from Wayfarer," Lara said. "They're quite a large group. Surely that will help."

Stuart Dare shrugged. "There are never any guarantees."

"Stuart, pessimism—"

"Calling it straight, hon." He stood to draw her close. When he pressed his lips to her hairline, the gesture seemed so tender and intimate that Val looked away.

He continued, "Prejudice doesn't respond to evidence, and there's six years of it stacked against Griffin."

Before his wife could respond, the door opened. Griffin

stepped in, and Val's heart clutched. She couldn't lose him. She wouldn't.

He wore no shackles today, as his dad had arranged. In the charcoal suit, white shirt, and red tie she and Hettie had found for him, he looked as dependable as a doctor. He smiled at her, but his mind stayed closed to the bond. Something was definitely wrong.

"Griffin." His mother stepped out from behind his father.

"Mom." Joy shot across his face as his mother darted into his arms. "I thought you'd been delayed."

"What good's money if you can't charter a plane?" Blinking back tears, she took his face in her hands and kissed him hard. "My sweet Griff. Finally." Her blue eyes narrowed. "You nail this thing, son. We want you home."

"That's the plan."

Smiling, she brushed a finger along his hairline. "You need a haircut."

"Nag, nag." He grinned at her. "Same old, same old. Caro thought I needed a shave, so I got one, and now you think I need a haircut. Want to complain about the suit they dug up for me?"

"What's not to like? You look like the successful artist you deserve to be." Her lips trembled, and she gave him a quick hug before turning away.

Her husband slid an arm around her. "With a little luck, honey, he can enjoy his success openly from here on out." He glanced at their son. "Wish I had a guarantee for you."

"I know, Dad. I trust you. Before we go in, though, I have to talk to Valeria. Alone." His eyes locked with hers.

She reached for him in the bond, but he didn't reach back. Dread bubbled in her gut.

"Only conversing with your legal team," his father said, "justifies your being out of the guards' sight."

"You can buy us a few minutes."

"If it's that important." Stuart shrugged. "But make it quick. Come on, everyone." He led them out of the room, leaving Val and Griffin alone.

"What's wrong?" She brushed her fingertips along his cheek. "Just tell me, Griffin."

"I know who the traitor is." Face tight with concern, he took her hands. "I'm so sorry, love, but it's Blake."

She stared at him, baffled, for a long moment before the words clicked. She took one step back. "What makes you say that?"

"I felt it when they were questioning me. Just a flash, but—"

"Flash of what?" She paced to the window, her body painfully tense, arms folded across her stomach. She didn't want to believe Griffin was right.

But Gene had spied on her. He'd voted against her and threatened her. For the good of the Collegium, he'd said. She'd wanted to believe that, but she'd felt uneasy about his motives all along.

Griffin stood close behind her but didn't touch her. "When they were trying to probe my mind, I told them I wasn't a traitor but someone on the Council was. Larkin felt shocked but uncertain. Blake, though, felt afraid. Guilty. I caught a flash from his mind of him with ghouls."

"You saw that in his mind?" *Oh God, no.*

"Nothing in words. Nothing explicit. But enough to make the accusation and force him to respond."

"You're sure."

"I can show you."

She didn't want to see, didn't want to know Gene could do such a thing. Just the idea made her queasy. Swallowing hard, she tried to steady her breathing. If Gene had betrayed their people and the Mundanes, persecuted Griffin to cover his own tracks, he had to pay for that.

Besides, the man she loved was asking for her trust. Val took a deep breath and turned to take his hands.

Full of love and regret, his mind touched hers. Then she was with him in the chair, waiting for Gene and Larkin to destroy him. She felt the crushing pressure on his mind, the constriction of his chest.

The love for her that had sustained him and now brought tears to her eyes.

I'm no traitor, he flung at his tormentors. *A councilor is.*

From Gene, *Bullshit.* Then that flash of fear and guilt, the image of the meeting, then *Don't let him con you.*

Heartbroken and fighting tears, she leaned into Griffin's shoulder. How could Gene have betrayed their people? Sent her to what might have been her death? He'd been the only father she'd known since the age of fifteen.

But her father would never have betrayed her. Or tried to have the man she loved executed for crimes he hadn't committed.

Griffin's arms closed tightly around her, offering refuge. His love for her and his grief over giving her this news brushed her mind in their bond. She held on to the solid, sheltering strength of his body and the steady warmth of his love, gathering herself, for a long moment.

Then she raised her head and kissed him. "Let's go," she said. "There's a reckoning long overdue here."

* * *

Griff kept a tight grip on Valeria's hand as the deputies escorted them to the assembly room. Thank God, she'd believed him, but it had cost her. That bright smile hid a heart ripped with disillusionment and loss. A reckoning was indeed due, for the way Blake had used her in addition to everything else.

When they rounded the last corner, a clump of people from Wayfarer stood with Caro and Hettie by the assembly room doors—Marc, Cindy and Molly, Sally from the Crystal Grotto, Todd and his sister Robin, Missy from the bakery. Sam Peters, a couple of the other farmers. Ben Hayes, the scruffy young publisher of the weekly Wayfarer *Oracle*. The mayor, Elijah Kimball, his dark, wrinkled face alight with interest. Stocky, graying Sheriff Burton, who ran the softball league in his minimal spare time. A handful of people Griff barely knew.

They were far more than he'd expected, and his throat closed. His eyes stung. Blinking, he set his jaw and swallowed hard. He couldn't believe so many of them cared enough about him to go to all this trouble.

Only Ben knew the truth. Valeria had needed him for her media push yesterday, but he'd sworn to keep the secret. The rest thought Griff was up for a seat on the board of the Georgia Institute for Paranormal Research, much lower stakes than he truly faced, but they'd come anyway.

Look at that, Valeria sent to him, *all these people are here because they care about you.*

He squeezed her hand but didn't reply. He couldn't trust his voice yet.

The squad of guards stepped back.

Griff nodded to his friends. "Hey, y'all." At least he sounded normal even though his throat still felt tight.

Little Molly beamed at him.

Hitching up the unaccustomed suit trousers, he crouched to flick his thumb over her chin. "Hey, punkin."

"Hey, Gray." She threw her arms around his neck for a quick squeeze that made him smile. Preening, she fluffed out her frilly pink skirt. "I got a new dress."

"A gorgeous dress. You look like a princess."

She twinkled in a way that promised trouble down the road for boys of her generation. "Todd's gonna be my prince."

Rising, Griff glanced at the gangly youth beside Cindy, Molly's mom. The boy showed no after-effects of his encounter with the demon hosts.

Griff directed a level look at him. "Okay, Todd?"

"Yeah." Todd gave him a solemn nod. "Thanks, Gray."

"My pleasure." They exchanged fist bumps.

"I'm here because you take time with the little kids—drawing, baseball, hoops, stuff like that." Robin's brown ponytail swung as she gave an emphatic nod. "It matters."

"I think so. Thanks, Robin."

Todd gave him a fierce look. "I'll tell 'em what you did for me, how you saved us. Tell 'em all about it."

If mage secrecy had to be blown with any group of Mundanes, the people in Wayfarer were probably the safest choice. Their laid-back attitudes and New Age interests made them more open to such prospects than most other Mundanes.

"Molly wanted to come." Cindy stroked her daughter's

hair. "We all did. But they said we had to wait out here."

Griff smiled down at Molly. "The first part's just for members of this group." Mundane ears shouldn't hear a debate about magical murder. "I can't thank you all enough for being here. It means a lot, regardless of how this turns out."

Marc stepped out of the knot of people. "We have your back. This is going to work out. I have faith."

"Me, too." Valeria slid her hand into the crook of Griff's arm. "We should go in."

He nodded to the group. "Thanks, everybody, for coming." He could feel their good will like a shield as he walked away.

The reeves stopped at the door. With his family and Hettie following, Griff and Valeria walked into the grotto and down the stairs. They took their seats at one of the two malachite tables flanking the obsidian chair.

Adrenaline hummed in his veins. His life was still on the line. No matter how things came out, though, the full assembly would have to listen to him, listen and know he spoke the truth. Whether they accepted it or not.

Judging by the hard looks people were directing at them, he had a big hill to climb. His fellow mages didn't look very forgiving, and what would that mean for Valeria when this was over? He'd done his best to convince her not to stick so close, but she had her own ideas. As usual.

"I'm proud to be with you," she murmured, "and I want everyone to know we're together."

Did she know what a high price she was paying for that? He couldn't let her be an outcast, not for him. Not when the Collegium had been such a big part of her life.

His father and Hettie took the chairs flanking Griff and

Valeria, with Caro and his mom sitting behind them.

Griff glanced sideways at Valeria. The sleek, royal-blue suit highlighted her trim curves, and lust punched him in the gut. He ached to take her to bed again.

If the strategy he and his dad had crafted could pull the rabbit out of the hat, maybe people would be more accepting than he feared. Maybe he really could have a future with her. If not, if the mages convicted him, he would find some way to protect her.

And to see Blake pay.

The High Council filled the opposite table, with the rest of the councilors again in front row seats. Griff's eyes met Stefan's encouraging ones.

A few minutes later, Will hurried down the stairs and squeezed into a seat a couple of rows from the front. He gave Griff the barest of nods. Javier Ruiz sat behind him, his dark eyes grim and focused. Javy's wife, Karen, was not a mage and so couldn't sit in on this proceeding. At the back, by the door, Lorelei sat with Chuck Porter and his wife, Dora, a high school English teacher.

Two rows below Lorelei and Chuck sat Tasha. Weapons were forbidden in here, except for the door wardens' spears, but Griff would bet she had something lethal on her somewhere. The rest of Griff's team was outside, in the overflow section on the lawn.

Sybil Harrison sat halfway up, with some of the other deputy reeves. Griff leaned over to Valeria. "Do you see Sybil?"

"Yes. Can't read her expression, though." She bit her lip. "I thought we were friends."

"I know, love. You will be again."

The loremaster, Gerry Armitage, came down the stairs and

over to Griff's table. His face showed only neutral disinterest, and Griff caught no hint of his mood in the magic. "Valeria, whether we proceed against you will depend on the outcome of Griffin's trial."

"I know. Thanks, Gerry."

He nodded. "Griffin, in accordance with the procedures laid down in the *Caudex Magi*, are you ready to answer the charges against you?"

"I am."

As Gerry crossed to the Council table, Valeria touched Griff's arm. "Nervous?"

"No." Not anymore. Not if he could nail that bastard, Blake.

Gerry turned to the audience. "The wards are set." He nodded at Will, who had helped set them. "A blue aura signals truth, green denotes evasion, and red, lies. After hearing the witnesses, the assembly will pass judgment."

He paused, power crackling around him as his gaze swept the room. "On you who are to judge, I lay this *geas*. You must vote only if your mind is open now, not judge on any preconception, and you will not speak of this, will not write of it, until you vote on the morrow."

The power of the *geas*, the binding, rolled through the room, encompassing the onlookers and giving each of their faces a brief, golden glow.

Gerry turned to Griff. "Griffin Rhys Dare, stand forth."

Valeria gave his hand a last squeeze before she released it. He rose, buttoning his suit jacket, and took his stance before the obsidian seat. Although his heart was doing quick time, he felt strangely calm. No more running, no more hiding, no matter how this turned out.

"You stand accused," Gerry said, "of the willful murders of Milt Alden, chief councilor of the Southeastern Shire Collegium Council, and of four deputy reeves, Terrence Lewis, Delia Swann, Max Argot, and John Darby, who attempted to stop you as you fled after killing Chief Councilor Alden."

Gerry continued, charging him with murdering Allie, Sykes, and Corin, too. The silence, the concentration, in the chamber pressed on Griff like lead. Without the shackles dampening his power, he could feel the vibrations of the spectators' magic in the air.

Finally, Gerry looked back at him. "What say you to these charges?"

"I accept responsibility for those deaths, but they were not murder." Even to him, that sounded absurd. How could you be responsible for eight people's deaths without being a murderer?

As though to taunt him with the question, Dan Jacobs, Griffin's predecessor as shire reeve, father to Corin and Mitch, walked down the stairs and squeezed into a seat. Dan looked tired, old. That scumbag Blake's treason had cost too many people far too much.

Gerry read out a list of other charges, all involving ghoul collaboration, all totally bogus, and Griff denied them.

"Finally," Gerry said, "you stand accused of conspiring to bring demons through the Veil into the land."

"I deny that, too. Shire Reeve Valeria Banning and I stopped ghouls from bringing demons through."

"Having heard the accusations and having answered," Gerry said, "be seated. Tell us what you would have us know." He walked back to his own place, a marble stool set in front of the councilors.

Griff settled himself on the black chair, resting his hands on his knees. Even without chains, this seat would never be comfortable.

"I did kill Alden, because he was in league with the ghouls. One of my deputy reeves who was injured in a failed raid knew he was dying and wanted peace. He admitted to helping Alden warn the ghouls. I accused Alden in the Council chamber, he denied it, and no one believed me."

He kept his voice steady, but the memory of what had come next still haunted him and probably always would. "In the firefight after that, four deputy reeves died. I consider that my fault for not managing events better."

Of course their families and friends despised him for that. They had every right.

"As for the rest, I categorically deny having any dealings with the ghouls except for trying to stop them. I categorically deny doing anything to favor or help them. I deny killing Allie or Corin, though I feel responsible because they were trying to help me. I did kill Sykes in self-defense, after he killed Allie.

"And I absolutely, on my life, damned well deny ever doing anything for the benefit of demons." His anger bubbled behind the words, and he let it. He'd had more than enough of being the mage world's favorite villain.

The aura held blue as it faded.

Blake rose to question him on the council's behalf. "Your father is one of our most esteemed attorneys, yet you never sought legal vindication."

"I considered it." Griff looked up at Dan Jacobs, Corin's father. "Acting Shire Reeve Corin Jacobs tried to arrange a hearing for me. He phoned me to say the Council intended to grant me one, but only as a lure. When I surrendered, they would kill me. While we were on the phone, someone killed him."

He let the pain of that memory show as he looked steadily at Corin's father. Dan's face tightened, with grief stark in his eyes.

Blake pursed his lips. "Corin Jacobs was killed with a staff weapon. You are the only mage in the Southeast who uses one."

"Only I use one regularly," Griff corrected. "Students sometimes train with them, and the Collegium has several in the armory." As Blake well knew. Griff took a moment to master his temper, then bit out, "You don't need much skill to blast a mage in the back."

"Who do you claim killed Corin Jacobs, if not you?"

Griff narrowed his eyes at Blake. "Since the killer was screened, invisible to scrying, that's the question, isn't it?"

"Only if one doubts you killed the man who pursued you doggedly. You're asking us to be conspiracy theorists." Blake gave the room a cool smile. "You may believe what you say, Griffin Dare, but that does not mean you are correct. What proof have you of Alden's supposed treason? Or anyone else's?"

"I have no proof of Alden's treason, as I'm sure you know. As for anyone else's..." Griff paused, leveling a hard stare at Blake. "Yesterday's session was illuminating."

"Do you wish to make an accusation?" Blake bit out the words.

Gerry stood. "Accusations must be made in their proper form and time. Griffin, if you wish to lay a charge, you may do so when this proceeding concludes tomorrow."

"Fine." Watching Blake, Griff bared his teeth in a wolfish smile. "I'll do that. As for the charge I made against Alden, I acted on a deathbed confession, as I said. It's not something I can reproduce for you here."

"Nor is it something we can verify. I assume you've tried scrying for proof?"

"I have. As we all know, scrying has its limits. It doesn't display sound. It can't reveal events that are screened or events yet to be. You can't exactly use Google to browse for what you want."

The crowd chuckled, breaking the tension. They might not like him, but a lot of them didn't hate him. He could feel that in the magic they all shared.

"So you have no proof," Blake repeated.

Before Griff could answer, a deep voice said, "I can corroborate the confession."

Chapter 23

Val jerked her head in the direction Griffin was glaring, toward the Council seats. In the center of their bench, Stefan Harper stood, his hard, brown eyes fixed on Gene's face.

Val leaned toward Hettie. "Did you know about this?"

"Only Stefan and I knew," Stuart said softly. "Griff would've forbidden it, but this is critical. It's the only way to clear him of murder in Alden's death. Once that's done, all the rest will follow."

"Yield the chair," Gerry ordered, glancing at Griffin.

Griffin's eyes held Stefan's for a long moment, and then he stood. His face stony, he walked back to his seat at the table.

Stefan took the black chair. His eyes swept the room. "I treated Deputy Reeve Zeb Vance. He was dying, wounded too badly for us to save, and he was angry. He told me he'd helped Alden send mages to defend ghoul nests. Alden never told the deputies of the consequences. Zeb wanted absolution before he died. I told the shire reeve at the time, Griffin Dare, and I've kept silent all these years at his insistence."

The aura around the chair glowed blue. The audience's

shock vibrated in the air, and only the crackling of the torches broke the silence.

Val slid her hand into Griffin's. He looked too grim for a man hearing testimony that could clear him. "What's wrong?"

"One of us with his ass on the line was enough."

Val sighed. "Someday, you'll realize you can't protect everyone you care about. And you don't have to."

Griffin said nothing, watching his friend, but he laced his fingers through hers.

Stefan again looked around the room. "He has paid a high price for trying to protect us. We cannot, in good conscience, condemn him for that."

"I'm sorry," Gerry said, sounding as though he meant it, "but you aren't to advocate while sitting there. That's for after, for the accused or his counsel."

Judging from the faces looking down at them, advocacy would be mere icing on the cake of Griffin's acquittal. He and Val might actually have a shot at a life together.

Anticipation was a fool's game, Griff reminded himself late that night, staring at the ceiling of his cell. He'd learned never to count on anything, especially anything good, until it arrived.

Yet he couldn't get Marc's words that afternoon out of his head. *As a man sows, thus shall he reap*, Marc had said, quoting the Bible, at the end of a somewhat embarrassing litany of Griff's activities in Wayfarer. Hearing it all felt good, though. It made him hope, whether he wanted to trust that or not.

At least he'd left a good mark somewhere, no matter how this trial turned out.

Something moved near the door. He sat up, and the cell's lights rose automatically.

Gene Blake stepped into view. Griff swallowed a triumphant grin.

"If you accuse me, they won't believe you."

Griff drew his unchained leg up, rested his bare foot on the bunk's edge. "We'll find out tomorrow."

The older man gave him a smug look. "Then you and Valeria ride off into the sunset and make lovely babies? You'll never be welcome here again, either of you. Even if they're foolish enough to let you walk."

"We'll see." Unfortunately, Blake had a point. Valeria might find her welcome here thin if she stuck with Griff, even if the mages acquitted him.

"The arresting mages said you told her you loved her before you flashed her away. If that's true, you should put her before yourself. Confess. Admit you killed willfully, conspired to bring demons through, that you tampered with the chair wards so they showed your lies as truth. I'll see you out of the country, give you a new start anywhere you choose."

"Geez, Blake, how powerful do you think I am? More to the point, how powerful have you convinced them I am?"

Blake was attempting to influence a witness. Where were the guards, that he would risk this conversation? Did he have them in his pocket?

Blake's smile was sinister. "You're strong enough to evade capture for six years, strong enough to send Valeria farther than the mage perimeter around that demon gate, strong enough to touch the orb and walk away sane. They'll believe."

"Maybe the gullible ones." The ankle chain dampened

Griff's precog along with his magic, but he didn't need it to know something was very wrong here. With no magic, no mobility, no weapons, he had the fighting chance of a fish in a barrel.

"Sign a confession, and I'll fix her life. And yours."

Give up, when all he'd longed for was within reach?

Griff let his grin erupt. "No deal. I'll have your ass for breakfast. 'And your little dog, too.'"

"Your mistake, Dare." Staring at Griff with cold, sharkish eyes, Blake said, "You won't see breakfast."

The ward dropped. Mitch Jacobs, Corin's brother, stepped into view, and sizzling blue energy shot from his sword.

Griffin. Griffin, please.

Valeria's voice knifed through the fog in Griff's head. *Wake up. Wake up, and tell us where you are. Griffin!*

He struggled to focus. *I'm awake. Shackled. Duct tape on my mouth—nothing like the tried and true, I guess.*

He felt, rather than heard, her gasp as her relief washed over him. *Don't joke. I felt them blast you. They must've had the cell ward down. I ran to the jail, but you were gone. Where's 'here'? What happened?*

Blake offered me a suck-ass deal. I refused. Now I'm in a van. On the floor. That reeve from the other night, Parker, two mages I don't know, blond man, sandy-haired woman.

He would pound them all to fucking paste, then do the same to Blake. He'd damned well had it with being knocked around. Being shackled. Having his life generally screwed with. *Shit, I smell ghoul.*

Her chilled reaction rippled through the bond. *Can you tell where you are? Where you're headed?*

Not yet...wait. We're stopping. Don't know where. What-ever happens, know I love you.

I love you, too. Valeria's spiking anxiety washed through him. Silent support came with it.

Light shone into the van. Pole lights. Voices in that direction, too. He closed his eyes, slowed his breathing. If he could catch them off guard, maybe he'd have a chance.

His captors hauled him out, carted him about ten feet, and dropped him on the ground. He managed not to tense. That shoulder would hurt tomorrow, though. If he lived to see another day.

"You sure you know how to do this?" someone behind him asked.

Griff opened his eyes to slits but didn't see anyone. The buildings around him looked familiar, but the angles seemed strange, the perspective...because he'd never seen it from inside. Now he recognized the ghoul nest near Vidalia.

"No mage has been drained in three hundred years, and never less than fatally," Parker's voice said, "but we'll have a go. What the hell—we kill him, one less for you to worry about."

Fuck that. *Valeria, ghoul compound outside Vidalia.*

Coming as soon as we can get a chopper. I sent Stefan after Gene.

Through the bond, he sensed her reaching for a phone, felt her gratitude for his worried friends gathered around her, all in combat gear. They'd come as soon as they could.

Meanwhile, he locked the bond down tight. If this went bad, he didn't want her feeling it. Besides, there was always a chance his captors might screw it up, give him a way to break free.

He tested his shackles. No give. *Hell.*

Valeria's tension, her fear and haste, teased his mind even with their bond locked down. She couldn't arrive in time to help, though. No way. Live or die, he was on his own.

He opened his eyes. His mage captors stood over him in a ring of ghouls.

Bastards.

"Hey, cutie." The mage woman set a small, wooden chest on the ground a few feet from him. With a tip-tilted nose, bow mouth, and sandy curls, she might've been attractive if she hadn't been in league with the enemy.

"Hope you don't mind an audience," Parker said.

When Parker bent over Griff's bound feet, Griff lifted them fast, shot them into the traitor's gut. Parker landed on his ass, but the other man pinned Griff onto his back.

Swearing, Parker chained Griff's shackled ankles to a wooden stake. It set up a tooth-grinding hum in the base of his spine, in the root chakra, the energy center that connected his power to the Earth, to nature. He couldn't feel the life forces around him anymore.

To cut him off that way, the stake had to come from a tree of power but with the wood dead, killed in some vile way.

They pounded another stake into the ground above his head, and pain lanced into the top of his skull. Tasting ammonia, he fought the pain. The stress was probably hiking his blood venom level up. He hadn't recharged in three days.

Now they'd disrupted the second crown chakra, his connection to the larger universe and the dimension where magic lay. Blocking those two energy centers effectively crippled him.

Shit. He forced his breathing to settle. Tried to think. He needed only a tiny break. Then they were all dead.

"Be sure you don't damage him." An older male ghoul spoke from behind the woman. He looked to be in his sixties, far older than most ghouls lived to be.

Weird, but Griff had bigger problems.

The ghoul continued, "Our deal was for breeding stock. Even if you have to stop short of draining him, we want him functional. We can always leech his energy periodically, as we do with other mage breeders, to keep him in line."

"Nope," Parker replied. "We got orders to see he can't ever be a threat again."

No way in hell he would breed for the ghouls. He'd kill himself first. He tried putting a tendril of power into the shackles. Nothing.

The woman smirked down at him. "The Dares have bred powerful mages for seven hundred years. He's functional."

Just let him get loose for a second. He'd show her how functional he was by kicking her ass into Canada.

"See that he stays that way."

"Yeah, yeah," Parker said. "You remember we get the first whelp he sires. Sue, get on with it."

The traitors were swapping mages for babies? Why?

The woman opened the chest while the men tied down Griff's bound arms. She pulled a green, cantaloupe-size orb—crystal, by the way it glinted in the light—from the chest.

"Parker." She tossed it to him.

Holding the orb, he stood at Griff's left shoulder.

She handed a magenta one to the other man. As he walked to Griff's right shoulder, she took position at Griff's head.

She held an indigo orb directly over his brow, over the chakra they called the third eye, the seat of his magic.

Oh, hell no.

The three built power in the orbs. It crackled between the spheres, echoed in Griff's body. He gritted his teeth, straining against the bonds. The traitors had pinned him well.

The spheres floated out of the mages' hands. Each rotated, gaining speed, until suddenly they whirled around as a group, like planets orbiting above Griff's head. Power flashed into the center of their circle, crashed into a rainbow.

The brilliant light stabbed into Griff's forehead like a rainbow lance. He cried out in agony behind the gag. Blind and deaf, he arched, thrashed, but couldn't escape it.

Burning pain ripped through his head, then spiked down to his heels. Along the way, it seared his skin as though peeling it from his bones.

It dug hot, sharp talons into his head and yanked. His blood ignited, then rushed to his head. Griff screamed.

Valeria!

Everything inside him twisted in a violent wrench, and then the world went black.

Chapter 24

Val crouched in the bushes outside the Vidalia nest with Will, Stefan, and the rest of Griffin's team. The handful she'd met at Tasha's cabin had been rounded out by eight others. The place looked quiet, but fear beat a constant pulse in her gut. An hour ago, a rush of agony had shattered her bond with Griffin, and then he was gone. The total silence in the bond, the emptiness, scared her down to her toenails.

"Griff will skin me if anything happens to you," Will murmured.

"Got it." She shot him a grateful look. He and his comrades shared her determination to think positively about Griffin's fate unless forced to do otherwise.

Will continued softly, "Don't make me sorry I agreed to this Trojan horse idea, even if it is our best shot."

"It'll work," Lorelei said quietly. "It has to."

Stefan gripped Val's shoulder. "I'll find you as soon as I can. You or Griff may need me."

"Thanks, Stefan. Everybody ready?" Val glanced around the group and got a series of nods. "Then let's do this."

Heart pounding, she stepped clear of the bushes.

The ghouls would surely suspect a trick when she walked up to the gate, but they'd probably let her in. They could always use another mage captive. Once she freed Griffin, they would breach the nest defenses from behind, opening the way for the rest of the team.

Still, the ghouls would be crazy not to shoot her up with enough venom to cripple her. If venom sickness overwhelmed her, she wouldn't be able to rescue Griffin or smash the front gate, so she'd tried Stefan's prototype vaccine.

She couldn't tell whether the drug was having any effect. The queasiness might be nerves.

She also had an injector for Griffin. He might already be dead, but as long as there was hope, she and his team would fight for him. She wouldn't let these ghouls stand between him and a new life. He deserved better than he'd had the past six years.

Too bad the idiotic Council had refused to trust the information he'd given her through the bond. They had Gene under house arrest in his quarters, no more. But that would change when she brought Griffin home.

If only she could sense him, let him know she was coming.

She didn't bother to shield, didn't let her stride falter as she stepped into the lights, into the cleared kill zone around the fencing. The nest was a typical one—a scattering of bungalows and a long, low, mostly windowless building that likely held offices and the breeding rooms. Ghouls didn't give their breeding stock windows. Why risk an avenue of potential escape?

No one challenged her, no one fired. So far, so good. She stopped about six feet from the gate and centered herself.

Showtime. Building power in her hands, she crashed them together in an explosion of red light that sent a thunderclap echoing off the buildings.

The doors flew open and ghouls peered out.

Val planted her fists on her hips. "Hurry it up, before I lose my temper."

Please, please do not open fire.

About two dozen male and female ghouls gathered ten feet inside the gate. A sixty-ish, graying male, very old for his kind, strode toward her. "You're on private property. Leave."

"I'm Valeria Banning," she snapped, enjoying the ripple of dismay that ran over their faces, "but you damned well know who I am. I've come for Griffin Dare."

"You're in the wrong place." The man sounded and looked calm, but with a snide edge to his words. "We're not holding anyone."

"Yeah, yeah, and the people in that long shed over there volunteered to breed your charming young." Good tone, hard, not showing the fear that gnawed at her insides. "Cut the crap, give me Dare, and we'll leave. No harm done."

His eyes narrowed. "Walk away, bitch, or die."

"That's 'mage bitch' to you." As he knew perfectly well. Yet here she stood, unharmed so far. Because of Gene? "I know you've got some kind of deal with Gene Blake. I don't care. All I want is Dare."

"There's no one here—"

"Bullshit. We're bonded. I can sense him." *If only.*

A younger female, brunette and slim, came out of one of the sheds. She whispered something to the man.

He smiled, sort of the way a cobra might. "Perhaps you'd like to come in and talk this over?"

Not as much as she'd like to kill them all and free their prisoners, but that would have to wait. Val nodded. "That's more like it."

She had to keep her face impassive, hide the dread curdling her blood. They opened the gate. Crunch time. Either the vaccine worked, or it didn't. She walked through the opening.

"Right this way," the man said.

She started after him. Suddenly there was a flicker of movement. Val wheeled toward it but didn't shield. She couldn't start a fight when she needed them to take her inside.

Someone's claws stabbed into her neck. Venom flooded from the wound down her arms, into her body. Gagging, shivering, and tasting ammonia, Val sagged into the arms of a stocky, blond male.

"No offense," he said. "Just a little shot to keep you in hand while we sort this out."

The vaccine wasn't working. If anything, she felt sicker than before, but they hadn't sucked her power. She still had a chance as long as they didn't search her and find the injector.

Her captor and the older male exchanged a look she couldn't read.

Something else weird about that older one—something wrong. Too much venom in her to sort it out, though.

The younger male carried her into the nearest building, the breeding shed. If they had Griffin, he was here somewhere.

Hurrying ahead of them, a female opened the door. The male carried Val into a small room with a padded leather table like the ones in doctors' examining rooms. No other furniture but a toilet and a sink. Nothing that could be used as a weapon.

He dumped her on the table and told the woman, "Strap her down. Stay with her while I call our contact and see what the hell this is about."

Val struggled, but the woman soon had her wrists and ankles secured to the table. "You look like good breeding stock." She stroked light fingers over Val's belly. "Our nest could use a mage womb."

Shivering, Val closed her eyes and tried to draw power. If she didn't break free, the team would have to charge the nest's defenses.

She would... Wait. She wasn't feeling sick or cold, only a little unsettled in the stomach. The ammonia taste was gone. The vaccine had worked, so it should help Griffin, too.

She peeked through her eyelashes. Her guard looked bored, was examining her nails. Val sent a tendril of power to the strap at her ankle.

It gave. Oh, yeah, she was going to do some serious head breaking. She had to be quick, though. She drew power from the life energy in the forest outside and burst the straps.

The ghoul looked up, mouth dropping open. Val flung herself off the table. Her hand shot for the woman's throat, and squeezed. No screaming.

The ghoul clawed at her face. Only Val's quick jerk backward saved her eyes. "*Morere*," Val snapped, feeding power into her throat hold. "*Morere*."

The ghoul slumped. The light in her eyes faded. Val eased her silently to the floor and slipped through the door. To be on the safe side, she tried to shield. Her power sputtered, providing only a feeble glimmer of protection. That weakness had to be a side effect of the vaccine. She'd have to tell Stefan.

Opening her senses, she found no one in the corridor, and—hallelujah!—the doors had names on them. Now to find Griffin. Anyone else came second this time around. *Benfield. Marshall. Delaney—*

Outside, something exploded. The building shook, and she stumbled against the wall. Shouts rang out, then more explosions. Will had decided not to wait, was moving in. To buy her time?

Solomon. Orser. Dare! But she caught no hint of his magic. She laid her hand on the doorknob and opened her senses, felt only one person inside. *Please let it be him*, she thought, and burst through the door.

He lay strapped to a padded table, and her heart seized. He still wore the gray prisoner jumpsuit. Lines of pain marked his face, and his skin looked jaundiced.

Val shut the door. "Griffin?"

He turned his head toward her, eyes closed, and made a faint, wordless sound. Val hurried to lay a hand on his cheek. It was clammy, a bad sign. "Griffin, love. I'm here with your team. We're getting you out."

Still no sense of his mind. She brushed her lips over his. His breath held a hint of ammonia that made her shudder. Even when his blood venom levels were high, she'd never smelled that on him, never tasted it. She reached into her undies and drew out the injector Stefan had given her.

"It's going to be all right, Griffin. It will." The stuff had worked for her. Surely it would for him. She set the point against his carotid, as instructed, and pushed the plunger.

His body jerked. He coughed. "Sick," he groaned, shuddering, his head thrashing. "Val...babe—"

He knew her, surely a good sign. Val sliced his straps magically and helped him to his feet. "Come on, there's a toilet. Just a few steps."

His knees buckled. He sagged against her. Bracing him, she gripped his waist. He groaned again. His fingers on her shoulder tightened. Dug in. *What—*

He straightened to slam his fist into her ribs.

Fighting for air, Val reeled backward from the blow, hitting the wall. He grabbed her shoulders, and she got her first look at his eyes. The clear blue was cloudy, surrounded by muddy, brown whites.

Val gasped. He'd turned. *No, no, no.*

He grinned, a parody of himself, no tenderness or happiness there. Frozen in dismay, she lost a precious instant. He slammed his body against hers, pinning her to the wall. His nails dug into her skin.

Icy lightning shot into her body. Racked by the pain, shivering with it, she pushed against his ribs. "Griffin, no."

She felt stronger, but even if she could form a shield, doing so while they were touching would put him inside it with her.

"Need to recharge, babe. Thanks." He ground his mouth against hers as her power bled away. The edges of the world went black.

She slammed her open palms over his ears, ramming air into his ear drums. He cried out, head jerking back. His grip loosened. Val shoved him away, then spun into a waist-level side kick backed by all her remaining power.

It knocked Griffin backward. He slammed into the table across the room, hit the wall, then collapsed. He had to stay down. Panting, she held her aching side. *Oh, God, please keep him down.*

The bond was gone. Useless.

Her heart screamed with love and loss, but she had to get ready, prepare in case he got up again. She drew power from the woods outside. The pain in her side eased. The misery shredding her heart did not.

Could she really keep her promise and kill him?

Oh, please, no.

"Banning!" Stefan's voice, from the hallway.

"In here, hurry!" She pushed away from the wall and managed, at last, to shield fully. But the protective aura felt unstable.

Don't hesitate, Griffin had said. *Take the kill shot.*

She'd promised him. But now that she had Stefan and his vaccine, there was a chance to save Griffin.

Stefan rushed through the door with a glowing sword in his hand. His eyes met hers, assessed her in a quick sweep, as he lunged toward Griffin.

"Careful." Panting, she drew more power from the woods. "It didn't work. You should shield, Stefan."

"I only do that in battle zones. I hate practicing medicine that way." Stefan dropped his sword. He reached for Griffin's pulse with one hand and touched his eyelid with the other.

Griffin's free hand shot toward Stefan's throat, and only Stefan's quick reflexes and long reach saved him from a fatal grip. His fingers tightened, white-knuckled, on Griffin's wrist.

Val dived for Griffin. Her shield flickered. As it died, she caught the arm he'd drawn back to punch. Snarling, he thrashed in her hold. He was still so strong, so hard to restrain.

"Griffin, please," she panted, clinging desperately and

drawing more power, "trust us. We love you."

Stefan grabbed the inside of Griffin's elbow, putting pressure and power into key points, immobilizing the arm.

Griffin's teeth bared in a snarl. He leaned toward her, trying to bite, but she managed to hang on and stay out of range.

Stefan yanked a large syringe from inside his camo tunic and jerked the cap off its long needle with his teeth. "Hold him," he gritted out.

Griffin bucked, trying to get his feet under him.

Stefan stabbed the needle through Griffin's coverall, into his chest, and pushed the plunger. Val cringed. The injection was necessary, but that had to hurt.

Griffin's body spasmed. His head fell back, eyes rolling. He roared in rage and pain. The muscles under Val's hands bunched. She pulled against his tug. He went with her pull and smashed his fist into her jaw.

Her head rocked back, crashed against the wall. White-heat rolled behind her eyelids, then red. She fought against the black. If she went down—

Standing, Griffin caught her shirt. Pain blurred his image. Whatever he'd done had knocked Stefan out. The doctor lay slumped against the wall.

As Griffin yanked her up, she locked her hands into one big fist, ramming it into his balls.

With a choked cry, he doubled over. His grip relaxed.

She punched him in the solar plexus.

He backhanded her.

Tasting blood, she wheeled for a kick.

He caught her leg. Upended her.

She slammed both feet into his stomach, knocking him back. She dragged herself up, drawing power again as tympani played in her head. If only she could shield. The thought tore at her soul. Part of her still couldn't believe she needed protection from him.

Snarling, he rolled to his feet. Nothing of the man she loved looked out of those muddy blue eyes, and the hatred in them tore her soul into bits.

He lunged.

Val sucked in a sobbing breath as she dodged. He crashed into the wall, clumsy, lacking that brilliant agility, and she banged her fist against the back of his skull. If only she could knock him out.

That wouldn't matter though. He wasn't himself, never would be again. The vaccine had been their last hope.

You'd be doing me a favor, he'd said.

So she'd promised him. But she couldn't. She wouldn't. Somehow, she'd reach him.

Another sob cracked through her chest, tightening it as though in a vise grip. "Griffin, please. You're my heart."

"Bitch!" he wheezed, straightening. "I'll fucking eat your heart." He lunged, hands going for her throat.

Tears glazed her eyes and mercifully blurred her vision. She ducked under his arms, lunging away. *Griffin, I love you.*

Nothing came back to her, not even a vague sense of him, and her heart cracked.

Val pivoted to punch him, but he wheeled faster than she would've thought possible. He caught her hair, yanking her back, trapping her against the wall.

With death in his eyes, Griffin closed his hands around her throat. He squeezed. Val gasped for air as blackness rolled across her vision. Desperately, she tried to force his arms aside.

There truly was nothing of his essence left. Either she stopped him now, or she risked letting him escape, dooming him to live as what he most hated, a perversion of everything he believed in.

No.

Her heart splintered, the shards driving into her lungs, her gut, her soul. Val drew power from the forest outside and slammed a hook punch into his left kidney.

He grunted. His grip loosened.

"*Morere*," she gasped, pressing her hands to his heart. She sucked in air, poured power into the contact, and screamed, "*Morere*."

His eyes glazed as his hands dropped. His knees buckled. Keeping one hand on his chest, pouring in power behind the command, she caught him.

They crumpled to the floor together. Blinded by the tears rolling down her face, she held his head to her breast even as her other hand kept up that lethal flow of magic. "I'm sorry," she choked through the grief and guilt clogging her throat, tearing at her soul.

"I'm so sorry." She'd done as he asked, but she'd failed him. There should've been some way to save him.

"Stop," someone shouted. "Banning!"

She couldn't stop. She'd promised. *Oh, Griffin.*

She pressed a kiss against his cool, clammy brow as her tears plopped onto his face. "I love you, Griffin. Love you with all my heart. Love you always."

The light in his eyes faded. For a moment, less than a heartbeat, his presence brushed her mind, warm and tender and probably imagined, and then he was gone.

Wrapping her arms around him, she buried her face in his

neck, against his soft, dark hair. His bay scent was gone, too.

An inarticulate, enraged roar came from her left.

Val looked up at Stefan. The tears in her eyes blurred his image, but his grief and fury thundered in the magic between them. His sword pointed straight at her heart with lethal energy crackling around the blade.

"Do it," she said. "Please."

Chapter 25

If Stefan killed her, she wouldn't have to live with what she'd done to Griffin. She used her sleeve to wipe her tears from his still face.

Stefan stood over them, breathing hard, his sword at the ready. "If we could've captured him—"

"Don't you think I would've preferred that? It was too late."

He searched her face for a long moment, then knelt in front of her and laid his sword aside. "Let me see," he said quietly.

Because he was Griffin's friend, she trusted him enough to raise her head, to lean out of his way, to let him touch that lax face. Looking grim, he felt Griffin's neck, checking for the pulse.

At last, he shook his head. "I was afraid he might turn. So was he." He drew her head against his shoulder with Griffin's body between them. "I'm sorry. I saw you, and I didn't think, just reacted."

"I would've done the same." Grief tore at him as it did her, and that was some comfort, that she wasn't the only one who cared.

Val swallowed hard to clear her throat, but nothing seemed to stop the tears. "I promised him, if he ever— Oh, God, I promised. I wish I hadn't."

The sounds of battle had died. Since she didn't hear any ghoul voices exulting in victory outside, the mages must've won. More of Griffin's friends would be along any moment.

Stefan gave her a reassuring hug. "For whatever it's worth to you, this was his greatest fear. You spared him that."

A fresh flood of tears streamed down her cheeks. Shuddering with their force, Val clung to Griffin with one arm and his friend with the other.

"I'll tell the others," Stefan said. "They knew about the venom. They'll understand, but better it comes from me."

Footsteps hurried toward them, with mage anxiety swirling in the magic and heralding Griffin's team. They halted in the doorway, but Val didn't look up.

"In here— Shit, no. No," a man's voice said.

"He'd turned," Stefan said bluntly. "There was no choice."

"Fuck!" Chuck Porter slammed his fist into a wall.

The shock, grief, and fury of Griffin's friends vibrated in the magic, a torturous mix that bore down on Val's soul like an avalanche. Would they forgive her? Could she ever forgive herself?

"I'll explain later." Stefan told them. "Anybody hurt?"

"We're all fine," Lorelei said shakily. "Bumps and bruises only. No need for you to tend us or for us to share energy. Tom and the guys from Atlanta are on guard."

Stefan nodded acknowledgment. "We'll clean him up before we take him home."

"Not to the Collegium, not to the people who hated and persecuted him." Val pressed a kiss against Griffin's dark head. "To Wayfarer. Miss Hettie." People who loved him. "His family will understand. They can meet us there."

"Much better idea." Stefan glanced over his shoulder, composed despite the pain in his eyes. "Will, I need your help. Chuck, bring me a set of camos from the helo locker. Griff's entitled to them."

Damned right, he was.

"We'll need a cleanup crew, too," Will said.

"On it," Tasha choked. She scrubbed angrily at her wet cheeks. "I'll go with you, Chuck." They hurried out of the room together.

Val released Griffin to Stefan and Will, then dragged herself to her feet as they lifted him onto the padded table. Will unsnapped the coverall.

Stefan said, "Someone get me a basin of water."

The shock was fading, letting her brain kick in. Gene, she remembered, and everything in her went cold and hard. "Griffin told me who the traitor is. I have to avenge him."

This must be how he'd felt when he'd buried his deputies and accused their killer and no one believed him. "Whether or not anyone believes me, that son of a bitch is going down."

Lorelei slid an arm around Val's shoulders. "He was the brother I always wanted," she said in a voice thick with tears. "Do what you need to. I'll have your back."

"You'll have lots of company." Will stripped off the coverall, and Lorelei tactfully turned her head away.

Griffin's arms lay limp at his sides, arms that wielded a quarterstaff with lethal skill yet tenderly cradled and comforted a homeless child. And Val herself. He'd held her in those arms, against that broad, scarred chest, in comfort, in easy affection, in driving, urgent passion.

Never again.

She clamped her lips shut against a sob, but she couldn't look away from him. "His hands," she said. "He dug into my neck, but—no talons."

"Let me see." Lorelei brushed Val's hair aside. "You have four red marks. He broke the skin, but they're long and narrow, not punctures. Not talons."

Val froze. "If he didn't go all the way, if he could've—we could've—maybe—"

"No," Stefan said flatly. "If the vaccine didn't work, we had nothing else to try."

So she'd thought, but—

"I'm the expert here," Stefan said. "Believe me."

Val scrubbed at stinging tears. Wiping her own cheeks, Lorelei hugged her.

Javier brought the basin of water. He turned away quickly but not before Val saw tear tracks on his cheeks.

Stefan thanked him. Stone-faced, with loss naked in their eyes, Stefan and Will set about cleaning up the residue of death.

"We'll tell everyone how he fought for our kind," Will said. "It's past time they knew and appreciated it."

Val said nothing. Gratitude was fine. But vengeance was better.

Medical personnel from the Collegium evacuated the ghouls' other captives. They would have their wounds tended and be sent home, with memory blanks when necessary.

Seventeen had been freed, quite a coup, but Val paid little attention.

About three a.m., Chuck and Javier settled the stretcher bearing Griffin's body on a rack near the chopper's rear hatch. Val curled up on the floor next to him. Soon she would have to give him up, consign him to the flames, as he'd wanted, and be without him forever. But she would take this one last ride holding his hand.

She reached under the blanket for it. Those strong, lean fingers were so cold. So limp. The change crushed her heart.

He wasn't turning green, which was a comfort. Stefan had said that could be because Griff wasn't born a ghoul.

"Mind if I sit with you?" Stefan's glance held pained comprehension.

When she held out her other hand to him, he settled on the floor beside her. He put his arm around her, and they leaned back against the equipment locker together.

"I also made him a promise." He raised his voice as the engines started. "An easier one than he asked of you. I promised him, if anything happened to him, I'd be here for you. Whatever you need, Valeria, you can come to me."

"You're doing it now." He was one of the few people whose presence wouldn't feel like an intrusion. The chopper lifted with a familiar lurch. Next stop, Wayfarer, Georgia, and the people who had given Griffin a home.

Val leaned back against Stefan's shoulder. She would have to tell Griffin's family. Miss Hettie. Marc. He would do the eulogy. Danny and Missy at the bakery could make the food.

Crystals and candles would come from Sally's and Lorelei's. Everyone who'd become part of Griffin's life would have some role in this, if they wanted it. Funerals, after all, were for the living.

Shielded from view by Stefan, she lifted Griffin's hand to her cheek and blinked back tears. She would do this for him, see it through, see that Gene was held accountable. Then she could fall apart.

"You know," Stefan said, "this team of fourteen took out a pretty big nest. Will says thirty-two ghouls live there. We've sent bigger groups against smaller nests and failed."

He was offering her a distraction, and she needed one from the boulder of grief that'd settled into her chest.

"We succeeded," she said, "because we weren't betrayed this time." Nodding at the flash of anger in his eyes, she continued, "I wonder why. Did the disinformation Will circulated about our destination protect us, or did the traitor decide not to risk drawing more attention to this nest?"

"Javier can dig into the computer records we seized, see what they tell us. He's an experienced hacker."

Suddenly, she felt a tiny twitch and froze. No. Not possible. *Get a grip, Val.* She kissed Griffin's cool palm.

His fingers curled around her chin.

Her heart stopped. Her breath caught in her chest.

Stefan leaned closer. "All right?" he asked softly.

Caught between hope and fear—was Griffin's hand warmer or just feeling that way because she'd held it?—knowing she was being pathetic, she choked out, "I… it…he moved."

The kindness in Stefan's eyes stung. "Probably just a shift in the helo we didn't feel. Shall I check him, though, just to be sure?"

Griffin's fingers shifted again, a hint of movement, not even really a twitch. *Stefan's right, probably just the helo.*

Mute, Val nodded. If Griffin had somehow revived, what would he be? She wanted him back, wanted him desperately, but not if he— Oh, please, not that.

Stefan reached for Griffin's wrist. His fingers found the pulse point, and his eyes lost focus, as though he were counting.

Only a few seconds ticked by, but every one of them drew the knot in Val's gut tighter.

Stefan turned to her with a kind smile. As his lips parted, he stiffened. His gaze shot toward the blanket over Griffin's face.

He eased around Val as she fought rising hope. If Griffin wasn't himself, if he revived as a ghoul, she couldn't bear it.

"You won't have to, no matter what," Stefan said gently, folding back the blanket, and she realized she'd spoken.

He lifted one of Griffin's eyelids, then the other. Holding the second one up, he drew a penlight from his pocket. He clicked it on and aimed it at Griffin's eye, and Val held her breath.

Stefan checked the other eye before he beckoned to her.

Afraid to risk the heartbreak of not seeing a change, she made herself rise on her knees beside him and look at Griffin's face. The whites of his eyes were just that, white, not muddy beige, around that deep, vivid blue. Stefan clicked the light on, and the pupil contracted.

Val's heart lurched. Carefully, she touched Griffin's cool cheek. He didn't react, and she shot an anxious look at Stefan.

"Sit here with him," Stefan said, "just as you were, and

we'll see what happens. This could be some weird thing from the venom in his blood."

"But you don't think so?" Her heartbeat roared in her ears, and her entire body ached with the sudden, desperate onrush of hope. She stroked Griffin's hair back from his brow.

"Just sit with him."

Stefan reached over her to grab his bag. Holding it so the others couldn't see, he withdrew his stethoscope and slipped the tips into his ears. His facial expression stayed neutral as he opened the camo shirt and tested different spots on Griffin's chest.

Val watched him. Maybe she was dreaming. Griffin hadn't moved, hadn't drawn a breath, in almost an hour. He couldn't be alive. She must've fallen asleep from exhaustion, imagined all this.

Stefan looked no longer neutral but amazed. "I hear a very, very slow heartbeat. Respiration, too, with the breaths faint and far apart, not enough to lift his chest, but there."

No. Not possible. It had to be a dream. Any minute, she would wake up and her heart would break all over again.

"Valeria." Stefan gripped her shoulder. "Do you hear me?"

"Yes. Yes, but…" She couldn't say it. Saying it might shatter the tiny possibility this was real.

"I don't know what's happening," Stefan said. "If I try to help, I may interfere with something important. We'll sit here and watch him, see where this goes. I have a garnet healing stone in my bag. I'll put that over his heart in a few minutes, but I want him stronger before I do that. Only if I think we're losing him again will I try anything more."

She nodded. Griffin's fingers curled loosely around hers,

and she bowed her head over their hands, choking back a sob. If this was a dream, if she woke up and he was dead—

"Easy," Stefan said, his grip on her shoulder offering much needed support. "He seems to be coming back as a mage, or at least a normal human, not a ghoul." He waited for her to look up at his grim face. "Even if that changes, though, it's not on you. Understand? I'm his doctor, and I'm responsible now."

Reluctantly, she nodded. A promise, after all, was a promise.

Faint chirruping sounds, night bugs. A distant creak. Slurping, like a dog drinking. Dim light from somewhere.

Griff turned toward the light. He wanted those sounds, wanted to see what made them, but his eyelids were too heavy. His brain felt mired in mud. He struggled against it, pushing. Reaching.

I'm here, Valeria told him. Her fingers twined with his, warm and firm. *Take your time.*

So tired. Yet he felt more alert now. *Love you.*

A muted sound, choked, and her lips brushed over his knuckles. *I love you, too. Everything's all right now, my love.*

His brain ratcheted up a notch. *Where are we?*

Your old room at Hettie's.

With Magnus on guard. Drinking.

Her chuckle rippled through his mind. *He wouldn't leave you. He spent the afternoon on your bed, bumped up beside you.* Sweet humor brushed over Griff, as though she smiled. *On the other side from me. He seems to think he has first dibs on you and the bed.*

As though summoned by the thought, the dog's padding

tread approached. His tags jingled to Griff's left. A heavy weight landed on the bed, shifted, probably as the dog did his traditional three-circle tromp. A plopping weight shook the mattress and put something big by Griff's hip, and a cold, wet nose poked his free hand.

Griff smiled and slid his fingers into the dog's thick, soft ruff. *He's a guy. He's territorial.*

"Let's not go there."

He caught the words more with his ears than his mind. At last, he pushed his eyes open.

Valeria sat beside him. The Tiffany bedside lamp washed rich gold and green over her face, but he couldn't see her features quite clearly, as though a thin, nearly transparent veil hung over her face.

"Welcome back." She leaned down to kiss him, her mouth soft and sweet on his.

The kiss warmed his heart but felt muted against his mouth. He slid his hand into the soft, thick hair at her nape and deepened the kiss.

With a sigh, Valeria sank onto him. Their arms slid around each other. Their mouths fused, bodies pressed close.

A long time later, the kiss broke. Valeria nestled against him. He pressed his lips to her temple, but nothing felt right, not her weight against his side, not the softness of her hair against his lips, not the big dog snoring by him. Something had turned down the volume, the intensity, not just in his hearing but in all his senses.

Maybe he needed a recharge. He reached for it, opened himself to the life around the house, the magic it bred.

Nothing came, no sense of anything beyond his body.

What the hell?

"I'm so glad to have you back." Valeria lifted her head and kissed him lightly. Although she smiled, her lips trembled.

He brushed a finger over her mouth and felt its soft warmth—but not as keenly. Later for that, though. Touching her, he could sense the misery knifing her heart. "What's wrong, love?"

She caught his hand again. Kissed it. "You don't remember?"

"Haven't tried." With his eyes on her face, he reached back, searching, and got a jumble of images. He pushed himself up in the bed. He'd never been this weak except from battle wounds. Even then, he'd been able to touch the magic.

"Griffin?" Valeria's brow furrowed.

"Wait." His father had come, they'd had a hearing, and then—"Fucking bastard Blake."

"We'll get him this time."

"We have to. He can't get away with this." He cupped her cheek. So warm, so smooth. Yet, again, muted. "Honey, I know this is hard for you, and I'll—"

Hard for her. Hard. Heart. Eat her heart.

Memory flooded into the bond. Draining. Rescue. Pain and rage. The agony in her eyes and, now, the guilt tormenting her heart. Aghast, he stared at her.

Valeria shrugged. She tried to smile and failed. Big tears welled in her eyes. "I'm sorry," she choked. "So sorry."

"No, love." Fool that he was, he'd laid this on her. Griff jerked her into his arms, and her pain roared through him, searing his chest and throat, writhing in his gut. "I'm the one who's sorry."

With a shuddering, gasping sob, she slid her arms around his neck. He lay back with her, stroking her, kissing her, while she wept into his shoulder. Loving him hadn't done much good for her.

"I shouldn't have asked you to do that," he said. "I was trying to protect you, convince you to protect yourself. If I'd known we'd fall in love, I…ah, hell."

If I'd known had become his mantra with her. She deserved better, someone who actually had the sense to see ahead. Someone who wouldn't cost her so much.

"No." She pushed herself up on one elbow. Tears streaked her face, and fury snapped through the bond. "Don't you go there, Griffin Dare. There can't be anyone else for me, not ever. It's you I love, you I want. Only you."

"I want you to have what you deserve," he insisted. The strain in her face, the pain quivering through her, said how much keeping her word had cost her. "As for what you did, I meant it when I said you'd be doing me a favor. I'm grateful. Don't have the words to say how much."

He brushed back her soft tresses. "I love you, Valeria."

Other memories were coming back, raking at him, images of mages glaring at her. Insulting her. Tarring her with his brush. But he couldn't deal with that now, not when she needed him to comfort her.

"I love you, too. Always, Griffin." Her grip tightened. "I'm so glad for the chance to say that to you again."

"Me, too, honey." In the bond, the echo of her pain, the searing memory, scalded him, too. He'd threatened to eat her heart, for God's sake. He pressed a kiss into her hair. "Clearly I suck in the last words department."

"Well, you get another shot at that." Valeria gathered herself, the effort resonating in the mind link, until she could raise her head and smile at him. "We both get another shot."

He wiped the tears off her cheeks with his thumbs. "We'll take full advantage of that."

Though the advantage might not be as much as he'd like. Even an acquittal, which had to be more likely now, wouldn't change most people's view of him. But saying so would only upset her. Instead, he kissed her.

She opened for him, forgiveness and love warming her touch. Griff let himself relax and take what she was offering. In return, he showed her the love that swelled his heart. He pressed slow kisses on her cheek, on her temple, her nose, finally on her mouth again.

Her lips pressed against his and flash fire rocketed through him. She was burning with him. Yet the intensity was muted, distant. *Damn it.*

He rolled above her, aware of her arms sliding down his bare back, her tongue fencing with his. Her honeysuckle scent and the absence of ammonia taste.

None of it felt right. He couldn't feel her, smell her, as keenly as before. He rolled to the side and tugged her to him.

"It will come back." Valeria must've caught his frustration in their bond. She brushed back his hair. "I know it will. You're still recovering. Besides, I love you completely, Griffin. Whatever comes back or doesn't."

"I love you, too, honey, no matter what." So he would do right by her, whether she liked it or not.

Now he remembered what Blake had said about the mages never forgiving her for siding with him. Shielding the thought, he tightened his arm around her. "Speaking of last words, what am I doing here?"

She settled against his side with her head a welcome weight on his shoulder. "Stefan isn't sure. Not long after the helo lifted off, you started coming back to us. That was a shock, to put it mildly, but none of us are complaining. Though Stefan has done a lot of muttering, seeing as you were definitely dead by any clinical standard."

Pain flickered between them, and she cupped his cheek. "Griffin, I—"

"Don't. You did what I asked, love. End of story." He gave her a direct look, willing her to feel his honesty.

Yet the awkwardness lingered between them.

Her eyes searched his, but she'd blocked off her feelings. He couldn't read her.

At last, she said, "What do you remember? Do you have any idea what happened?"

"Not much." Stroking her hair, wishing he could feel it the way he used to, he stared up at the ceiling. "That heart shot of Stefan's hurt. Then…I was angry. Something sizzled through me. Tore at me. Strengthened me, too. When you grabbed me that last time, the tearing was harder."

She flinched, and he kissed her.

"Don't," he said. Stroking her hair again, he struggled to remember. "The tearing, then…I saw you. Saw us, you holding me. Then Stefan pushing himself up. I called out—tried to reach you. But I was falling away, rushing away. How long was I out, anyway?"

"You started coming back to us about an hour later. In the chopper. That was around three this morning, and it's nine twenty at night now." She slid her fingers over his cheek, her eyes grave. "I was so afraid to believe it, to hope. But now I have you back, and I would do it all again for that."

She laid her palm against his cheek and let him feel her sincerity in their bond. "Believe that, Griffin."

"I'll try to." Stroking her back, he knew she was telling him the truth, which made him far luckier than he deserved.

Desire warmed her eyes and flowed between them. He lowered his head to hers, lost himself in the touch and taste of her, the love she gave him. But the distance, the muteness, filtered the contact.

For her sake, he forced a grin when he raised his head. "I'm sure Stefan, and probably Will, will poke at this sixteen ways from Sunday."

"I should call Stefan. Your folks are here, too, and the team. They're all going public about their loyalty to you, and they've been very good to me."

"They'd better be."

Sliding off the bed, she smiled at him. "Are you hungry? Miss Hettie made chicken pie and has watermelon for the side. Your mom made peach cobbler. She says this combo is your favorite meal."

"Yeah." His answering smile came from his heart. He hadn't eaten homemade chicken pie or cobbler since he'd gone rogue. "But wait, what about the splice at the old Adams place? Tonight is the dark of the moon. What if something tries to come through?"

"Collegium mages are on guard, and they told Will no one has shown up to answer that summons. Destroying the orb must've voided it, for which we can be thankful. The Collegium mages know we're here but not much else. We're playing our cards close."

"I knew I'd hooked up with smart people."

"Indeed. Oh, and Stefan said you're to stay in bed until morning." With a grin, she added, "I'm sure Magnus will watch over you, especially since I'm bringing back pie."

The dog's ears lifted, and he thumped his tail on the bed. Grateful for the small pleasure, Griff scratched the big golden's back. Magnus laid his head on Griff's thigh, the familiar bowling-ball weight reassuring although, again, damnably muted.

Griff leaned back in the bed and reveled in the quiet pleasure of the moment. He really was here, alive. Not a ghoul. With her.

"You and I will eat in here with your folks and Hettie. The others will come see you after. If you're up to it."

"Just try to stop me." He grinned at her as happiness pushed into his throat. Dinner with his family. A little thing, except he hadn't had it for a long, long time.

"I'll be right back." She kissed him quickly and left.

As she walked out the door, he enjoyed the view of her superb ass. His blood stirred, surely a good sign, and he reached mentally for her.

Reached, and got nothing. Because she wasn't touching him anymore? He still felt unusually tired. Still couldn't feel the magic. Or even the life energy of the dog he was scratching.

Heart pounding, Griff stretched one hand out in front of him and summoned power. Nothing. No glow, not even a spark.

Well, shit. The bastards had drained him, after all. Why hadn't that killed him?

Regardless, he'd come back from the dead. His power probably would, too.

If it didn't, though, then what?

He blew out a slow breath. One problem at a time. First, nail that fucking Blake.

Chapter 26

Odd, Griff thought, that a globe of crystal, a neutral, inanimate thing, might signal the end of his hopes. *The world ends not with a bang but a whimper*, like T. S. Eliot said. Except Griff didn't even have a whimper's worth of power in his hands now. Without it, he couldn't make the crystal glow.

With Valeria on the camelback sofa beside him and Stefan across from them and morning light pouring into Hettie's parlor, he felt strangely distanced from the two people who were so dear to him. He'd never been this close without sensing their magic.

His neck tensed. He bit back a curse.

"Take your time with it." Stefan leaned forward. "Draw the magic first, then channel it into the ball."

"Yeah. It's the first part that's the problem."

"If I touch you," Valeria said, "activate our bond and let you draw magic through it, would that help?"

"Worth a try." At least he'd managed to sound as if the idea of being unable to tap the power without her didn't burn him. At least she had recovered her ability to shield this morning. If only she'd been able to protect herself from him yesterday.

Her hand slid onto his forearm. The magic she drew warmed the bond, warmed his mind the way sitting by a fire in winter warmed his face. He opened to the power, reached for it…and nothing came.

Well, hell. Gently, because this wasn't her fault, he closed the bond as her dismay rose to match his.

"No joy," he said for Stefan's benefit. He set the crystal globe carefully in the tripod holder on the coffee table.

Valeria reached for his hand. He laced his fingers through hers and silently, in his own head, damned whatever muted the sensation, as though he were wearing gloves. Defying it, he raised her hand to his lips to brush a kiss over her knuckles.

Her fingers tightened on his. *It will be all right*, she thought to him.

If only.

Stefan frowned at him. "I feel magic in you. It's there. If the bond you two share can still function, even if you have to touch to activate it, there's still magic in you. They didn't manage to drain all of your power, maybe because of the venom."

Griff glanced at Valeria. "That would be ironic."

"And then some," Stefan agreed. "It may also be that your third eye may've been different from most mages' in some way that let you do things we can't—translocate farther, move faster, tolerate such a high venom level in your blood."

Griff raised an eyebrow. "'May have been'?" The brow

chakra, or third eye, was the seat of magical ability. If it was damaged…

Anger flamed in Stefan's hard eyes. "Whatever they did blew your brow chakra to hell. Instead of the single segment Mundanes have, we have five. Or should. You have only one of the five now, with a bloblike shape that looks like a big scar where the other segments should be."

"Can you realign?" Valeria asked. "Retune the chakras?"

Stefan shook his head. "I can't realign what isn't there anymore." Bitterly, he said, "I'm sorry, Griff."

That sounded about as final as things could get. Valeria's hand tightened on Griff's, but he kept his mind closed to her. How could he stand beside her, let alone shield her, if he couldn't match her in a fight? "Then I'm done, finished as a mage."

"I don't like to say finished."

Griff shrugged. "Facts, Stefan. Though none of that explains why I'm still alive." Alive but useless. He couldn't win justice for his dead if he couldn't fight.

"The draining ritual," Stefan said, "usually involves one globe, appropriately colored, for each chakra. That's why it's fatal. Maybe it wasn't this time because the mages tapped only three chakras, drained your power but not your life."

His power gave his life meaning, made it vivid and full. Without the magic, he might as well be blind and deaf.

"As for why you came back to us," Stefan continued, "near as I can tell, you did something mages haven't been able to do since before the Burning Times. You went out of body, what our kind once knew as astral traveling."

"What's that?" Valeria asked.

"It's a way to travel to distant places in moments, see what's happening there, and even communicate, if the old legends are correct. Mages used to send messages to their kindred that way, but we lost the knack, the knowledge of the method, in the Burning Times."

"I didn't have any control over it, though." Griff glanced at Valeria and winced at the guilt in her eyes. *Not your fault*, he reminded her silently.

A wry smile twisted Stefan's mouth. "I wouldn't recommend the combination of venom, vaccine, and lethal magic. We were lucky to get you back."

"Still," Griff said, "that could be useful."

"Damned risky to figure out, though." Stefan shook his head. "Without magic, maybe impossible."

"I'll try anything," Griff said.

Staring into the distance, Stefan rubbed his chin. "You had no talons," he said thoughtfully. "Your skin didn't turn green. Then you revived, after almost an hour clinically dead, with no brain or major organ damage."

Just magic damage, Griff thought.

"There's something about your physiology that's different in key ways." Stefan shook his head. "We'll keep digging at this. You work with your staff, try to recharge. Maybe the wall will come down. Maybe you have self-healing abilities we don't yet know about."

"Maybe." Griff wasn't betting on it, though.

"I have a friend who's a medicine man in the Eastern Band, Cherokee Nation, up in North Carolina. He may be able to help, but we need to finish your trial first. Some of the Council are pressuring me to bring you back, wanting me to certify you fit to continue."

Griff was sick of the Council and all their maneuvering. If not for Valeria, if not for the need to accuse that bastard, Blake, he would walk away from it all.

"Let's get it done, then," he said.

That afternoon, the tribunal convened in the ritual grotto. Griff watched the mages file in. If there was any justice, he'd be acquitted, but he'd stopped trusting in justice long ago.

Valeria's warm hand gripped his. If he was convicted, could his dad get her acquitted?

You aren't going to be convicted, she sent to him firmly, but he could feel that small worm of doubt, of dread, that nagged at her, as it did at him.

He didn't need magic to feel the tension in the air, especially when Blake entered under guard. The guards escorted him to the High Council table. One or two of them looked at him askance.

Otto Larkin shook his head, refusing to meet Blake's eyes, but that could mean anything.

Gerry Armitage stood before the obsidian seat, facing the assembly. "Come to order," he called, and the room stilled.

Because of the *geas* he'd laid on them, only those who'd started the process with open minds, about seventy-five or eighty mages, remained in the rows of seats.

Griff's mom and sister and his team, including Will and Stefan, stood in the walkway behind the uppermost seats with the others who couldn't or wouldn't vote. His dad and Hettie, as counsel to the accused, flanked Griff and Valeria, all of them standing for the verdict. None of them could vote, either, because they'd come into this with their minds set.

"All who find Griffin Rhys Dare guilty, beyond doubt, of any charged offense will now rise," Gerry said.

Griff's heart pounded. He couldn't read anyone's expressions, had no idea what they were thinking. Could evidence trump six years of prejudice?

The assembled mages shifted, some exchanging irritated glances. Halfway up the center section, a woman stood. A man farther down and to the left followed suit. Another farther up, then two mages, a man and a woman, on the right. No more.

Justice could still prevail occasionally. If a man had the right allies.

Five. Only five. Exultation rang in Valeria's thoughts and eased the tightness in Griff's chest.

"This assembly," Gerry stated, "finds the accused not guilty of all charges. He is free to go. So is Valeria Banning, who was charged as an accomplice."

With a glance at Griff, Gerry added, "I personally hope he will come back to us. Griffin, do you have anything to say?"

"I have a charge to lay."

At Gerry's direction, Griff took his place in the obsidian seat, hands on his knees. He looked directly into Blake's angry eyes. Behind the anger lay fear.

The bastard deserved to be terrified, but Griff kept his voice even, letting no hint of triumph show. "I accuse Chief Councilor Gene Blake of treasonous collaboration with ghouls against our kind. I accuse him of the murders of mages who died on raids because he warned the ghouls they were coming. I accuse him of ordering my kidnapping and of turning me over to the ghouls."

He ignored Stefan's scowl. Stefan had wanted him to include his loss of powers, but this was for his dead, not about him. He wouldn't have mentioned himself at all if his friends hadn't insisted on it.

"On what grounds do you bring this charge?" Gerry Armitage asked.

"When he and Councilor Otto Larkin attempted to probe my mind, I saw into the chief councilor's. I saw a memory of him meeting with ghouls."

The aura glowed blue around the chair, for truth. Shock vibrated in the chamber. A clamor of voices rose.

Gerry lifted his hands for silence. Only when the last mutter died did he turn to Blake. "Your response, Chief Councilor?" he asked in a flat, neutral voice.

Blake stood. "I deny it all," he said, staring at Griff with malice in his eyes, "and I demand my ancient right to prove my innocence in magical combat against my accuser."

"I accept," Griff snapped before anyone else could break the shocked silence in the chamber.

Valeria's cry of "No" was almost lost under Stefan's roared "The hell you do" and Will's furious "Fuck that!"

Again, excited voices created a din as the seated mages turned to each other.

Griff met Blake's sneer with a hard stare. The bastard knew, or guessed, Griff hadn't regained his powers. Regardless, this was his fight. He'd find some way to win it.

"Order," Gerry shouted. The door wardens banged the butts of their spears against the floor, the sound echoing in the vaulted space.

As Valeria ran to Griff, Stefan translocated, a breach of the rules in this chamber, to stand in front of him. "The accuser has no powers—"

"Shut up," Griff hissed, grabbing him.

Stefan shook him off. "His powers were unlawfully stripped from him, at the orders of the accused."

A gasp rose from the watching mages, then a babble of voices.

"Stefan, no! Stop." Griff hadn't wanted anyone to know, though maybe that was pointless since the traitors probably did.

"He has the right to choose a champion," Will shouted, charging down from the back. "I volunteer."

"So do I," Stefan rapped out, as Valeria and Tasha cried, "I'll do it." Even Lorelei, who hated hand-to-hand combat as much as Stefan did, called out above the babble of spectators' voices, "Let me!"

Valeria's fingers dug into Griff's arm. Her eyes pleaded with him. "Let me do this. The bastard used me, too."

"Not a chance," he said as his dad snapped, "It's my fight."

Chuck grabbed Griff's arm. He must've run down the stairs. "Griff, let me knock his ass to hell for you."

"Stop, all of you," Griff shouted. Nobody else was dying for him. Or risking death on his account.

The boom of the door wardens' spears slamming into the stone floor smothered the cacophony of voices. The echoes faded into silence thick with anticipation.

Gerry turned to Griff. "Is this true, that your powers are gone?"

"It is." Damn Blake to hell and back again.

"Then you may choose a champion." *You should*, Gerry's level stare said. "This is a duel to the death unless one of you recants."

"Like I said, this is my fight," Griff stated into the tense quiet, "one long past due. I stand by my accusation, and I decline, with gratitude, all offers to serve as my proxy."

At his side, Valeria made a stifled sound. She bit her lip, and he gave her shoulder a quick squeeze.

"Barehanded or with weapons?" Gerry asked.

Blake could kill from a distance, while Griff could now do so only at close range. But Blake would fry him in direct contact. Better to risk the amplified energy of Blake's sword and have a chance to force some distance with his staff if he needed it.

"Weapons of choice," Griff said. "One each, and only one. I choose my staff."

"Sword," Blake grunted. He stared at Griff with narrowed eyes, as though suspecting a trick.

Gerry looked up at the door warden. "Have the weapons brought and these tables removed."

"What the hell are you thinking?" Stefan demanded.

"That I'll win." Griff gripped Valeria's shoulders and looked into her pale, angry face. She had to believe him. "Somehow, I'll win."

"Please don't do this," she said.

"I'm committed now." He cocked an eyebrow at Will. "Right?"

"Yes, damn it." Will scowled at him.

"We just got you back," his mother said from the circle of his father's arm. Tears glistened in her eyes. At her side, Caro stood tight-lipped and pale.

Griff looked around at his friends' faces, at his parents and sister. His heart ached with love for them.

He hadn't let himself think how much he loved his family, his friends. When he'd been at constant risk of losing them forever, he hadn't dared. But now he couldn't avoid it, not when the next few minutes would decide whether he kept his new-won freedom or died here.

"I wouldn't do this," he said, "if I didn't think I had a good shot." He let his gaze travel over the little knot of people who cared about him. "While Blake rode a desk these last six years, I've regularly fought for my life. I still have the moves, even a fair amount of speed, just not the power."

Okay, so that sounded laughable, but he plowed on. "I owe the dead." He wanted justice for what Valeria had suffered, too, but she would discount that argument.

He set a hand to her cheek to activate the bond, staring into her wide, worried eyes and willing her to feel his resolve. "I'll be fine."

The doors opened. More mages streamed into the room behind the ones bringing his staff and Blake's sword. Talking quietly, the newcomers filled the great chamber.

Griff's heart pounded. Time to do or die. Better to fail in his quest for justice than to let anyone he loved stand as his shield.

He kissed Valeria quickly, accepted hugs from his family and slaps on the back from his friends, then stepped away from them. They walked up the stairs to the first row of seats to wait.

Griff stripped off his jacket and tie, unbuttoned his shirt collar and rolled up the sleeves. As an afterthought, he shed his shoes and socks. Bare feet had better traction on the dirt floor than dress shoes. He set his discarded clothes against a wall.

The tables were gone, but the obsidian seat remained, fixed in place as it had been for centuries. If he was lucky, it might provide him with strategic cover. Or not, but it was worth a try.

Doing two things at once in a fight, like attacking while defending, took practice. He had that skill. If Blake didn't, the odds were more even than the traitor could know.

"Take your places," Gerry said, indicating spots on opposite sides of the chamber.

Griff took his position, the raked dirt cool and soft under his bare soles. A stern-faced deputy reeve brought him his staff. As usual, Griff wrapped his hands around it so the *P* shape of *thurisaz*, the rune for power, and slanted *H* of *hagalaz*, power and harm into healing, lay under his palms, along the life lines.

Could he truly feel the magic in the staff, or was that wishful thinking?

As the man turned away, he murmured, "Good luck, Dare."

Griff blinked in surprise but had no time to respond because Gerry was speaking.

"The mages assembled will ward the floor. The ward will not drop," he said, glancing from Griff to Blake, "until one of you recants or dies."

Griff nodded acknowledgment. So did Blake.

The traitor mage had removed his suit coat and loosened his shirt collar and cuffs. He held the sword in a relaxed grip at his side. He'd probably try to take Griff out with a lethal blast first thing.

Gerry stood by the first tier of steps. He raised his hands, channeling the assembly's power. It rippled over Griff's skin as the air shimmered from the ground up, forming a dome above the floor and sealing Griff and Blake in together.

"Make ready," Gerry said.

Griff raised his staff to a guard position as Blake did the same with his sword. Blake glared at him, but Griff wasn't watching his face. The body's position was a better guide to intentions. If Griff didn't read Blake's right, he was dead.

Chapter 27

Begin," Gerry called. Griff took a single step, as though to charge, as power sizzled along Blake's sword and flickered into a shield around his body. The traitor's eyes narrowed. His blade rose.

Griff dived left, behind the obsidian seat, but fire seared his thigh—energy blast. His leg screamed in pain.

His eyes teared, and he clamped his jaw shut. Had to breathe through the pain. Block it.

Blake was circling the stone, coming for him.

Teeth gritted, Griff pushed himself up. He jerked to the side as a stream of green power ripped past his face. Too close.

Blake jumped onto the seat. Lost his fucking shield—*Oh, yeah!*—as he slashed power down at Griff.

Griff jumped the whipping bolt. He used his staff like a bat, slammed it into the flat of the blade. Knocked it clear. Whipped the staff around to take out Blake's kneecap.

The traitor mage screamed as the joint buckled. Griff spun

the staff for a head strike, but Blake dodged. He shot a stream of green energy from his palm. Griff flung himself flat, rolled aside and into a crouch behind the seat.

As he popped up, he swung the staff at Blake's head.

Blake ducked, his face dark with rage. He shot another stream of energy at Griff.

Griff dodged the bolt, lunged forward, punched Blake's gut. Jabbed the staff into his thigh.

Falling, Blake shot a stream of magic at Griff's face.

Griff dived aside, but not fast enough. The stream knocked him back against the stone chair, seared his chest. Pain roared in his head, then Blake's hands dug into his neck. Burning. Crackling with power.

"Suffer," Blake panted. "Die."

The stench of burning flesh seared Griff's nose as agony blazed in his throat. Black heat roaring in his head blocked his vision and stole his breath.

If he passed out, he was dead.

His scrabbling fingers caught his staff. He rammed one end into Blake's chest.

Blake whoofed. He lost his grip and stumbled back a pace. Griff's strike into his belly pushed him back. He fell to his knees. Wheezing, he shot green at Griff's face.

Griff dodged left, but he was too slow. The bolt scalded his right shoulder. His arm blazed, then went numb. He pivoted on his good leg. Had to use the injured one to kick Blake's face. White heat from the impact roared up the leg.

Blake collapsed. Groaned.

Griff staggered, then fell to his knees from the pain. God, if he could only draw a decent breath.

He could still deliver a deathblow with his left hand. A

staff strike to the Adam's apple, hard and precise, would take the bastard out. He shortened his grip on the staff, then rammed it backhanded at Blake's throat.

Blake scrambled up. The blow struck him midchest with a hideous crack of breaking bone.

Blake fell backward. Panting, Griff pressed his staff to the traitor's throat. "Confess, you bastard, or I will happily kill you."

"Impor—portant," Blake choked. His breath gurgled, and blood trickled over his lip. "We're...dying out. Fewer...every generation...recessive...gene, ghouls...like rabbits, made deal like...like Alden."

"What deal?" Griff demanded.

Blake drew a shuddering breath. "Access to...research, custody every...third...child. Engineer mage gene...dominant."

"In exchange for protecting them." Griff's hands clenched on the staff, but he kept his voice level. "You alert them when mages are coming to raid. You sent Valeria's team and Healey's to their deaths."

"Important...breeding center, had to relocate." He swallowed hard. "Val...too curious."

"You set her up, you bastard."

"Sorry," Blake muttered, "but...future at...stake."

His eyes rolled up in his head. With a last, rattling breath, he stilled. The ward around the arena dropped.

Griff planted his staff and used its support to haul himself to his feet. The adrenaline rush faded, and pain blazed anew in his shoulder and thigh, in his burned neck. He had to lean on the staff to stay upright.

Valeria jumped to the floor and ran to him. With the others behind her, she gripped his arms, standing close but not touching his injured body. "You're hurt—"

"I'm alive. As promised." He kissed her, long and hard. *I love you.*

I love you, too.

Careful of his wounds, he drew her face to his good shoulder, then took a minute to savor her honeysuckle scent, to absorb the sweet pressure of her body in the circle of his arm.

She lifted a hand to his face, the skin to skin contact activating the bond, and he realized she was fighting tears. He tightened his hold on her.

You okay? he asked.

She nodded. Her power flowed over his neck, easing the pain. *I can't fix that altogether, it's too deep, but—*

It's better. Thanks.

I need a minute. She scrubbed her face against his shoulder.

He kissed her temple and let his hand drift up her back. Holding her close, he gloried in the silken softness of her hair against his cheek. He'd avenged his dead and hers, and served justice once again.

Behind her, Stefan knelt, checking Blake's carotid pulse. With a slight head shake, he rose. "Dead," he confirmed.

"Griffin Dare's accusation is upheld," Gerry said to the watching crowd. "Justice has been served, and this proceeding is at an end."

"Hey." Stefan touched Griff's shoulder lightly. "Let me see to those burns, check your leg."

Valeria gave Griff a quick kiss and stepped aside.

Stefan set gentle hands on Griff's neck. His eyes lost focus. "Fixable," he murmured. "You knocked him back in time."

Healing energy flowed over the skin, repairing the damage, tingling in Griff's nerve endings.

"Kinda blew confidentiality to hell when you told everybody about my powers," Griff said.

"Not like it was a secret, not when Blake and his buddies already knew. And it won you some PR points."

"Maybe." But done was done, and Stefan had meant well.

Teresa DiMaggio, the weaponsmistress, Gerry Armitage, Joe Healey, and Dan Jacobs waited at the fringe of the group around Griff and Stefan. But most of the crowd filing out didn't look at Griff. Those who did wore doubtful or disapproving expressions. Not a good sign. *Not guilty*, after all, did not mean *innocent*.

He couldn't let his relationship with Valeria cost her any more than it already had. He owed her too much to let her tie herself to someone most mages still considered untrustworthy.

"That'll hold you." Stefan gripped his shoulder and shook him lightly. "You lucky bastard."

"Not lucky." Griff flashed him a grin. "Skilled."

When Stefan moved aside, Dan Jacobs stood before Griff with tears in his eyes. Griff braced himself, but Dan thrust out his right hand. "I'm sorry about Mitch," he said, "but Corin would have welcomed this day."

"Thanks, Dan. That means more than I can say."

"Congratulations, Griffin," Teresa said, offering her hand to shake. "I can use your help training students."

Griff thanked her. This was the last place he wanted to spend much time, but she meant well. So did Healey and Gerry, with handshakes and congratulations, though Healey's were maybe political. Behind them came Darren

Hale, the young mage he and Valeria had helped at Americus.

As they left, Will swept Griff into a bear hug. The next few minutes became a blur as his family and friends followed Will's example. Griff endured it all, his mind reeling, trying to absorb his victory. He'd won, for himself and his dead. His name was clear. He was off the mage most wanted list.

Valeria touched his arm. "Meet me in my old suite?"

"Sure. Honey—" But she was turning away with Sybil. Good. Maybe she could salvage something.

He smiled at his beaming friends. "Meet you later."

"In my suite," Will said. "Beer and champagne on ice." With a sidelong glance at Tasha, he added, "And Pepsi."

She wrinkled her nose at him, then grinned. "For this occasion, I can deal."

"I'll help you set up," Hettie offered. "I brought peach cobbler and watermelon."

His father grinned. "We'll be up soon."

As Griff's friends hurried out, laughing, his mother hugged him. "I'm very proud of you." Cupping his cheek with one hand, she peered into his face, and in the lines around her eyes he saw the worries she'd carried during his years of exile.

But she was smiling at him. "You scared a decade off my life, Griffin. I want you to come home, give us some time."

"I'd like that." Especially since he wouldn't have to look over his shoulder anymore. Unless ghouls came after him. No point worrying about that now, though.

They started for the steps, and his mother added, "Valeria is welcome to come, of course. We all want to know her better, and I want to hear all about your painting, see some pieces." She paused, staring hard at him, and her gaze sharpened. "Tell me what's wrong."

"Caro." Griff waited until her face turned toward him. "What were people saying in the halls today?"

To his parents, he added, "Don't look so surprised. She's quiet, so people overlook her. She can't see, so they act like she can't hear, either. Spill it, Caro."

"They were surprised by your testimony and Stefan's," she said. "Many of them were admitting they misjudged you—" She stopped abruptly.

"Go on," he said. "Let's have it all."

She frowned, brows knitting. "Some were saying nothing excused your killing those mages when you went on the run. They're glad you don't have your powers. And some idiots think Valeria should be kicked out for helping you instead of bringing you in."

"Thanks for that, but if we were talking about a stranger, none of us would blame them for feeling that way."

"I would," she insisted.

"Yeah," he said, trying to lighten the mood as they neared the steps, "but you're special."

"About time you figured that out." But her half-hearted tone meant his effort had failed.

"We're at the stairs." He tucked her hand through his elbow for the climb. "Step up."

His father frowned at him. "People take time to come around. Most of them, however, will. Look at Gerry and Dan. Teresa. Healey. And that young man who followed them."

Griff shrugged. "Five out of two hundred in here." Plus the mage who'd given him his staff, maybe. The guy hadn't stuck around to congratulate him.

So few wouldn't help Valeria. This was her home. He'd made her unwelcome here. And for what? He'd killed one friend and four deputy reeves, lost Corin and Allie.

If he'd come to his father, done what Corin urged him to years ago, would those friends still be alive? Or would his father have died, as Corin did, for trying to help?

"Top of the stairs, sis." He squeezed her hand.

She released him and activated her laser cane.

"I don't like this mood," his mother said. "Griffin, you've won your life back. Can't you be glad of that?"

"You heard Caro, Mom. And I'm done as a mage anyway."

"Maybe not," Caro said. "Stefan has a friend—"

"Stefan," Griff interrupted, "feels a misguided sense of obligation to me. He won't give up even when sanity dictates it. Even so, he admits he's taking shots in the dark. Better to face things and deal."

"Nice." Stefan stepped inside in the doorway, his eyes cool. "I want to talk to you, Griff."

"We'll clear out," Stuart Dare said. "See you upstairs."

Griff's mother kissed him, his sister hugged him, and then he was alone with Stefan.

"Even a shot in the dark can hit the target," Stefan said.

"The odds aren't great." Griff shrugged.

Before Stefan could reply, a male voice in the corridor said, "Dare is one brave bastard. I hate to think we didn't do right by him."

Shock widened Griff's eyes, but another man said, "Maybe." After a moment, he added, "I'll grant you the sumbitch is brave, but they wouldn't have pinned so much on him if he hadn't done something. Smoke, fire, you know. And he killed all those deputy reeves."

"I dunno. Blake put his own ass in a sling out there."

"Doesn't mean Dare is clean as driven snow."

The two men walked on. Griff's eyes met Stefan's angry ones.

"People will learn," Stefan said. "You have to give them time."

"Maybe." While Valeria remained an outcast among their people? Griff was used to being one. She wasn't, and she had dreams she could attain only here. Losing her would tear out a piece of his soul, but he couldn't let her give up anything else, lose out on anything more, because of him.

Stefan stared hard at him. "I don't like your mood, either, and I know how you think better than your parents do. Don't blow the best stroke of luck you've ever had."

Stefan gave him a curt nod and turned on his heel. Griff glared after him. Everybody was so damned worried about him. They should think about Valeria.

Even she probably wasn't thinking about her own best interests. But he would.

"I'm glad you're okay," Val told Sybil as her friend helped her line a box with newspaper. No one had offered her the shire reeve job back, and she wasn't going to count on it. She'd left the door ajar so there'd be no questions as to what she was doing here.

"Thanks." Sybil sighed. "Look, I don't like what you did, siding with Dare, keeping secrets. He should've gone through the proper channels to handle Alden, precog flash or no. When you had the chance, you should've brought him in, not covered for him."

"Sybil, he—"

"But what he did today, going up against Blake with no powers, that's one of the bravest things I've ever seen. He was right, too, about there being a traitor."

"He's a good man. One of the best." Yet some people still distrusted him, even after all he had done. With time, he could prove them wrong. They could, together.

"Maybe you're right," Sybil said. "I don't know what to think, Val."

"He's done so much, lost so much. I love him, Syb. Give him a chance. Please."

Sybil hesitated. "Well, for you, okay. If you trust him, that's a point in his favor."

"Thank you so much. You won't regret it."

"I'd better not." Sybil gave her a wry grin and a hug. "I'll see you later, huh?"

"Later." As Sybil walked out, Griffin came in. The two of them exchanged tentative smiles. That was good.

Griffin closed the door behind him, and her heart plummeted. A man who'd come to celebrate with his lover would be grinning, hurrying toward her. Not standing with his feet braced and his face grim. She drew a slow breath.

"I'd be dead without you," he said.

"We're even on that score." If he would stay, agree to fight for their future—

"It's good of Harrison to give me a chance," he said. "Most won't."

"Some won't."

"They still don't trust me and may not ever. There's no sense in sugarcoating that fact."

"Is that why you're planning to dump me?" The words surprised her. She hadn't meant to say them out loud.

He looked startled. "You deserve better than you'll get if you're with me."

"And you deserve better than you've had." Val took a step closer, willing him to believe her. "Together, we can show them—"

"Maybe when hell freezes over." The denial and pain in his eyes made her throat ache with frustration. "I love you," he said, "and loving me is wrecking your life. I can't do that to you."

The last of her hope withered, but she had to give it one final try. "I never told you I was engaged once, to a man who wanted me to give up my dream of being shire reeve. He wanted me to do something safer. At least he had the balls to admit his fear was the problem and give me a choice. If you love me, you'll respect my right to decide what I'm willing to face. Make a stand with me."

His jaw tightened. At last he said, "That you'd choose me and all my baggage means more to me than I can say. But too many people have suffered terrible losses because of me. I couldn't save them. I can save you."

"So I'm paying your karmic freight for everybody? That is such bullshit." Despite everything, she couldn't believe he'd ask her to accept that. That he could accept it.

"Eventually you'll see it's not. People ostracized Allie. I won't be the cause of that happening to you."

He was adamant. Val took a deep breath that didn't ease the heaviness around her heart. "Allie didn't have you with her. With you beside me, I can face anything."

He shook his head. "This way, you'll have your job back. I know you will. You deserve it."

"I'm not sure I still want it. If I do, I'll find a way."

"Your road'll be easier without me."

She didn't want easy. She wanted him. If only she could make him see that. Make him believe in what they could have together.

"You know, you're protecting me again, and I like it even less now than I did before. I'd hoped that would change when you were acquitted. Since it hasn't, I guess things wouldn't have worked between us anyway."

Pain flickered in his eyes before they became unreadable again. "Maybe not," he said.

"What will you do?"

"I'll go home with my folks for a while. Meet my brother-in-law." He shrugged. "There's always another mural for Gray Walker or Simon Ishmael to paint. I'll be fine. So will you. I'm doing this for you."

Val shook her head. "No, you're not. Doing what's best for me would mean building a life together, whether it's here or somewhere else. You're doing this for yourself, so you don't have to feel guilty."

She took a deep, painful breath. "Good-bye, Griffin. Good luck."

He looked at her a long moment, and sorrow filled his eyes. "Good luck to you, too." He walked out, closing the door quietly.

Val blinked back tears. Sometimes love really wasn't enough.

Chapter 28

During Griff's two-week visit with his parents, he'd been antsy to get back to work, but painting didn't offer the refuge it once had. Dabbing white on the stream, he frowned at the big canvas. His unreliable mind kept putting Valeria on the flat rock.

At least he had no memories of her here, in his new home.

He'd had to give up the place in the swamp. He couldn't defend it if ghouls came hunting, but he'd found a refuge half a mile from the swamp that he could buy at a good price, a rickety old farmhouse with a sturdy, much newer barn. He'd set up a studio and living space in the barn and dived back into work because he wasn't sleeping.

Griff dabbed blue in the water. She looked good in blue.

It had been a month since he'd seen her, half that long since he'd come back to Wayfarer. In time, she would realize he'd done the right thing.

Stepping back, he forced himself to think only of the painting. He had the trees roughed in, the stream almost done. Maybe he should've chosen another scene for his own mural, but this was one of his favorite places. Eventually, it would become a comfort again, a memento when he knew she'd moved on, a way to hold a bit of what they'd shared.

How pathetic.

Scowling, he chugged Coke. He'd grown to like it, even though he no longer had issues with the ammonia taste. With both the magic and venom in his system low, they seemed in balance. Finally. Hell of a price to pay, he thought, staring at the unoccupied rock he'd painted.

Shit.

Maybe that was justice, too. He'd killed people who hadn't deserved death. If his powers were the recompense the universe demanded, he was getting off lightly.

He stalked to the window, where an air-conditioning vent wafted cool air through. With recharging not an issue, he could indulge the pleasures of climate control. When he had time, he'd maybe fix up the house, but the open space down below was fine for now.

Before heading out with his parents, he'd hired contractors from Wayfarer to build a kitchen, bath, and a couple of closets on the ground floor. They'd also built a real staircase up here to the loft, and put up drywall throughout. Which he still hadn't painted.

He'd let his mom, who was desperate to do something, anything, for him, choose furniture. The big, cushioned pieces upholstered in blues and burgundies went together better than the secondhand hodgepodge he'd had before.

At least his paintings still looked as vivid as they ever had, despite the loss of his magic. At least to him. And the canvases he now had the time to do were selling well.

Stefan's steel-blue BMW coupe crunched its way down

the newly graveled drive. Odd, that he hadn't called first. Stefan parked and climbed out, his expression one of grim purpose.

Had something happened to Valeria?

Griff set his brush aside and clattered down the steps from the studio to the main floor. He flung the door open while Stefan's hand was raised to knock. "What's wrong? Is it Valeria?"

"No," Stefan replied, studying him. "Interesting that she's your first thought."

"Shove it." Griff stalked back up the newly stained and waxed stairs. He'd bought the banister, with its smooth top and carved dragons swirling along the sides, from a local folk artist.

Stefan followed. "Nice to see you openly enjoying your success at last."

"Yeah. The painting's going well, but I have to take care that it doesn't squeeze the shelter kids out of my day."

"Can't have everything."

Or even the one thing he wanted most.

At least he'd kept his promise to make up to the kids for running out on them the night Valeria was hurt. "I've turned the magic tricks over to Will, but I bring goodie bags."

They reached the loft. Griff shut the door, closing the cool air in. "Want a Coke? Beer?"

"No, thanks." Stefan nodded at the painting. "That looks good, almost like I could walk into it."

"Thanks. In this, at least, I seem to be normal. I guess the art wasn't due to magic after all."

Griff considered the mural. Maybe a little yellow in the water, for sunlight. He picked up his brush again. "So what brings you to my corner of the swamp?"

"A promise I made you."

What promise? He hadn't— Oh, fuck, yes, he had. Griff wheeled around, shoulders tensing. "So there is something wrong with her. Damn it, you should've said so."

"It's nothing that isn't normal," Stefan said.

"Good." Griff relaxed.

Stefan added, "For a woman dealing with a broken heart."

Griff scowled at Stefan to hide the way the words gouged his soul. "Stay out of this, bro. I'm warning you."

"I promised I'd see to whatever she needed, and she needs you. I think you need her, too." Stefan slid onto a stool.

"I need her to be happy," Griff ground out. "Secure. She has a better shot at both without me."

"That must be why she's losing weight and always looks tired and drawn, as though she isn't sleeping. Why she keeps to herself." At Griff's sharp look, Stefan shrugged. "The Council hired her to lead a new task force, uncovering traitors in the ranks, working on the demon problem. She recruited Javier and, for part-time, Tasha. She's already rousted half a dozen from intel and recon in the shire reeve's department."

"I could've told them she'd be great."

"And she is, at the job. But she keeps to herself. I guess it's because she's so damned happy and secure that she won't have anything to do, at least in her off hours, with people who don't forgive you. Doesn't even do much with her team, Javier says."

So she was lonely anyway. Tired and heartsore and lonely. The image flayed Griff's heart. His fingers tightened on the brush.

"You don't look so great, either," Stefan added. "You need

to stop trying to atone for things that aren't your fault and start liv—"

"Shut up!" Pointing with his brush, Griff said, "We're grown-ups. We deal." Even though he couldn't sleep without her and when he did manage to sleep, he dreamed of her. "In the long run, this is best."

"I saw her kill you."

The quiet tone, the pain behind it, stole Griff's breath.

"I tried to stop her," Stefan continued, "but I was dazed, too slow. I was ready to kill her. I had the power in my blade to fry her, more than enough. She was sitting on the floor, cradling you in her arms."

Griff couldn't breathe. He turned his back and snapped, "Enough."

"She and I lived it. You can hear about it. I was about to blast her when she looked up at me. Tears ran down her face. Poured down, but her voice was steady when she said, 'Do it. Please.'"

"Okay." Griff pushed the word through his tight throat. "I get it."

"If only. That's when I realized what had happened, when she said that, and then she told me about her promise. Later, in the chopper, when you started to revive, she was terrified that you wouldn't be you, that she would be honor bound to do that again, and she didn't think she could. Hell, I don't think I could've done it the first time."

Griff's throat tightened. He cleared it, hard. "So now she doesn't have to worry about that."

"You're bonded to each other, Griff. Do you know how rare that is?"

"We *were* bonded. The traitors took care of that."

Stefan made an impatient sound. "For a smart guy, you are so fucking stupid sometimes."

"Hey—"

Stefan grabbed him, swung him around. Griff's hands rose, fisting, but the pain in Stefan's face stopped him.

"Griff, there's no moving on from what she did for you. I bet she thinks you don't forgive her. Maybe she doesn't forgive herself."

Griff could see it, could feel the echo of that pain, both Stefan's and Valeria's. That didn't mean, though, that being with him was good for her. "Okay," he muttered. "I understand."

"I hope so." Stefan released him. "What matters is what you do about it."

What if Stefan was right? Four days later, the question still gnawed at Griff. The mural was progressing, and he'd resolutely finished the flat rock as an empty one. But the idea of Valeria suffering haunted him.

He'd thought she would get over it. She was strong. It had only been a month. Surely her friends would come around if he stayed away. Surely she would unbend toward them.

He feathered sap green along the branches of a pine tree. Her eyes were green, with flecks of golden brown.

You're doing this for yourself, she'd said.

Was he? He'd killed four under-reeves doing their duty. Allie, Corin, and Sykes wouldn't have died if not for his choices. He couldn't let Valeria also pay for what he'd done.

His phone rang, and Hettie's number appeared on the caller ID. He picked up the phone. "Morning, Gorgeous."

The familiar snort came back to him. "How come I haven't seen you since you been back, boy?"

"I'm working. Painting, something I'm free to do partly thanks to you."

"I got your letter, your offer of a freebie. I'd love a picture of Magnus. If you want to come take some photos of him, I'll have fresh biscuits in the morning."

"You can always bribe me with food."

"Counting on it. I'll have eggs, cantaloupe, and some of Elijah Kimball's home-cured bacon. See you at nine." As Griff winced, she added, "Don't tell me that's too early for you artsy types."

"Even if it is." Over her snort, he said, "Any news I should know about?"

"Bunch of mages have been messing around the old Adams place. They say it's safe, but they're keeping an eye on it. I've been taking 'em cold drinks." She paused. "That girl of yours is there now."

Valeria. His chest constricted. "How is she?"

Not what he'd meant to say, but he had to know.

"Come to breakfast and see for yourself. I'm inviting her, too, since she's meeting with the mayor and town council late tomorrow morning."

God, how he wanted to. Ached to. "That's not a good idea. I'll take Magnus's photo another time."

"Bullshit. Chicken shit, too."

Anger flared white hot in his chest, pushed through the pain in his heart. "You have no idea—"

"You listen to me. Your mama and daddy won't say this to you. Too worried about you, too glad to have you back, but you know I don't pull punches."

"So you've all talked about Valeria and me. Blast it, Hettie—"

"That girl deserves better than this from you. Lawyers deal with a lot of angry people, and I've had my share. But I've never seen anybody so damned furious, and so damned scared, as she was when we were trying to stop them from killing you."

Damn it, could no one see? "I'm trying to give her the future she deserves. I owe her that."

Yet she kept to herself, Stefan had said.

"Sell yourself that crap if you like." Another snort. "I'm not buying it, and she doesn't want it."

"Has she said—"

"Of course not. Got her own share of stiff-necked pride, that one. I know grief when I see it, though." Hettie's voice softened. "And I'm telling you, it's eating her up. You think about what you really owe her."

Hettie hung up. Lips tight, Griff snapped his phone closed.

Turning, he spotted his car keys on the bar. Well, they would just stay there.

It's eating her up, Hettie had said.

First Stefan, now Hettie and, by implication, Griff's parents. The way things were going, Magnus would weigh in next.

Maybe they all had a point, though. He'd meant to protect her, to keep her from paying a price for loving him. She'd paid one anyway. He was trying to keep the cost down, but was he fooling himself, as Hettie implied? Was he really making things worse for Valeria?

* * *

Leaders didn't run, and Val hadn't either. Nothing she could face as task force director would be harder than coming here, looking down the rutted, overgrown lane to the spot where Griffin had finally said, *I love you.* But she'd done her duty, seen the countering ritual performed, felt the residue of Chaos magic so she could recognize it again.

Now the job was behind her. One more thing down.

One more tie with him severed.

She'd found a reliable tracker and learned Tina Wallace and Jim Barcan had been murdered by rogue mages. The young deputy reeve she and Griffin had saved, Darren Hale, helped her prove it.

Computer records from the Americus nest had shed light on the ghoul breeding program. But there was no explanation yet for why the ghouls now used explosives at their nests, how they'd come to ally with Void demons, or what they planned.

Meanwhile, Will and his parents, who were famous archaeologists, were studying the amulet the ghouls had used on her. So far, they'd had no luck figuring out how it was made.

"Hey, boss." Javier trotted toward her. "Looks like we're done. Anything else before we head back?"

"I'll check the monitoring crystals. You and Leah can go."

"Thanks. See you at home."

He jogged toward the portal site, where Leah probably waited. The guy never walked, now that Val thought of it. He must have a hell of a lot of nervous energy.

Hettie's blue pickup truck bumped its way down the lane.

The older woman had kept the working mages supplied with iced tea, lemonade, and homemade cookies. And she'd never once mentioned Griffin.

"There you are." Hettie stuck her head out the driver's side window. "Got a minute?"

"Sure. I have only a couple of things left to do." Val strolled around the truck to Hettie's side.

Magnus bounded from the truck bed and dropped an icky tennis ball at Val's feet. She tossed it into the woods. With a joyous bark, he gave chase.

Hettie peered over her glasses. "Since you're meeting with the town council tomorrow, would you like a bed for the night? I'll give you a good country breakfast in the morning."

Stay over in Griffin's second home? In the bed she'd shared with him? No way.

"That's very kind, but I have a room at the motel on the highway. Breakfast sounds great, though."

"Suit yourself." Hettie shrugged. "See you round about nine, then."

"Thanks." Val hurried to check the crystals and leave before Magnus thought to bring back that slobbery ball.

After a sleepless night, Griff headed for the shelter. He could fall in with whatever the kids were doing, or help Marc if he needed it. Yet he couldn't stop thinking about Valeria or wishing she was with him. But seeing him would only hurt her, and he'd done enough of that.

She needs you, Stefan had said, *and I think you need her.*

He wanted her, no doubt about that. But maybe Stefan and Hettie were both wrong. Now that she'd had time to think, she might realize she'd made a mistake in falling for him.

She'd called his reasoning selfish. He'd been sure it wasn't, but maybe he'd been fooling himself. Hettie'd called him a chicken shit. Maybe he just didn't have the balls to see Valeria face an uphill climb at the Collegium because of him.

He stopped to let Sam Peters pull his battered red pickup out of the market square. Sam gave him a toot of the horn and a friendly wave, and Griff answered with a two-fingered salute. At least he still had the town and could move around it openly now.

Suppose he called her, tried to see her. She was at Hettie's now. He could settle this today. If Valeria would talk to him.

She'd tried, more than once, to tell him how she felt, and he hadn't listened.

Regret and longing squeezed his heart. He couldn't put this off. Griff swung into a U-turn and put the hammer down.

Chapter 29

Griff drove down the bumpy dirt drive with its live oak trees laden with Spanish moss and past the two-story, white frame house to his usual parking spot in back. Opening the car door, he looked up, and his heart jolted.

Valeria sat on the back porch steps with a glass of iced tea in her hand and Magnus snoring beside her.

He climbed out of the car, into a humid morning that promised to become sweltering as afternoon approached. Griff took his sunglasses off. He wanted a good look at her.

Magnus shot to his feet, tail wagging, and leaped to the ground. Scratching him was the fastest way to get past him, so Griff obliged, but he watched Valeria covertly.

She took his breath away. Green shorts showcased those long legs, and her yellow tank not only clung to her breasts but let those gorgeous, toned arms show. His scrutiny reached her face, her blank expression, and his enjoyment faded.

He wanted to touch her. Ached to.

Needed to.

Stefan had been right. Griff needed her. He had to fight for her, suck it up and deal, even if that meant watching her take flak sometimes. If she would take him back.

She stood, brushing off the seat of her shorts. "I'll tell Hettie you're here. Unless she's expecting you?" Her eyes narrowed.

"She isn't. I came to talk to you."

"Oh?" She raised one eyebrow.

Clearly, she wasn't going to help him out, but she'd gone more than halfway already only to have him knock her back. "I'd like to apologize."

"Oh."

Couldn't she say any damned thing else? Pushing on, he explained, "For not being the kind of man you wanted."

"We are what we are." Her voice held steady, but her lips trembled, the pain they betrayed an ice pick in his soul.

Was she hurting at seeing him? Or because she regretted ever loving him? "It's...I miss you." Great, another weak lead-in.

Maybe she feared he'd turn ghoul again someday and put her through that hellish wringer again.

"I'm sorry." Her throat moved in a hard swallow, and her eyes darkened with misery she couldn't or wouldn't hide any longer. "I can't be your pal, Griffin, if that's what you want. Not now and maybe not ever. As for anything else..." She shook her head. "I can't be with someone who doesn't trust me to handle myself or believe in what we have together. So you can go in and see Hettie or toss the ball for Magnus, or you can leave. But we're done here."

She turned toward the door. His heart clutched.

She looked so sad, so lonely. He'd done that to her. He'd cost her more than anyone ever should've and denied her the one thing she asked in return.

"I'm an asshole," he blurted out, and he started after her.

A vision flashed over his sight—Valeria standing beside him, fighting dark, smoldering foes with her sword as he swung his staff, a staff bright with magic.

The vision winked out. It might've been precog or imagination or wishful thinking. He would worry about that after he'd put things right with her.

At the door, Val froze, blood roaring in her ears. "What did you say?" He probably was just trying the same song, different key, not changing anything. Sometimes hope was a viper.

She heard the sound of his footsteps as he came up onto the porch and stopped behind her. He was so close she could almost feel his body heat in the muggy air.

"You were right," he said. "About my not respecting your choices. About my giving you up too easily. About you deserving better. I didn't listen. Hence, asshole."

Hope sank its fangs in, and she didn't have the nerve to turn around, to make the bite sharper if this wasn't going where she wanted it to.

He took an audible breath. "I hear you've got this task force. That you're maybe hiring. I could use a job."

"What?" She turned to him. The longing in his face hit her like a jab to the heart.

"A job," he repeated. "Under your command."

He looked serious. But was he?

"You know that means I decide who takes point. You're okay with that?"

"Yes. I'll type and file if that's what you want. I'll hate it, especially if something happens to you, but I'll do it. I'll even live at the Collegium if that's where you're headquartered."

She stared at him. If she yielded now, and he let her down, he would break her heart again.

"I love you," he said. "I don't know what's going to happen to me, with the magic. I don't know if ghouls will come after me. But I do know that I want you. For better or worse, powered or not, for the rest of our lives." Could she believe him? Trust him one more time?

"I mean it." He held out a hand to her, his eyes pleading. "Touch me. Connect with me, and you'll see."

Hesitantly, she laid her fingers in his warm, callused palm. Their bond flared to life and in it rang the truth of his claims.

Joy burst out of her in a shuddering, elated gasp. She flung herself into his arms.

Holding her close, he groaned, and then his mouth found hers.

"Well." Hettie spoke from the doorway.

They let their kiss break but not the embrace. Smiling against each other's lips, they took one last, whispery taste before they looked to her.

She grinned. "Took you long enough, boy."

"Too long." He planted a kiss on Val's hair. "Sometimes I'm slow."

"We're working on that." Val leaned into him, and his chuckle flicked happiness over her heart.

"About time, too." Hettie surveyed them over her glasses. "In my day, goin's on like that meant wedding bells. We do right nice weddings hereabouts, especially in October, when the weather cools down some."

That sounded perfect to Val, but she looked at Griffin, checking.

He smiled with happiness lighting his eyes. "You did realize that was a proposal?"

"It sounded like one, but I guess I didn't formally accept. So yes, I'll marry you." As his smile spread, she added, "In October if you like."

"I do." He lifted her hand to kiss it, then folded it against his heart.

"Excellent." Hettie gave them a sharp, approving nod. "Griffin, I'm sure your folks'll have ideas. You just let me know however much or little y'all want me, or any of us, to do. The gazebo out back is pretty, or that little chapel in town. Whatever you want, we'll do it up right, 'cause you're family."

Her lips curved slowly. "Now I'm going back to my biscuits and y'all can go back to sparkin'." With another little nod, she marched into the kitchen.

Val smiled up at the man who held her heart. "Sparking?"

"I think that's what they called serious making out at one point." Grinning, he turned, tugging her body against his definitely aroused one. A jolt of pleasure and need almost melted her knees.

"Whoa." She clutched at him, wrinkling her nose at the satisfied smile on his face. "Okay, I'm with the program."

"Good, because we need to make up for lost time."

His head swooped down, and he took her mouth. No tenderness this time.

Breathless, Val laid her head on his shoulder. "You know," she said, listening to his heart beat, "she's right. We are family here, with her, her nutty dog, and this town. More than I ever felt at the Collegium."

"Me either, obviously." He rested his cheek against her hair. "It's a nice feeling, having a place to belong."

"I tried to tell you that you had a place with me."

"Yeah, yeah. And that's your last *I told you so.*"

"For now." Glorying in the closeness of his body, his arms around her, his mind and hers mingling, she laughed up at him. "By the way, you're hired. And don't worry, I'm too smart to waste your field experience on an office job."

"A wise move since I'm a lousy file clerk." Grinning, he slid an arm behind her knees and lifted her. "Let's go upstairs and seal the part about belonging to each other."

"But Hettie's inside fixing breakfast."

"She won't mind. She's family."

"Besides," Hettie called from the kitchen, "I want little ones around here again. Y'all get a move on."

Stunned, Val stared at Griffin, who laughed. "One thing at a time," he called back as he started down the hall. "Let me get her married first."

"I like the sound of that." She brushed his hair out of his face and let her fingers linger over the thick, soft strands. *My husband,* she thought, and his hold tightened.

"According to your father, acknowledging our bond publicly makes us as good as married in the mage world."

"That's great, but we're taking care of the Mundane world, too, rings and all." He grinned, and his satisfaction rippled through her mind. "Forever used to be a pretty grim prospect in my old life, before you. Now I can't wait."

"Neither can I."

In the bond they shared, happiness reverberated, spinning and glistening through them. He walked into his old room, kicked the door shut, and laid her on the bed.

He smiled as he stretched out beside her. "You promised me I would go home one day, that we both would." His eyes softened. "Today, with you, I'm home. Finally."

"We both are." She drew him down for a long, tender kiss, their first on the road to forever.

FBI agent Camellia "Mel" Wray is a straight by-the-book investigator who doesn't believe in magic.

But a supernatural murder case forces her to confront a gorgeous doctor who is secretly a mage—and the one man she vowed she must never love again…

See the next page for a preview of

Guardian

Chapter 1

Wayfarer, Georgia
Present Day

*T*oo late, too late, too late.

The refrain pounded through Special Agent Camellia "Mel" Wray's brain. Each repetition slammed into her heart. She took a slow, deep breath that didn't ease her pain or her guilt.

She should've been here, should've come when Cinda first asked her, not let work get in the way. Sick in the depths of her soul, she hitched up the knees of her gray slacks and knelt in the grass by her music teacher's crumpled body.

On Cinda Baldwin's other side, the medical examiner, Dr. Harry Milledge, also knelt. The thin, gray-haired man watched Mel over his glasses but said nothing, giving her time to process. Somewhere behind her, the sheriff and two of his deputies waited.

Headlights from the sheriff's department cruisers cast harsh shadows over Cinda's face, and the blue flashers gave her contorted features an eerie tint. Her agonized expression eliminated any hope she'd had an easy death. Mel brushed a strand of white hair off Cinda's cold forehead.

"You all right, ma'am?" A stocky deputy who looked to be in his midtwenties crouched beside Mel. Hastily, he corrected, "I mean, Special Agent."

Ma'am. So familiar and, in the South, so automatic. Cinda had been *ma'am* until Mel grew up enough to become a friend and not just a student. She'd been the only person outside the family who still called Mel by her old, more girlish nickname of Cami.

Mel sucked air into her tight chest. If only the night weren't so muggy. But what could you expect in Georgia in September, a few miles from the vast, wet expanse of the Okefenokee Swamp?

"I'm fine, thank you." Guiltier than homemade sin, as people back home would've said, but not about to hurl. This wasn't the first murder scene she'd attended, just the first involving a friend. Why the hell hadn't she driven the four-plus hours from Atlanta sooner? Her team had cracked the human trafficking ring's code at midday, but Mel had waited for the busts, for the feel-good moment when the first of the teenaged victims was reunited with her family.

If Mel had left sooner, arrived here before Cinda's assailant, Cinda might still be alive.

Mel locked the guilt away. Later for that. "I confirm this is Lucinda Baldwin, the owner of this property."

At least this cottage in the woods was far enough out from the town to avoid curious onlookers. Only Mel's silver Toyota Camry, the sheriff's two cruisers, and an ambulance sat in the drive. The yellow crime scene tape ringing the front yard seemed unnecessary.

"How well did you know her?" The deputy had his notebook out now, and a pen.

"We're from the same town, Essex, up in eastern North Carolina. She was my music teacher for ten years." She was also the only person who'd encouraged Mel to pursue playing her flute even though her dad scorned it as impractical. "We kept in touch, visited once or twice a year."

"What brings you here tonight?"

"A visit, as I said earlier. I'd planned to spend several days with her." Mel hesitated. Saying Cinda wanted an FBI agent to check out some weird things wouldn't win points with the locals, but they should know she had been nervous. "She said she'd seen some strange things, odd-looking people, eerie lights back in the woods at the full moon. Did she ever report any of that?"

"Not so's I know, but I'll check." He pursed his lips. "Lights mighta been the local Wiccans, especially at the full moon, but you never know. Lots of strange things been seen in the swamp for centuries. Right many Indian legends about it."

Wiccans and swamp hoodoo. Mel swallowed a sigh. No wonder the town of Wayfarer, Georgia, had a New Age weirdo reputation.

She glanced at Dr. Milledge. "What can you tell me?"

"Officially, nothing." He waited for her nod of acknowledgment before he added, "Seeing as how you carry that federal badge, though, I don't mind saying she has strange wounds." He opened Cinda's blouse to reveal four deep punctures on the right shoulder.

Mel's head went light. She took a deep breath and forced herself to focus on the punctures and not the fact this was Cinda. "Not much blood for wounds like that."

"No. There's a fifth on the back of the shoulder, as though

from a grip. Five more at the base of the spine with what might've been the thumb dead center, by eyeball estimate, on the lumbosacral plexus."

The description, the reference to that nerve junction in the lower back, jiggled something deep in Mel's brain, but she couldn't bring it forward.

"Shoulder wounds are just about over the brachial plexus," he continued, indicating the nerve junction at the right shoulder. He unbuttoned the checked cotton the rest of the way and gently folded the right side back. With one finger, he traced a deep, short abdominal cut. "Under here's the liver."

"The killer meant to cut out her liver?" Mel jerked her eyes aside and swallowed hard against a sick taste in her mouth. *Focus, damn it.* She hadn't survived in the FBI by being squeamish.

Then again, a murdered friend could never be just another case. The guilt and the loss and the bone-deep outrage over what Cinda had suffered threatened to choke her. She shut her eyes to stem angry tears. Later for that, too.

Blowing out a hard breath, she looked back at the doctor. The kindness in his eyes deepened her guilt because she didn't deserve it. If only she'd left Atlanta sooner.

"I couldn't say what was intended," he replied, "not from this wound alone. It's odd, though."

Odd, yes, and another poke in the depths of her brain, another fuzzy image she couldn't bring clear.

"Cause of death?" Mel asked.

"No guesses." The doctor shook his head. "Not until I take a closer look. We're ready to transport, if you're done."

"Yes. Thank you, very much, for talking to me." She might

be a Fed, but she had no jurisdiction over a local murder. The sheriff and his team had allowed her this much out of professional courtesy.

Mel stood and made herself turn away. Her hands were shaking. She jammed them into her pockets.

The deputy offered her a cup of water. She took it with a word of thanks. She hadn't realized he'd gone to get it.

"Can you help us find next of kin?" he asked.

"She doesn't have any family left. I'm her executor." Knowing what that might imply, she looked the deputy straight in the eye. "Aside from small personal bequests to friends—including me, unless she changed that—she left everything to the North Carolina School of the Arts."

"But she lived here in Georgia?"

"She liked the atmosphere in Wayfarer." Until lately. "She had a friend down here. Hettie...something with a *T*."

"Miss Hettie Telfair?" The young man's brows rose.

"That sounds right. I'd have to see Cinda's address book to know for sure."

"I guess that's it for now, ma—uh, Special Agent."

"'Ma'am' is fine." Any term of respect would do. At age thirty, Mel had been on the job long enough to lose the insecurity that came with being young, female, and a law enforcement officer. "I'll let you know if I think of anything else, of course."

"We'd appreciate that."

As the deputy pocketed his pad, Sheriff Dan Burton walked over to her.

"Odd case," the short, burly man said.

"Yes. Worse when it's a friend." Mel kept her back to the bagging and lifting going on behind her. The idea of Cinda in that bag clawed at her heart. She tried to focus, convince herself this was a routine investigation. "Any witnesses?"

"The woman who called 911 was driving by when her headlights hit a white male bending over Miss Cinda. He ran right in front of the car. Description puts his age as midtwenties, height around five six, blond hair."

He paused, frowning. "She said his eyes were purple, swore to it, but I'm thinking that's a trick of the light."

"Or contact lenses," Mel said. "Some people try hard to look freakish." Even murderers.

The sheriff eyed her speculatively, his face tense in the eerie light. "Seein' as the deceased was a friend, you gonna try to pull the Bureau in on this case?"

Mel shook her head. "No grounds, and we both know it. I want in, though." She met his narrowed eyes with a level stare. "Unofficially. I'm on leave from the Bureau for the next two weeks. When I saw you all here…I'm not too proud to do legwork, and I know how to take orders from the officer in charge."

He studied her for another few seconds. "I'll need to get a look at that will, of course. If you're clear, I got no problem with you helping out."

Clear meant not only that she inherited too little to be a motive for murder but also that she hadn't had time to come here from Atlanta after work, kill Cinda, and then pretend to drive up after the sheriff's crew arrived. That was okay. That was procedure.

Mel nodded. "Thank you, Sheriff Burton. You've been very kind. If you can suggest a motel nearby, I'll write down my work and travel schedule for today and get out of your way."

She'd planned to stay with Cinda, but that would never happen again. Mel set her jaw against a rush of grief.

Sometimes justice wasn't enough. This was going to be one of those times, damn it, but seeing the killer punished was the only thing she could still do for Cinda.

Every turn of the chopper's rotors, every breath Dr. Stefan Harper's badly wounded comrade drew brought them closer to the Collegium, the mages' base near Brunswick, and its state-of-the-art operating suite. The equipment there would give Stefan's patient, his friend, a chance to live. If they reached the OR fast enough.

"Stay with me, Javier," he murmured, praying the unconscious man would hear him. Stefan knelt by the stretcher, both hands over Javier's heart. His magic infused the slight, dark-haired mage's chest, sealing the damaged blood vessels as best he could, keeping the heart beating and the lungs pumping.

"Blood pressure," he rapped out. He couldn't check it himself without losing focus on his task.

"Seventy-two over forty-eight and dropping," Ellie Ferris, the petite, blond medic kneeling across from him reported.

Hell. That was way below the bottom of normal. Over his shoulder, he called, "Someone get an ETA from the pilot."

The shrapnel wounds in Javier's chest were too numerous for Stefan to stop all the bleeding. They had to reach the OR fast.

"Josh says thirteen minutes, give or take," Tasha Murdock reported grimly. Her boy-short auburn hair and long bangs were tangled, matted with sweat from the morning's battle, but she didn't seem to notice. "What can I do? Do you need a power boost?"

Stefan shook his head. More power wouldn't block the leaks, and the shrapnel would wreak further havoc if he simply summoned the little bits of metal out. A sword wound would've been so much simpler to heal.

At least he could use magical CPR, not drive the shrapnel deeper with chest compressions and make things worse. That was too dangerous to try until they were at the OR. Unless Javier died. If that happened, magic wouldn't work anymore, but the Mundane, or normal human, technique might.

Damn it, he could feel the BP dropping. He glanced at Ellie, who pumped air into the cuff on Javier's arm.

"Fifty-one over thirty," she said, her voice flat.

Hell. They weren't going to make it. Only one very dangerous strategy might push the chopper home in time. "Get us a tailwind."

"On it." Tasha sprang toward the front. "Batten down, everybody, now," she shouted over the rotor noise. "Darren, with me. Leslie, Max, open the doors."

Stefan heard her as though from a distance, his attention still focused on the pale, unconscious father of two. But he couldn't think about Javier's kids now. Better to focus on the vitals while Tasha and Darren hooked up safety harnesses, leaned out the doors, and raised the wind.

Stefan and Ellie braced themselves while holding onto Javier's stretcher. At least the other wounded were stable. Their injuries, various venom-tainted slashes from ghoul talons, needed more treatment but weren't likely to be fatal.

The three others on stretchers were strapped in. By now, as the doors ground open and wind rushed through the chopper, the eleven who were uninjured or walking wounded were buckled in or hanging onto something. None objected to the risky maneuver, not when Javier's life hung in the balance.

Midmorning sunlight streamed into the cabin. The whoosh of the rising breeze drowned the *chukka-chukka* of the rotors. The helo leaped forward, canted sharply to one side and jerked before the pilot mastered it again. Good. They weren't going to crash, but would they gain enough speed?

The weather workers had to limit the power they poured into the atmosphere. If they didn't, they could screw up area conditions and cause a tornado or worse. Destroying Mundane homes to save a mage was not an option.

"Someone get me our ETA," Stefan shouted over his shoulder.

A few moments later, Max James's deep voice said, "Ten minutes out, Doc."

Shit. "Keep me posted on the time," Stefan ordered.

Their dawn raid on the ghoul nest had better be worth it. They'd wiped it out completely, seized all documentation, but didn't yet know whether those records contained any useful information. Like whether the ghouls' allies, demons from the Void between worlds, still meant to open a gateway to Earth. They'd tried last month without much success and at a high cost to the mages.

"ETA, eight minutes," Max reported.

Not fast enough. "Stay with me," Stefan murmured. Maybe they'd get lucky and nature would boost their tail wind.

Ghoul use of dark magic left them unable to eat anything

other than fresh kill or to breed among themselves, so they kidnapped mages and Mundanes as breeders. And occasionally as snacks, though they usually kept animals for food. The raiding party Javier led had liberated nine humans, two mages, and assorted livestock. It was damn good work, no matter what the captured records did or didn't reveal.

"BP forty-six over twenty-three," Ellie said.

Max added, "ETA, five minutes."

Too much time.

"Radio ahead," Stefan said. "Order a surgical team to assist me and have a suite prepped. I want the elevator on the ground floor, doors open, and a crash cart by the landing pad. When we land, this stretcher goes on a gurney, *stat*."

Too bad they couldn't translocate to the infirmary. Every building on the property was warded against such incursions. Or excursions, for that matter. Even if that weren't so, the systemic shock of the maneuver would likely kill someone in Javier's condition.

"ETA, three minutes."

"Forty over—no reading."

"Come on, Javy," Stefan ground out. Steeling himself for the worst, preparing to fight it, he heard the landing gear come down. Felt the chopper descend.

Javier's heart faltered, then stopped.

Stefan managed not to flinch at the final gurgling wheeze, the trickle of blood on his friend's lips. The still silence of his chest.

The chopper touched down. Staffers in scrubs scrambled through the open doors, grabbing for the stretcher, pulling it onto a waiting gurney.

"Crash cart," Stefan shouted, leaping out. Electricity plus

shrapnel would cause burns, but those were easy to heal. He grabbed the paddles from a tall orderly, checked the charge, and snapped, "Clear."

The jolt of electricity succeeded. Javier's heart restarted.

"Bag him," Stefan ordered as the heartbeat faltered again. He vaulted onto the gurney to straddle his patient.

Orderlies flanked them, ready to roll as soon as the respiratory bag mask was in place. Stefan started chest compressions while Susan Miller, one of his staff doctors, applied the mask.

"Go," she said. She ran beside the gurney, pumping air into Javier's lungs to Stefan's count as the orderlies rushed them into the building, down the corridor to the elevator. They dropped one level for the OR and shot down the hall to it.

Dr. John Parkhurst waited there, his dark face grim in the fluorescent lights. "Callie has a team waiting in the OR. How bad?"

Stefan gave him a quick summary, too aware this all might be in vain. "Take over while I scrub." He hopped off the gurney as John picked up the CPR.

The organic damage it caused could be corrected easily now that they were home. If only Javier's system hadn't endured more than it could withstand.

Stefan ran into the locker room. Yanking off his bloody fatigues, grabbing clean scrubs, he couldn't help remembering more was at stake than one mage's life.

The Void demons didn't have a portal to this world. So how were they communicating with the ghouls? There had to be some method.

Maybe the demons have evolved, said the unpleasant voice

of logic in his brain. We have. Why shouldn't they?

Because stopping them was hard enough without their gaining new powers. They'd never given up easily. Odds were, they'd try to open a portal again in order to bring Void demons to Earth, bringing plague, terror and death.

If that happened, the world was seriously and totally fucked.

Three hours after landing, Stefan stuffed his bloody surgical gown and gloves into the disposal bin. Javier had survived the surgery. Now all they could do was wait. At least magic could speed healing, and Stefan's very competent staff would take over that part.

Stefan had called Javier's wife, Karen, and caught her en route from Athens. When she arrived, she would want an update, so no use trying to rest. He couldn't anyway, not after surgery.

Instead, he wandered down to his office and through the door marked DR. STEFAN HARPER, CHIEF PHYSICIAN. The anteroom was empty. His assistant was out, probably at lunch.

Stefan glanced at the wall clock. Was it really just one thirty? His mind might still be keyed up, but his body felt as though he'd put in a full day's work.

Visitors didn't see this part of the building. They were only allowed in an area rigged to look like a paranormal research lab. The Georgia Institute for Paranormal Research was the cover identity for the mages' Collegium, the headquarters for the Southeastern U.S. Shire. And wouldn't there be hell to pay if Mundanes ever learned about that?

The Burning Times, the witch hunts of the seventeenth

century, had provided a salutary lesson. Some humans could be trusted with the truth but only a small, almost minuscule, few. Open practice of magic was dangerous, and not only to magekind.

As Stefan had more reason than most to know.

He shoved the memory aside and sat at his desk, punching the button for voicemail. Nothing much interesting there, a couple of speaking invitations, an offer to cowrite a paper.

"Stefan," the fourth message began in the Wayfarer sheriff's familiar, gravelly tone, "it's Dan Burton. We got an odd murder case here, could use some help. Deceased is missing a lot of blood and has an unknown toxin in what's left of it."

Now, that was intriguing. Stefan focused as the sheriff continued, "I know you've done some consulting. Cathy Lamb at GBI recommended you for this. If you're interested, give me a call. Word's out about the wounds somehow, so I've set up a press conference for late this afternoon. You can get an idea what they're talking about in the *Oracle*."

Weird wounds and strange toxins sounded ghoul-related. Stefan turned to the computer and pulled up the Wayfarer weekly *Oracle* newspaper's site. The murder was splashed across the homepage. The victim was an elderly woman, a retired music teacher.

The sheriff's department was withholding details. Of course they were, or at least they were trying to, but there was a reference to a purple-eyed suspect and a description of deep, curving wounds, as though made from talons.

Cold prickles rose on Stefan's neck. Purple eyes as in Void demon host? Talons as in ghouls?

The article said the woman had moved to Wayfarer from

Essex, North Carolina. That was Camellia Wray's hometown.

He could still see Cami's face, pale, gray eyes wide with hurt and fear as she accused him of cheating on her.

"*Marry me,*" he'd said in desperation, "*and I'll tell you where I go on those missing weekends.*" If she would commit to him, he'd thought, maybe he could trust her with the truth. Maybe she loved him enough not to freak out if he told her he was a mage, that he went away to study magical healing techniques with a mage physician.

"*Tell me,*" she'd flung back at him, "*and maybe I'll marry you.*"

Maybe hadn't been enough for him to take the risk. Instead he'd kept his silence and lost her.

Stefan frowned at the screen. He'd been over her for years, of course, but he still remembered that kick in the gut she'd delivered, first by doubting him and then by leaving him.

He'd bet there weren't many music teachers in a town the size of Essex.

So what if this woman had taught Cami Wray? Cami had nothing to do with this case. Even if she came to the funeral—likely with a husband and kids in tow—he wouldn't see her because he wouldn't attend. Thinking of her shouldn't make his gut clench. That had to be tension from the hard day he'd had, one that was far from over.

The picture accompanying the article showed the victim's bright eyes and kind smile. She'd lived a quiet, ordinary life but died with a weird toxin in her blood, a toxin whose nature Stefan could probably guess without seeing the labs. A toxin he needed to sample, one no Mundane doctor could properly identify.

If Stefan was right, Dan Burton and his crew would be up against a foe they couldn't hope to beat. Stefan picked up the phone.

"Thanks for clearing me so quickly, Sheriff Burton." Considering the suspicion many local cops nursed toward any and all Feds, Mel wouldn't have been surprised if he'd sat on her request. Instead, here she was, midafternoon, the very next day. "I appreciate your bringing me in on this."

They stood beside the corner desk he'd assigned to her, the only uncluttered one of eight in the room. With deputies serving as courtroom bailiffs, patrolling the county, and managing the press out front, she and the sheriff had only the dispatcher and clerk at the front counter for company.

"I'm glad to have the help," Burton said. "I ran that wound pattern through the National Crime Information Center and got a match with a case up near the Great Dismal Swamp in North Carolina. Another one down in the Everglades, although not identical to ours, has similarities."

So they couldn't know yet whether they were hunting a serial killer. Mel nodded. "I knew the wound pattern seemed familiar. I can't access NCIC from my laptop, so I left a message asking a colleague to do it, but he hasn't gotten back to me yet."

Frowning, the burly man shook his head. "Damnedest thing. Anyway, I asked the Atlanta office to bring you in on this. Brunswick office is our usual contact, but you're already here."

"I appreciate that, Sheriff."

He laid a manila folder on the desk. "Copies of the reports are in here. Bottom line, we found nothin' new."

"I'm sorry to hear that. What can I do?"

"For starters, you can back me up at the press conference. I guess you noticed the mob out front. Dr. Milledge did the autopsy first thing this morning. I'm thinking somebody at the hospital just couldn't help flapping their lips."

Mel and the sheriff exchanged a glance of mutual frustration. She said, "Judging by the chatter at lunch, I'd say you're right."

Some people in the café—the Goddess's Hearth, across the street from the Wayfarer *Oracle* newspaper, names doubtless adding to the town's New Age-y reputation—had speculated the murder was some kind of Satanic ritual. They might be on track. Those blaming otherworldly creatures absolutely were not. What was it with this town and woo-woo?

"There's other strange factors we've managed to keep a lid on," Burton said. "Report's in your file, but I'll go ahead and tell you, most of Miss Baldwin's blood was gone, and what was left had a strange substance in it Milledge couldn't identify. Like the Great Dismal case."

Mel shook her head. "'Curiouser and curiouser,' as the saying goes. But you think the yard is the murder scene, even with no blood?"

"We do." Rubbing his chin, he added, "There's signs of a struggle in the grass. Anyway, Milledge recommended a toxicology consult, so I phoned the Georgia Bureau of Investigation. Their top choice is a fellow who's just an hour or so away. And here he is."

Before Mel could turn, a man spoke in a rich, clear baritone behind her. "Good morning, Angela, Corey," he said to the clerk and dispatcher.

A shiver of recognition rocked through Mel. But surely

this couldn't be Stefan Harper. She risked a quick glance over her shoulder at the man strolling around the end of the counter and into the territory reserved for those with badges and weapons. Oh, God, it was him.

Her heart skipped a beat. A buzz filled her ears, and she lost the thread of the sheriff's comments. Stefan Harper. Voice of an archangel, hands of a sex god. Or so she'd once described him.

"Hey, Stefan." Sheriff Burton walked forward to meet him.

Mel turned hastily back to the desk, toying with the paper in the file. She was so over him, had been for years. So why wouldn't her breathing settle? It must be the shock of seeing him. It could only be that.

Instead of the jeans and T-shirt combo he'd favored in med school, when she'd known him, he wore a charcoal suit that fit as though it'd been tailored for him. Otherwise, he looked the same. Same thick, dark hair neatly combed but in need of a trim. Same strong chin and straight, aristocratic nose. Same serious brown eyes with gold glints that never showed in photos.

Same generous mouth so adept at arousing her body.

Once so adept. That was totally over.

Breathe, damn it.

"Thanks for coming," Sheriff Burton said, his gravelly voice a sharp contrast to Stefan's almost liquid one.

"I don't guess you've had a chance to go to the hospital yet."

"No, sorry. I'll listen in on the press conference from the back, then talk to the crime scene unit before I go to the morgue. Milledge agreed to meet me there."

"That works. Come on, I'll introduce you to the FBI agent working with us on this."

Footsteps came closer. Mel steeled herself. *Deep breath. In. Out. In.*

"Stefan, this is Special Agent Wray. Mel, meet Dr. Stefan Harper, our medical consultant."

Mel squared her shoulders and turned to greet the man who had broken her heart.

About the Author

Nancy Northcott's childhood ambition was to grow up and become Wonder Woman. Around fourth grade, she realized it was too late to acquire Amazon genes, but she still loved comic books, science fiction, fantasy, and YA romance.

Nancy became an attorney but eventually realized her internal superheroine needed more room to play. She left the legal profession to teach at the college level and to write freelance articles and novels, most recently blending her extensive knowledge of fantasy into her own stories. A sucker for fast action and wrenching emotion, Nancy combines the romance and high stakes she loves in her new contemporary mage series.

Married since 1987, she considers herself lucky to have found a man who not only enjoys a good adventure story but doesn't mind carrying home a suitcase full of research books. Nancy and her husband have one son, who also likes a good adventure story.

For more information, visit Nancy's website, www.nancynorthcott.com.

Withdrawn

For Every
Individual...

Renew by Phone
269-5222

Renew on the Web
www.indypl.org

For General Library Information
please call 275-4100